Book Two of the
Deer Creek Mystery Series

Ice Quest

by
Karin
Richardson

ICE QUEST is also available as a Kindle edition from Amazon.com

10 9 8 7 6 5 4 3 2 1

ISBN 978-1-57550-072-0

Printed in the United States of America
Cover Art by Johanna M. Bolton

ICE QUEST is a work of fiction. All the characters and events portrayed in this book are fictional, and any resemblance to real people and incidents is purely coincidental.

Karin Richardson is also the author of the first Deer Creek mystery novel, BLUE ICE.

BLUE ICE

Ruth Ann's life was finally on track. Her children were grown up and doing well, she had a great place to live, her business was taking off, and she was dating two of the town's most eligible bachelors.

So what could go wrong?

Apparently everything!!! For starters, Ruth Ann inherits a rare aquamarine necklace, but before she can claim it, the bank is robbed and the necklace disappears. Now everyone is looking for the necklace, and some of them are not so polite about it!

With millions at stake, the under currents of the quiet little town of Deer Creek, Colorado are surging into a raging torrent bullets and fists are flying as old feuds erupt and people start taking sides.

Here's what readers have to say about BLUE ICE, Richardson's debut novel:

5-STARS

Jaw Dropping – kept me on the edge of my seat! (TT)
This book was so suspenseful from start to finish. The voice of the characters was so strong I felt like I was right there with them all searching for the necklace! Awesome, quick read!

☆

Couldn't put it down (AJ)

I loved this book. Every time I thought I had it figured out there was another twist and turn. A great read and now I anxiously wait for the next one!

☆

Great Story! (by Avid Book Reader)

☆

Love the dialogue between characters. East to pick up if set it down. Keeps you guessing.

☆

A charming mystery!!

☆

A great read. Perfect for a book club. Looking forward to the next one in the series!

☆

What a great, fresh, new read by an up and coming author!

☆

Great read! (Jml)

☆

Great read!! Love Ruth Ann! Can't wait for the next book!

A Deer Creek Mystery

BLUE ICE

Karin Richardson

It began with the letter & took them on a desperate race from Colorado to Sweden, searching for an heirloom necklace. Was this fabulous gemstone really cursed?

BLUE ICE is available from Amazon.com as either a paper book or for Kindle

I dedicate my second book in
The Deer Creek Mystery Series
To

Wilma Longman
for her grueling work editing
ICE QUEST.

Once again, I would like to thank
Johanna M. Bolton for her extraordinary work with
the artwork, formatting, and her painstaking effort in
making ICE QUEST a success!

RECIPE INDEX

Warning: Neither the author or publisher will be responsible for any weight gain due to the abuse of the recipes included in the book! They are truly delicious and the temptation to over-indulge is considerable. They should be consumed only under the careful supervision of a responsible adult!

Chapter 1

"**B**ut Bert, Ms. Prunella said it was okay to have *two* butlers!"

"Inga," Bert snapped. "I will *not* be second butler to anyone, especially to this Sherman person."

"There isn't a first or second butler, Bert," Inga protested. "Ms. Prunella would never get rid of any of the staff here just because she brought her own butler over from Sweden." Inga added, "I'm from there, too."

"That's different. The other housekeeper, Bertha, went and got herself killed."

"She was a horrible person, Bert. I can't believe you didn't know that after all the years you two worked together."

Bert didn't like Inga's accusation and stormed out of the kitchen. I watched the entire conversation and chose to stay out of it. It wasn't my house and even though I had quite a bit of influence with my cousin Prunella, it wasn't my place.

It was hard to believe what had transpired over the last few weeks. It began when a lawyer in Sweden sent a priceless family heirloom to our small town's bank in Deer Creek, Colorado. It was supposed to be handed over to me, however, the bank President, Doug Albertson held onto it because of a letter that was attached to the piece. Before Doug could contact the police chief, John Wilkinson, about the letter, he was attacked in his own bank and severely injured.

I reached down to my neck and felt the large gem I was currently wearing, even though it was a priceless antique. It's hard to believe such a beautiful piece of jewelry could have caused such tragedy and brought me so much happiness at the same time. Everyone who came into contact with it believed it was cursed. I don't believe in curses.

Over the course of the week after Doug was attacked I was kidnapped and brought to Stockholm to help retrieve the necklace from a ruthless businessman, Axel Eklund. The Eklund's and my family, the Liljestrom's, fought over the necklace for decades and Axel would go to any lengths, including murder, to get the necklace back for himself.

Axel's main residence was in Stockholm where he ran a humongous shipping empire, but he also purchased a large estate about twenty minutes outside of my town, Deer Creek, Colorado. He only bought the estate to get ahold of the necklace, but in the end he didn't win. Axel ended up dead after a long battle back in Sweden involving me, Ruth Ann Conroy, John Wilkinson, the Chief of Police in Deer Creek, and a few other important people I'll be mentioning. One of them was Inga, Axel's housekeeper back in Stockholm. She grew to despise her employer because of the way he treated his second wife, Prunella.

Prunella happened to be the reason why I was brought into the picture in the first place. She was much younger than Axel Eklund, but very much in love with him until he turned on her and threatened to murder her for possession of the necklace. Prunella had to fake a terminal illness with the help of Inga, Sherman the butler, and a doctor named George, to keep Axel from killing her.

The problem was Axel thought we had the necklace and we thought he had it. We were both wrong and discovered that a housekeeper in the Colorado household, Bertha Angstrom, was the one who actually had possession of the necklace. She obtained it from her evil brothers who ran a pawnshop in Stockholm. They were sent to Deer Creek to steal the necklace and bring it back to Sweden for a lawyer back there. In the end, Axel Eklund killed Bertha and her brothers.

As I previously stated, Prunella was the reason for my involvement. Prunella sent me the necklace with the help of her lawyer because of everything that was occurring back in Axel's Stockholm residence. Prunella thought it would be safer with me far, far away. That's when Bertha's brothers came to town and bashed Doug's (the president of the bank) head in and stole the necklace. Axel wasn't aware what happened to Doug and thought I had the necklace all along. He had me kidnapped and finally, in the end, after a long battle, the necklace was brought safely back to Deer Creek. I also brought along Prunella, Inga the housekeeper, and Sherman the butler.

Back to the current dilemma; we now have two butlers -- Sherman and Bert -- at Prunella's estate in the mountains. I forgot to mention that Prunella inherited both the Stockholm and Deer Creek Estates, along with all of Axel Eklund's money and business. She was still married to him, and it left Prunella a very wealthy young woman.

Prunella has tried repeatedly to share her wealth with me. I told her all I wanted was to share the necklace with her. Prunella wasn't accepting my decision, however, and insisted I help organize her assets since she moved to Deer Creek for me.

Now, back to Inga and Bert's conversation in the kitchen. "What's the matter, Ruth Ann?" Inga asked, switching from Bert to me. She had caught me deep in my own thoughts.

"Oh, nothing, Inga. I was thinking about everything we've been through the last few weeks, and here we are with our only problem being Bert and Sherman's fight over the butler's job."

"It's silly isn't it?"

"Yes, Prunella promised all of you that you never have to worry about where you live or about your positions in her household. Even when you're too old to work she'll let you live here free of worry."

"She's a kind and generous person. I hope she can find someone to share her life with and maybe eventually have a couple kids."

"I agree, Inga," I said, wondering what I could do to help bring Inga's wishes along. "We need to find Prunella a husband."

"It's too bad George decided he wanted to stay back in Stockholm. Ms. Prunella was devastated, but we can help her now. We have to make sure whoever it is doesn't marry her just for her money."

"We can handle that. We won't let anyone take advantage of her."

Prunella walked into the kitchen and asked what we were talking about. "Just the ongoing battle of the butlers," I answered quickly so she didn't suspect Inga and me of matchmaking. I didn't think Prunella would appreciate Inga and me trying to marry her off just yet so I omitted that part of our conversation. Her husband had just been killed, and even though they hated each other for some time it was still her husband.

"Let them work it out themselves," Prunella stated. "They know where I stand on the topic, and if they don't figure it out soon I'll hire a third butler."

"Oh, that would put them over the edge, Prunella," I replied, laughing.

"So, Ruth Ann, what's our plan for Halloween tomorrow?"

"I'm glad you asked. I'd like you to go to the town's Halloween party over at the resort. You haven't met anybody yet and my daughters have been asking to meet you."

Prunella hesitated for a moment and smiled sweetly. "I'd love to meet Nancy and Lynne. I can't believe you have thirty-year-old twin daughters. That's not much younger than me!"

"I'm just sorry my sister, Irene, is still out of town. She won't be back until spring. I think she and her husband have had it with cold, Colorado winters and prefer the hot sun in Arizona."

"That'll give me plenty of time to adjust to living here, Ruth Ann."

We sat down at the kitchen table and Inga poured us some hot tea. I couldn't help but go deep into my thoughts again. Halloween was tomorrow and I had so much to do. My antique shop was under control with my assistant, Meme, running it.

I opened a shop on Main Street last year and it was only a couple doors down from my daughter Lynne's bakery, Sinful Sweets. Lynne was a magnificent baker and she loved trying new treats. Unfortunately, I loved eating all her treats and my clothes kept trying to tell me to stop, but I have zero willpower. If chocolate was put in front of me there would be no way I wouldn't eat it. It's just my thing, sweets and more sweets.

My other daughter, Nancy, was a high school teacher. She taught American History over at the local school. Nancy was quiet and serious while Lynne was social and funny. They're extremely close even though their personalities are so different. I always tried to stay out of their lives especially living in such a small town, but they think I stay out of their lives too much! They tell me it's because *I* get into trouble and don't want them to know about it. Like the last few weeks. Lynne and Nancy were left out of the necklace adventure because I was afraid for their safety. They didn't take kindly to my decision-making, and they are still punishing me. At least they were safe and happy, however, neither one of them was married. I guess I needed to get them married off along with Prunella, too.

Our town, Deer Creek, is a small town. One very long Main Street with businesses running up and down along it. In the middle of the street is a huge plot of land where a ski resort was built. Dick and Carol Dickson run Deer Creek Resort. The mayor only allowed one resort in town even though we could've used more. Once ski season begins our town thrives, and if we could just house more tourists I believe we'd become a prosperous area. Oh well, the mayor didn't want it that way, and he felt we should remain a quiet little town in the middle of nowhere.

We're located at the base of Deer Creek Mountain. It's a vast mountain with no other resorts around. Most people have never heard of it, but once they do they usually return every year. Carol and Dick run a full service hotel for the skiers. Even local residents stay at the hotel to pamper themselves from time to time.

Besides the business part of town, most residents lived on the few streets behind Main Street. It's pretty simple, there's one long street and on the back of one side is the mountain and road up and around it that would lead to the nearest town, Grand Junction, and the other side are the houses and apartments for the residents.

The end of Main Street is where our schools are located. It was the only area a large, flat field could be laid out for sporting events and other social activities. The school complex consists of a grade school, middle school, kiddie daycare, and the high school.

I currently reside in a ranch house a couple streets back off of Main Street. My daughters don't live with me anymore. I encouraged them to move out, so they rented separate apartments not far from here. They chose to live on their own instead of together, but their apartments are very close together.

"Ruth Ann," a voice called out to me. "What are you thinking about? You haven't heard a word I've said!"

"Oh, sorry, I'm just figuring out what I have to do before tomorrow's party." I said, smiling at Prunella. "We need to get you and me some costumes."

"Costumes?" she asked, confused. "You dress up at this Halloween party?"

"Of course," I replied. "We've always dressed up in costumes for Halloween."

"I have no idea what to be," Prunella said anxiously.

"Don't worry, we'll come up with something. Just give me a little more time."

"We don't have much time," Prunella answered. "What about Inga, Bert, and Sherman? Can they come too?"

"Of course, the more the merrier."

"Are you going with John?"

"He'll be there I assume," I responded, wondering the same thing myself.

John was the Chief of Police in Deer Creek. He went over to Sweden to rescue me and succeeded. Without his help, and a detective I haven't mentioned yet, we might not be alive to celebrate the upcoming holidays.

John and I have dated on and off. He would like us to be more serious, but I've held him off. I knew I cared for him a great deal, but I wasn't ready to settle down and remarry just yet. Until the last few weeks I thought I had lots of time, but a new detective was in town, Judy Lynch. She and John were old friends and Judy was brought in to help out with the last case. John's much older than Judy, but he felt a bond with her since he was friends with her parents and helped her become a police officer. She used to work in a large police station as a detective. Deer Creek's just a small town, and I never thought she would remain here, but John informed me that Judy was offered a full-time position and she accepted.

As you might be able to tell I have a slight case of jealousy when it comes to Judy. She's too perky and touchy feely when she comes into contact with John. I know she works for him, but they definitely have a close bond. I just hope it's of the professional nature and not personal.

"Ruth Ann," Prunella called out to me again. "You're doing it again. Is there something on your mind because you keep wandering off?"

"I'm sorry, Prunella. I was just thinking about John and wondering if Judy will be attending the Halloween party, too?"

"Ah," Prunella said, grinning over at me. "You're really jealous of her, aren't you?"

"No," I snapped back in a hurry. "I just didn't know if they had to work or not."

"Sure, Ruth Ann. I see the way John looks at you. I don't think you have anything to worry about. He's crazy about you. Judy's just his friend and co-worker. He treats her like a guy friend not a girlfriend."

I perked up a little at Prunella's assessment. "So you think he's not attracted to her? She's young and I guess you could say she's pretty."

"Please, she's got nothing on you!"

"Thanks, Prunella, I sure am glad you're around."

I left Prunella at her estate and headed back into town. I wanted to pop over to the resort and ask Carol if she needed any help. The resort's ballroom was large enough to fit up to 200 people, and I'm sure Carol already adorned the room with her scary Halloween decorations.

It took me about twenty minutes to pull into the parking lot over at the resort. I noticed the lot was pretty full, but there was barely enough snow for skiers yet. Maybe there was another reason for all the cars here. I hurried up to the front doors and entered into the grand lobby. Dick and Carol did a great job making their resort feel luxurious, yet warm and comfortable. The wooden log structure boasted soaring ceilings in the lobby with chandeliers made from several antlers joined together and a roaring stone fireplace. I felt instantly at home as I walked up to the front desk where I spotted Dick.

"Hi, Ruth Ann" Dick said, smiling up at me from the paper he was reading.

"Where's Carol?" I asked, looking around the lobby.

"She's in the ballroom finishing up last minute decorations."

"Can I go in there?"

"Of course, Ruth Ann, Carol would love to see you. We're still so grateful you're alright."

"As good as ever," I responded. "Thanks to John. He flew all the way over to Stockholm to save me."

"I'm sure glad that business is over with," Dick said, then eyed the necklace around my neck. I realized I didn't take it off before I left the estate and give it to Prunella. We were currently sharing it with each other. It may seem silly, but we felt we both deserved to wear it. "Is that the famous necklace, Ruth Ann?"

"Yes, it is, Dick. I forgot to take it off and put it in a safe place. I really enjoy wearing it, but I shouldn't wear it out too much."

"Why not?" Dick inquired.

"John would tell me it's not safe and I could be robbed. Doug would tell me it's worth too much money and it should be locked away in his safe at the bank."

"Good point. Maybe you'd better stop off at the bank and keep it in a safe deposit box."

"No way," I responded grabbing a hold of the gleaming, blue stone. "Why have something if you can't enjoy it? I guess I don't like being as practical as others think I should be."

"Well, be careful." Dick was about to go back to his paperwork when he asked one more question. "So, is our new resident coming to the party?"

"Who, oh wait, Prunella?" Dick nodded to my question. "Yes, Prunella said she'd come as long as I find us some costumes. Also, her staff will be attending too if that's alright with you and Carol? I know it's a few more people than we said were going to come."

"The more the merrier," Dick answered happily. "Oh, I know where you can get some costumes last minute if you want."

"That'd be great. Where?"

"Over at the high school. Their prop room's filled with costumes from the plays they put on. I bet they can help you out in a pinch. Why don't you call Nancy and ask her to help you?"

"I didn't even think of that. Thanks, Dick, I'll call her as soon as I'm done with Carol. See you later…" I walked down a hall off to the right of the lobby and pushed open a set of large, wooden doors. Carol was in there on top of a ladder. She was about ten years younger than me, but tall and thin with bright red hair.

"Carol," I called out. "Be careful up there."

Carol jumped a bit and I realized I probably startled her more than I should have. "Sorry, Carol. Didn't mean to scare you." Carol climbed down the ladder and walked over to me by the entrance doors. "No biggie, I'm fine."

I looked around the ballroom decorated with black balloons, and orange and black streamers draped around the crystal chandeliers. "The place looks great, Carol."

"Thanks," she answered. "I've still got more to do, but it's coming along."

"What else do you need?" I asked. "The tables look perfect with the black tablecloths and candelabras." I glanced around some more and noticed the skeletons hanging from the ceiling at different heights. "Nice touch," I said, regarding the skeletons.

"Oh, those are a bit of a surprise for later. They won't be hanging down at the beginning of the party. But when they do appear I hope people don't bump into them too much because it'll be quite dark in here."

"You're going to keep the lights down at the party to give it a scarier affect?"

"That's the plan. I've got all the tables filled with candles and I can't really turn on the chandeliers with the streamers. I don't want to start a fire."

"Good point," I responded. "You can turn on the wall sconces if you need more light, too."

"That's what I still have to do. I'm changing the bulbs over to orange ones. It'll be a nice glow in here, don't you think?"

"I think you got it covered, Carol. I was going to ask if you needed my help, but I think you have it all perfect."

"Thanks, again, Ruth Ann."

I left Carol to her decorating and headed back into the lobby. I pulled out my cell phone and dialed my daughter, Nancy. There was no answer when I realized she was still teaching a class. I shot out a quick text telling her I'd stop by the school before she left for the day. Nancy responded to my text and said that would be fine. I had about an hour to kill so I decided to stop over at my antique shop and see if Meme, my very young, but very capable assistant, needed me. I left my car at the resort and walked to the store. It was only a short distance down Main Street and it was sunny outside, but cool. I went around to the back of my store and entered through the alley into the storeroom. Meme wasn't back there so I headed to the showroom.

"Hi, Meme," I said, walking over to her while she was straightening up a curio cabinet full of porcelain figurines.

"Ruth Ann," she called out as I came near her. "What are you doing here?"

"It's my store!" I declared laughing.

"You're supposed to take some time off, remember?"

"Oh, yeah, I kind of forgot about that. It's silly anyway. I'm perfectly fine and John's just being overly cautious."

"Don't forget Doc Albert told you to take it easy for a few more days."

"I can't," I said. "The Halloween party's tomorrow and I need to get costumes not only for myself but for Prunella and the staff up at the mountain estate."

"Prunella's going?" Meme questioned.

"Why not? It's a good opportunity to meet people in town and I suggested she bring along Bert, Sherman, and Inga, too."

"The butlers and housekeeper?"

"Yep, I think Prunella will be more comfortable with them there watching over her."

"Well, can't they get their own costumes?"

"If I don't go back to the estate with costumes in hand I doubt they will go. They only arrived here a few days ago, and I've talked them into going. In fact, I don't think Prunella has even told the others about tomorrows' party."

"That'll be interesting meeting all of them."

"Prunella isn't much older than my daughters. I hope they can form a close relationship. Plus, the three of them need to meet some men."

"Speaking of men, Ruth Ann…"

"Not you, too," I snapped. "John just did his job as Chief of Police rescuing me over in Sweden."

"Oh, yeah, right, Ruth Ann," Meme laughed. "Most local policemen fly all the way over the ocean to rescue a kidnapped woman. I don't think so. He really cares for you. When are you going to give the guy a break?"

I didn't have a response for Meme. She was right, but I was so wrapped up with Prunella and getting her and the staff settled I hadn't seen much of John since we got back into town. I wondered how his new detective, Judy, was doing, too?

"Ruth Ann," Meme called out. "Are you okay?"

I shook my head and said, "Sorry, just thinking about what you said. I do need to call John and see if he's coming to the party tomorrow."

"I'm sure he is, everyone's going. Even that new detective, Judy Lynch."

"Ya, I figured she would go."

Meme saw the disappointment on my face and said, "You don't like her much do you?"

"I should be grateful to her. She was with John in Sweden and helped save our lives. There's just something about her that makes me dislike her so."

"Could it be, and don't get mad at me for saying this, but are you jealous of her?"

"What, me?" I exclaimed. "She could be John's daughter. I don't think Judy's more than thirty or thirty-five years old."

"Another one that's not much older than your own daughters."

"Thanks for reminding me of their age, Meme. It makes me feel so old."

"Sorry, Ruth Ann, that's not what I was trying to accomplish."

I could tell Meme felt badly. I smiled sweetly at her and said, "I'm just kidding with you. I know Judy's too young for John, and it would be great if Prunella, my daughters, and even Judy became friends."

"Great attitude."

"I guess so. Well, I just wanted to stop and see how the store was coming along. Any customers today?"

"Oh, yes, Ruth Ann," Meme said. "I think people buy antiques to decorate their homes for Halloween. You know, some of the older items can look kind of creepy."

"As long as we're selling I don't care what they think!"

"Funny, Ruth Ann. Well, you better get out of here before John or Doc Albert catches you. They wanted you to take it easy for a while after your kidnapping."

"That's just silly. Anyway, I'm heading over to the High School to see if Nancy and I can rummage up some Halloween costumes. The theatre department has tons of choices and I should be able to come up with something." I turned to Meme and asked, "Are you going tomorrow night?"

"No, I don't have a babysitter for Elijah."

"Oh, I wish I could help you with that. Let me think about it and see if I can find someone to babysit for you."

"That's okay, Ruth Ann. I don't really want to go."

"Why not?"

"I'm too busy raising Elijah and don't have time for social occasions. Maybe in a few years."

"Meme, you're so young. You need interaction with people your own age."

I watched her expression go from sad to hopeful. "Well, it would be nice to hang out with friends once in a while. But most of them don't have children yet."

"You were very young when you had Elijah," I said. "But you're a terrific mother and he's a wonderful little boy."

Meme perked up and said, "He's perfect, Ruth Ann. He's two and a handful, but I wouldn't change anything about him or my choice to keep him."

I gave her arm a little squeeze and headed back into the storeroom. My office was just off the back room. I walked into the office knowing that if I went in there I might be tempted to stay. The papers were beginning to pile up on my desk, but I chose to ignore those until after the weekend. It was time to head out to the high school.

I walked back over to the resort and picked up my car from the lot. I drove out to the school and spotted Nancy standing outside the front entrance. She was tall and thin, once again, opposite of her mother. She was wearing a cute sweater and slacks.

"Hi, Nancy," I called out walking over to her.

"Hi, Mom, I didn't know if you were going to show. I was about to call you, but then you pulled up."

"Oh, I'm sorry, I stopped in at my store and had a little chat with Meme."

"You weren't supposed to go there for a few more days, Mom."

"I wish everybody would stop treating me like I was injured. Nothing happened to me, I'm perfectly fine to resume my normal activities."

"That's not what Doc Albert told us, and you know that."

"He was talking about emotional trauma."

"That can be just as severe as physical trauma," Nancy replied solemnly.

"I know you're just worried about me and I do appreciate it. However, the best thing for me is to move forward. I have a hard time when I'm alone thinking about what could've happened. It's better for me, and I'm only speaking for myself, that I remain busy."

"Oh, I do get that," Nancy replied cheering up, and then changed the subject, thankfully. "What do you need here at the school?"

"Oh, yeah, I almost forgot! I need some costumes for the party at the resort tomorrow night. I was told that the theatre department has lots of them and maybe I could borrow a few?"

"That's a great idea. So good an idea I already did that for myself!"

"Terrific, what are you going as?"

"You'll have to wait and see," Nancy responded giggling. "Why did you say you needed *costumes*? You need more than one for yourself?"

"No, I 'd like to see if I could bring some to Prunella and her staff. There are three others who work for her that I'd like to come. It would be the perfect opportunity for them to meet people in town."

"That's a great idea, Mom. I can't wait to meet Prunella. You've told Lynne and me so much about her."

"I know I should've brought you up to her estate to formally meet, I just wanted to give her some time to settle in up there before overloading her here in town."

"It's just Lynne and me, Mom," Nancy said, a little perturbed.

"I'm sorry, Nancy. I should've brought you girls right up there to meet Prunella. She wanted me to but I thought we all needed a moment to breathe before diving back into our normal lives."

"I guess I understand," Nancy said quietly, but then perked up and stated, "Let's go look at some costumes."

We walked back inside the school and headed for the area behind the gym. That's where the prop room was located and loads of costumes were hung up on several long rods. "Wow, look at them all," I exclaimed.

"You shouldn't have a problem finding something to wear. For whom do you need them?"

"Prunella, Bert and Sherman, who are the butlers, and Inga, the housekeeper. Oh, and I need one, too."

"She has two butlers?"

"Please don't ask. When I left there they were both fighting over who should remain as the butler? Prunella wants them both to stay, but I don't think they like that plan very much."

"She must be loaded to afford that whole estate and staff."

"She's extremely wealthy so keeping on two butlers is nothing to her. She wants them to be safe and happy."

"Must be nice, Mom," she answered.

"You and your sister aren't deprived my dear. You should be grateful for what you have."

"Oh, I know. I'm sorry, I didn't mean to sound insensitive. Just wondering what it's like to be *filthy* rich."

"She wants to give me half of everything," I blurted out accidentally. I didn't plan on saying that!

"What did you say?"

"I said…Prunella has offered me half of everything she inherited from Axel, her husband."

"WOW!" Nancy shouted loudly. "Are you going to take her up on her offer? Hey, why didn't you tell Lynne and me this?"

"Because I refused to take it."

"But why? She has more than she'll ever need according to you. Maybe it's what she wants."

"That's what Prunella said, too. Let's give this some time and let her settle into life here in Deer Creek. She may hate it here and want to return to Stockholm."

"I doubt that. It sounds like her life was miserable over there. Plus, she has a whole new family here."

"I agree, dear," I said walking over to the racks of costumes. I pulled one off and held it up to me and said, "What about this one?"

"Seriously, Mom, a maid's outfit. Aren't you a little old for that?"

"I'm not old!"

"Sorry, I didn't mean to say that out loud. I just meant it's a bit revealing for a mother of grown-up women."

I held up the short, black dress with the white apron and said, "I guess I shouldn't wear this anyway. I don't want to offend Inga. She really is a housekeeper and I don't want her to think I'm making fun of her."

"Good choice," Nancy said, walking over and grabbing another costume. "How about this one?"

I took the outfit from her and held it up to myself. "You want me to wear a soldier's uniform?"

"I guess not," Nancy said, stuffing it back on to the rod. "How about one of these dresses from the Thanksgiving program. You could be a Pilgrim?"

"No, thank you. I don't want to be that covered up. I want to live a little, maybe show a little more leg or something."

"What do you mean or something?"

"I didn't mean anything by it. I just don't want to look old and boring."

"Oh, I get it. You want to impress John, don't you?"

"No, well maybe," I answered. I did have to compete for his attention against a much younger woman than myself these days.

"Okay, let's find you the perfect costume," Nancy said, pulling another one of the rack. "How about this? I think it's perfect."

I took the outfit from Nancy and held it up. "This could work," I replied, checking it out from top to bottom. "Let me slip it on while you look for Prunella and the others."

I walked over to a floor length mirror and slipped the dress over my head. I kept my clothing on, but I was just trying it on to see if it would fit. I wasn't a large person, especially where I wish I had a little more. It didn't look too bad, and I could make it more or less seductive depending on my mood for the evening.

"Perfect, Nancy," I said. "This nightclub singer's costume fits me like a glove."

Nancy turned away from the rack and eyed me suspiciously. "Wow, that does look good, Mom. I hope you'll wear a tank top or some other undergarment that covers you up a bit."

"Why?" I asked jokingly. "It's a bit low cut, but not enough that would be considered inappropriate."

"I guess so," Nancy responded slowly. "I grabbed a few costumes for the others. Come and have a look."

I pulled off the dress and walked over to Nancy. "This'll be perfect for Prunella. How did you know her size?"

"I didn't, I just guessed based on everything you've told me about her. I picture her as a tall, beautiful, blonde bombshell with a perfect body."

"That's her," I said. "Unfortunately, I didn't get those genes from our family."

Nancy laughed as I took the stretchy, scaly, mermaid costume from her and put it with mine. "Okay, Bert and Sherman's will do. They'll love being pirates. They can fight it out over their position," I said, chuckling.

"What about this one for Inga? I picture her as a larger woman who comes across kind of tough?"

"You pegged her," I responded. "But what exactly is it?"

"It's a Saloon owner's costume that happened to be worn by an older female."

"Older as in my age older or as in much older woman?'

"I think it was a character about fifty or sixty. It was used in our pirate production during the bar scene."

"Well, whatever it is it's perfect for her."

"Are you going up to Prunella's estate now?" Nancy inquired.

"Yes, I have to go and bring these up there and see if there's anything else they need."

"Can I go with you?"

I didn't want one daughter to meet Prunella without the other one. I was about to say yes when I wondered if Lynne would be available to go, too. "Only if your sister can come too."

"She's over at her bakery, let's go ask her," Nancy said, excited. "I really would like to meet this person. She's my family, too."

"Yes she is, Nancy."

We hopped in my car and headed over to Sinful Sweets. That was the name of my daughter, Lynne's, bakery. "I hope she can take the time off to come with us," Nancy said.

"If it's slow I'm sure she'll want to. She's as eager to meet Prunella as you are."

We walked in the front door and first looked to see how crowded it was. "Not too bad," Nancy said, glancing at the few tables with customers. "It's late afternoon and most people don't come in here now. Her busy time is the mornings."

"True," I responded. "There's Lynne," I said, pointing to the long, white counter she was wiping clean. She wasn't as dressed up as Nancy. Lynne was wearing a red, long-sleeved t-shirt with a large black outlined cupcake in the middle with the words Sinful Bakery imprinted. Lynne was not at all like Nancy. Lynne was shorter, but not as short as me, and athletically built. She was quite the tennis player when she was young, and has always kept up her fitness regime. I would guess she would have to owning a bakery! Unlike Nancy's bright red hair, Lynne had a beautiful, golden brown shade of hair. She got her coloring from her mother.

"Hi, Mom, Nancy. What are you two doing here?"

"Mom was getting some costumes over at the school and she's bringing them up to Prunella's estate. I want to go with, but she won't bring me without you."

I interrupted Nancy and added, "I want the both of you to meet her at the same time."

"I get that," Lynne answered. "I can go."

"Great," Nancy shouted. "Let's go…"

"Wait," I said first. "Let's get some sweets and bring them.   Prunella will love to try out some of your baked goods."

"Good idea, Mom, I'll wrap up an assortment and we can head up the mountain."

Chapter 2

I drove the three of us on the only road out of town, up and around the mountain toward the city of Grand Junction. About twenty minutes up the winding road there was a turnoff onto a small gravel drive. This was Lookout Mountain Road, and it's where Prunella's new home was located.

Lynne and Nancy have never been here before. I, unfortunately, had some negative experiences here when Prunella's husband, Axel Eklund resided here. He and his bodyguard, Finn, who also happened to be his cousin, held me and a security guard named Paul as prisoners. Paul was tortured and thrown down a hole in the ground in the basement. I was chained to a wall. Not much better, but Paul clearly got the worst of the accommodations. Paul was a good friend to go along and protect me when I went on a wild goose chase up here. He was protecting me from Axel and Bertha's brothers who were running around town murdering innocent victims.

Paul went back to his security firm in Grand Junction. I think his experience in our small town scared him to death. The Chief of Police, John Wilkinson, was the person responsible for bringing Paul to our town. He didn't think I would corrupt, but Paul listened to me over John. Oh, well, back to where I was.

I turned down the gravel road that led to Prunella's estate. We drove about a quarter mile and pulled into a circular driveway with a large fountain in the middle. The fountain was covered with tarps for the upcoming winter season. I stopped the car right in front of the steps that led to the massive, front double doors.

"Wow, this place is unbelievable," Lynne commented, gazing around the front entrance. "I knew it was a large house, but this is a mansion!"

"I know; this place is too large for Prunella. That's why she keeps asking me to move in here with her."

"She did what?" Lynne asked, taken off guard.

"Oh, I forgot I told your sister about Prunella wanting to share the wealth with us. I refused, of course."

"You did what?" Lynne cried out. "Why would you turn down all that money?"

"We don't need it."

"Maybe you don't, but we could surely use it. Maybe we'll need it in our futures," Lynne declared.

"You know, you're right, Lynne. I'm sorry for not asking you girls first. I was only thinking about my answer without consulting the two of you."

"Yeah," Nancy added from the backseat.

"I'll talk to Prunella about her wishes again if you both agree?"

"Yes!" Lynne and Nancy exclaimed in unison.

We walked up the stairs and before I could grab the brass knocker the door opened up. "Ah, Ms. Ruth Ann, you made it back," said Bert, the original butler here in Deer Creek.

"Yes, Bert," I replied. "Where's Sherman?"

Bert was shoved aside by an arm that reached around him. "Hi, Ruth Ann," Sherman said in a cheery voice. "I see you finally brought your daughters along."

"Yes, this is Lynne and Nancy," I said, grabbing both their arms and putting them front and center. "These two gentlemen are Bert and Sherman, the butlers." Bert grunted and turned to leave in a huff. Sherman, on the other hand, smiled and took both their hands in his and heartily shook them. "Nice to meet you both."

Lynne smiled and whispered, "We like you much better, Sherman. What's the problem with the other guy?"

"Bert, dear," I said to her. "His name's Bert, and he's not too happy that Prunella brought Sherman over from Sweden to work here, too."

"Oh, I see," Lynne, answered. "Bert's mad that there are two butlers and he feels this is his place, right?"

"You said it perfectly," Sherman said. "Ms. Prunella's expecting you, Ruth Ann. She's in the dining room about to have dinner. I'm sure she'll be delighted to have the three of you joining her."

"Oh, that would be lovely," I said, following Sherman down the hall to the left and entering the dining room.

Lynne and Nancy followed behind me as we entered the large, formal dining room where Inga spotted us. "Ruth Ann," she said thrilled. "I'm going to run and set more places at the table for you and your daughters."

"Thanks, Inga," I said, turning my attention to Prunella who was seated not at the head of the table, but the first seat to the right. "Hi, Prunella!"

Prunella popped up out of her chair and hurried over to us. "Ruth Ann, I'm so glad you're here! These two beautiful women must be Lynne and Nancy, right?"

"Yes, Prunella, I brought them here to meet and get to know you," I said, reaching down under my shirt and pulling out the necklace I forgot to take off. I handed it to Prunella and she put it on. Lynne and Nancy stared at it but didn't say a word.

The three women said their hellos and we sat down to a long, wonderful dinner. Lynne had brought dessert, and after we finished Inga's lasagna dinner we dug into an assortment of fudgy brownies, chocolate chip cookies, and Lynne's special hot fudge cheesecake.

"Wow, Lynne," Prunella said, with her mouth stuffed. "These brownies are to die for!"

"Thanks, I have a few secret ingredients in there that makes them extra chocolaty."

"Whatever it is they are dangerously good. I can't stop eating them."

LYNNE'S SPECIAL
3 INGREDIENT BROWNIES

The key to these brownies is simple. Just a few changes in the original recipe on any box of store bought brownie mixes.
- 1 Box Brownie Mix (Any brand, but I like to use the 9 x 13 pan size)
- 2 egg whites (yes, just the whites)
- 1 Container Chocolate Pudding Cup

Place mix, 2 egg whites, and pudding cup in a bowl and mix thoroughly. Dump into 9 x 13 metal pan and bake according to directions. *

*I always bake mine at 350 degrees for just about 20 minutes. We like our brownies chewy and a little underdone!
**You can also add in any other yummy ingredients such as chocolate chips or your favorite candy bar chunks. A little layer of frosting always helps, too. Try the recipe on page 40.

The evening flew by and before I knew it the time was after ten. "I almost forgot, Prunella. I have costumes in my trunk for the party tomorrow night."

"How exciting," she answered. "What did you bring us?"

"I'll go and get them and see if you like them." I left the three girls alone and hurried to my car. Sherman went with me, but couldn't figure out why I had so many costumes. "One's for Prunella, and the others are for you, Bert, and Inga."

"We're going, too?" Sherman asked, surprised, but in a positive way.

"Of course, Sherman. You need to meet people here in town."

"That sounds like a lot of fun, Ruth Ann. I'll bet Bert won't want to go though."

"Prunella will order him if he refuses," I said, chuckling.

Sherman grabbed the costumes from me and we walked back into the foyer. Inga was waiting for us and told us to go into the library. Prunella and the girls went in there with hot tea.

"Perfect," I said, thanking Inga. "Actually, Inga, come in there because you need to hear this, too."

"Me?" Inga inquired curiously as she spotted Sherman with an armful of clothing.

"Yes, let's go," I said, pulling her into the library with us.

Prunella and my daughters were sitting on one of the couches in front of the large stone fireplace. The last time I was in here Axel Eklund was holding me captive. Axel and I sat on this very couch and had a long talk about the necklace and his first wife. At that time, I didn't even know Prunella existed. It wasn't until I was taken to Stockholm, and placed in his estate that I met Prunella, Inga, and Sherman.

The girls spotted Inga, Sherman, and I walk in. "There you are," Prunella said. "You have the costumes!"

Sherman walked over to the couch and laid the costumes over the back. "Ruth Ann tells me we all are going to the party?"

"Yes, I think it'd be fun."

"I get to go, too?" Inga asked, excited.

"Yes, of course, Inga," Prunella answered. "Bert, too."

"Where is Bert?" Sherman asked, looking around the room.

"He's sulking in the kitchen," Inga answered. "I'll go get him if you'd like."

"Yes, please do," I answered for Prunella. "I'd like to see the expression on his face when we tell him he gets to dress up as a pirate!"

"Pirate?" Sherman chimed in. "Am I a pirate, too?"

"Yes, you are, Sherman. Is that okay with you?" I asked.

"Oh, yes, that'll be great!"

"Good. Now we have to convince Bert." Prunella stated.

Inga disappeared after checking out her costume and loving it. Prunella held up her costume and turned to me, "What on earth is this?"

"It's a mermaid costume," Nancy answered for me. "Look, there's the fin on the bottom, but your feet have a separate opening so you can walk in it."

Prunella studied it for a couple minutes and I began to think I made a huge mistake when she smiled broadly and exclaimed, "I love it!"

"Phew," I said. "I thought for a minute we were going to have to run over to the high school and pick out something else."

"No, it's perfect." Prunella looked at all the costumes and added, "So these are on loan from your high school, Nancy?"

"Yes, from the theatre department. We have tons of costumes there, but mom thought these would be perfect for all of you."

"They really are," Sherman said, holding up his pirate's hat. "This could turn out to be a fun party."

"Of course it'll be fun, Sherman. Just because it's a small town doesn't mean we're boring."

"No, no I didn't mean it that way. Sorry, Ruth Ann," Sherman pleaded. "I only meant that I was worried people would look at Inga, Bert, and me as the help and not as guests."

Prunella rushed in and answered for me. "Sherman, you're my family… you, Inga, and even Bert. Soon Bert will feel more comfortable around us and he'll realize how close we are."

Suddenly the library doors flew open and Bert stammered in. "Inga informed me that I am to attend a town Halloween party tomorrow night. And that I have to wear some ridiculous pirate costume?"

"Yes, Bert, that's true," I replied, trying hard not to react to his snotty attitude.

"I absolutely refuse to attend such a party."

"You don't have a choice, Bert," Prunella answered softly. "It'll be fun and you need to get out of this house and mingle with normal people."

"I don't like *normal* people," he declared, as he stared directly at me.

Prunella noticed his glare, mainly at me, and said in a stern voice, "Well, now you're just being rude, Bert. I will not tolerate that; do you understand me?"

Bert lowered his head and stared at the library floor. "Yes, ma'am."

"That's better," she said. "You *will* go to the party tomorrow night and you *will* enjoy yourself."

"Yes, ma'am," Bert responded in a weak voice.

"I don't see why you're being so hostile with us, Bert. It's as if you would rather have Axel bossing you and the staff around."

"Well," he began to say raising his head up high. "It's just that he led a more formal lifestyle. You and the others (Sherman and Inga received a nasty look) have no sense of routine and act *too* friendly with each other."

"That's because we *are* friends, Bert. Actually, Sherman and Inga are like family to me. I was hoping you would come around and want to be a part of our family, too."

"I doubt that will happen, ma'am."

I was confused by Bert's behavior. He was a butler who expected lots of rules and formalities, but Prunella was telling him to relax and he just couldn't do it. "Bert, Mr. Eklund's gone now. You don't have to be so rigid. Prunella has extended a welcoming hand so why don't you try and be nice?"

Bert shrugged his shoulders and picked up his pirate costume.   He walked out of the room mumbling, "Ridiculous costume… me, a pirate… really…"

Once Bert left, Sherman said, "Ignore him. He's just a big stick in the mud. Maybe the party will do him some good and he'll end up having a fun time."

"Good luck with that one," Lynne said giggling. "Why don't you just get rid of him, Prunella? He doesn't want to be here anyway."

"I won't do that, Lynne. I promised myself that whoever was left after the fallout from Axel I would keep on and treat with as much kindness as I could. However, Bert does try my nerves."

Lynne, Nancy, and I said our good-byes and headed back into town. I told Prunella that we could meet at my house since it was closer to the resort. Sherman offered to do the driving and we decided to meet at 6:30 tomorrow night. The girls said they would just meet us over at the resort.

I went to sleep that night feeling happier than I had in a long time. Too bad it wasn't going to last.

Chapter 3

I woke up feeling refreshed and ready for a fun, but most likely, a long day. It was Saturday, Halloween, and my store was open for a half day only. Meme was going to be in early with me and then I'd go home and get ready for the party at the resort this evening.

I picked up the phone and called Lynne over at the bakery. I knew she'd be hard at work since she was helping bake for the party. "Hi, Lynne," I said.

"Hi, Mom," Lynne responded. "What do you need? I'm swamped and don't have time to chat."

"Just wanted to let you know I'm available to help you after my shop's closed if you need me?"

"Nope, I'm good. Nancy said she'd come over and between Julie, Nancy, and me there's not much room in the kitchen. Thanks though…"

"Okay, what are you making for Carol over at the resort?"

"I'm making cookies and cupcakes that are decorated for Halloween, and I've made pumpkin balls dipped in white chocolate and covered with orange and black sprinkles."

"Oh, I love those. Have you and Carol talked about your opening a shop inside the resort lately?"

"No, maybe after this party she'll be ready to negotiate some space for me."

Lynne had expanded the sweets at her shop to include an assortment of dipped chocolate balls (some would call them truffles, but Lynne calls them balls). She makes a wonderful assortment of these balls including Oreo, pumpkin, gingersnap, and peanut cookie. All she does is crush Oreos and mix them with cream cheese and form them into little balls. Then after some time in the freezer she dips them in milk, dark, or white chocolate and decorates. So simple, but she was selling them so fast she didn't have time left over for her every day baking.

I had suggested a few weeks ago that she talk with Carol Dickson, the owner of the resort, and that she open a small bakery there and call it, "She's Got Balls." Lynne loved the idea and I offered to bankroll the whole deal. I didn't want Lynne to feel I'd interfere with her business if I paid for it. I had better mention that to Lynne again. Maybe that's why she's been hesitating about going to Carol again.

SHE'S GOT BALLS
RECIPE #1 - PUMPKIN BALLS
3 INGREDIENT RECIPE

- 1 Package spice or pumpkin flavored cookies (preferably with the white filling inside)
- 1 (8 oz) package Neufchatel Cheese
- 1 bag of white candy melts or chips

Crush the cookies in a food processor or in a large plastic bag with a rolling pin. In a mixer, throw the cookie crumbs, the cheese, and combine thoroughly. This can be done by hand, too! Cover and Chill about 30-60 minutes to firm up.

Roll into golf ball size or smaller balls and put on waxed paper lined pan. Freeze around 30 minutes.

Melt the candy/white chips in microwave safe bowl for 30-60 seconds then stir. If not completely melted, microwave at 15 second increments. Be careful, white chocolate can harden quickly if overheated!

Dip balls with a spoon in melted white chocolate and place back on waxed paper lined sheet. Place back into freezer for 10 minutes and then ENJOY! Keep in plastic bag or container in refrigerator. Usually lasts a week to two weeks - no problem.

I hurried and grabbed a quick bowl of bran flakes (that was my way of combatting all the sugar I eat!) before heading out to my store. I didn't think there would be much business on Halloween morning. The town's residents were getting busy for the Trick or Treaters and the party afterwards.

The antique Store, Ruth Ann's, was only a short drive away. I could've walked, and should've, but didn't. I pulled out of the driveway in my yellow SUV and drove two blocks over to Main Street. The resort parking lot was across the street from the intersection and I considered popping in there to have a quick chat with Carol about Lynne. I decided against it since she was probably busy with party details.

About a half mile later I pulled into a side drive that led to the alley behind my store. All the stores, except the resort, had access from the alley that ran up and down the backside of Main Street. I unlocked the back door of the store and passed through the storage room to get to my office.

"What a mess!" I said out loud to myself.

I pushed aside a large pile of papers and grabbed a notebook where I kept the financial records for my store. Business had been pretty good since I was kidnapped. Meme, my assistant, couldn't tell the story of what happened to me enough. She was a smart employee, because as she told the harrowing adventure she would point out merchandise she felt the shopper should purchase. I smiled, as I looked at all our sales for the last couple weeks.

"Not bad," I said, again out loud. But this time I had a response. I popped my head up and saw Meme standing in the doorway of my office. "Hi, Meme."

"You don't have to hang around here if you have other things to do. Remember, Doc Albert doesn't want you overexerting yourself too soon."

"I feel terrific, Meme."

"I know. You look great, almost glowing."

"I don't know why, just have tons of energy and lots of things I want to accomplish."

"Like what?"

"Well, I'd like to clear out all the Halloween decorations and start putting up Thanksgiving pieces around the store. Then I need to get Lynne serious about opening up another shop over at the resort."

"You're so generous to bankroll that for her."

"It's what I want to do. I've been fortunate to have the means to help." I turned to Meme and added, "And it's time I give you a raise, too."

"But it's not time for my annual review yet."

"I had a life changing event recently and I want to thank and help as many people as I can. So it's time I officially made you Assistant Manager."

"Oh, Ruth Ann, you don't know how much I appreciate that. Raising Elijah costs a lot of money and this'll really help."

"I know, and I'm sorry I didn't help you sooner."

"You're the best boss ever!"

"I just wish I could convince you to go to the party tonight."

"Sorry, no babysitter."

"If I think of someone reliable will you go?"

"Maybe the Holiday party in December, Ruth Ann. I like staying home with Elijah. He's only two and needs me so much."

"But you need to have a life, too."

"I'm young still. It'll happen."

I put Meme's problem in the back of my brain and went back to the books on my desk. Once I felt I had most of the paperwork under control I headed into the showroom and spotted Meme with a couple customers in the middle of the room. Oh, no, it was Lulu Hamilton, the Mayor's wife. She was a tall, young, brunette with way too much makeup on for this time of the morning. She was standing with Meme and another woman I didn't recognize. I walked over to the group and noticed Meme looking frazzled.

"I'm sorry, Mrs. Hamilton, we don't have any more black candelabras. We're sold out with Halloween."

"Where am I supposed to get some then?" she asked with a condescending attitude.

"Lulu," I interrupted. "What do you need the candelabras for?"

"Oh, hi, Ruth Ann. I wanted to put a creepy looking candelabra near the front door so when the kiddies come to trick or treat they see it next to the candy bowl. I have orange and black candles but no candelabra."

"I have an idea, Lulu. Why don't you buy those brass candlesticks that are upstairs on the dining room tables? They're tarnished already so they'll appear old.   When you're done with Halloween you can polish them up and they'll look shiny as new."

"I don't polish anything, Ruth Ann," she snapped.

"You can have your housekeeper do it then. How about it?"

"Well…that could work," Lulu Hamilton muttered. "Meme, will you go and grab all the candlesticks you have?"

Meme stormed off towards the staircase that led to a second floor showroom. "Now, that should settle your dilemma. Anything else I can help you with?"

"Nope," she replied.

I looked at the middle-aged woman standing next to her and asked her, "May I assist you with anything Miss…"

"Oh, this is my personal shopper from the city. She brought me a slew of costumes that I can wear for tonight's gala."

"You have a personal shopper?" I asked curiously.

Lulu looked strangely at me and said, "Of course. I don't have time to search the stores for costumes. I have too many duties as First Lady to shop!"

Really? This woman shopped non-stop as far as I could tell. She was always wearing the most current trends of clothing and jewelry. Plus, her large home was always being renovated. I wasn't quite sure what 'duties' the woman had, but she was a customer of mine so I kept my mouth shut.

Meme came back down with her arms full of brass candlesticks. "I have seven," Meme stated, plopping them down on a table near Lulu, her personal shopper, and myself.

"That'll do," she said, picking one up and inspecting it closely.

"Meme, why don't you take Mrs. Hamilton and check her out?" Meme nodded and grabbed the other six candlesticks and headed to the register near the front door.

I said my good-byes and went into the back storeroom. A few minutes later Meme entered and said, "I know I should be nicer to that woman, but I just can't. She's a horrible person, Ruth Ann!"

"She's a snob, but she doesn't mean any harm. Why do you have such a problem with her?"

"That's a long story, Ruth Ann. Let's just say she hasn't made my life with Elijah any easier."

I didn't want to pry, but told Meme whatever happened she could always count on me to support her and her little boy. Meme smiled and told me everything was all right and hurried out of the storeroom. Hmm, I wonder what that was about? Something else to add to my lists…find out what Lulu Hamilton did to Meme and her son.

The time passed quickly and before I knew it noon had arrived. I told Meme to head out and enjoy the rest of the weekend. I walked over to Lynne's bakery, Sinful Sweets, and found a closed sign in the window of the front entrance. I knocked on the front glass door and nobody answered. I hurried around to the back alley entrance and knocked on the back steel door. Within seconds, Lynne opened the door and let me in.

"What are you doing here, Mom?" Lynne asked.

"I just closed my shop and thought I'd see how it was going here. Is that all right, dear?"

"No problem, c'mon in. Join the crowd," Lynne said, with a bit of a scowl on her face. What was her problem?

I entered into the kitchen and discovered the reason why my daughter appeared upset. Lulu Hamilton was standing in the middle of the kitchen with her personal shopper next to her.

"What are you doing *here*, Lulu?" I asked curiously.

"Well, I came by hoping to purchase some goodies for the kids and found your daughter's store closed. I pounded on the door for several minutes before someone came and opened the door."

"Lulu," I began to say. "Lynne has a lot of baking to do for the party tonight. She closed up early to get it done. Why didn't you come by yesterday for treats?"

"Because, Ruth Ann," she said with a sneer. "I wanted *fresh* treats, and if I bought them yesterday they wouldn't be as good."

Lynne was standing with her arms crossed across her body watching my exchange with Lulu. I could see her temper rising and knew I had to get this woman out of here. I suggested we go into the front of the bakery and see what we could figure out. Lynne followed us out there and left Nancy and Julie (Lynne's assistant at the bakery) working hard with the order for the party tonight.

"So, I'm not sure Lynne will be able to help you, Lulu."

"I'm sorry, Mrs. Hamilton, but I closed early today to bake for tonight. I need the order to be fresh for the party."

"Well, what am I supposed to do?" she barked.

"Why don't you pop over to the grocery store and buy some bags of candy or better yet, large candy bars? Kids love the larger size candy bars. Your house will be the most popular out there," I said, hoping my suggestion would lure her out of here.

Lulu Hamilton smiled and I could just imagine how her mind was beginning to work. "That's a great idea, Ruth Ann! I'll do just that. Good-bye." Lulu turned and stormed out the front door with her personal shopper. Lynne finally took a breath.

"Thanks for that, Mom," Lynne said. "I had nothing for her and she wouldn't take no for an answer. My minds on tonight's order and not her candy bowl!"

"She only took my suggestion because I mentioned their house would be the most popular around. She's a total snob and you have to cater to her on her level. Forget about it and tell me what I can do to help?"

"I figure you won't take no for an answer and just rest, huh?"

"Nope," I declared, tired of everyone telling me to rest when I was full of energy.

"Let's go," Lynne said, walking back into the kitchen. "You can frost the cupcakes. Do you know how to work a pastry bag?"

"I do," I answered, happy that she picked out something I really did know how to do."

Lynne handed me a pastry bag filled with orange frosting. She told me to frost the chocolate cupcakes with the orange frosting and the white cupcakes with the black frosting. They looked delicious as the buttercream frosting oozed out of the bag. I couldn't help myself and squirted some frosting onto a spoon. "Mmm...this is really tasty frosting. I wish I could get my own frosting to taste this good!"

LYNNE'S FABULOUS BUTTERCREAM FROSTING

- 1 Large bag powdered sugar (might not need entire bag, but always good to be prepared with lots of sugar!!)
- 2 Sticks butter (sometimes I use a little

less, takes practice)
- 2 teaspoons vanilla (or almond or 1 teaspoon of both!) extract
- Splash of milk

1. In a large stand mixer (or a hand one) whip the butter for a couple minutes (3-5 is best).
2. Adding 1 ½ cups at a time, slowly add powdered sugar, half the extracts, and a tiny amount of milk.
3. Once mixed in, turn up power and whip the frosting.
4. Slow it down then add another 1 ½ cups powdered sugar, other half of extracts, and a tiny more bit of milk.
5. Mix, then whip.

If it's not to your liking, either add more powdered sugar (1/2 cup at a time) or more milk (if too dry) until it reaches the consistency you like. Makes enough to frost a 2-layer cake or 2 dozen cupcakes.

*If it's a white buttercream, use only clear vanilla extract or your frosting will have a brownish tint to it.
**If you want to add color (orange or black or whatever color) add at very end, slowly until mixed thoroughly
***For chocolate buttercream, add ¼ to ½ Cup Baking Cocoa powder

Frost away (and do as I do, a lot of taste testing!). Store remaining frosting in the refrigerator.

Lynne, Nancy, and Julie laughed as I wiped the orange frosting from my mouth. "Sorry, couldn't help myself."

"Just don't eat it all. I need enough for a hundred orange frosted and a hundred black frosted cupcakes."

"Why so many? You have other desserts, don't you?" I asked.

"Yes, but cupcakes are easy to eat so people may eat more than one."

Nancy asked how many people were coming to the party and I told her Carol said at least a hundred people. "That's the entire town's population," Nancy said shocked. "Everyone in town is coming?"

"Quite a few of them Carol said. Some people are bringing guests along like me."

"That's right, Prunella and her gang are coming, too," Nancy said.

"After here I'm going to pop home and get ready so I'm ready when they show up."

"They're meeting at your house later?" Lynne asked, forgetting she was there when we made the plans. "Nancy, Julie, and I will meet you at the resort since we have to load my van with all the desserts."

"I know, dear. You told me you'd be going separately when we were at Prunella's estate."

"Oh, sorry, got a lot on my mind."

"Do you need extra hands to help load and unload the van?"

"We can get it into the van but when we get to the resort I'll need some help. Dick said he would grab some guys and help unload."

"Sounds perfect to me. Dick and Carol run a tight ship over at their resort," I replied.

I continued frosting and frosting cupcakes for the next two hours. By the time all the cupcakes were frosted I felt like my hands were going to disconnect from my wrists. It was late in the afternoon and I was about to leave for home. Lynne was happy with my job and thanked me. "I didn't realize how time consuming it would be to frost two hundred cupcakes. I couldn't have done it without you, Mom."

"Thanks," I said, feeling glad I was able to help. "I'm heading out, see you at the party!"

"Oh," Nancy said stopping me. "Is John escorting you to the party?"

I turned away from the back door and said, "I haven't talked to him in a couple days. I assume he'll be there, but he didn't ask me to go with him."

I left wondering why I hadn't spoken with John. I know he's busy as the Chief of Police, but he's usually very attentive when it comes to me. Hmm…I wonder if Judy had anything to do with that? Ever since Judy went with John and saved my life I felt a change in the atmosphere regarding my relationship with him. He was all over me when we were in Sweden and he played the hero, but ever since we returned he had hardly spoken to me. I wasn't going to let that dampen my night. It was my time to show Prunella and her three staff members how to have some fun.

Chapter 4

I only had two hours before Prunella, Inga, Sherman, and Bert were to arrive. I took a quick shower and threw on an old, comfy, fleece robe. There was a definite chill in the air and I couldn't wait to sit down and have a cup of hot tea. Normally, I would grab some chocolate to eat with my tea, but not today. I had enough orange and black frosting to make my stomach a little sick, but I only had myself to blame.

I turned on the TV and watched one of my food competition shows. I usually watch these when I'm exercising, but with all that happened over the last few weeks I was way behind. Just as I was relaxing my cell phone rang. It was Doug, the President of the Bank, here in town.

"Hi, Doug, what can I do for you?"

"I know it's last minute, Ruth Ann, but would you like me to pick you up and take you to the party?"

I wasn't prepared for his question and hesitated a moment too long. "Ruth Ann? Are you alright?"

"Oh, I'm sorry, Doug. I'd love to accept, but my cousin Prunella and a few of her staff are coming to pick me up and we're going to party together. We can meet up there if that's okay with you?"

"Sure, Ruth Ann. I ran into John earlier at the bank and I assumed you'd be going with him, but he said he hasn't talked to you lately. I was quite surprised at his answer so I thought I'd take a chance and ask you myself."

I was shocked by what he said about John. Doug sensed this and said, "I'm sorry, Ruth Ann. I shouldn't have said anything about John. He's probably got his mind on another case or something."

"Or someone," I muttered.

Doug heard my comment and asked, "*Who*?"

"Oh nobody, Doug. I'm sure I'll see John over at the party. Make sure you save a dance or two for me!"

"Sure will," Doug happily answered. "See you soon."

With that we hung up and I jumped out of my comfy leather recliner and headed to my bedroom to get dressed for the party. Suddenly, dressing up as a nightclub singer wasn't what I wanted to be. I looked through my closet and searched for something better. "I guess I'll just have to make do with what I have."

I put on the low-cut silver sequin dress that went all the way to the floor and looked at myself in the mirror. "Actually, not bad, for being in my fifties," I said to myself. My hair was set up in a loose up-do and I put on a heavier coverage of makeup than I was used to. Suddenly I felt like I looked like an aged, nightclub singer! Well, maybe not that bad.

At 6:30 on the nose, I spotted the black stretch limousine pull into my driveway. I opened the front door and waited for the three of them to come up to the front entrance. Sherman was driving and stepped out immediately and opened the door for Prunella. Inga was sitting in the back with her and she opened up her own door and stepped out. Bert was in the passenger front side and reluctantly got out of the car and walked behind the other three towards my house.

"Hi there," I called out. "You all look terrific!"

"Thanks, Ruth Ann," Prunella said, stopping dead in her tracks once entering my front foyer. "Whoa," she said staring me up and down. "That's quite the costume."

"Is it that bad or good?" I asked, scared to hear if I was wrong picking out such a revealing outfit.

"It's fantastic!" she blurted out.

"Yeah, Ruth Ann," Sherman said, ogling me and making me feel a little cheap. "You look hot!"

"Really?" I replied stunned, but flattered. "You don't think it's too much?"

"No way," Prunella replied. "Every male in the place will be checking you out tonight."

"Oh, I don't know if I want that, but…"

Prunella read my mind. "You just want John to notice you, don't you?"

"No," I answered untruthfully. "I just felt like stepping out of my comfort zone a little."

"You sure did that," Bert exclaimed. "You're not in your twenties or thirties anymore!"

Prunella turned and glared at Bert. "What did I tell you about your behavior this evening?"

Bert lowered his head and stared at the ground. "Yes, Miss, I will watch what I say and what I do."

After checking out Prunella's beautiful appearance in her mermaid costume, and Inga's saloon outfit, I laughed at Sherman and Bert's pirate costumes. They were wonderful, and Sherman was grinning from ear to ear, while Bert scowled at my compliments. Bert's black belted top hung so loose he looked scrawny compared to Sherman's fitted white shirt, open to the waist (wouldn't have been my suggestion to keep a button down shirt open down to his waist at his age and physical appearance, but not me to judge). Inga was proud in her voluminous dress, and Prunella's skintight-scaled dress showed she had a perfect body!

I gave the group a quick tour of my house. Compared to Prunella's estate mine was tiny. "It's lovely," Prunella stated politely, even though I could tell from her constant smiling that she was probably wondering how I could live in such a small house. "I could see you being very comfortable here."

I took them from the front foyer into the great room and kitchen. Then we went down a hallway that led to two bedrooms. Mine is tastefully decorated and large enough to support a king size bed, a little sitting area with a loveseat, and my elliptical trainer.

"Ruth Ann," Prunella said, warming up to the place, "I love the bright floral colors in here. It's such a cheery room."

"Thanks," I replied. "I keep my elliptical in here so it's a constant reminder to use it."

"That's a good idea," she said, admitting she never exercised a day in her life!

Inga and Sherman were very quiet during the tour. I turned to them once we got back into my compact kitchen. "I know it's nowhere near as large as what you are used to, but it's mine."

Inga looked around the kitchen and said, "It's very small, but you don't seem the type of person who would cook a lot anyway." Well, that was Inga, blunt, but honest!

"Oh, I do, and it's just fine in here for what I need."

When I first me Inga she frightened me. She's a large, intimidating woman who didn't like me very much. It wasn't until I proved my loyalty to Prunella that I saw she had a big heart, but shoved deep down. Inga didn't show it often, but I have seen her when she's kind and friendly almost. Sherman, on the other hand, was open and honest with me from the start. He'd give his life for Prunella if it came to that. I wasn't so sure about Bert. He claimed he was a stickler for rules, yet he broke the law with his former boss, Axel Eklund. He knew and participated in my kidnapping. I wasn't quite sure why he wasn't arrested for the part he played in that. John tried to explain it to me, but I still wasn't buying it. I figured in time he'd be so frustrated with Prunella and the rest of us that he'd quit.

We piled into the limousine and Sherman drove us to the resort. I was hoping a few people were there as I took myself out of the limousine. What a kick to get this ride for only a few blocks.

Many people in town have already heard the tale that led to Prunella coming to Deer Creek. I'm sure most of it was inaccurate. I'm hoping that after everyone meets and gets to know Prunella they'll welcome her and include her in the towns' many activities.

"Here we are," Sherman called back to us as he pulled up to the front entrance of the resort. "I'll let you out in style, and then park the vehicle."

"We'll wait for you inside the front doors, Sherman," Prunella explained. "You don't know this place and there'll be so many people it may be difficult to find us."

"Sounds good," Sherman stated, getting back into the driver's seat and pulling away.

Prunella, Inga, Bert, and I entered the resort. As we stepped inside the lobby, Dick, one of the owners of the resort was there to greet us. "Hi, Ruth Ann," he said, eyeing the group and then bringing his gaze back to me. He looked me up and down and a huge smile adorned his face. Maybe I didn't look as old as I first thought.

"Hi, Dick," I said. "Love the costume. What are you a vampire?"

"Yes," he said, dropping a set of fanged teeth out of his mouth into his hand. "It's obvious, isn't it?"

"Oh, yes, it is. The purple velvet cape misled me for a second, but then I saw your teeth with the fangs."

"Carol thought the purple color would 'pop' out in the darkened ballroom. It's not what I would've picked out," he said, looking like a young boy who was ordered to wear it.

"It's fine, Dick. Be confident in it then nobody will question it at all."

"Good advice, Ruth Ann, thanks." He quickly added, "This must be Prunella, your cousin…"

"Yes, Prunella, this is Dick, he and his wife, Carol, own and run the ski resort."

Prunella held out her hand and Dick grabbed it and gave it an awkward little shake. "Nice to meet you, Dick."

"And this is Inga, her housekeeper, and Bert, one of the butler's at her estate here."

Dick looked confused and asked, "*One* of the butlers? Your place's that big it requires more than one butler?"

Prunella let out a loud, but sweet laugh that would melt any man's heart and said, "Oh, you're funny, Dick. Bert worked for my late husband here in your town. I brought Sherman, my butler from Sweden, with me and I would never let anyone go because they worked for my late, horrible husband." Bert glared at Prunella, but stayed quiet.

Dick looked around and asked, "Where's your other butler, Sherman, you say his name is? Didn't he come tonight?"

I jumped back into the conversation and answered Dick's question. "He's parking the car. He should be here…ah…here he is."

Sherman walked proudly through the front doors and met up with us. "There you all are," he said, dressed in his pirate costume with a plastic toy sword dangling from his side.

"Sherman, this is Dick, he owns the resort," I mentioned.

"Nice to meet you Sherman," Dick said holding his hand out. I noticed Carol didn't waste any effort with poor Dick's costume. As he held his hand out to shake Sherman's hand I noticed his nails were painted black. I pointed to them and said, "Nice touch." Dick rolled his eyes and hurried his hands back under his purple cape.

"Let's go into the ballroom. I can't wait to introduce you to people around town," I said, pulling Prunella by the arm and leading her down the hall to the main ballroom.

We were about to enter the closed double doors when I heard my name being called out from behind. "Oh, it's Lynne," I said turning around. She was pushing a cart filled with sweets for the party. Right behind her was Nancy and Julie pushing two other carts. "Wow, that's a lot of desserts!"

"A hundred people can eat a lot of cupcakes, cookies, and pumpkin spiced balls," Lynne said, meeting up with us. "Hi, Prunella, Bert, Sherman, and Inga."

Prunella answered for the group as Sherman reached around and grabbed a black frosted cupcake. "Sherman," Prunella said, slapping his other hand lightly. "You should wait until she actually serves them."

"Oh, it's perfectly all right, Sherman," Lynne replied cheerfully. "I'm always happy when someone wants to eat my desserts. Go ahead, eat away…"

Sherman did just that. In one huge bite he shoved the entire cupcake into his mouth and nodded his head in delight. We watched in amusement while he tried to chew and swallow. "Wow, Ms. Lynne, these are the best cupcakes I've ever eaten!"

Lynne, obviously pleased, said, "Thank you, Sherman. You should try the orange frosted ones. They're on the chocolate cupcakes."   Sherman didn't waste any time grabbing an orange cupcake, but this time he ate it in two bites.

We let the girls go ahead and enter the ballroom to set up their assortment of desserts. The rest of us followed and when we walked into the room I was taken aback by its ambience. The chandeliers were off, but surrounded with orange and black streamers, and there was an orange glow from the sconces on the wall. "This is so cool," Inga exclaimed. "I've never been to a Halloween party."

"I'm glad you were open to coming here tonight, Inga," I said to her. "Let's go in and meet some people."

Bert pulled Sherman aside and I heard him ask, "Do we have to go through with this? I'm too old for this nonsense."

I didn't let Sherman answer. I grabbed Bert's arm, firmly, but not too roughly, and told him, "Look, Bert, what's your problem? Prunella was kind enough to include you when it's apparent you would prefer to be back at the estate working for your abusive, former boss."

He pulled his arm out of my grasp and told me, "I do not work for you. If Ms. Prunella doesn't like my behavior she can tell me, not you."

Well, Prunella overheard Bert's rude comments and it finally put her over the edge. She took Bert to the side, away from any people and had a quiet talk. I couldn't overhear what she said, but figured it was a pretty good scolding from the expression on Bert's face. He glared at Prunella and I could see her face turning red. She must've said something to change the situation around because suddenly Bert's demeanor changed and his head bowed to the floor. I saw him nod several times then Prunella turned away from him and marched back to us.

"That should take care of him," she stated without an explanation. She turned to me and with a huge smile on her face said, "Let's have some fun!"

"All right," I said, pulling her toward the first person I saw.

"Hi, Carol," I said.

"Hi, Ruth Ann," Carol replied checking out my costume from head to toe. "Now that should turn some heads tonight."

I flushed a little, but ignored her comment. "Carol, this is my cousin, Prunella," I said, pointing to Prunella in her mermaid costume.

"Now, Ruth Ann, Prunella may also turn some heads tonight." Carol laughed and squeezed my hand. "It's so nice to finally meet you, Prunella. You look absolutely stunning in your costume. Don't tell me that came from the High School theatre room, too?"

"Yes," I answered, watching Prunella try and walk without tripping on the scales that dragged on the floor. I grabbed Inga's arm and introduced Carol to the rest of the group. Carol was nice enough not to bring up the whole double butler position. We didn't want another tantrum from Bert.

"Go on in and enjoy yourselves," Carol said, giving me a slight push into the room. "The food's on the opposite wall and the bar's open and over there, too." Before we walked toward the middle of the room Carol pulled me aside and whispered, "John's here, Ruth Ann."

"He is? What costume is he wearing?"

"He's a western sheriff from the olden days. Not too imaginative." Carol looked around her making sure the coast was clear and added, "He walked in here with that detective lady, Judy. She was dressed as one of those saloon singers. Kind of like they planned it together."

"Really?" I asked, quite a bit shocked.

"Are you okay with that, Ruth Ann? I mean if they came together and all?"

I stood a little taller and declared, "He can do or see whomever he pleases!" And with that I stormed into the middle of the room and found myself smack dab in the middle of the dance floor.

It was early still and nobody had started dancing so I felt a little foolish just standing there. Thank heavens for Prunella when she grabbed my arm and kept me walking straight toward the bar. "I think you could use a drink," she said.

"I think so, too," I said, trying to pull it together.

At the moment, I couldn't see very well with the darkened room and my fury with John. Plus, the ballroom was beginning to fill up quickly. Prunella and I pushed through a few people without stopping until we made our way to the bar.

"Have a drink and it'll loosen you up a little. I still want to meet people so you can stay busy with me all night, Ruth Ann."

"Thanks, Prunella. I know I don't have an exclusive relationship with John, but I find it hard to believe he would do that to me."

"Maybe there's another explanation. Wait and see what he has to say."

I ordered my favorite drink, a Dirty Shirley. I don't like the taste of alcohol so I tend to pick fruity drinks like Pina Colada or Margarita's.

DIRTY SHIRLEY
(At least my version and it's quite tasty)

- One shot (or two) cherry vodka (can use plain, just add some liquid from the maraschino cherry jar)
- Lemon-lime soda
- A cherry or two (or three or four!)

Stir and Enjoy! Be careful…you can hardly taste any alcohol, and it will sneak up on you

A Dirty Shirley packs a good punch for me because I don't taste any alcohol at all. Prunella thought it sounded good and ordered the same drink.

"Mmm, this is pretty good, Ruth Ann," Prunella said, sipping the cocktail from the tiny straw. "I don't taste the vodka at all."

"That's the danger in this drink so be careful not to have too many."

We stepped away from the bar and found Inga, Sherman, and Bert in line at the food tables. I wasn't hungry yet and had a feeling John and Judy would be hanging around the food. He has a huge appetite and I wasn't ready to see him yet. Maybe after one more drink. Prunella and the others grabbed their plates of food and we went to a table and sat down. All around the dance floor were tables set for four to six people. We grabbed a table for six that was near the bar and sat down. Carol had the candelabra centerpieces glowing with orange and black flameless candles. The tablecloths underneath were a combination of orange and black plastic sheets.

Prunella noticed I didn't grab any food and said, "You'd better eat something, Ruth Ann. That drink may go straight to your head."

"I hope it does," I replied, sucking down the last of my cocktail. "I'm going to get one more. Anyone want one?"

Prunella said she would wait a little while and Inga, Bert, and Sherman said they would go get their own as soon as they were done with their first plate of food.

Carol put on a great buffet. There were chafing dishes full of mummy wrapped hot dogs, burgers with ketchup oozing down the sides, and cotton candy webs surrounded the dessert plates. She went all out. Lynne's dessert table was separate from the main food items. I don't know if Lynne cared for the cotton candy stretching all around her cupcakes and cookies because it made it difficult to grab one without getting stuck in the cotton candy. Oh well, it made for a good effect.

I stood up and went back to the bar and waited in a longer line this time. I counted four people in front of me and one of them was none other than the Mayor and his lovely wife, Lulu Hamilton. I never understood why Henry, who was a few years older than me, married such a young snob. She wasn't much older than my daughters, but tried to act overly mature, which came across as pretentious. From what I heard she came from a mid-western town and had no money until she met and hooked Henry. What men will do to catch a younger woman!

Henry and Lulu finished ordering their drinks and walked by me. "Hi, Ruth Ann," Lulu called out to me. "I wanted to let you know that trick with the candlesticks worked out perfectly, and I did like you suggested and took all the king sized candy bars the grocery store had left. The kiddies loved it! Thanks for the suggestions."

"No problem, Lulu. You and Henry look festive this evening. Are you two dressed as a King and Queen?" How fitting I thought to myself.

"Why, yes we are," Lulu said, smiling proudly and readjusting her bodice that flashed a little more flesh than was necessary. But who am I to talk, I'm told my costume was a tad inappropriate, too.

Henry eyed my body up and down and grinned. "You look lovely this evening, too, Ruth Ann."

"Thank you, Henry," I said, feeling a little dirty the way he just checked me out.

"I hear you brought your cousin and her help along tonight," Henry said.

"Really, Henry? You make it sound like we're living in the nineteenth century! Their names are Inga, Sherman, and Bert. They work for my cousin, Prunella, up at her estate. They're here tonight to meet people from our lovely little town. You know, our friendly town?"

"Oh, yes, that's what I meant, Ruth Ann," Henry said, correcting himself quickly. "Why don't Lulu and I wait for you to get your drink and we'll go over to your table together. I'd like to introduce myself to your new family member and friends."

"That would be lovely," I said, regretting I said anything to them. "I'm next in line and I'll be right with you." Henry and Lulu stepped to the side and waited for me to get my second Dirty Shirley.

"That looks tasty, Ruth Ann," Henry mocked. "A kiddie cocktail?"

"With a bang!"

We walked over to my table without spotting John and Judy. Prunella watched my face, as we were closer to the table. I was rolling my eyes and grimacing as I introduced the Mayor and his lovely wife, Lulu. "Nice to meet you both," Prunella said with the utmost of grace, standing up and holding her hand out.

Henry took the cue and gently received her hand and brought it up to his lips to kiss. Lulu didn't look overly thrilled with Henry's reaction to Prunella. I had to admit it made me chuckle.

"Welcome to our quaint little town, Ms. or Mrs...." Henry stopped and looked at me for the right response.

"Prunella," I corrected. "Prunella Eklund."

Prunella smiled, and then turned to the others and motioned for them to stand with her hands. "This is Inga, Sherman, and Bert. They live with me up at my mountain house."

Henry looked at them with the biggest, phony smile, and welcomed them to our town and told them if they ever needed anything to stop by his office. They made a hasty retreat and I took my seat at the table. Prunella told me again to go get some food since I was on my second drink without eating. "What would your daughters say to you?"

"They wouldn't," I declared. "They know better!" I laughed and Prunella eased up a bit. We sat for the next hour or so talking with people that came over to our table to meet them. Inga and Sherman headed for the bar after a while and grabbed a couple beers. Bert disappeared into the crowds of people and Prunella didn't stop him. "Let him go," she said. "Maybe he'll meet somebody who needs a crabby ole butler."

"Only if you're lucky," Inga said, guzzling her bottle of beer. "I'm going to get another... Sherman?"

"Sure, why not. I won't be driving for a while, and I'll only have these two. "Sherman and Inga stood up when I noticed the line for the bar grew even longer.

"They'll be a while, Prunella. Why don't we get up and mingle a bit? I'd like to walk over to the dessert table and talk with Lynne. Nancy may be helping out, too."

We left our table and I noticed as I stood up and walked over toward the desserts that I felt a warm sensation run through my body. It must be the cherry vodka. I haven't had two drinks in a while, and it must be affecting me. Felt pretty good, actually. I may just have another.

"Hi, Mom," Nancy said before we reached the table.

"Nancy," I began to say. "Aren't you helping your sister serve desserts?"

"Nope, she said she didn't need any help. I'm just hanging out with some of the other teachers. It's so dark in here I couldn't find you before. Where were you sitting?"

I pointed to our table near the bar and noticed Inga and Sherman were sitting there. Inga was holding her bottle of beer and Sherman looked to be drinking water. Good for him, I thought. He was our chauffeur for the evening.

Nancy took off and headed back to her friends. Prunella and I walked over to the dessert table and spotted Lynne and Julie serving the sweets. I was about to grab an orange frosted chocolate cupcake when a large hand pressed on my right shoulder. I whipped around to see John, larger than life, staring at my outfit.

"That's some outfit, Ruth Ann," John said, smirking. "Trying to get *someone's* attention this evening?"

"Don't be absurd, John," I snapped. I wasn't in the mood for his teasing, and the fact that he ignored me up till now truly upset me.

John eyed me suspiciously, "Did I do something wrong, Ruth Ann?"

"You'll have to answer that one yourself," I told him. "Prunella, let's get some cupcakes and bring them to our table."

Prunella didn't dare say a word while I grabbed a large plate and piled about ten cupcakes on it. I was fuming mad at John for having the nerve to show up here with a date, Judy the Detective, and flaunting it in front of me. He told me not more than a week ago that he couldn't live without me. I'm going to seek out Doug and have him join me.

We hurried back to our table and I dumped the plate of cupcakes down on the table, knocking a few off the plate, and told them I'd be back in a minute. I saw the astonished looks on their faces as I turned away. Before I was too far away, I turned back to them and said, "I saw Sherman pop two in his mouth before we made it in the door tonight. I figured you could eat two each so there's plenty there for everyone."

I stormed off angry at the world and went over to Carol who was at the front door greeting guests. "Hi, Carol," I shouted out over the loud music.

"Hi, Ruth Ann, isn't this band great?" She said, screaming at the top of her lungs. "A bit loud, but they're really good. I like 80's and 90's music, don't you?"

"Yeah it's great, but maybe they can turn the volume down just a tad."

"I'm going to find Dick and ask him. He'll handle it. We want people to still be able to speak to one another." Carol was about to walk away and find her husband when I grabbed her arm and asked, "Has Doug made it here tonight?"

"Yes, he got here about a half hour ago. He asked for you right away and I told you you were with your cousin and her friends. Check over by the food, maybe he's getting a plateful."

"Thanks, I will," I said.

"Ruth Ann, I could tell by the way you marched over here that you saw John and Judy?"

"Yes, well at least John. He was rude so I walked away from him."

"Is that why you want to find Doug? You want to make John jealous?"

"No, I promised Doug a dance earlier and I just want to let him know I'm available, very available."

"Ooh, gotcha!" Carol giggled a little and then stopped when she noticed I wasn't smiling. "Sorry, Ruth Ann, it's just one of the oldest tricks in the book."

"I don't plan on using Doug, just dancing with him. If John happens to see us I guess it'll be his loss."

"In that costume it sure is his loss. You really do look terrific!"

"Thanks, Carol." Before I left to search for Doug I asked Carol one last question, "Any surprises for tonight?"

"Like what?" she asked curiously.

"Halloween pranks or scary creatures coming out of the ceilings and all?" I remember what she told me about the skeletons that'll fall from the ceiling at some point.

"Ah, you'll have to wait and see. It's still early yet."

Carol left in search for Dick, and I went looking for Doug. Carol was correct and I found Doug at the food table, but he wasn't alone. I walked right up to Doug and put my arm through his and stood there waiting for a response.

I surprised Doug, but he handled it beautifully. "Hi, Ruth Ann, where've you been hiding the last few minutes. I missed you."

Putting it on little thick I thought to myself, but I went with it. "I was having a chat with Carol."

John, still speechless at my actions, and Doug's comments, finally found his voice. "You two are here *together*?"

Doug answered for me as he wrapped his arm around my waist, "Why not?"

"Uh…I didn't know you two were seeing each other."

"I never said we were," I replied tersely. "Doug was kind enough to ask me to the party tonight."

"Oh, yeah, I guess I…" John couldn't speak. He muttered a few incoherent words and walked away from the two of us.

"Wow, that should do it, Ruth Ann," Doug exclaimed.

"Do what?" I questioned. "You did ask me to the party, and I did tell you I'd look for you and ask you to dance."

"Yes, you did, Ruth Ann. But you know you put on a show for John to make him jealous."

"Doug, I really do want to dance with you and I didn't mean to put you in a bad position with John. I'm truly sorry, and if you don't want to dance with me I understand."

"Seriously? I have no problem with you exploiting my intentions. I've been trying to get you to date me for years!"

"I don't think Shirley would appreciate hearing that."

"Shirley, Doc Albert's nurse?"

"Yes, she has quite the thing for you, and she mentioned she was spending some time with you lately."

"Oh, we've had coffee and lunch a few times, but nothing serious. I hope I haven't given her the wrong intentions."

"She's cold as ice to me because she knows you've asked me out before. I don't think she likes me very much, but Doc Albert swears she's a terrific nurse and he doesn't care too much about her social life. She's always been so protective over Doc I thought she might have a thing for him, too."

"I'll be sure to be more careful with her, Ruth Ann. Let's go dance."

"First, we need to stop by my table and check on Prunella and the others."

We walked over to the table and Inga was alone. "I'm sorry, Inga, I didn't mean to leave you alone."

Inga was rocking back and forth to the music and smiling. "It's okay, Ruth Ann." She must've had a few more beers. "Prunella and Sherman are out on the dance floor, just look at them!" Inga pointed to the center of the dance floor and laughed as she watched Sherman attempting to dance with Prunella. He was jumping up and down like an uncoordinated bunny rabbit!

"Where's Bert?" I asked.

"Haven't seen him in a while. Let him be, we don't need his negative vibe around us anyway."

I introduced Doug to Inga and I could read Inga's mind. He has nothing on John. John was tall, muscular, and handsome while poor Doug was short, stout, and bald. What Inga didn't know was Doug's personality was much kinder and gentler than John's. John was loud, pushy, domineering…I do like the way he takes charge though.

I noticed Dick must've told the band to turn it down a little because it was much easier to hear. I grabbed poor Doug's hand and said, "let's go dance." He willingly followed me onto the dance floor and we cozied up to Prunella and Sherman.

"Hi, Ruth Ann," Prunella shouted, dancing to a fast paced song I've never heard before. Sherman was so out of breath he didn't have the strength to speak. I tried introducing Doug to the both of them, but with all the people on the dance floor pushing and bumping into one another it made it impossible. Prunella did give me a shrug of 'who is that, it's sure not John.'

Doug and I danced a couple more songs, thankful that one of them was a slow song. We made our way to the table and Doug asked if anyone needed anything from the bar. Inga asked for another beer, Prunella and I had another

Dirty Shirley. Sherman stuck to water and Bert was still missing.

"Where do you think he went?" Prunella inquired eyeing the room. "It's so hard to make anyone out in here."

"They do have it pretty dark in here, but that's because it's a Halloween Party. They want it to look scary."

"Oh, makes sense," Prunella said. "Maybe I'll go have a look around."

"Wait, here comes Doug with our drinks. Why ruin the evening getting Bert back?" Doug borrowed a small bar tray and handed Prunella and me our drinks, then handed Inga her bottle of cold beer. "What's your drink, Doug?" I asked.

"It's a vodka and tonic."

Doug took the chair between Prunella and me. Inga was on the opposite side of the round table and Sherman was next to her. It didn't take long for Prunella to start asking Doug questions. At first it was questions about his work over at the bank. Boring, but Prunella appeared interested. Once that topic was exhausted, Prunella started in on Doug's social life.

"I don't have much time for a social life, Prunella," Doug answered moping a bit. "Being the President of the bank requires most of my attention."

"Is that why you never married?" she inquired.

"Yes, that and I never met the person who I was meant to be with for the rest of my life," Doug replied, turning to me with a huge grin on his face. That was when he said the most shocking statement. "I've tried to convince this lady to settle down with me, but she's a difficult cookie to crumble."

Prunella's mouth fell open, but no words came out. It was the perfect time to change the topic. I wasn't about to go down the marriage road with Doug, not when my feelings for John still existed. At least they used to, I'm not quite sure where they were at the moment.

"Doug, why don't you set up an appointment with Prunella so she can do her banking here in town? I'm sure that would boost profits here in town with all her money."

"Ruth Ann," Doug said. "I don't want Prunella to think I'm only being nice to her to get her business."

"Oh, no," Prunella interrupted. "I do need a bank here so why not yours?"

"Oh," Doug said, perking up. "Come down to the bank on Monday and we can set you up."

"Perfect," she answered. "I'll bring Ruth Ann in, too."

"Ruth Ann doesn't have to be there, Prunella. Unless you feel more comfortable with her being there."

Prunella looked over at me then back to Doug and said, "Yes, she does because half of my fortune's going to her."

"What?" Doug cried out. He looked directly at me and asked, "Why haven't you told me this, Ruth Ann?"

"Because I haven't accepted that most generous offer yet, Doug," I retorted. "Prunella and I need to have a long talk first."

"Yes, yes, of course. Just let me know what you both decide and I'll help you out," Doug said, apparently shocked at Prunella's statement. What would it matter if I were rich? Would that change how Doug felt about me?

Prunella sensed the tension at the table and hopped up and asked Doug to dance. "Me?" Doug questioned. "Yes, I'd love to." I watched as the two of them disappeared into the crowd on the dance floor. I looked at my watch; it was almost ten o'clock in the evening. I wondered when Carol and Dick's surprises were going to begin? I didn't have to wait long…

Chapter 5

While I watched Prunella on the dance floor with Doug there was a flicker of the orange colored sconce lights on the walls. I wondered if they were planned or was there a problem with the electricity? Sherman and Inga noticed it too and we waited to see if the other lights were going to flicker and go out. "What happened, Ruth Ann?" Sherman asked me.

"Maybe just a fuse went out," I said, having no idea. "Nobody seems to mind."

As we watched the chandeliers and lights around the bar and food tables glow in their orange illuminations I was unaware that a body sat in the chair next to mine. It wasn't until Inga cleared her throat loudly and nodded her head in the direction of the newcomer at the table. I turned my head around and found John sitting closely next to me.

"John," I blurted out. "You startled me. Don't sneak up on a person like that."

"I'm sorry, Ruth Ann, but you've been avoiding me all evening."

"Why would I want to interrupt you and your date?" I snapped.

He grabbed my closest arm to him and pulled me in. "Let's go and have a private chat." I refused to budge until he added, "Please, Ruth Ann, can we go and talk privately?"

I agreed so he wouldn't make a scene. We left the ballroom and walked down the hallway into the lobby. We found a quiet corner where there were a couple chairs looking out through floor to ceiling windows onto the mountain and the well-lit ski lifts. "What do you want, John? Your actions the last couple days and this evening have said it all to me."

"What actions? I don't know what you're talking about."

"If you don't then this conversation's a waste of time. I'll just go back to Inga, Sherman, and Prunella." I started to stand and he pulled me back down into my chair.

"No, you may not go until I get a word in. Listen, I do admit I haven't been paying you the attention you deserve this last week. I was so behind from being in Stockholm saving your behind that I lost track of time. Plus…" I interrupted him and said, "Even a text or a call would've explained that, John."

"I'm truly sorry, Ruth Ann. You know me; I get carried away and lose all sense of time when it comes to my job. Now, let me get to the other misunderstanding."

"You call your dating Judy a misunderstanding?"

"Let's get this perfectly straight. I am NOT dating Judy. We're NOT here on a date. I wasn't planning on coming here at all tonight. I was working, like I've been doing every day and night when Judy came into my office with this ridiculous Sheriff's costume. I told her she was crazy and I would never wear that outfit."

"But you are," I interrupted.

"Yes, she made a good case. She pointed out I haven't slept, eaten, or done anything but work. It would do me some good to get out of the station and attend the party for a little while. She even pointed out that YOU would be here and maybe we could spend a little time together. So you see, Ruth Ann, Judy was thinking of you, not herself, when she suggested I show up here tonight."

"How kind of her," I commented sarcastically.

"Yes, it was," John snapped loudly. I looked around to see if anyone was listening to our conversation, but the lobby was fairly empty since everyone was in the ballroom having fun.

"Okay, fine, Judy was being nice but that doesn't explain why she didn't tell me any of this."

"She sensed you were pretty ticked off at me and decided to stay away from you until we got it straightened out."

"Oh, well, then I'm sorry for behaving poorly to her, but it doesn't get you off the hook for avoiding me since we've been back home."

"I agree, and I apologized for that part. However, I do recall Doc telling you to take it easy, and from what I've heard around town you've done anything but."

"Doc's advice was wrong. I'm not the kind of person who benefits from 'taking it easy.' You of all people should know that."

"You're right about that, but it wasn't advice Doc gave you, it was his orders as a physician. You had an enormous trauma while in Stockholm and your mind and body needed a little rest."

"Then take me away to some tropical island!"

"Excuse me?"

"That's the only thing I can think of to make me sit still. Lying on a warm, fluffy, sandy beach overlooking the blue-green Caribbean waters. Drinking a Pina Colada would help, too!"

John grabbed my hand and said, "I can't think of anywhere else I'd love to go, it just isn't the right time. I was gone in Sweden and can't get away until the station gets back to running smoothly. Lou and Dave did a good job, but Dave's still a rookie and Lou's a young guy. Smart as a cop, but hasn't had much supervisory experience yet. Soon, he's getting better every day."

"Until then, I plan to keep myself busy. That's my healing, John."

"Understood, I won't bother you about taking it easy again." John gave me one of his 'can't resist' smiles and asked me, "Am I forgiven?"

I couldn't fight him and told him, "Of course, but don't ignore me because I don't handle that well. If you're busy just tell me so, I'll understand."

"Agreed," John said, standing up and reaching his hand out for me to grab.

We headed back into the ballroom to find complete and total chaos had broken loose. "What's happening in here?" John yelled over the loud screams.

"I don't know," I said, panicking. "We need to find my daughters and Prunella." I took John's hand and pushed through the people trying to leave the ballroom. I needed to get to the other side of the dance floor where I left Prunella, Inga, and Sherman. The dessert tables were over there, and I hoped to find Lynne and Nancy.

John looked confused and bellowed, "What happened and why are people trying to leave the ballroom, but nobody's getting out? If there was a problem, we would've seen people flooding into the lobby."

"I don't know, John," I said, about halfway across the dance floor. "It's so dark in here I can't see much at all."

Between the costumes people were wearing and all the hysteria I couldn't tell who was who. There were giant papier-mâché spiders dangling down from the ceiling on black wires. "This must be one of Carol's surprises she told me would happen," I said, knocking one out of the way from my path across the floor.

"That can't be why people are panicking."

"The lights are flicking on and off from the sconces and the spiders hanging and look...skeletons dropped down from the ceiling, too." I pointed to several plastic skeletons that had dropped down over the dance floor. "It must've scared people," I said, making it over to the empty table where I left Prunella and the others. "Where'd they go?" I asked John.

"You stay here. I'll find out what's going on," John ordered as he took off toward the bar area.

I wasn't going to stand still until I found my family members. I hurried over to the food tables or what was left of them. The two dessert tables had been knocked over and cupcakes, cookies, and other pastries were spread around the floor. Most of them were smashed from people stepping on them. I couldn't find Lynne or Nancy anywhere. I ran into Lulu Hamilton as I stood by what was left of the dessert area. She looked at me with wild, scared eyes and screamed, "It's horrible, just horrible."

I grabbed her arm and swung her around to look at me and begged her to tell me what was going on. She was too distraught to speak, but pointed in one direction. "Just horrible, I need to find my husband..." and off she ran toward the dance floor and exit.

I ran over to the bar where Lulu had pointed. What could possibly be so horrible over here? There was a large group of people in a circle just in front of the bar area. I heard a loud, authoritative voice holler out, "People, just back off a little." It was John's voice. I pushed my way through the circle of people and found John, and most of my family.

"What happened here?" I cried out terrified.

Prunella was on her knees looking at something on the ground. She hurried to stand up and tried to pull me away. "No, what happened, Prunella? Please tell me!" I demanded.

"There's been a ghastly accident, Ruth Ann."

"What or who should I ask?"

"C'mon, maybe you should see this for yourself," Prunella gently took my arm and led me towards John." I was on my tippy toes looking over Inga, Sherman, and John trying to get a look at what they were staring at on the floor. I was so frustrated with my short stature that I wanted to jump over them just so I could see what the hype was about. Prunella said it was a terrible accident, but I knew it wasn't anyone in my family because I spotted Lynne and Nancy in the group of onlookers opposite from where I was standing.

"Ruth Ann, I need you to stay back. Can you take your friends away, too?" John asked calmly.

"Not until you tell me or show me who's on the ground."

"Fine, but let me warn you it's gruesome," John stated. He pushed Sherman aside a little and made way for me to take a look.

What I saw made my knees buckle and I fell to the ground. If John didn't grab me as I went down I would've cracked my knees open. "Oh, my God," was all I say before I almost passed out.

"Ruth Ann, I told you it was bad," John said, trying to pull me further away from the scene.

"No, John," I said. "It was just the shock of it that made me fall. I'm fine, now." I stood back up and stared at the dead, disfigured body on the floor.

"It's Bert," Sherman said to me. "He's been murdered."

"Why... and who would do this to him?"

Prunella stood next to me and we turned to look away. "I didn't even recognize him, Ruth Ann. He's been so badly burned that if it wasn't for Sherman I wouldn't even know it was poor Bert."

"How did Sherman identify him?" I asked curiously.

"Yeah," John chimed in. "Sherman, how did you know this was your friend?"

"He's not my friend," Sherman snapped. "I only knew it was him because he still has on the gold ring from his pirate's costume."

I turned to look again and noticed the gold skull ring on a finger. I quickly glanced at the rest of Bert or should I say what was left of him. The body lay on the ground in a perfect S shape. Whoever did this to Bert tried to make him look like one of the other skeletons that fell from the ceiling. Most of him was unrecognizable because he had been burned from head to toe. It was the most disgusting thing I've ever seen or smelled in my life. I covered my mouth with my hand to try and keep some of the rotting flesh smell away.

John called Dick over and asked him for his purple vampire cape. He laid the cape over the scorched body and asked people to back away, but not to leave. This must be why most of the people didn't leave the ballroom. Somebody must've told them to stay inside the room. That someone just walked over to John. It was Judy Lynch.

"John, I couldn't find you anywhere so I tried to secure the area and keep people in the ballroom."

"That's the right thing to do, Judy," John stated. "We need to take statements from everybody here."

Dick turned to leave, but John stopped him. "How did a human body happen to come falling down from your ceiling, Dick?"

Dick looked pale from the sight of the body and exclaimed, "I didn't plan this, John. Carol and I only had fake spiders and skeletons rigged up to fall at ten o'clock to scare people a little. I have no idea how this happened, and why anyone would play such a sick joke."

"I need you to go over to the front doors and tell people to stay inside here. Then turn on the normal ballroom lights so we can see better in here."

Dick took off and did what he was told and within a couple minutes the room illuminated and I saw the faces of terrified residents of Deer Creek hovering by the front doors begging to get out.

John walked to the middle of the dance floor and hollered at the top of his lungs, "People, quiet please." He waited for everyone to be quiet. It took a number of times from John to get people to listen to him. "Please, I need your full attention."

Finally, everyone stood still and paid attention to what John was about to say. "Listen, there's been a horrible crime committed. Nobody can leave until Judy or I have talked with each and every one of you. I don't want anybody playing a fast one and exiting. If you do, you'll be arrested, do I make myself clear?"

I wondered how John would know if someone had snuck out, but then it dawned on me that Carol kept immaculate records and she knew everyone who signed in this evening. So if John or Judy didn't interview them they would be sought out, questioned, and possibly arrested.

Chapter 6

Halloween night has now become a true horror night in Deer Creek. Most of the town had gathered together to celebrate and dance the night away at the only resort's elegant ballroom. What they didn't pay for was a real life terror story.

Prunella, Inga, and Sherman sat themselves down at the table we had occupied earlier that evening. I grabbed my daughters and asked them to join us until we were released from the ballroom. Lynne declined because she wanted to clean up her ruined desserts that were spread out over the floor. Nancy and Julie, her assistant at the bakery, offered to help her clean it up. I could see them clearly from where I sat so I felt they were perfectly safe.

I settled myself down into a chair next to Prunella who sat staring out into space. "Prunella, are you alright?"

Inga answered for her and said, "No, I don't think she is, Ruth Ann. Bert was just brutally murdered and Prunella blames herself for that."

"What?" I asked, astonished at Inga's insensitive remarks. "Why would Prunella blame herself? She had nothing to do with his murder."

"Yes, Ruth Ann," Prunella quietly said. "I made him attend this party tonight. If I just left him alone he'd still be alive."

"This isn't your fault, Prunella," I responded. "Bert was making all of your lives miserable. I'm not saying he got what he deserved. I'm saying that he had a way of making people dislike him and somebody took it too far."

"Dislike him?" Sherman asked. "I despised the guy."

"Sherman!" Prunella cried out. "This isn't the time to talk like that."

"But it's the truth," Inga chimed in. "He was a miserable, rude pain in the...somebody killed him to shut him up."

"But who?" I asked. "Nobody knew him except for us."

"Exactly," Inga said, looking at the three of us. "Maybe one of *us* did it?"

"Be serious," Prunella declared. "None of us did this to him. We were together all evening."

"Ah, good point, Prunella. Sherman, Inga, and you were never apart, were you?"

"Not long enough to burn a body, figure out how to hang him up from the ceiling, and have him released the same time as the spiders and other plastic skeletons were," Sherman stated.

"That would take a lot of time and planning, wouldn't it?" I asked.

"Yes," John answered, sitting down at the chair next to me startling the others and myself. "Sorry, didn't mean to surprise you all, but Ruth Ann has a good point. When was the last time you saw Bert tonight?"

We looked at each other and I spoke up first. "I haven't seen him since we arrived here this evening. We grabbed this table and I don't think he ever sat here, did he?" I looked at the others and they shook their heads.

"No, he took off on his own the minute we walked into the ballroom," Prunella stated. Inga and Sherman nodded their heads, but didn't speak.

"So, when you got to the resort tonight did you talk to anyone before you came inside the ballroom?"

"Just Dick, I believe," I answered. The other three nodded their heads in agreement.

"You two can speak up, too," John mentioned to Inga and Sherman.

"We don't know anything," Sherman snapped. "Bert was being a pain and didn't want to come this evening. We forced the guy to come and once we got here he stormed off. Knowing Bert's personality, he probably ticked off some disturbed person and they killed him."

"What do you mean Bert's personality ticking somebody off?" John inquired.

"He's an old snob of a butler and he wasn't happy working for Prunella. He missed his former boss," Sherman answered.

"You're talking about Axel Eklund?" John asked.

"Yes," Inga replied for Sherman, wanting him to be quiet. "He was very loyal to Mr. Eklund, but he died back in Sweden. Bert could've left but he didn't."

"I don't know why he didn't quit since we were brought here under Prunella's leadership and we didn't need two butlers," Sherman added resentfully.

"Sherman!" Prunella shouted. "Stop that, now."

John, shocked at Prunella's outburst and Sherman's lack of sympathy for a dead man, watched as the two of them battled it out. It was an old trick for a cop to let people's true feelings come out in chaotic times. I wanted to stop both of them, but then John would be furious at me so I let them continue their bickering back and forth.

"Ms. Prunella, you know he's been a complete, excuse the word, jerk, to you, Inga and me."

"It doesn't matter how he acted, Sherman, nobody deserves to be killed in such a horrific way."

"He got what he deserved," Sherman mumbled.

"What did you say?" John asked, wondering if he found his killer already.

"Nothing," Sherman bitterly said. "He was a miserable human being, that's all."

"You wouldn't happen to know what happened to him, Sherman?" John asked him intently.

"*Me*?" Sherman stuttered. "Why would I know? I was with them all evening," Sherman answered pointing to Inga and Prunella. Realizing he was looking guilty he added, "You think *I* killed Bert?"

"Did you?" John asked bluntly. "You sure hated the guy, and Bert didn't know too many people in town, right?"

"I did NOT murder him and I don't know who he knows in this town. I just arrived here and Bert had been here for months. Maybe he was involved in something illegal here, he's done it before."

"What do you mean he's been involved in illegal behavior before?" John asked, knowing Bert had been involved in my kidnapping earlier on.

Sherman shouted out, "He helped kidnap Ruth Ann, didn't he? Plus, he worked for Axel Eklund, and most of what that man did was illegal."

"Okay," John replied coolly. "I want you three to stay here until all the other guests have been interviewed." He stood up to leave and then added, "and that means not leaving his ballroom, got it?"

"Of course, John," I answered for the group. "We'll stay right here at the table."

"Wow, that went bad," Inga, declared. "We sure look guilty."

"No, we don't," Prunella replied. "There's no way Sherman could've killed Bert. He was with us all evening."

"Not the entire evening," Inga commented. "Sherman did go off on his own for a while."

"Hey," Sherman bellowed. "I went looking for Bert because Ms. Prunella asked me to. I wasn't gone that long."

"Maybe not long enough to burn him and set him up as a ridiculous skeleton piñata," Inga said.

"That's sick," Sherman snapped.

"Sorry," Inga said, regretting her words the minute they left her mouth. "I didn't mean to speak ill of the dead. I don't want to curse myself for saying bad things."

"Curse?" I asked curiously. "Why would you think you would be cursed?"

"Because, it could happen," Inga spat out. "I'm disrespectful of Bert and how he was such a despicable person, and then I made a joke about how he was killed. He could come back and haunt me."

"Ridiculous," Sherman snorted. "I'm the only guilty looking one right now. I'm in serious trouble aren't I?" He looked to Prunella and me for a response but we didn't give one. We sat in silence for the next couple of hours watching John and Judy talk with the other guests. Most of them were allowed to leave once they were finished with their interviews. Slowly the room was emptying except for Bert's body. Why weren't they taking it away? I couldn't bear to look in that direction anymore.

Finally, around midnight, the coroner loaded the body into a black vinyl bag, and with the help of a couple of John's men picked him up and dumped him onto a gurney. They wheeled him out and I took a long deep breath. It felt like the first breath I took all night. First, fighting with John,

then Bert falling down from the ceiling looking like a
skeleton. I wanted to go home and close my eyes and wake
up believing this evening was a horrible nightmare.
Unfortunately, that wasn't the truth.

Chapter 7

John escorted us out to the front of the resort and watched as Sherman went and retrieved the limousine. "Ruth Ann, where are you staying tonight?"

I looked at him strangely and told him, "At my house, why?"

"I didn't know if you were planning on staying up at Prunella's place or not. I'd feel more comfortable if you weren't alone. I don't know why, but I really don't want to go down this path again."

"What path?" I asked him, confused. "Why would I be in any danger? Bert was killed and I had nothing to do with him."

"You did a few weeks ago. That man aided in your kidnapping, remember?"

"But Axel Eklund was killed back in Sweden." I reminded him.

"I'm not so sure that happened, Ruth Ann," John admitted. "My sources have confirmed there was never a body found at the prison."

"You're just telling me this now?" I snapped.

Prunella overheard what John said and asked, shocked, "You think my husband's still alive?"

"I didn't say that," he replied carefully. "I just said his body was never recovered. He was a rich, and resourceful man, who knows what stunt he could've concocted."

Sherman drove the limousine around and got out to open the doors for us. He caught the tail end of John's explanation. "I'm just saying, I'd feel more comfortable if you stay with Prunella. If Eklund did make it out of prison he could've come back here and murdered Bert. You could be in danger."

"Why would he murder Bert?" I asked curiously. "Bert was on Axel's side?"

"Who knows what could've went down? Maybe Bert had been in contact with him and he wasn't cooperating with Eklund, so instead of risking being caught alive he killed him."

"That's the most ridiculous story I've ever heard," Sherman responded to John. "Bert was a jerk and he answered only to Eklund. Eklund would never kill him because he knew Bert would do anything for him. That's if Eklund's still alive, which I think is ludicrous."

"Thanks for your opinion, Sherman," John declared smartly. "You'd think you'd like that option since it releases you of any suspicion."

"Oh, I…didn't mean to be disrespectful," Sherman quickly said. "I guess it could have happened that way."

"No way," Prunella demanded. "He's dead and never coming back."

"I'm sure he's gone, Prunella," I said, trying to reassure her. John put a frightening thought back into her head, and now she'll worry about it until the truth comes out whether Axel's dead or alive.

"He has to be gone," she said quietly. "He'd be using his money, and my financial guy back in Sweden would've contacted me about any activity with his accounts."

"True," I said. "John, there's no way Axel's still alive. You need to find somebody else to blame for Bert's death and not Sherman!"

"He has the motive and a missing piece of time when he went looking for the guy. Sorry, Sherman, but you are as of now my only suspect."

"Am I under arrest?" Sherman asked, distraught.

"No, but if you try and leave Prunella's estate without permission I'll find you and you'll be locked up. Do you understand what I'm saying?"

"Yes, but I didn't do it. I hated the guy, but I didn't kill him."

"Whoever murdered Bert's a sick and disturbed person, John. Sherman has done nothing to show he's that kind of person," I said supporting Sherman.

"I agree," Prunella stated emphatically. "We'll find out who did this if you don't."

"Oh, no, we aren't going there again, ladies," John said, glaring at Prunella and me. "You just got back from your last escapade, this time the murder investigation's my territory. Understand me clearly?"

"Sure, John, whatever you say," I said smirking, knowing I would do what I wanted, and since Sherman was now a close friend of mine I'd help him anyway I could. Prunella caught my quick glance over at her and winked back at me.

"I saw that!" John yelled. "If I have to put an officer at the front and back doors of Prunella's place, and put you all under house arrest, I'll do just that. Don't push me, Ruth Ann."

"Calm down, John. I'm sure you'll find out who did this to Bert and we won't be a part of it in any way." I looked toward the front door of the resort and spotted Lou, John's next in line at the station besides Judy, looking over at John. "Uh, John, I think Lou wants you."

John spun around and waved Lou over to us. "What'd you find?"

Lou looked from John to all of us and said, "In front of them?"

"Yes, you might as well. They'll find out anyway."

"Okay, we opened up the ceiling to see how the owners rigged up the wiring for the spiders and skeletons to fall. They were on the same remote control so when it was time, Dick or Carol just had to push a button and the items would fall down from the ceiling. Everyone would be surprised, you know, a hokey Halloween trick."

"Ya, so what about the human body that fell?" John inquired.

"That's just it, he wasn't hooked up to the remote wiring and that means whoever killed him was up in the ceiling waiting for the time when the owners dropped the other stuff."

"That makes no sense, Lou." John added, "Is there room up there for a person to hang out?"

"Oh, yes," Lou said excitedly. "Above the ballroom ceiling is a catwalk that can be used to hang props from the ceiling. In this case, the killer knew about it and knew about what time the other Halloween items would fall from the ceiling, too."

"So the killer must've obtained that information from Dick or Carol, right?" I asked.

"Appears so" John said, confused. "I could ask Dick or Carol if they told anyone about their little surprise at ten."

"John," I interrupted his thinking out loud. "I did kind of know about it."

"What?"

"Well not *exactly* when it was happening. I came by earlier and saw some of the spiders hanging. That's when she told me there was going to be surprises happening. She didn't tell me anything else. Who knows what other information she revealed as the night went on. Maybe she told the killer without thinking much of it." I stopped for a moment and then hurriedly added, "That means Carol knew the killer!"

"Maybe, Ruth Ann," John said. "We don't know if Carol told anyone anything as of yet." John turned to Lou and asked, "Have you spoken with either Dick or Carol lately?"

"No, we spent our time trying to figure out how the body fell from the ceiling."

"What about the body being burned? Have you found where that occurred? It had to be somewhere here at the resort."

"Good point," I said to John. "Where could someone burn a body so it looked like that?"

John turned to Lou and ordered him and the other cops to search out behind the resort and see if there was any sign of a fire. "Also, check the kitchens, the basement, and see if any smoke alarms were tripped during the party." Lou nodded and hurried back into the resort.

John turned his attention back to us and told us to get in the limousine and head back to Prunella's. He had too much to do here and didn't want to worry about us. "Stay together, just in case," he added, shutting the back door of the vehicle.

"I'm sure glad we're out of there," Inga stated. "But it feels weird leaving without Bert."

"I know," Prunella agreed. "We didn't like the old man, but he didn't deserve to be killed so brutally."

"Sherman, you have to agree with that, right?" I asked him.

"Oh, yes, I did hate the guy, but this…nobody deserves what happened to him."

"Good," I said then sat back while Sherman drove us over to my house so I could pack a bag and head up to Prunella's estate.

Chapter 8

By the time we reached the estate it was well after midnight. "I'm glad it's not Halloween anymore," Inga said. "That holiday gives me the creeps, and now we have to worry about Mr. Eklund possibly coming back here!"

"Let's not go there tonight," I said. "I'm exhausted and we could use a good night's sleep. We'll think clearer in the morning."

As Sherman pulled into the circular driveway I noticed a police car parked near the front door. "What's this?" I questioned.

"Maybe they came to arrest me," Sherman panicked. "I don't know what I'd do if they took me away to jail."

"I'm sure that's not why they're here," I said as Sherman parked the limousine behind the police car. "It can't be John, we left him and Lou back at the resort." The three of us hurried out of the limo and walked up to the police car. Just as I was about to peek inside to see who was in there a familiar voice called my name from the opened front doors of the estate.

"What...how did they get inside?" Prunella asked furiously. "I don't care if they're the police, they have no right to break into my house!"

I couldn't believe my eyes, it was Judy Lynch, the newly hired, permanent detective at the Deer Creek Police Station! She was still dressed in her Halloween costume as saloon performer. Judy was waving for us to come over to her. Prunella didn't wait for Sherman, Inga, and me. She marched up the wide-set front brick steps and declared, "You had no right breaking in here."

Judy gave Prunella a most innocent glance and stated, "I didn't break in."

"We've been gone this evening. How did you happen to get inside my house then?"

"She let me in," Judy replied, grabbing the arm of a person who was hiding behind the door. "C'mon," Judy said, struggling to present the mysterious person behind the door. Finally, a young woman appeared holding her head down to the ground. "This is Helena."

"Helena?" Prunella inquired, confused at the sight of this woman dressed in a black and white uniform. "I don't know you."

"If you would just come in I'll explain," Judy said, exasperated. She turned to Helena and shouted, "Stop fidgeting, they won't be mad at you once I explain everything."

The young woman held up her head and I couldn't help but stare at the beautiful face that looked out at us. She couldn't be more than twenty-five, tiny body with long dark hair pulled up into a high ponytail. She had the most amazing turquoise green eyes that stared at us so innocently.

Prunella was the first one to enter her house. I followed suit, then Inga and Sherman. Judy dragged poor Helena alongside of her as we went straight into the library. Prunella wanted to establish her control of the situation and went to sit behind her late (hopefully) husband's large executive desk. "Well, we're all here so please tell me what this is about."

The rest of us either sat in the two chairs that faced the desk or stood behind them. I, of course, sat in one of the chairs and so did Inga. Judy went to the side of the desk and hopped on the edge. Poor Helena stood directly behind me with Sherman close to her.

"It's a bit of a long explanation, but here goes," Judy started to say. "Helena worked here for Axel Eklund. Don't go accusing her of anything until you hear what I have to say." We looked at Helena whose head dropped back down. "Axel hired Helena from a shelter and brought her back here and she became the second string housekeeper under Bertha."

Helena's head popped up when she heard Bertha's name. "I know Bertha was a very bad person. You need to believe me that I had nothing to do with her. I just did my job and I had nothing to do with your kidnapping." Helena stopped talking and pointed at me. "Please, I am a good person and not like those others, Bertha and Bert."

"You knew Bert?" I asked quickly.

"Yes, of course," she answered matter of fact. "He was Mr. Eklund's butler. We didn't really speak much. He scared me, actually."

Judy interrupted and asked her, "Why would Bert scare you?"

"He always looked at me like I was a nothing, you know, worthless, that's the word. He treated me like I was a piece of garbage and he was better than me. Bertha did the same thing. I hated both of them, but I did my job and kept my mouth shut."

"We've heard your statement before so you don't have to explain anymore," Judy said. "Let me get back to my explanation. Helena was a maid here before you returned from Sweden. She wasn't involved in Ruth Ann's kidnapping. We've thoroughly checked out her story and it's true."

"But if she worked for my late husband, where has she been since we've returned from Sweden?"

"Once the chief and I took off to Sweden after Ruth Ann, and Bertha for that fact, we placed Helena with a local resident to try and help her find a job. Unfortunately, Helena doesn't have a lot of experience so she insisted we place her back as a maid. The problem is that there aren't too many locals here that require a maid."

"Except for the mayor and his wife, right?" I asked Judy, knowing what she was going to say next.

"Exactly," Judy said, smiling. "That didn't go over too well with Mrs. Hamilton, the mayor's wife."

Helena added, "She was very mean to me!"

"Because she didn't want a young, beautiful woman in the house with her husband," Judy declared. "But that's another story…"

"I understand that," I said smiling over at Helena. "Henry can be a bit of a flirt. His wife, Lulu Hamilton, brought out the claws and kicked you to the curb I bet."

"Huh?" Helena responded with a baffled look on her face.

Judy blurted out, "The wife would be too jealous of you so you didn't get the job. It wasn't because you weren't good enough, you were too pretty."

"Oh, I get it," Helena answered proudly. "I didn't like them anyway. I like it here."

"So, now we have two housekeepers instead of two butlers?" Inga asked frustrated. "It can't end the way it did with the butlers!"

"What do you mean?" Helena asked. "Where's Bert?"

We looked at Judy and I asked her, "You didn't tell her?"

"No, I was waiting until we knew if Prunella would be so kind to keep Helena here as help?"

Prunella, being the kind person we all know she is, smiled sweetly and told Helena, "Of course you can stay. I would never kick somebody out that used to be a part of this household. That's what I kept telling Bert, but he wouldn't listen to me and now it's too late."

"Too late for what?" Helena asked panicking. "Where's Bert?"

Judy answered Helena's question for the group. "Bert had an accident tonight and won't be coming back."

"What kind of accident? Is he in the hospital?" she asked harmlessly.

"He's dead," Sherman blurted out without any sympathy in his voice. "Somebody murdered him tonight at the Halloween party over at the resort. So that's why there's only one butler now."

"Murdered?" Helena asked, falling against the back of my chair and grabbing onto it.

"Sherman, help her!" Prunella cried out.

"She's fine now, right?" he asked her without lending a helping hand.

"Yes, I'm all right. I just can't believe somebody killed Bert. Who would do that? He was old and basically harmless."

"That's what we need to figure out," Judy replied.

"Have they any suspects?" Helena asked.

"Me," Sherman announced. "They think I did it because I couldn't stand the guy."

Helena moved quickly away from Sherman and stood on the opposite side of the desk from Judy. "Did you?"

"Of course not," Sherman spat out. "I hated the guy, but I would never kill him. I just wanted him to leave Ms. Prunella's home. He didn't fit in here anymore."

"Sherman!" Prunella bellowed. "That's not up to you. Bert would've had a job for as long as he wanted. Just like you Helena. You are welcome here as long as you want."

"Thank you, ma'am," she said quietly, smiling.

"Please, call me Prunella."

"Oh, no, I could never do that."

"Okay, then Ms. Prunella. I won't take anything else."

Helena beamed and backed away from the desk. We turned our attention back to Judy and I asked her, "So, is that why you're here? To bring Helena back?"

Judy laughed and said, "Don't you wish, Ruth Ann."

"Please explain," Prunella said with authority.

"John felt it necessary that you have protection up here. The station is at least twenty minutes away and he didn't want anything happening without police protection."

"Because of me?" Sherman inquired.

"You happen to be a prime suspect, Sherman," Judy answered truthfully. "But I think it's more about who may come up here."

"Who?" I asked.

"Yes, there's a killer out there lurking around and he happened to murder your butler. Think about it. Nobody knows this Bert except for you all. Why would a complete stranger want to murder him in such a gruesome manner?"

"That's your job to figure out," Prunella snapped. "Why do we need police protection *here*?"

"I'm just going to say it…the chief's worried that Axel Eklund is still alive and may be lurking around here."

"What?" Helena screamed and almost fainted again. "He's a horrible man. Do you think he killed Bert?"

"It's a strong possibility," Judy acknowledged. "That's if he's still alive."

"He's not," Prunella stated strongly. "There's no way he can still be alive and letting me live here using his fortune."

"That's a good point, Prunella," I said. "Have they discovered any missing money? I mean I'm sure the police have checked his financial records, right?"

"That's not your concern, Ruth Ann," Judy said.

"Of course it is! If Axel's still alive and he's touched some of his money that would mean he's coming here to finish us off."

"And that's why I'm here, Ruth Ann."

"You think you're going to stop Axel if and when he comes here?" Prunella inquired with sarcasm.

"I'm a detective, it's my job." Judy hopped off the desk and said, "Enough of this, it's late and you need to get some rest. John said he'll come by here in the morning and we'll discuss our plans. I'll be wandering around the house throughout the night, and there are a couple policemen doing surveillance outside. You are safe."

"I'm tired," I said, rising from the chair. "I'll just go up to my room and see you in the morning. Prunella?"

"Yes, I'll come with you." Prunella pushed the large desk chair back and stood up. Inga trailed behind us as we left the library, and then Sherman, Helena, and Judy followed.

"What do you think?" Prunella asked me as we headed up the main staircase to the second and third floors.

"It's obvious they think Axel's a threat to us or there wouldn't be police presence here."

"Unless they want to watch Sherman," Inga suggested quietly as Sherman went up to the third floor alone.

"They would've arrested him if they really thought he was dangerous," I replied.

"I agree," Prunella stated. "If Axel's alive, he won't rest until I'm dead."

"Me, too," I said.

"And me," Inga added. "I've betrayed him and he knows my loyalty's with you, Ms. Prunella."

"I wouldn't have made it this far without you, Inga," Prunella said, as we walked down the long second floor hall to her master bedroom. "Do you want to stay with me tonight, Ruth Ann?"

"No, I'll just go next door and crash. I'm exhausted so it won't take me long to get asleep. My problem's if I wake up before it's light out I won't be able to fall back asleep."

"Come in here, then," Prunella said. "I don't know if I'll sleep a wink!"

"I'll sleep on the couch in here, Ms. Prunella," Inga announced.

"No, Inga, go upstairs and sleep in your own bed. Helena will be up there and Sherman, too."

"I don't want to leave you alone," Inga stated. "Mr. Eklund knows his way around this place. If he wants to get in without the police seeing him he will."

"Thanks for making me comfortable, Inga," I said, mockingly.

"I'm just saying it might help if we stay together," Inga demanded. "I'll sleep on the couch and you two can share the bed. It's a huge bed so it shouldn't be a problem."

"Well, what do you say, Ruth Ann? Inga does make a valid point."

"It does make better sense to stay together," I admitted. "Judy's good, not that I would ever tell her that, but Axel's one sneaky man. I wouldn't put it past him to survive and come back to finish us off."

"That's reassuring," Inga said.

"Okay, Inga, Ruth Ann and I will take the bed and you can sleep on the couch if you want to. Run up and tell Helena and Sherman where you'll be for the night so they don't worry."

Inga left the room, which gave Prunella and me a little alone time to discuss what happened to Bert privately.

"So, do you think Sherman's guilty or do you believe Axel came back from the dead and finished Bert off?" I asked Prunella seriously.

"I know Sherman didn't kill Bert, but if Axel's alive we all have a lot to worry about."

"I agree, but it seems so unlikely that Axel could still be alive."

"Ruth Ann, I've known Axel a long time and it wouldn't surprise me. He was kind and gentle to you one minute, and then stabbing you in the back the next minute. I didn't think I was capable of marrying such a monster."

"So, when you and Axel first got together he was still married, right?"

"Yes," Prunella replied. "I know it was wrong, but his wife was horrible to him and he wanted to divorce her, but she wouldn't let him without destroying everything he owned."

"Now it seems so silly because they're both dead, well at least that's what we're supposed to think."

"The more it sits on my mind the more I'm convinced Axel may still be alive," Prunella said and headed into the bathroom attached to her bedroom. She came back out in a gray t-shirt and some black yoga pants. "The only thing that keeps me from totally believing Axel's back is the way Bert was murdered. I know he was ruthless and cruel, but he never did the physical part of hurting someone himself."

"What do you mean?"

"He never tortured or killed anyone, he had Finn or one of his thugs do it for him."

"So what you're saying is that if Axel's back so are his men?"

"That or it's not him," Prunella said, hopping into the king-sized bed and getting under a fluffy, down comforter.

"Hmm, maybe he hired some new men to do his dirty work. Who knows, maybe he's ordering the hit from Sweden!"

"I doubt that, but it would make me feel a little better."

"Not me, I would worry more about professional hit men," I said. "Forget that I said that, it was a ridiculous theory."

"Nothing's out of bounds when it comes to him. If he wants to pay me back and take back what is his, he will. Even if he has to have someone kill to get it."

"That's not making me feel any better, Prunella," I said, retreating into the bathroom to clean up and put on some pajamas.

By the time I returned Prunella was sound asleep. So much for her not sleeping tonight! It was extremely late so I carefully got into the other side of the bed. Inga had returned and she was lying on the couch watching me creep around the bed. "You startled me," I whispered to Inga. "I didn't know you were back."

"You were in the bathroom when I came in. Prunella was already asleep so I tried to be very quiet."

"Well, not much more we can do until morning. I'm going to try and get some sleep." I got inside the warm cozy bed and thought I would fall asleep immediately. It was a long day and a horribly long evening. Normally, at home I would turn on my television or read until my eyes felt heavy. But since I didn't want to disturb Prunella or Inga, I chose to lie here until I dropped off. It was 2:00

am…2:30…3:00…3:30…Ridiculous! I couldn't calm my brain down.

Once I'm focused on something during the night I cannot shut it down. There have been times I wake up in the middle of the night and start thinking about the silliest things. Once these thoughts are in my head, it's almost impossible to stop them. I can't tell you how many nights I've laid awake because I forgot to write something down on my grocery list or if I needed to change what I wanted to wear the next day. Worst is when I lie there thinking about how I really have to go to the bathroom, but do I get up? No, I suffer and lie awake until I can't take it anymore.

So, should I just get up and go downstairs? I didn't want to wake Prunella or Inga, but I was a tiny bit scared to venture downstairs in the dark by my lonesome. I decided to give it a chance and go down to the kitchen to make myself a cup of tea. Maybe that would soothe my nerves and I could catch a couple hours of sleep.

I ever so carefully pulled the comforter off me and swung my legs off the bed. I glided my feet into a pair of slippers I put next to the bed and walked toward the door. Just as I was passing the couch an arm reached out and grabbed my leg. I wasn't prepared for what came next. My leg gave out and I landed smack dab on top of Inga on the couch.

"What the…" I cried out as quietly as I could and pulled myself off her.

"Sorry, Ruth Ann," Inga whispered. "I saw you trying to leave and I had to stop you."

"Why? I just wanted to go make some tea because I can't sleep."

"You shouldn't go anywhere alone, especially in this house."

"Why not?" I questioned. "Are there ghosts?"

"Not funny, Ruth Ann," Inga snapped. "There may be, but that's not why I stopped you. If anyone knows how to get around here it's Mr. Eklund." Inga threw the cotton blanket aside and stood up next to me. "I can't sleep either so we can go down together."

"Fine, but we need to be quiet. I don't want to wake Prunella."

"Neither do I," Inga snapped back at me. "She's very fragile."

I looked at Inga with a stunned expression on my face. "Why would you say that? Prunella's young, strong, and a very intelligent woman."

"She's been through a lot over the last couple years."

"Remember Inga, she faked an illness with Axel. She wasn't actually sick."

"Sometimes I forget it was a sham. I envision her lying in that bed up in the attic in Mr. Eklund's home back in Sweden. You're right, she isn't fragile."

"Let's get out of here before we wake her up." We took off down the dimly lit hallway of the second floor and headed for the staircase that either led toward the grand foyer or back to the kitchen. Inga took the lead and we went down the back staircase, which ended in a butler's pantry that led to either the kitchen or dining room.

"I'll start some tea," Inga said, walking toward the stove and grabbing the stainless steel kettle sitting on it.

"Make mine decaf, please," I asked. "I need to get some sleep still and don't want any caffeine."

"That's what I was going to do anyway," Inga said grouchily.

We left the lights in the kitchen off and just made our way around from the light left on above the massive stove. The room had an eerie glow and I was happy I wasn't alone in here. "Kind of spooky down here at this time, isn't it?"

"That's why I didn't think you should go alone," Inga said, opening a cabinet and pulling out a couple mugs for the tea.

"Grab three mugs," a voice called out from the door that opened to the butler's pantry.

Inga juggled the two mugs in her hands trying not to drop them as I jumped off of my stool at the island. "Sherman!" I exclaimed. "Don't do that."

"What?" he said. "I came down here to do the same thing you two are doing since I couldn't sleep." Inga recovered herself and grabbed another mug. "Come and sit down, Sherman."

Sherman sat down on the stool next to mine and said, "I can't get the image of Bert out of my head. The burnt skeleton of a body and the way he lay crooked on the floor. That image is permanently embedded in my head."

"Me, too," Inga said, and I nodded in agreement. "The smell was horrible, too."

"Please don't talk about that, Inga," I asked. "My stomach hasn't recovered from it yet and I'm hoping the tea will settle it down."

The whistle on the teapot squealed and the three of us jumped. "We're all so tense," I said, dumping my tired self back down on the stool. Inga poured the tea and grabbed a plateful of almond biscotti and plopped it down in front of us on the massive marble island. "Those look good, Inga," I said. "I do love a good biscotti! I used to make those all the time, but had to stop because I couldn't stop eating them. A very dear friend of mine gave me a delicious recipe for them, but they were deadly for my weight!" I snapped my lips shut after seeing the astonished looks on Inga and Sherman's face. "I didn't mean to use the word, deadly!"

Chapter 9

After a quiet cup of hot tea, the three of us went back to our beds and made another attempt at slumber. I have to admit the tea did the job for me. My stomach settled down, possibly from the biscotti, and I slept until late the next morning. I awoke with a start and found myself alone in Prunella's bedroom. "Where's everyone?" I asked myself. Once dressed, I flew down the back staircase and entered the kitchen. Helena was at the sink washing the mugs and plates from the night before. I asked her where everyone else was and she pointed toward the dining room. "Thanks," I said, and rushed through the butler's pantry into the dining room.

I spotted Prunella at the head of the table. Her back was to me and Inga was at the side table making a plate of food for her. Sherman was at the opposite side of the room bringing in Judy. "Hey, where were you last night?" I asked her curiously. I didn't remember running into her when we came down here for our late night tea.

"What do you mean, Ruth Ann?" Judy asked innocently. "I was here, walking around the house and keeping everybody safe."

"Really? Sherman, Inga, and I were down here during the middle of the night and we didn't see any sign of you."

"Oh, when was that?" she asked, taking an empty chair to the right of Prunella. I noticed that when she grabbed the chair her hand was slightly shaking.

"Around 3:00 in the morning," I replied. "We didn't hear any sign of you. Where were you?"

Unexpectedly, Judy knocked her cup of coffee off the saucer spilling half of it on the table. Inga rushed over to clean it up with a damp cloth. "Oops, clumsy me," Judy said chuckling. "I didn't have any sleep last night. I'm always clumsy when I pull all-nighters."

Once Inga cleaned up Judy's mess I asked her again where she was at about 3 in the morning. "I really can't say, Ruth Ann," Judy said a little less cheery. "Maybe I was checking with the guys posted outside the house. I did that, too."

"That makes sense," Prunella said, motioning for me to sit on her other side. "Let's get some food in us and wait for John to show up. He can fill us in on what's been happening with the investigation and Bert."

"I'm not too hungry," I said, remembering the sight of Bert last night. I wondered if I'd ever be able to rid my brain of Bert lying on the floor, literally burnt to death.

"You need to eat to keep up your strength. We're all running on little to no sleep," Prunella said.

"Okay, what'd you make for us Inga?" I asked her.

"Helena made most of the food since I was upstairs with you two."

Helena popped into the dining room hearing her name and hurried over to Inga. "I made scrambled eggs, bacon, toast, and some French toast." Helena stood up as tall as her five-foot frame would allow and smiled broadly.

"You did well this morning, Helena," Prunella said to her. "If your food tastes as good as it smells you won't have to worry about your position here." Inga glared at the small woman and even at Prunella. I didn't think Inga wanted any competition when it came to her job after the butler fiasco. Look at what happened to Bert when Sherman and he fought constantly.

"Inga," Prunella said, sensing she upset her. "You know you'll always be very important to me and you never have to worry about your job here."

"Thank you," she muttered. She wasn't happy, but she took it in stride. "What do you want, Ruth Ann?" Inga asked after serving Prunella her eggs and toast.

"I'll have the French toast if you have syrup for it."

"I'll just pop in the kitchen and grab it," Helena replied, darting out of the room and returning immediately. "Here, I found it."

Inga grabbed the bottle from Helena and spoke to her in a low, quiet voice, "Don't try so hard to look good. Do you understand me?" Helena backed away from Inga and made a plate for Judy.

"Thanks," Judy said, taking the plate from Helena's shaking hands. "I'll eat whatever you make me."

Prunella, not appreciating Judy's comment, said, "Just how long do you plan on staying here?"

"Until the killer's caught or the Chief tells me not to."

"Oh, well, I'll have a nice chat with your chief when he gets here," Prunella remarked.

"Have a chat about what?" a voice called out from the other side of the room.

"John," I cried out. "Doesn't anybody ring doorbells anymore?"

"I did knock, but nobody answered so I tried the door and it wasn't locked." He looked over at Sherman and stated, "Isn't that your job, Sherman?"

"Huh?" he asked confused.

"To make sure the house is safe and secure?"

"Oh, yes, I just thought with the police around it *was* safe and secured."

Trying to get past this conversation I asked John to sit next to me (not Judy) and tell us what was happening since we left him last night.

"The coroner gave us his preliminary results on Bert." Inga plopped a plate of eggs, bacon, and toast in front of John and he momentarily stopped talking so he could put some food in his mouth.

"These eggs are so creamy," he said, then shoving an entire piece of bacon in his mouth.

"John," I said irritated. "Please get back to Bert."

"Yes, I will, Ruth Ann. I haven't eaten in hours and the food smelled so good I just wanted a couple bites. Then I'll tell you what I can."

"Oh, here we go with this again," I said.

"What do you mean by that?" asked Judy.

"John reminds us that we aren't privy to *all* the information. He'll tell us a nibble to keep us satisfied." I smiled over at John and reminded him, "How did that work out last time?"

"Not well," he said, swallowing his coffee with a big gulp. "Think what you want, I'm the Chief of Police and I'll tell you what I think you need to know. If there's other information out there we feel needs to be kept under wraps, we'll do just that. Unless you've recently gone through police training?" He looked from me to Prunella then to Inga and Sherman.

"Go on," I snapped. "Just tell us what happened to Bert, and if you know more about who did this to him?"

"The obvious assumption was that Bert was burned to death, tied to some fishing line, and hung from the ceiling to be dropped with the other props."

"Yes, that much we know," Prunella, said.

"The coroner said Bert was already dead before he was burned."

"What?" I cried out. "How'd he die?"

"He had a stab wound. He died instantly, then the killer set him on fire out back of the resort. We found the spot."

"That's horrible!" Prunella remarked quietly. "How could someone stab a person then set him on fire?"

"It gets worse," John said, stuffing a whole piece of French toast in his mouth. "The killer purposely didn't burn him all the way. Just enough to burn the skin and blacken it so he would hang and look like a Halloween prop."

I wanted to get sick. The little bit of French toast I was able to get down stirred in my stomach, and I felt as if it was about to come back up on me. I excused myself and ran out of the dining room into a bathroom just off the kitchen. I was able to hold off getting physically sick, but my face and neck were clammy as I bent over the oval clam shaped sink and splashed cold water over my face. "Better," I said to myself. I wiped my face off, took a few deep breaths and opened the bathroom door. John was standing there.

"Oh, I didn't see you, John," I said, almost running into him. "I'm fine, just needed to splash my face with some cold water."

"You don't have to pretend to be so strong all the time, Ruth Ann. You've been through a huge ordeal recently, being kidnapped and held prisoner back in Sweden. This is too much and too soon for you. Why don't we go and have you lay down somewhere?"

"No, I want to go back to the dining room. I want to continue the conversation with everyone."

"They left the dining room and are reconvening in the library. Let's go in there, when you're ready."

"I'm ready, I'm ready," I repeated, walking out the kitchen door into the hall that led into the foyer.

"This place is enormous, Ruth Ann," John said, looking around. "There's like three doors just to leave the kitchen."

"I know, this house was built to employ a full staff so there's an entrance from the main hallway, the butler's pantry, the back door to outside, and one to the basement."

"That's more doors than my one-bedroom apartment has."

My stomach relaxed with John's silliness as we made our way to the library. The double doors were wide open and everyone was sitting around the large stone fireplace. "Come over here," Prunella called out patting the couch to me as we walked in.

"This room's much better than the dining room. I don't have to smell any food when discussing Bert," I said, sitting myself down on the brown leather couch next to Prunella.

Judy was leaning against the stone fireplace staring at the flames lost in thought. John stood behind me and sat on the back edge of the couch. Inga and Sherman also stood waiting to serve us in any capacity, but dared not leave in case they would miss something of importance.

"Let's get back to how Bert came to his death," John said in a careful manner. "I won't go into any gruesome details."

"So Bert was stabbed and that's how he died?" Prunella asked.

"Yes, he didn't suffer," John, said. "It was quick and that's the only reassuring part of his death."

"I'm glad for that," Prunella said. "Not that he was murdered, but he didn't even know. The other part is sickening." Prunella looked over at me to make sure I was still doing okay.

"I'm good," I said, reassuring all of them. "I just couldn't eat the French toast and hear the details at the same time."

"Inga," Prunella said looking around the room to locate her. She was leaning against the large desk and stood upright upon hearing her name. "Could you pour Ruth Ann some hot tea from the pot?"

"Of course," Inga said, walking to a serving cart near the doors.

"Just black tea, please," I said, smiling to Inga.

The tea was perfect. Hot, soothing, and calming for my stomach. I felt much better and even ate that biscotti Inga stuck on the saucer. "Okay, John, tell us more about what the coroner said."

"The time of death he estimated was somewhere between 7:30-8:00."

"That's right after we arrived!" Sherman declared. "How could he have ticked somebody off so fast that they wanted to kill him?"

"Exactly," John commented. "Good deduction, Sherman. I thought that myself and what does that mean…anybody want to guess?"

"That it had to be someone Bert knew," Inga blurted out. "He must've willingly gone with the murderer because he knew and trusted him."

"That would be my theory, too," John said, looking over at Sherman.

"Wait," Sherman exclaimed. "Each of you looked at me when Inga said it had to be somebody Bert knew. You all think I did it, don't you?"

"No, Sherman," I said as loud as I could over Sherman's rant. "That means you didn't do it! Don't you get it?"

Everyone but John and Judy looked at me confused. John smiled and told me to go on. "If the coroner said Bert was killed around 7:30-8:00, Sherman was with us during that time. Sherman didn't go looking for Bert until much later. Therefore, Sherman has an alibi…us!"

Sherman, stunned by what I just said, opened his mouth and shut it. "It's okay, Sherman," I said. "You can relax and be assured that nobody will think you're the murderer anymore."

Sherman inhaled then exhaled a deep breath of fresh air. "I'm grateful that you all didn't think I could be so awful."

"I never did, Sherman," Prunella reminded him. "I told you from the beginning we didn't think you were guilty."

"I know. It's just that the evidence was pointing right toward me."

"Not really," John interrupted. "It would've been almost impossible for you to lure Bert outside, stab and burn him, then drag his body back inside and place him in the ceiling. Not to mention hook him up with fishing wire and sit there and wait until the other props fell. You were never gone that long."

"Ya, you're right," Sherman answered staring out into blank space, finally realizing he wouldn't be blamed anymore. "But if I didn't do it, who did?"

Judy, who had stayed quiet so far, walked away from the fireplace she was leaning against and sat on the arm of the couch. "It has to be someone this Bert person knew," she said. "But you claim Bert didn't know anybody else?"

"We were gone for a week or so while we were in Sweden. Bert stayed here at the house so maybe he did know someone else," Inga reminded us. "Maybe one of Mr. Eklund's men is still around here."

"Or Axel," I said quietly. "Don't rule him out completely."

"John," Prunella jumped into the conversation again. "Isn't there any way of finding out definitively if my husband is alive or dead? I mean they should be able to locate a body."

"We're working on that, Prunella," John answered. "If Axel Eklund did make it out of prison, I'll find out for sure. I'm waiting for Dave back at the station to give me a report."

"How long could that take?" I asked frustrated. "There was either a body in the cell or not?"

"There's more to it than that, Ruth Ann," John replied. "Eklund was allegedly stabbed by another prisoner while awaiting his transfer to a maximum security prison. He was supposed to stay in prison until the trial began. The police had him transferred to the hospital, but there was an accident along the way. According to my sources over there the body of Eklund went missing."

"Missing!" Prunella shouted. "That's ridiculous. How could they be so irresponsible over there? It's Axel's ammo to fool people and it sure sounds like to me he just pulled off a huge escape. Obviously, he had some inside help."

"We were told Eklund had inside help at the police station," Judy said.

"So then it's really possibly that Axel survived or didn't even get stabbed?" I asked, stunned at the possibility.

"Yes," John admitted.

"Why didn't you tell us this earlier when you got here, John?"

"I planned on telling you everything, but when Ruth Ann got sick over the coroner's findings, I wanted to wait to add this bad news. It's not looking good, but I won't say any of this is fact until Dave contacts me."

"What can Dave do?" I asked.

"He's been talking with the police over there and they've admitted there have been a few of their own cops who had been paid off by Eklund. It's a huge mess and it's taking time to get solid information." John excused himself to call Dave to see if there's been any news. He walked out of the library and shut the double doors.

"So that's it?" Prunella questioned. "Axel never died and he's back here trying to get what's his?"

"Sure sounds that way," Inga replied. "He has to be the one who murdered Bert, but why? I still don't understand why he would murder Bert?"

"If Axel's back, he's brought back one or more of his men to do the dirty work. We need to find a way to catch him and get rid of him once and for all," Prunella announced.

"How can we do that?" I asked Prunella. "We have to let the police handle catching him. Axel's dangerous, and if he did come back here he'll be out for revenge, in a big way."

"Agreed, but we can't depend solely on the police," Prunella said quietly so Judy wouldn't overhear. "Look what's happening back in Sweden. He's got a way of getting even officials to back him."

"He did it here, too," I admitted. "He got Bertha out of jail and told me he had help inside John's station."

"I told you!" Prunella cried out. "Wait, what about that young maid here, Helena?"

"Where is she anyway?" I asked.

Inga answered, "She's in the kitchen cleaning up after breakfast."

"Oh, but can she be trusted?" I asked. "She was here with Axel, Bert, and Bertha."

"She seems so incompetent," Inga snapped. "I don't see her as a threat or even being qualified to help Mr. Eklund."

"Maybe that's her plan," I said back to Inga. "She could be pretending to be naïve."

"Humph," Inga muttered. "Maybe I'll stick a little closer to her and see if she wanders off or tries to contact anyone outside of us. I could have a look around her room, too."

"That sounds wrong, Inga," Prunella replied. "I'd feel bad if she was an innocent victim and we invaded her privacy."

"What if she's not so innocent?" I asked. "It may be worth it to have Inga take a peek in her room."

"I'll do it," Inga stated. "I'll give her a time consuming project, like cleaning the silver, and then I'll search her room."

"I don't know," Prunella said, thinking it over. "If we're wrong, I'd feel horrible."

"Better safe than sorry," Inga stated.

"We don't have a choice, Prunella," I said. "If Inga gets caught I'll confess to Helena that it was all my idea."

"Absolutely not," Prunella demanded. "It's my house, my staff. I'll be the one to confess. Maybe she'll understand if we don't find anything then we can take her into our confidence."

"Sounds like a plan," Inga said, walking away from us toward the doors. "I'll go find her and get her started cleaning the silver. That should take a couple hours. Sherman can keep an eye on her in the kitchen. Okay, Sherman?"

"I'll find a reason to come and go from the kitchen. She won't suspect a thing."

Just as Inga was about to grab the doorknob the door flew open and John re-entered the library. "Where are you going, Inga?" He demanded.

"I'll tell him, Inga," I said. "Just get going with our plan."

"What plan?" John demanded. "What are you up to now, Ruth Ann?"

"It's not just Ruth Ann," Prunella interrupted. "Ruth Ann, Sherman, Inga, Judy, and I agree that Inga needs to check out Helena's room upstairs."

John glared over at Judy, who was still unnervingly quiet today, and yelled, "What?"

Judy awoke from her trance-like state and said, "What, oh, what's the big deal, John? They want to make sure Helena isn't hiding anything, and I doubt Inga will find anything anyway."

"You gave your *approval* for Inga to break into Helena's private space?" John asked, stunned. "That's not for them to do."

"I gave *my* permission, John," Prunella intervened. "It's my house and Helena's a guest in my house. Her room's my property and I ordered Inga to search it."

John, dumfounded, looked from Judy to Prunella and shrugged his shoulders. Finally, he said, "If there's anything, and I mean anything, found in her room I'll be told immediately."

"Agreed," I said. "Judy?" I called out, watching her stare into the dwindling fire. "What's the matter with you? Ever since we got here you haven't been paying any attention to us."

"Yes, Judy," John agreed. "What's the matter with you?"

Judy, who had gone back to leaning against the stone fireplace, turned her head from staring into the fire to her boss. "I'm fine."

"Why so quiet? It's not exactly like you," John said.

"Just thinking about the case, that's all."

John seemed to accept her excuse and said, "Fine. Let's get back to why I left the room in the first place."

"Oh, that's right," I blurted out. "Did Dave give you more news about Axel?"

John's expression changed and his cheeks flared a deep shade of red. "I can't believe what I was told. I've never been more disgraced to be a cop!"

"What happened?" Prunella cried out, hopping up from the couch and walking over to John who was standing by the library doors. "Wait, don't tell me...he got away with it?"

"Apparently," John admitted. "Dave found out that the two policemen who were driving Eklund to the hospital after his alleged stabbing were under his pay. The original report was that Eklund died on the way to the hospital, and his body was delivered to the morgue. The two cops went back to the station and filled out the report and the case was closed. It wasn't until we contacted the station asking questions that the chief over there found out the truth. It took some time trying to locate the two cops who were off duty and now gone missing."

"Missing!" I shouted. "That means they're here with Axel!"

"The chief contacted the hospital and he was transferred to the morgue and guess what?"

"No body," Sherman answered.

"Yes, no body," John said. "The chief admitted that it was those two cops who worked for Eklund who set up the entire plan up. Eklund and the cops are now missing."

"This is a nightmare," Prunella said almost faltering, but John grabbed her arm and led her back to the couch next to me. "Now what?"

"We have to assume Eklund and the two cops made their way back here and they're the ones who murdered Bert. I'm not sure why they would kill the one ally they had here, but Bert must've said or done something to make them doubt his loyalty."

"I can't believe this is happening, again," Prunella said in tears. The pain in her eyes said it all to me. She had been through so much with this man and the thought that he may be after her again might be too much for her to bear.

"We're prepared now, Prunella," John said, standing behind the couch and putting one hand on her shoulder and the other on mine. "I won't let him do anything to you or the others. I promise you as the Chief of Police, and as your friend, that we'll catch him before he causes any more harm."

"That's a gigantic promise to make, John," Prunella said, turning her head around and wiping a tear from her cheek. "I'm all right, I just had to get over the initial shock."

"I don't blame you," I said. "We've only had a week free of the man and we're back in it against him."

"I'm going to call your friend, Paul, Ruth Ann. He'll come and stand guard. We need all the help we can get and I know Paul will do anything for you, right?" John said squeezing my shoulder and smiling down on me.

"Yes, John, I get it." I turned to Prunella and Sherman to explain about Paul Welch. He was the security guard assigned to protect me from Axel before we left for Sweden. Paul watched over me at my antique store and I kind of talked him into coming up here to see who actually lived at this house. I was under John's watch over at the police station when my life had been threatened. Paul was guarding the store while I was at the police station. I contacted Paul and asked him to go along with a wild plan that would allow me to get away from John and go investigate this estate. Paul only agreed because I told him I would give him a large bonus, which I did, and I needed some protection just in case.

Unfortunately, we got ourselves caught and Paul was thrown into a dirty hole in the ground. We both made it out okay, but I was taken prisoner again by Axel and brought to his estate in Sweden. We made it out alive and Paul was rewarded for his bravery. John did have a long discussion with him about who he took orders from and needless to say it wasn't me.

"It would be great to see Paul again," I smiled. "He's a loyal, brave guard and I don't think he'd let Axel get the better of him."

"As long as he follows the rules, Ruth Ann," John said, giving me an accusatory glance.

"I understand, John," I agreed. "I do wonder if he might choose to turn you down, though."

"Why? He was rewarded handsomely by you and he made it out alive."

"But I made him go against his principles and he was thrown into a hole in the ground."

"He survived and it gave him quite the story to tell to the other guards," John said, laughing. "He'll do it."

"I'd feel safe if Paul was guarding us, Prunella," I said to her.

"I think we need more than one security guard to protect us from Axel and two rogue cops."

"We'll have more, Prunella. Judy, Lou, Dave, and I will take shifts here and I'll borrow some police from our local stations around here. It'll work out."

"So, now what do we do, John?" I asked, but he never got to answer me because Inga pushed through the unopened library doors and ran frantically into the room.

Chapter 10

"She's...she's gone!" Inga bellowed. "Helena isn't anywhere!"

"Gone? Gone where?" John asked, desperately trying to grab Inga's arm as she ran into the room.

"I don't know," she replied, stopping dead in her tracks next to John. "I went to find her to ask her to clean the silver, but she wasn't in the kitchen. I hurried up the back stairs and checked her room, but she wasn't there either."

"Maybe she's somewhere else," I said. "This place is huge. She could be anywhere from the basement to the third floor cleaning."

"No, she's not," Inga, declared. "I went through the third floor and the second floor and she hasn't made any of the beds or cleaned the baths. She must be gone, but where? She doesn't drive and we aren't near any neighbors."

"She must be here somewhere," Prunella declared. "We need to search the entire place."

John agreed with Prunella and gave us sections to check thoroughly. Prunella and Judy were to check the main floor. Inga and Sherman were to check the top two floors. John and I were going into the basement. "Why me?" I asked.

"You know what happened to me the last time I was down there."

"It'll be okay, Ruth Ann. I'll be at your side the entire time."

I reluctantly agreed even though I was terrified. The last time I was in the basement I had been kidnapped with Paul, the security guard. Axel's right hand man, Finn, tortured poor Paul and that's when he was thrown in that dirty hole. I was shackled to a wall while Finn watched over me, laughing and mocking us the entire time.

We separated and agreed to meet back in the library in no more than a half hour. John and I went through the kitchen toward the basement door. I hesitated as John started down the dark stairway. "C'mon, Ruth Ann, nobody's down here anyway. I doubt Helena would have any reason to go into the basement."

"Unless someone forced her down here," I mumbled.

"What?" John asked me.

"Nothing," I said. "Let's just get this over with."

I took my first step onto the old, wooden step and it creaked with my weight. A couple steps ahead of me, John was shining his flashlight to guide his way. "Can you see anything yet?" I inquired taking another step down.

"No, it's pitch black down here."

"There's a light after you reach the bottom. Shine your flashlight up and you'll find the string for the light."

"I remember, Ruth Ann," John said reaching the bottom of the staircase. "Are you coming?"

"I'm almost there," I answered.

John found the string and pulled it. "The bulb must be burned out, I can't get it to turn on."

"That's just great," I said, reaching the bottom finally. "Maybe we should go back up and see if the others discovered anything."

"No, I have a flashlight. We can go on from here with the light it shines." John turned around and held out his hand. I grabbed it tightly and we walked toward the wall I remember so well. "I'm going to shine the flashlight against the cement wall, you feel for the button that opens up the wall."

I remembered watching Finn open up the wall by running his grimy hand along the wall in a certain area. We walked over to approximately where we thought it was and I started rubbing my hands over the cement wall. John was shining the flashlight, but it wasn't giving me enough light to see where it was. "This is useless, John," I stammered. "I can't see anything, and this is a big wall to search."

"We know about where the button should be, Ruth Ann, keep trying."

Finally, after several minutes I felt a tiny nub against the wall and pushed it. Up popped a section of the wall. It made a loud, crunchy sound as it rose. "It's dark in there, too," I said, peeking inside the room where Paul and I were held prisoner only a short couple weeks ago.

John shone the light into the room and found the string dangling from the ceiling. "Got it," John yelled out to me. I remained at the doorway waiting for him to give up so we could go back upstairs.

He pulled the string and the room illumined and momentarily blinded both of us. "Oh my God!" John exclaimed. "Don't come in here, Ruth Ann."

I couldn't help myself. I had to look inside once my eyes adjusted to the light. What I saw will be burned in my brain forever. "John!" I screamed, but nobody else could possibly hear me because cement walls deep into the basement surrounded us. "What happened to her?"

John hurried to my side and instructed me to go upstairs and get Judy. "Now!" he ordered.

"But we have to get her help right away, John," I cried out. "Maybe we can still save her!"

"No, Ruth Ann," he said. "She's dead."

I backed out of the room leaving John with Helena. I went through the pitch-black room with only John's flashlight to guide me upstairs. I tripped on most of the stairs on my way up, but not because I couldn't see. The scene in the back room of the basement was horrible; the blood was splattered all over the wall where I had once been shackled. "How could someone do this?" I said aloud as I reached the top of the stairs and pushed open the door to the kitchen.

"Thank God," I said, rushing into the room and finding Judy and Prunella standing against the island. "Hurry, we need you in the basement!"

"You found Helena?" Prunella inquired. I nodded and turned around to go back down to John. Prunella and Judy followed right behind me. "What happened, Ruth Ann? You look awful."

"Slow down, Ruth Ann," Judy said. "I can't see a thing. I'm pulling out my cell phone and turning on the light. It'll make it easier to see." Judy stopped on the top step and turned on another light to help us see. "Where's John?" She asked, shining the light around the room at the base of the stairs.

"Oh no, don't tell me," Prunella started to say. "He's in that secret room of Axel's, isn't he?" I nodded. "And Helena's back there, too, right?" I nodded, but didn't speak. As soon as we stood between the first room in the basement and the secret room I halted. "Prunella, stay back in here. Let Judy go in."

"Why, what happened in there?"

"Helena was brutally murdered." I answered.

"What?" cried other voices from behind. Inga and Sherman heard the commotion in the kitchen and followed us down here.

"John and I found Helena," I said. "She was murdered, recently."

"How do you know it was recent?" Inga asked curiously.

"It just was," I snapped, letting Judy go inside. "We need to let John and Judy do their job. They'll tell us everything when they're done."

"I want to go in and see," Inga demanded. "I can handle it."

"No, I don't think so. I only got a quick glance and it was horrible, utterly horrible."

"Tell us, Ruth Ann," Prunella demanded. "If we can't see her for ourselves you have to tell us."

"John and I found the button on the wall to open the secret room. When the wall slid up it was pitch black in there. All we had was John's flashlight. He went in search of the string to pull to turn on the light bulb. I remembered there was one when I was held captive in there."

"Oh, Ruth Ann, I'm so sorry. You and the security guard were held prisoner in there. This has to be terrible for you," Prunella exclaimed.

"I've had nightmares about being in here, but now with this, they will get worse." I hesitated a moment and stepped away from the entrance to the back room. Inga, Sherman, and Prunella followed me over toward the bottom of the stairs. The light from the flashlight barely showed the fear and anguish in my face. I couldn't believe this nightmare was happening again. How could Axel be responsible for two murders in the last twelve hours?

I shook off the thoughts of how Bert and Helena were murdered. I knew they wanted details about Helena so I sucked it up and told them what happened. "Once John turned on the light, our eyesight took a moment to adjust from the darkness. I was standing just inside the doorway while John was in the middle of the room."

"Was he near the hole your friend Paul was thrown into?" Sherman asked, shivering at the thought.

"No, the hole is on the farthest end of the room. John was near the wall where I was shackled, but the shackles weren't empty."

"Oh, no," Prunella cried out. "Helena?"

"Yes, Helena had been shackled to the wall."

"Why is that so gruesome?" Sherman snapped. "We can handle that."

"That's not all, Sherman." I said slowly. "At first, my eyes noticed Helena against the wall, but then my eyes caught glimpses of splattered blood all over the cement wall and floor."

"Blood!" hollered Sherman. "If she was shackled and left there to die, why was there so much blood?"

"That's it, she was stabbed numerous times."

"No?" Prunella questioned, horrified.

"I only saw her for a second. John jumped in front of my view and ordered me to stay away and bring Judy down here. That's when I took his flashlight and ran up the stairs to find you."

"How could this happen?" Prunella asked. "And right under our roof."

"It must've happened right after breakfast," I stated. Suddenly, John walked over to us and said he was going up to call the crime into the station. We were to go upstairs with him and wait in the library.

"I don't want any one of you to leave the library until I give you permission, do you understand me?"

"Yes, but why are we being sequestered, John?" I asked him.

Sherman blurted out, "You suspect one of us, don't you?"

"I didn't say that, Sherman. I don't believe any of you could've committed this crime. You were together, with me, too."

"Yes, we were," he said, realizing his accusation was unfounded. "Are we allowed to serve some tea or coffee in the library?"

"You and Inga may go into the kitchen and bring the beverages into the library, but then stay put."

We followed John upstairs and left Inga and Sherman behind in the kitchen while Prunella and I headed into the library. John disappeared out the front door to make his calls. Prunella grabbed my arm and led me back to the couch in front of the fireplace. The soaring fire had turned into steaming, sparse embers. The room once warm and inviting, felt frigid and dark. The curtains were open but the sun had disappeared under clouds that threatened a looming snowstorm. "Brrr..." I said, sitting next to Prunella. "It's freezing in here. When Sherman comes back he can get the fire going again."

Prunella reached her hand around the back of the couch and pulled the hand-made crocheted afghan and gently put it over my lap. "Aren't you cold, too?" I asked her.

"Yes, but I want the cold air to keep my head fresh. I'm so confused, Ruth Ann. Twenty-four hours ago we were excited about going to the Halloween party and meeting people in town. Now, there have been two murders and all because of us!"

"It's not our fault, Prunella," I said, exasperated. "We're the innocent victims in this."

"Yes, but Bert would still be alive if I didn't come here from Sweden. Poor Helena, too!"

"We had no idea Axel would still be alive or free for that matter. We left Sweden full of hope for a bright future for you and the others."

"I guess, but I still blame myself for Bert and Helena losing their lives."

"All we can do now is prevent any more violence."

"Ruth Ann, how can we possibly do that?" Prunella asked, looking at me as if I was crazy.

"I don't exactly have a plan yet, but I will. Plus, we have John and Judy on their home turf now and they won't let anything happen to us."

"He's gone after the help so far, Ruth Ann. First Bert, his loyal butler, then Helena, an innocent maid. That doesn't make any sense. Why would he want those two so brutally murdered?"

"That's it!" I bellowed. "We find out what Bert and Helena had on him, and then we'll have an idea of what we're up against."

"Don't you think we should leave that up to the police?"

"Yes, they'll be looking into that angle, but we can help by searching their rooms a little closer."

"John told us not to leave the library, Ruth Ann."

"He'll be occupied for a long time with Helena. Once Sherman and Inga get back in here let's talk to them and see if they're willing to help."

"I don't know Ruth Ann. John will be furious if we aren't in here when he returns. Why don't we wait for him and ask if it's all right for us to leave the library and look for some clues upstairs."

"He'll just tell us to back off, Prunella. I want to go now while it's still fresh and undisturbed."

"That's what the police want too, and if we go into Bert and Helena's rooms we'll disrupt their investigation."

"Oh, like leaving our fingerprints and messing things up in their rooms?" I asked, knowing she was right, but I didn't want to sit in here either.

"Yes, exactly."

Inga and Sherman returned with a tray full of chocolate croissants, a bowl of cut-up fruit, and a fresh pot of hot tea and coffee. I motioned them to bring the two trays over to us and set them on the coffee table. "Inga, you know those chocolate croissants have to be kept far away from me!" Inga knew chocolate was a sure way of calming nerves after a horrific event. Seeing Helena stabbed and hanging from the shackles qualifies as a horrific event in my book. I reached over and grabbed a croissant. They were still warm and the dark chocolate was oozing out of the ends. I put it to my mouth and licked the warm chocolate and then took a large bite of the croissant. The butter-flavored pastry melted in my mouth while the chocolate gave me comfort that only chocolate can do.

"I needed that, Inga," I said, wiping a spot of chocolate off the side of my mouth with a cloth napkin.

Prunella smiled and watched me devour the croissant while she sipped a cup of hot tea. The only calorie Prunella ingested was the squirt of honey she put in her tea. No wonder she had a perfect shape. "Are you going to mention to Inga and Sherman what you plan on doing, Ruth Ann?"

"Yes," I stated, putting the plate down on the tray. I picked up the teapot and poured myself a steaming cup and settled back against the couch shoving the afghan aside. Eating the chocolate croissant and now holding the hot cup of tea warmed up my whole body.

"I think it's time we stop this nonsense and catch Axel Eklund before he does any more harm. What do you all say? Are you with me or should we let the police handle it?"

Chapter 11

"**A**re you serious?" Sherman roared, forgetting his position in the house.

"Excuse me?" I said, eyeing him suspiciously. "I'd think you of all people would want Axel caught. It would get you, and in fact any of us, off the hook for the murders."

"I *am* off the hook, Ruth Ann," he declared. "Your chief cleared me, and I have no intention of putting the spotlight back on me."

"You're right, Sherman. You've been completely cleared. I just thought it would benefit us if we help find Axel."

"How would that benefit us?" Inga asked, surprised at my explanation.

"By keeping us alive," I stated. "The longer he's on the loose, the more chances for one of us to be harmed next."

"You mean killed, Ruth Ann," Prunella corrected me.

"I just didn't want to use the word killed in the same sentence with any of us."

"I agree," Prunella replied.

"You agree to what I just said or to us helping out with the investigation."

"Both."

"You're kidding, right?" Sherman exclaimed looking from Prunella to me and back to Prunella. "I'm not having your chief catch us outside of this library. We need to stay put and behave."

"Forget it, Sherman," Inga said, finally entering the conversation. "I don't see the harm going and having a look around the house. I was up in Helena's room, but I didn't have time to search it. I was looking for her."

"I think we stick together and search Bert and Helena's rooms. If John does find us he can't be too upset if the four of us stay together. What do you say?" I looked over at Prunella, and then Inga and Sherman. Prunella smiled and nodded. So did Inga. Sherman was still shaking his head saying he didn't think it was a good idea, and that we should wait for John to give us permission. "Well, Sherman, you can stay here, but we're leaving."

I stood up and headed for the library doors. Prunella followed me and Inga stood next to Sherman awaiting his response. "Fine," he blurted out of thin air. "I'll go just to keep us together, and you should have a man along just in case." He stomped to the door with Inga behind him in case he changed his mind. She had a wild look in her eyes that told me she would force Sherman to follow along if needed.

I opened the doors to the library and peeked out into the foyer. The room was clear and dark. There was no morning sun entering the foyer anymore and when I glanced outside I noticed light snow beginning to fall. Once winter hits Deer Creek it's here for months and months.

I waved the others to follow and we hurried over to the main staircase. I could hear voices coming up from the basement and kitchen area. John must've gotten his forces up here quickly and they were deeply involved down in the secret room. "Let's go," I called out to the others.

We went directly to Bert's room first. His was on the third floor along with Helena's, Sherman's, and Inga's. I went to grab the doorknob and Inga knocked my hand out of the way. "Stop," she exclaimed.

"What is it?" I demanded, rubbing my hand from the hard slap. "You didn't need to hit my hand so hard!"

"Sorry, but you can't touch that doorknob. You'll get your fingerprints all over it."

"Oh, I didn't even think of that," I replied, feeling guilty for not realizing that, too.

"But haven't they already been in there and searched?" Prunella inquired.

"That's right!" I said, quickly grabbing the knob and trying to turn it before Inga hit my hand away again. "Hey, it's locked. Why would they lock it?"

"Because it's part of a criminal investigation," Sherman answered bluntly. "They don't want anyone in there, hint hint."

"Why didn't John tell us what they found in there?" I asked, wondering if he would've told us anyway. He has a tendency of clamming up when things get dangerous.

"Because we're not the police, Ruth Ann," Prunella reminded me. "John doesn't have to tell us anything."

"I don't care," I said. "Can any of you pick a lock? I can but I need something to use."

"I have a hairpin," Inga answered pulling out a small black pin from the severely tight bun on her head. "This should do."

I grabbed the hairpin and played around with the lock. It jiggled a few times and I thought I had it, but it wouldn't budge. "I can't seem to get it."

"I'll try," Inga said, taking her hairpin back. "Sometimes it takes just the right…touch. There," Inga said turning the knob and opening the door.

"Great job," Prunella called out.

Inga opened the door about a foot and the four of us peeked inside. The room was dark since the heavy, emerald colored curtains were still drawn. "I'm going to get some light in here," I said, walking over to the window and pulling the curtains open. "There, this should help."

The room lit up quite a bit because of the heavy snow falling outside. "Wow, look at it snow!" Sherman bellowed. "We're getting quite a storm."

"Looks like whoever's in this house isn't going anywhere," Prunella said, staring out the third floor window. "You get a lot of snow here, don't you?"

"Yes, Prunella, we do," I answered. "Our town thrives when it snows since the main business here in town is the ski resort. The one we were at last night actually," I couldn't help reminding them.

"I wonder what the murder at your town's resort will do to the tourist season," Sherman mentioned.

"Hopefully, the owners will keep it out of their brochures, Sherman," I replied sarcastically. "Once the police finish their investigation, I'm sure nobody will mention it again. Everyone in town benefits from a busy tourist season."

"Almost as if Bert never existed," Prunella said sadly. "What about any family of his? I have no idea how to contact them."

"Maybe we'll find something in here," I said, looking around the room to see where I wanted to look first.

"We'd better get moving if we want to search both rooms," Sherman said. "I'm going to take his closet," he stated and headed to the large walk-in closet.

"He's a butler, I'm surprised at the size of his closet," Inga said, glancing inside after Sherman went in there and flipped the light switch.

Sherman answered her, "All the bedrooms in this estate have large closets, Inga. Bert's is pretty empty though. He has several pairs of black pants, white shirts, black vests and his tie rack only holds black ties."

"That's it?" I called out to Sherman.

"No, there's shelving in here that contains his pristine black shoes, undergarments, and some casual tops and pants. I don't see anything that could help us in here. Wait a minute!"

"What did you find, Sherman?" I asked.

"There's a large trunk at the very back of the closet. I didn't see it at first because the lighting in here stinks. I'll bring it out to the room so we can look at it closely." Sherman took the trunk and dragged it into the bedroom. We stood around him as he set it on its back so the top would open up. "It's locked!"

"Pick it," I said, looking over at Inga so she could grab another hairpin.

"It's not that kind of lock, Ruth Ann," Sherman explained. "It's a padlock, and a very large key is needed to open it. We need to find that key."

"Let's keep searching the room and hopefully one of us will find it," I said, walking over to the nightstand next to Bert's bed. "It feels strange searching Bert's personal belongings with him being dead."

"Even alive it would be strange," Sherman muttered. "He was a strange bloke after all."

"Sherman, behave," Prunella ordered, but in a sweet voice to show she understood his feelings about Bert. "We don't have to worry about you two bickering any more so let's just get this job done so we can get out of here."

I opened the nightstand drawer and found blank pieces of stationery, pens, cough drops, and keys! I found a brass ring with several keys attached. "I found the keys!" At least

I hope I found a key that would work in the trunk. I hurried over to Sherman who was still working on the lock with Inga's hairpin just in case.

"Give me the key, Ruth Ann," Sherman demanded. "I mean, please give me the key."

I handed the key ring over and Sherman eliminated three of the five keys because they were too small. "That leaves two that could possibly work," he said, putting the first rusted, old key inside the padlock. "Not this one," he said, grabbing hold of the last key. "Wish me luck," he said, putting the shiny, silver key into the hole on the lock. "It worked!"

"Open it, Sherman," Inga excitedly cried out. "I can't take the suspense any longer."

"Okay, okay, I'm doing it." The lock clicked open and Sherman pulled it off the trunk. I wondered why the key was shiny and new looking, but the trunk looked old and beat up. It was large enough to hold two of my biggest suitcases inside. What could Bert possibly have in there? Maybe it was everything he owned after coming here from England.

Sherman slowly opened the lid of the trunk while the rest of us bent over watching. "Wow," Sherman exclaimed. "There's not much in here considering the size of the thing. Why would he need such a large trunk if it's only a quarter full?"

"What's in there, I can't see," Inga snapped. "Is it more clothing?"

"No," Sherman stated. "There's a few books, papers, pictures…hey!"

"Pictures?" I questioned. "Of his family?"

"I don't know. We need to look at them. There are quite a few in a yellow manila envelope."

"What else is in there?" Inga anxiously asked. "There has to be more!"

Sherman dug deeper into the trunk and pulled out a small leather case. Like the kind men use for toiletries, but there was definitely not a toothbrush and toothpaste in there! "WOW," Sherman cried out. "Look at all this cash!"

"Cash?" Inga inquired. "How much cash?"

"Has to be thousands...more," Sherman said, pulling out one hundred-dollar bill after another.

Prunella got on her hands and knees and ignored the pile of cash. She stared at something else in there. "What is it, Prunella?" I asked her curiously.

"Look at this," she said, pointing to a deep colored stain on the bottom of the trunk. "It looks like dried blood!"

We stopped watching Sherman count the money and redirected our attention to the large spot in the trunk. "Maybe something leaked in there. It doesn't have to be blood," I said, reaching out to touch it but Prunella pushed my hand away.

"Don't touch it, Ruth Ann," she said. "Until we know what it is we should leave it free of our fingerprints."

"You're right, Prunella," I said, backing my hand away and sitting back on my knees. "There isn't anything else in there."

"Nope, just the pictures, cash, books, and some papers."

"We should check out the pictures and see if we can spot Bert in any of them. Maybe there'll be names on the back or dates." I suggested.

"You and Ms. Prunella go through them," Sherman said. "Inga and I need to keep looking around the room."

Prunella grabbed the yellow folder and went and sat down on the overstuffed, navy loveseat against the wall near the door. She opened the folder and dumped the pictures out next to her on the couch. I sat down on the other side of the pile. "These must be from his childhood," I said, picking up an old, yellowed photo of a young boy in dress shorts, shirt and tie, standing next to a smiling young couple. "It must be Bert with his parents. Look how happy they were, Ruth Ann."

"It was a long time ago, Prunella. Something horrible must have happened to Bert when he was young to have made him such a cynical, negative person."

"Maybe this is what happened, Ruth Ann," Prunella said, holding a small piece of paper in her hand.

"What is that?" I asked.

"It's a death notice from a paper over in England. I think his parents were murdered when Bert was just a young boy. The obituary says that there was one surviving family member, a young boy of fourteen."

"Oh, that's awful," I said, holding another picture of Bert with his parents. But in this one Bert had to be about ten or so. He was on a bike with each of his parents next to his side. "They looked so happy, I wonder how the parents were killed?"

Prunella grabbed another piece of an old, yellowed newspaper and read the article. Bert's parents were murdered while the young boy watched from under the parent's bed. "They were murdered in their sleep, Ruth Ann," Prunella said horrified. "But why was Bert under the bed in the first place?"

"I don't think we'll ever know, Prunella. But watching your parents be stabbed to death has to make quite an impact on a young teen."

"I wish we knew more about this when he was alive. I think we'd be a little nicer to Bert," Prunella announced loudly so Sherman would overhear.

"It's terrible what happened to him, Ms. Prunella, but I don't think we would've liked him any better," Sherman responded.

"It doesn't matter anymore," I said before Prunella scolded Sherman for his harsh words. "Bert's gone and it appeared he had no other family…wait," I hollered. "Look at this!" I held up a picture and waved it high in the air so they all could see.

Inga and Sherman rushed over and took a look at the picture I was holding. It was an old photo, but not as old as the previous ones. The man in the picture looked like a younger Bert, but he was holding a boy on top of his shoulders. "Look at the face of the young boy!" I exclaimed.

"No, it can't be," Prunella quickly said.

"How can it not be?" I replied, waiting for Sherman and Inga to give their opinions.

"Why, that looks like Mr. Eklund as a boy," Inga said, stunned. "But why would he be on Bert's shoulders?"

"Exactly," I declared. "Why indeed?"

"So they must've known each other for a long time," Prunella concluded. "I wonder how long and what was their connection?"

"You don't think Bert was Axel's father, do you?" I questioned carefully.

"No way!" Sherman shouted. "That's outrageous."

"Maybe not so outrageous," I said, holding up another photo.

Chapter 12

"This makes no sense," Prunella said. "I thought Bert was closer in age to Axel."

"Maybe Bert was a young father. He could've been eighteen when Axel was born. That's not too big of an age gap," I said staring at another picture with Bert and a clear picture of Axel around the age of twenty. "This changes everything."

"Why would Axel kill his own father?" Sherman questioned. "We must be missing something, but I can't see what."

"I didn't think we were going to find anything in here," Inga expressed. "I thought Helena would be the one to hide something of importance."

"Why?" I asked curiously.

"There was something about her that I didn't trust. I don't know what, just a feeling. She acted too naïve and innocent for me."

"We're running out of time. Let's get over to her room and check it out, just in case," Prunella said, heading toward the door. She stopped at the doorway and turned, "Sherman, can you put the trunk back into the closet? We don't want the police to know what we did in here."

"We have to tell John," I told Prunella. "He needs to know that Bert and Axel might have been father and son."

"Maybe he was his uncle or some other kind of relationship." Sherman mentioned.

"It's possible," Prunella agreed. "Let's get through Helena's room, and then we can talk about what we should reveal to the police."

Prunella, Inga, and I left Sherman to put away the trunk while we headed down to Helena's room. There was still police tape stuck to the door, but when I grabbed the knob, this time it was unlocked. "That saves us time," I said, opening the door to Helena's bedroom. "This one is so much brighter and cheerier than Bert's."

"The curtains are still open and her room's painted a light yellow. It really makes it look cheery and bright," Prunella explained. "Also, her bedding is all white. White sheets, pillowcases, and even the thick down comforter are white."

I looked around Helena's bedroom and from what I saw it was hard to believe she could conspire with Axel. The room was decorated for a young, sweet girl not a criminal. However, she must've done something to make Axel and his men want her dead. We need to find out what that was. "I'll look over by the bed and nightstand," I decided walking towards the opposite wall from the door.

"I'll go into her closet this time," Prunella declared as Sherman entered the room.

That left Inga and Sherman to check out the bathroom and the rest of her room. I pulled back the neatly made bed and looked under the sheets and the bed. There was nothing hidden under there so I moved onto the glossy white, wooden nightstand next to her bed. On top of the table was a reading light, a pair of sunglasses, a partially drunk bottle of water. Inside the drawer there was nothing, not even a piece of paper.

"That's so strange," I said, closing the drawer. "Her nightstand drawer is totally empty. I wonder why?"

"Maybe the police emptied it, Ruth Ann," Inga reminded me. "They were in here earlier."

"That's a good possibility. But Bert's wasn't emptied."

"I don't know, Ruth Ann," she replied. "I can't see anything out of the ordinary over here either," Inga called out as she was putting the pastel colored couch cushions back on the couch. "I'm going to see if Sherman needs help in the bathroom."

She didn't get time to help because Sherman came out holding a few items in his hands. "The only thing I could find in here are some empty pill bottles," he said, holding the bottles up for us to see.

"What are they for?" I asked.

"One is for Xanax, and this one is for migraines, and the last here is…whoa, no way!"

"What is it Sherman?" I asked, rushing over to him.

"You won't believe this? It's a bottle of prenatal vitamins!"

"What?" Prunella shouted loudly from the closet doorway. "Did I just hear you say Helena was taking prenatal vitamins? That would imply she was, you know, pregnant."

"This keeps getting weirder and weirder," Inga exclaimed. "I thought we wouldn't find anything in here and now we come to find out she was pregnant."

"Oh, that's horrible," Prunella, cried out. "That means when she was murdered her baby was murdered, too."

"Do you think that's why she was killed?" I questioned. "Maybe it was Axel's baby?"

"No, he's too old," Inga, commented.

"He's about seventy, but he can still get a woman pregnant," I answered.

"We can't ignore what we've uncovered up here," I stated. "We have to tell John that we went snooping." I added, "If they didn't find out what we did John will be furious with his staff for letting amateurs outdo his own men."

"They must know about her being pregnant," Prunella stated. "That's probably why the pill bottles are empty. They had to have sent the pills out to be tested."

"Yes, that has to be what happened. But why leave the empty bottles in the medicine cabinet?" Sherman asked curiously. "I'm going to put them back where I found them. I don't want to get further in trouble once they hear we've been in these two bedrooms. Your chief's going to blow a gasket."

"Probably," I replied. "But if we uncovered information they didn't know then he can't be too upset."

"I sure hope so, Ruth Ann," Prunella said going back inside the closet. She informed us that there was nothing in the closet except for clothing. Helena might've been a housekeeper, but she sure wasn't organized in her closet. There was a huge pile of old, worn clothes on the floor of her closet.

"We should get back downstairs," I suggested. "It's been a while and John might've already gone looking for us." We agreed and closed up Helena's bedroom and hurried back down the stairs. We made it back into the library just in time. Within seconds, John and Judy showed up at the doorway and stared each of us down. I was leaning against the desk, a tad out of breath, and Prunella sat in the chair that Axel once occupied. Inga and Sherman were hanging around the tea cart pouring us cups of tea. "So," John said. "You have been good it seems?"

"Why would you ask that, John?" I questioned, feeling guilty about what the four of us had been up to.

"Your track record isn't so clean, Ruth Ann," he said smiling. But only for a moment because I was planning on breaking the news to him that I wasn't so well behaved.

"Well..." I started to say, but Judy interrupted me after my first word.

"I told you, John."

I glared back at her and almost, for a second, changed my mind about confessing to our adventure up on the third floor. Guilt won out over Judy so I continued, "We didn't stay in here the entire time." I spun my head back towards Judy and asked, "Is that what you were implying, Judy? That I couldn't keep my word and stay here like a good little girl?"

Judy looked from me to John not knowing how to respond. John chose to answer for her and said, "Easy, Ruth Ann, Judy just mentioned she didn't think you'd be able to stay cooped up in the library for long. She didn't mean you any disrespect."

"Sure she didn't," I mumbled.

"Let's get back to what you were just saying, shall we?" John asked. "Did I hear you say that you *didn't* stay in the library the entire time? What's that mean?" John's gaze went around the room and waited for the one who was going to break down and confess. "I'm waiting..."

I was still fuming about Judy and wasn't ready to talk yet. Prunella sensed my anger and took over the conversation. She sat in Axel's desk chair with a coolness I hadn't seen before. Prunella motioned for John and Judy to come all the way into the room and take a seat at the chairs in front of the desk. John nodded to Judy and she followed him over to the chair and slowly sat herself down. "Go ahead, Prunella," John said curiously.

"We did as you told us. We originally came in here and had a cup of tea. As time passed we got to talking about Bert and Helena. We *collectively* decided to take a short trip up to the third floor and have a look in their bedrooms." John was about to interrupt abruptly, but Prunella wouldn't let him. "As I was saying, John, we *all* decided to do this. It was not Ruth Ann's idea. She wanted to talk to you first, but we convinced her it might be a while with the investigation down in the basement. Once we decided, we went up and searched both rooms."

"You did what?" John jumped out of his chair and shouted. Surprisingly, Judy grabbed his arm to bring him back into his seat. "Let them explain, John," she said quietly. "I'm suddenly interested in what they have to say."

"Yes, John, we acted against your wishes, but once we tell you what we uncovered, I'll bet you'll forgive us."

"You found something? What? Wait, first tell me one thing," John hesitated, took a deep breath and asked, "Did you have to break the lock to get into Bert's room?"

"Yes, we did, John," Prunella stated calmly. "It wasn't that difficult to unlock the door." She waited to make sure he was over our first illegal betrayal before she continued. "All good?" No response from John except that he looked like he was going to explode. "Yes, so we entered the room and had a look around. Not much was in there until Sherman discovered a large trunk in the back of the closet."

John quickly looked at Judy to see if she was aware of the trunk. She shrugged her shoulders implying she had no idea about the trunk. John lowered his head and shook it back and forth. "You got to be serious? You missed the trunk in the closet?" Judy slowly nodded her head.

"How could you miss it?" Sherman exclaimed. "It was gigantic!"

"I don't know, John," Judy said, trying to defend herself and the other cops who missed the trunk. "I'll talk with the others who were up in the room."

"Prunella, did you open the trunk?" John asked her, ignoring me completely.

"Yes, but we had to find a key. It was locked and picking it wouldn't work. Ruth Ann found a set of keys in his nightstand and one of them worked. Sherman unlocked the trunk and we looked inside."

"Do I want to know what was in there?" he asked reluctantly. "This is very illegal, you know that, don't you?" John looked at each one of us, but his eyes stopped on me the longest.

"Enough, John," I stammered. "We found some interesting things in there. If you want to know what it was just ask. I don't want to be reprimanded like a child any longer!"

"Fine, Ruth Ann," he said, calming himself down. "I would like very much to hear what was inside the trunk."

I took it from here and said, "We found a bunch of papers, cash, and pictures."

"So?" Judy asked sarcastically. "The way you all were talking I thought you found a gun or incriminating evidence he held onto against Eklund."

I scowled back at her, but she kept her mocking smirk. "Maybe, just maybe Judy, there was incriminating evidence in one of the pictures. Did you ever think of that? Especially since you and your guys missed the trunk all together."

"Enough," John bellowed. "What was in the pictures, Ruth Ann?"

Prunella picked up a piece of paper from her desk and held it up for us to see. It was one of the pictures of Bert, when he was a young boy, with his parents. "They appear to be happy," was all John could say. "Is there more to this?"

Prunella held up the newspaper clipping with the obituary announcement of Bert's parents. John reached over the desk and grabbed the fragile piece of news and read it silently to himself. "So, they were murdered when Bert was young?" He handed the slip of paper to Judy and she read it quietly. John turned back to Prunella just as she was holding up another picture of Bert. This one was a shock to both John and Judy.

"That looks like Eklund!" Judy screeched. "But why would he be on top of Bert's shoulders?"

Prunella didn't' stop there. She held one last photo up for them to see. "This one should clear matters up a bit more," she said.

"It's Eklund around the age of twenty standing with an older Bert," John said, studying the picture in his hand. He turned it over and found there was no writing or dates written or stamped on the back. "This is crazy." John looked up at us and asked, "You think Bert was Axel Eklund's father?"

"I guess he could've been an uncle or something, too," Sherman announced.

"Highly unlikely," Inga said. She looked over at Prunella and me and gave us a funny look. "There's more, remember?" She saw our faces and added, "About what else was in the trunk…"

"Oh, yeah, I don't know how I almost forgot," I cried. "There was a dried, dark reddish stain in the bottom of the trunk. We didn't touch it just in case you wanted to test it."

"A red stain?" Judy asked, feeling even worse than before. "How could we miss such a crucial piece of evidence?"

John gave her a nasty look and said, "It does make our department look like a bunch of amateurs, Judy. It's a big item to overlook."

"I know, I'm very sorry, John. I really don't know how it was missed."

"Forget about that!" Prunella shouted. "We have more."

"More?" Asked John, shocked at Prunella's announcement.

"Not in regards to Bert, but in Helena's room," I said.

John's face went pale and he said, "Please tell me we didn't miss something in there, too?" I saw him glance at Judy and she appeared stunned by Prunella's statement.

"Well," Prunella began to say. "I'm not sure if you missed it or emptied it."

"Emptied it? What are you talking about?" John questioned confused.

"Her bedroom was pristine," I said. "Full of life with the bright yellow and white. Also, so neat and clean, except for her pile of clothes in the closet."

"Oh, no," John said. "What was in that pile of clothes?"

Judy interrupted quickly and stated, "We checked that pile of clothes. There was nothing out of the ordinary in there. In fact, the clothing was unusually worn and old."

"It shows she didn't have much before she came here," Prunella said sadly. "She was so young and my husband ruined her."

"How did Eklund ruin Helena?" John inquired curiously. "Wasn't she just a maid for him?"

"Ha!" Inga declared loudly. "Not exactly."

"Would one of you please tell me what's going on?" John demanded. "Obviously Helena did something to tick Eklund off enough to kill her. So what did you find out?"

"She was pregnant," I cried out bluntly, blowing away John and Judy. They didn't say a word, but stared at me after my declaration. "Did you hear me? I said Helena was pregnant, and it was more than likely Axel's baby. He murdered her because of it, don't you think?" I looked around at everyone and they all nodded except for John and Judy who were still too shocked by what I announced.

"Wait," John said, trying to regain control. "How on earth did you come to this conclusion?"

Prunella pulled out the emptied pill bottles from a pocket in her sweater. "This is why." John reached over the desk again and grabbed the three bottles of pills.

"Where did you find these?" he asked, studying the bottles.

"In the medicine cabinet in her bathroom," she answered. "One's a mild sedative, the other for migraines, and the third bottle is..." Judy grabbed the bottle quickly from John and said, "Prenatal vitamins."

"I don't believe it," John said reading the labels on the bottles. "Why are the empty?" he asked curiously, studying them intently.

"That's what we were going to ask you," I replied. "We kind of thought your staff emptied the bottles to test them and see if they were really what they said they were."

Once again, John looked over at Judy who replied, "No, I'm sure whoever searched her bathroom earlier didn't think it was important. They were empty and Helena obviously didn't die of an overdose."

"NOT IMPORTANT?" he yelled, scaring the lot of us.

"Easy, John," I said, trying to calm him down. "It was probably pure luck that Sherman found these. I'm sure whoever searched the bathroom had it written in the report they were there."

"Judy, get me the cop who searched Helena's bathroom. I want to see the report and speak with him NOW." Judy took off out of the library in a hurry. She didn't want the fallout from this to land on her. "I don't understand; how did we miss so much?" John asked quietly. "Something doesn't feel right."

"I agree," I said, sitting in Judy's chair next to him. "We'll get to the bottom of it. Let's go over everything we know so far."

Prunella took the lead again. "First, Bert was viciously murdered last night. This morning we went looking for Helena, and you and Ruth Ann found her stabbed to death in the secret room down in the basement. Right so far?" John nodded attentively. "Next, you ordered us to stay in the library, but we didn't follow your order." John shook his head in disgust, but agreed with Prunella that we didn't follow his direct orders. "Then, Inga, Sherman, Ruth Ann, and I went up to the third floor and searched both Bert's and Helena's bedrooms."

"Let's not forget that you broke into Bert's room, and ripped off police tape to get into Helena's bedroom," John stated.

"Yes, yes, we did, John," I said. "Let's get past the fact we broke into their bedrooms."

"Go ahead Prunella," he said, ignoring what I just said.

"In Bert's room, Sherman discovered a large trunk hidden in the back of his closet. Your people overlooked the item." Disgust rose in John's face again. "Inside the trunk we found newspaper clippings and pictures telling us that Bert and Axel were either related or very close since Axel's childhood. We also learned that Bert's parents were brutally murdered in their bed while Bert hid under their bed."

"I'll have to verify these events before we can conclusively state them as fact," John added.

"Yes, I'm sure we understand that, John," Prunella agreed. "Next, we entered Helena's room and found three empty pill bottles in her bathroom. One of these was for prenatal vitamins, implying she was pregnant. Ruth Ann's theory is that she was pregnant with Axel's baby, and he killed her because of that." Prunella glanced out at the group before she added, "Are we good, John?"

John rubbed his head a few times before he said, "Yes, I have everything you told me written down. What I need now is to find Judy to see if when she and my other men searched the rooms they also noticed the pill bottles."

"And the trunk with the blood stain on the bottom," Sherman added.

"Yes, Sherman, I hope for their sake they knew about the trunk, too." He stood up from the chair and told us to stay here. He was going out to look for Judy and would return momentarily. "No leaving this room this time. Do we understand clearly what I'm *ordering* you to do?"

Collectively we responded, "Yes."

Chapter 13

John took off from the library while the rest of us sat around in silence for a few minutes. So much had occurred we didn't know what to do or think. Do we let the police take over and search for Axel and his men or do we get involved on our own and try and find him? I know John would have a complete meltdown if I mentioned we wanted to help with the investigation. I could just hear him now. "He has murdered TWO people in twelve hours, Ruth Ann! He didn't just murder them, he brutally, viciously, tortured, and then murdered them!" Somehow, Prunella and the rest of us had to discreetly find a way to bring Axel down, permanently.

I decided to mention my thoughts to the group before John and Judy returned. "Are you saying you *want* to go and look for Axel?" Prunella asked, stunned.

"Yes, kind of," I said non-committedly. "We obviously can't mention this to John, but we have to protect ourselves, too."

"I agree with Ruth Ann," Inga pronounced. "They couldn't even find the trunk or the pill bottles. Those were huge clues."

"That's true," Sherman said, coming around to my way of thinking. "If we go on with the initiative we also protect ourselves in case he comes after one of us, too."

"Exactly," I said. "I'm not saying we go out and actively search for Axel. Just be prepared, and maybe we can help the police catch him."

"How?" Prunella asked curiously.

"I'm not sure yet, but we need to think of a plan and quickly."

"You know John will insist on us leaving the house, don't you?" Prunella asked.

"Possibly," I answered. "Or he'll post plenty of his men in and around the estate."

"Mr. Eklund knows how to get around his house without being spotted," Sherman declared. "They won't be able to protect us unless they're at our side at all times." Sherman looked directly over at me and asked, "He wouldn't stick a guard on each one of us would he?"

"He doesn't have the manpower, unless…" I hesitated a moment and said, "Unless he brings back Paul, my security guard friend?"

"Maybe he'll bring back Paul plus more guards," Sherman suggested. "He would need more than one I would think."

"I'm not going to suggest anything to John. All I want to do is stay in this house. It's a big place and we can stick together and defend Prunella's home."

"It's a good idea, Ruth Ann, but it's risky," Prunella said. "Axel could overthrow any security guard John threw at him, plus get to us more easily here than if we stayed at your house back in town."

"Maybe, but I don't want to involve anyone from town, especially my daughters."

"I agree with you about your daughters," Prunella said. "Do they know what's going on?"

"Just about Bert last night. I haven't spoken with them today. We've been a little busy with Helena's murder."

"I'm sure they'll want to speak with you soon," Prunella began to say. "Maybe you should just call to reassure them you're all right. Tell them you'll be staying here for a while and that you'll talk with them during the week. It may get them off your case and far away from all of this."

"Yes, good idea, Prunella. We don't want the girls involved. That's another reason I have to convince John that we need to stay put here."

Inga interrupted our conversation regarding my daughters and anxiously asked, "What are we going to do here? Your chief will be back soon and I think we should have a plan."

"Any suggestions?" I asked.

"We can try and lure him out of hiding," Sherman suggested out of the blue. "I don't know how, but we can come up with something, can't we?"

"I think if we knew why he killed Bert and Helena we can get Axel to come out of hiding," I said.

"Then he'll come after us," Inga declared.

"That's kind of the idea," I said. "I don't want him to get ahold of one of us, just as you said...but lure him out and then catch him."

"Sounds pretty dangerous to me," Prunella commented. "If we do actually uncover why he killed Bert and Helena, we'll become his next potential victims."

"Not if we're ready for him," I said. "I know, it sounds dangerous, but I don't have any other ideas." I looked around the blank faces of the group and said, "It looks like you don't have any better ideas."

"Nope, not at the moment," Prunella said, resigned. "I don't like this though, Axel's very smart and extremely dangerous."

"Let's see what John suggests before we make any moves, agreed?" Inga, Sherman, and Prunella nodded and we waited in silence for John and Judy to return.

I started to get antsy waiting for John to return to the library. He left so angry, but at least it wasn't at us. If Judy and the men she used to search the two bedrooms didn't take the pills from the bottle or notice the trunk in Bert's closet, all hell will break loose. I began pacing around the library constantly glancing over at the doors to the foyer. "It's been a long time, hasn't it?" I asked, stopping in front of Prunella who was still sitting at Axel's desk with her head resting on her hands on bended elbows.

"He's been gone about an hour," she answered looking at the time on her cell phone.

"I'm getting hungry," Sherman protested. "It's time for Inga and me to prepare lunch. Maybe we should head out to the kitchen and get some food going. There's quite a few people hanging around here still, and I bet they could use some food."

"After John comes back, Sherman," I said. "He really meant it this time for us to stay where we were. I think we pushed him when we left to search the bedrooms upstairs."

"I think so, too," Prunella commented. "If John's staff didn't uncover the same clues that we amateurs did, he'll be in no mood for us to disobey him again."

"Fine, but they better get back here soon," he snapped and immediately the library doors flew open. "Uh-oh," Sherman whispered. "He looks furious."

"Well," John said. "I have to say I'm a little less furious (eyeing Sherman whose comments he heard), seeing all of you still in here. What, no bodies to uncover yet?"

"Not funny, John," I retorted. "I understand you have a serious case on your hands, and your staff made some huge mistakes, but don't take it out on us."

"You're right, Ruth Ann," he said, calming down slightly. "I'm not happy about the lot of you breaking the law earlier by entering two secured rooms, but you did uncover some vital information that my staff overlooked."

"Where's Judy?" Prunella inquired. "I hope you weren't too hard on her."

"She was in charge of the search up there," John snapped. "Even though it wasn't her that missed the clues, she should've double checked their work."

"So your department didn't empty the pill bottles to test them?" Prunella asked.

"No," he answered flatly.

"I wonder if someone flushed them to get rid of them," Inga suggested. "But why would that matter?"

"I can't think of any reason why the pills would've been flushed if they left the bottles in the medicine cabinet," I said.

"Unless the pills weren't what they were supposed to be," John hinted.

"Oh, you mean someone put different pills in the bottles from what they were supposed to be?" Prunella asked curiously. "Why? Wait...maybe Axel put a pill in the prenatal vitamins that would cause her to lose the baby?"

"That's what I thought so I contacted the coroner and he's going to flush her stomach and see what's in there. Also, he's doing a quick blood test to see if anything in her blood answers our questions."

"I thought toxicology reports take weeks?" Sherman asked.

"They do, but he can do a quick check that may disclose basic information. If we're lucky, we'll know something soon."

"I'm sure glad I found the pill bottles," Sherman announced, happy with himself. "I am also the one who discovered the trunk in the closet."

"Maybe you should change professions," Inga spoke sarcastically. "But you're too old, aren't you?"

"Hey," Sherman hollered, but I stopped them before John blew another fuse.

"Can Inga and I get lunch together for everyone? That would require us to leave the library and go all the way to the kitchen, by ourselves."

"Don't get smart, Sherman," John barked.

"Can we?" he asked, changing his tone somewhat. "You have how many cops wandering around the estate?"

"Let's see…Judy, me, plus two outside cops, two in the basement still going over the crime scene, and one guy walking around the inside."

"So, that makes…seven plus us four so eleven we need to prepare lunch for," Inga said. "We can get something simple together and it will be ready within thirty minutes if you'd like."

"Go," John decided waving them out. "But just to the kitchen and the dining room to set up. No going back up to the third floor, got it?"

"Yes," Sherman said, taking a hold of Inga's arm and dragging her out of the library. As he left I noticed a funny look he gave Prunella. I must've been seeing things because I would've sworn I saw Prunella give Sherman a slight nod of her head. "We'll ring when it's ready," he said, as he closed the library doors and left Prunella, John, and me alone.

"So now what?" I asked John, forgetting about what I might or might not have seen. "What are your plans for us, John?"

"My gut's telling me you should pack your bags and move into town."

"I live in town already, John."

"But you've been staying here quite a bit. I understand that you're trying to get to know your cousin, Prunella, but it's not safe here."

"I don't think we'd be safe anywhere, John," Prunella added. "I don't want to leave my new home."

"You can't stay here alone," John said. "And I don't have the manpower to protect you 24/7."

"What about hiring Paul and other guards at his company?" I suggested. "I don't think we're in as much danger as you believe."

"How could you say that, Ruth Ann?" John questioned her, exasperated. "Two people were brutally murdered in less than twenty-four hours. They're directly associated with all of you!"

"But they must've been in contact with Axel all along, John. We haven't seen or talked with him since we were back in his office in Stockholm," I said.

"John," Prunella started to say. "We need to find out why Axel killed Bert and Helena. Then, and only then, will we understand what's going on around here? If Axel survived to come back and take what's rightfully his, he would've made a move on me, not Bert and Helena."

"Unless Bert and Helena caught sight of Axel and threatened to tell you he was here," John suggested. "He might've killed them to keep them quiet."

"Possibly, but sounds like a long shot to me," Prunella answered. "He wouldn't worry about threats from a butler and maid. He would come straight for me."

"Why don't we agree that we need to find out where Axel is and why he hasn't tried to get his money, property, and business back?"

"And why he killed poor Helena and Bert," I added.

"Yes, that too," John admitted sullenly. "Those two were murdered for no reason. I hate when I have to investigate such violent murders."

"It doesn't happen very often in a small town like, Deer Creek," I said. "Until my family drama came to town."

"That was my fault, Ruth Ann," Prunella said, turning her attention to me. "If I didn't involve you with our family's necklace a couple months ago, none of this would've happened. I'm sorry that so many people have been hurt and killed because of me."

"It wasn't because of you, Prunella," John stammered. "It's your supposed dead husband's fault, and his alone!"

"Thanks, John," Prunella said, smiling sweetly at him. Her expression quickly changed to show her anger and determination. "Let's get him, once and for all."

"That's the plan."

Chapter 14

John paced the library for a short time mumbling until he stopped, turned, and stated, "I've got a plan." He walked quickly toward us and dumped himself into one of the chairs facing the desk. Prunella sat down behind the desk in Axel's over-sized chair, and I sat down next to John in the other wingback chair.

"Tell us," I said, excited. "What can we do to catch this creep?"

"We?" he asked, surprised. "*WE* don't catch him, I do."

"You need us John, admit it," Prunella said calmly. "I think I should put myself out there so he can attempt to get at me. It's the only solution."

"That's ridiculous!" I hollered. I looked from Prunella back to John and back again to Prunella. I saw this strange connection between the two of them. It was as if Prunella read John's mind before he could tell us his plan. "John, you wouldn't use Prunella to lure Axel out of hiding, would you?"

"Hmm…" he murmured. "I think it's our only option. We'll protect Prunella so she'll be safe. My only problem's how to do it? How do we safely construct a scheme where Prunella's open for Eklund to come after her?"

"Are you two cracked?" I shrieked. "No way will I allow Prunella to be caught by that man! It's out of the question!"

"Excuse me, Ruth Ann," Prunella said, oh so gently. "I want to start by saying I understand you have only the best intentions when you said that. However," Prunella said raising her hand before I could protest. "However, it is my decision and I want to go for it."

"What?"

"Yes, it'll work," she said confidently. "I just need a good enough reason for him to catch me."

"Let's think about this carefully," John said. "Axel pretended to be dead back in Sweden. He escaped jail and flew back here to pick up his life again. Including his money, business, and possibly his wife."

"He doesn't want me as his wife," Prunella swiftly responded. "He wants me dead so he can control his assets again. I never signed an agreement, what's it called again?" She hesitated trying to think of the word for signing a document that states what she gets in case of death or divorce. "A prenuptial agreement. That's what it's called."

John and I stared at one another in amazement. "You never signed a prenup?" John asked shocked. Prunella nodded her head slowly while smiling.

"Not very bright of Eklund, is it?" John inquired. "What that tells me is that he was either so much in love with you that he wasn't thinking clearly when the two of you got married or…"

"He knew I'd be dead before him!" Prunella stated finishing John's sentence.

"This is ridiculous!" I exclaimed. "Nobody needs to lure Axel out of hiding. We know he's after Prunella, possibly me. Keep us covered and eventually Axel will make a mistake and you'll catch him."

"We could do that, but at what cost?" John asked. "We can't afford another life to be lost, Ruth Ann. This man will kill anyone who even remotely gets in his way. You need to know if we can figure out a safe way for Prunella to assist us. It'll be the best solution, once and for all."

"Yes, once and for all, Ruth Ann," Prunella repeated. "I can't live like this anymore. I'm afraid for you, Inga, and Sherman. He'll try and kill you before he gets to me."

"He could've killed me many times before," I reminded them. "He never hurt me, in fact, he was kind to me until the very end."

"That's how he operates, Ruth Ann," Prunella responded. "He lured me into marriage, and I actually believed he loved me in the beginning."

"Maybe he did," I said. "Something must've snapped in him."

"I'll say," John chimed in. "The man's a cold-blooded murderer, Ruth Ann. Don't be fooled by him."

"Oh, I'm not, John," I said. "I was only stating that when Axel first held me captive he wasn't violent. Something changed to turn him into this monster."

"What?" John questioned. "I guess getting caught back in Sweden and losing his precious family necklace to you and Prunella set him off the deep end."

"That's it!" I yelled out. "He's trying to get to our necklace, Prunella." I looked over at her and her eyes were wide opened. "I'll bet he tried to get Bert and Helena to steal back the necklace."

"Why didn't we think that?" Prunella asked, appearing not to be surprised about the necklace. "The man, along with his past family members, have taken enormous risks to keep the necklace in their possession."

"Where's our precious family necklace anyway, Prunella?" I asked curiously. "I haven't seen it recently."

"With Halloween and the party I put it safely away," she answered. "In a new safe I had installed."

"Where's this new safe?" John asked, intrigued. "And when is the last time you checked on it?"

"Yesterday, before the Halloween party," Prunella replied. "It was just as I left it."

"That's good, but maybe we should check on it again," John suggested. "My immediate thoughts were that we should take it away from here and put it in the station for safekeeping until we catch Eklund."

I agreed. The necklace held a priceless gem that went back many generations in both my family and Axel's family. Many people have been hurt or even killed trying to keep possession of the gem. It was a brilliant, sky blue, rare, emerald shaped aquamarine that was almost 13 carats. Most people wouldn't understand why an aquamarine would be worth such a violent history, but it has been conveyed to me that it's almost priceless. We've had appraisers after the gem besides the Eklund's and my family, but at this very moment it was Prunella's and mine. I wanted to keep it that way.

John stood up from his chair and told us to follow him. "Are we going to eat?" I asked.

"Not just yet," he said, opening the double doors from the library into the grand foyer. "We're going to check on your necklace first."

"Now?" Prunella questioned him. "I'm sure it's fine, let's eat first, I'm starving."

John and I glanced briefly at one another. I bet we had the same thought…something's up with Prunella. First, she barely eats at most meals I've had with her, and second, why the hesitance with the safe? "It'll just take a second, Prunella," John said, motioning us into the foyer. "I don't want to remove it from your safe, just make sure it's still in there."

Prunella shook her head. "I don't want to divulge the exact location of my safe just yet."

"What?" I exclaimed. "You don't want *me* to know where the safe is?" Prunella didn't answer me and I reminded her, "It's my necklace too, Prunella. I have a right to know where it is."

Prunella wouldn't budge. "I don't trust what's going on around here. If we go together, I feel it opens the possibility for someone else to know where it is. Can't we please eat lunch first, and then I promise I'll go and check on it? I'm sure it's just fine."

"Now you've got me feeling suspicious, Prunella," I said, feeling very exasperated. "You and I have become so close, why are you shutting *me* out?"

"I'm not, really," Prunella pleaded. "After lunch, I promise."

John nodded, and so I gave in. "Fine, but right after lunch, and you're not going alone. If you don't want John following you, you'd better let me come along." Prunella nodded and we went through the foyer to the dining room. Inga and Sherman were setting trays of food onto a large buffet set along the side wall.

"Ah, you're here," Inga said, placing a silver tray with sandwiches down on the buffet. "We're almost ready. I just have to grab the coleslaw from the kitchen."

Prunella confidently went to the head of the table and sat down. John and I sat on either side of her across from each other. "Do we serve ourselves?" John asked, eyeing the assortment of sandwiches, relishes, chips, and now a large glass bowl heaping with coleslaw. "I'm hungry."

"Me, too," Prunella said, waiting for Inga to grab a plate and prepare her food. I felt it wasn't necessary to be served so I motioned to John and we stood up and walked over to the buffet. I grabbed some Swiss cheese and made a sandwich, adding a few slices of ham. Then I scooped up a pile of coleslaw and plopped it on my plate. I was about to return to my seat when Sherman popped in with a silver platter full of frosted brownies and ooey, gooey looking chocolate chip cookies. "I can't even get away from chocolate up her!" I said, grabbing one of each. John laughed and grabbed two brownies and two cookies. "I don't diet," he said, shoving an extra cookie into his mouth.

"I'm not on a diet," I snapped. "Do you think I should be?"

"That's a loaded question, Ruth Ann," John mumbled coughing on the cookie in his mouth. He looked over at me as I sat down and added, "You always look great, Ruth Ann. You don't need to be on any silly diet, ever."

Good answer, but I knew he was only being polite. I wasn't heavy by any means, but I could use to lose a few pounds…or ten! "Thank you," I answered anyway as I took a bite of the warm, soft, cookie before I touched my sandwich.

"Prunella," I said, looking at her sorry plate of food. "I thought you said you were starving."

She looked down at her half a cheese sandwich and spoonful of coleslaw. "This is just to start. I'll probably eat more."

Sure she will. Something very strange was up with her. She wasn't willing to talk in front of John, but maybe I could get her to tell me what was up if we were alone. But what could be her problem? She was fine until John and I mentioned the necklace. "I hope so," I said. "That's not enough food to fill up a toddler."

John ignored Prunella's plate issues and continued to eat from his own. He went up to the buffet for seconds and after finishing another plate of food, stood up and declared it was time to check on the necklace. Just as John said the words, Sherman dropped an entire half-filled platter of sandwiches. "What?" he yelped as the tray hit his foot. "The necklace?"

Prunella glared at him and he shut up and bent over to clean up the mess on the floor. Inga stood frozen next to Sherman, but didn't speak a word. Sherman hoisted himself up and as he started to walk towards the kitchen Inga grabbed his arm. "What's this about?" She demanded. "Why are you and Ms. Prunella shooting daggers across the room about her necklace?"

"*Our* necklace," I corrected everyone, again. "And I'm with Inga, what's up?"

Sherman's eyes pleaded with Prunella for her to speak instead of him. She took the last bite of her half sandwich and chewed it slowly while looking at each one of us. She wiped her mouth daintily with her napkin, and then set it on her plate. "C'mon, Prunella," I snapped. "This is ridiculous! We haven't kept any secrets from one another since we met. Why now?"

"I can't tell you why, Ruth Ann," Prunella finally spoke and admitted.

"Aha! So you admit something's up?" John hollered. "This isn't time to keep secrets, Prunella. Two people have been murdered."

"I know, that's why I'm doing what I am," she said. "I can't tell you anything else."

"Wait a minute," I cried out. "You've had contact with Axel, haven't you?"

John practically fell off his chair after I accused Prunella of deceiving us with Axel. "I suggest you answer her, Prunella," John demanded. He stood up and hovered over her chair until she spoke.

"Back off a little, John," she requested curtly. "I won't answer any of your questions at this time. You have to just accept it and in time I can tell you everything I know." Prunella glanced over at my expression of utter astonishment and begged me to understand. "Please, Ruth Ann, I don't want anything to come between us, but I need a little more time, and then I'll tell you everything."

"No!" I stammered. "I will not give you more time." I glared at Sherman who stood holding the dropped tray of food. I pointed at him and said, "He knows something, doesn't he?"

Sherman didn't speak a word, but waited for Prunella to talk. "I needed his help, and, before you ask, he was the only one I could ask."

John, frustrated, sat back down and pleaded with Prunella to confess. "This is crazy," he exclaimed. "You and Sherman aren't qualified to handle Axel and his men. They'll use you both, and then kill you. Don't you see that?"

"No, I'm finished here." Prunella stood up and left the dining room through the kitchen doors. Sherman immediately followed her out of the room. I looked at John in horror and he shook his head in disgust. "I'm totally confused, Ruth Ann," he admitted. "Why would she turn on us?"

"I don't know but I'll find out one way or another," I said, stomping off into the kitchen and leaving John and Inga speechless in the dining room.

Chapter 15

I entered the kitchen and it was empty. Where'd they go? I was only a few seconds behind them. I hurried back into the dining room and yelled, "They're gone!"

"Gone? How could they be gone?" Inga replied, dropping the silver tray on the table and rushing into the kitchen. John and I followed her into the kitchen and watched her open a door that led to the back of the house. "Where's she going?" John asked hurrying over there.

"Inga," John yelled as he exited the house. I was right behind him and just as I stepped onto a red brick paved patio, I caught John holding onto Inga's arm forcing her to not go any further. "Where are you going?" he shouted at her.

"They took off, look," Inga pointed over to a three-car garage in the backyard. "They left!"

"John, you need to go after them!" I shouted. "Call your men to follow them! Quick, there's no time to waste!" We grabbed our coats from the front hall closet and ran to the garage. Inga was correct. The garage doors were on the opposite side of the house so we couldn't see them leave. There was a grass driveway so the sounds were muffled from the car. Inga said there were only two cars left in there now, but earlier there were three. "They took the large, black sedan!"

"Call it in, John. You know what kind of car to look for. We can't let them get away!"

John took a hold of Inga's arm and turned her to face him. "Where did they go, Inga?"

"How would I know?" she hollered. "Didn't you happen to notice I'm as much in the dark as both of you are?"

"Leave her alone, John," I demanded. "She was duped by the two of them, too. We need to know what direction they went. Maybe your man in the front saw which way they went."

John let go of Inga's arm and took off toward the front of the estate. Inga stood frozen in disbelief over the fact that Sherman and Prunella excluded her in their plans. "How could they?" Inga asked me pathetically. "I've given up my entire life for her." I took a gentle grasp of her arm and led her back into the kitchen. We sat down at the table and I reached for the pot of coffee in the middle. "No, no coffee, Ruth Ann. It'll make me jittery and I'm already shaking."

"How about some tea? I can heat up the kettle and we can both have a cup and discuss what happened." Inga nodded, so I stood up and went over to the stove. I really wanted to run out front and find John, but Inga was so distraught I didn't think it wise to leave her alone. Who knows what she would've done? Maybe take one of the other cars and drive helplessly around looking for them in an unfamiliar town.

"I've never made you tea, Inga. What do you want in it?"

"Just black tea, please," she said pathetically. I poured the steaming hot cup of tea and we both sat and sipped silently trying to think what we should do next.

"You have no idea what they've been up to?" I questioned her.

"None."

"I don't get it. How could they do this to us? We've been in this from day one together. What could possibly have happened to change their minds?"

"Obviously, Mr. Eklund got in contact with one of them and gave explicit instructions to not tell anybody or they would be killed."

"Or he threatened us," I suggested. "Don't you believe Prunella, and even Sherman, would do whatever he demanded to protect us?" I waited for Inga's response, but she sipped her tea without answering me. "I believe they had our best intentions when they chose to betray us."

"That makes no sense, Ruth Ann," Inga replied bluntly looking up from her cup. "You think they excluded us because they wanted to protect us?"

"Yes, I do."

"So do I," a voice called out from the kitchen back door. It was an out of breath John coming inside. "I put out an alert for them, Ruth Ann. Also, I spoke with Dave who happened to be on duty out front."

"Did he see them?" I inquired anxiously.

"Yes, he did. They sped by him almost running him down."

"Who was driving?" Inga questioned.

"Sherman."

"Was Ms. Prunella sitting next to him in the front or the back?" Inga asked curiously.

"Why does that matter?" I asked.

"Because if she's in the back she wants to look like she's a lady being driven by her chauffeur. If she's in the front they're on equal grounds going after Mr. Eklund."

"Interesting observation, Inga," John said. "Just so you know, Prunella was sitting in the front seat."

"That's not good," Inga responded. "They're running right into danger."

"I agree," John said.

"What do we do next?" I asked, frustrated. "We can't just sit here and wait for them to return or worse...not return."

"Once again, *we* don't do anything," John said, frustrated. "We wait until we hear news on where they were headed. If we hear, that is."

"Why wouldn't we hear?" I asked, angry that he didn't want to take off after them. "Which way did they go? Dave must've seen them."

"After he recovered from nearly being hit by their car, he ran after them, but by the time he got to the main road they were gone."

"So we don't know if they were headed into town or toward Grand Junction?" I asked.

"Nope," John answered. "My guess is they went toward town."

"Why would you say that?" Inga questioned.

"I just have a gut feeling. I've been a cop for a long time and usually my hunches are correct."

"Then let's head back into town, John," I suggested hopping out of my chair.

"I think the best solution for the both of you is to come back into town with Judy and me."

"Really?" I asked, surprised that John readily agreed with my suggestion.

"Yes, safety in numbers. Plus, there was a murder here this morning and I don't like leaving you here without me."

"And me?" Inga added.

"Of course," John said. "I meant the two of you. Once we locate the sedan, we can make our next move."

We followed John into the grand foyer. The other policemen were finished in the basement for the time being, and John instructed them to get back to the station and keep a lookout for the black sedan with Prunella and Sherman inside. Judy came down the staircase from re-searching the two bedrooms on the third floor. After filling her in on what had happened she said, "We've done a thorough job up there. All we've got is the trunk and the empty pill bottles. Forensics will test the stain from the bottom of the trunk, but my guess it's blood."

"But whose blood?" John questioned.

"It could be Bert's blood. Maybe just a simple accident he never cleaned up. We'll make sure though," Judy answered.

"Get everybody out of here except two men," John ordered after he explained what happened with Prunella and Sherman. "I want to keep this place closely monitored while we're gone. Just in case Eklund or one of his men comes back here."

"I'll be happy when he's locked up for good," Inga declared.

"Me, too," I said. "Let's get going. We need to find Prunella and Sherman before they do something they'll both regret."

"They already have done something they should be regretting," John snapped. "They took off and didn't inform any of us."

John, Judy, Inga, and I got into John's police cruiser and headed back into town. We kept a close watch for Sherman, driving the sedan. There was one moment I thought I spotted a car off in a ditch, but it was an abandoned pick-up truck rolled on its side. With the help of the lights and sirens, we made record time into Deer Creek. The first sight arriving back in town was my daughter, Lynne's, bakery, Sinful Sweets. Today was Sunday, it was closed and I was thankful for that. I hoped Lynne was at her apartment near her sister's apartment recovering from the previous night's disastrous party at the resort.

"Everything looks quiet," Judy announced as we passed my antique store, Ruth Ann's. I missed my normal routine working six days a week at my store. It was also closed, being a Sunday. Meme, my assistant manager, has been running the store since my adventure in Sweden. She's young, but very ambitious and intelligent. Meme's only distraction these days was her two-year old son, Elijah. When he's not at daycare, he's usually in a controlled area in the store.

"Maybe we should take a look at the resort's parking lot?" Judy suggested. "We can look at the cars parked there. Maybe they went there since it was the place where Bert was murdered last night."

"Possible," John said. "But if they had to return there, why wouldn't Prunella just come out and say so?"

"Who knows," Judy replied. "Maybe there was some evidence they knew about and wanted to get a hold of? Or, Eklund's hiding out somewhere near and it's a public place."

"Ski season has begun," I said. "There'll be lots of strangers in town throughout the season. Last I heard, Carol said her resort was booked solid for months."

John pulled off Main Street into the parking lot and drove around searching for the luxury black sedan. The enormous, log cabin resort loomed ahead. "The lot's pretty full. Everyone keep a sharp eye out for the car."

We spent several minutes going up and down the lanes without success. "I was hoping we'd find their car here," I said solemnly. "Where else can we look?"

"What about your house, Ruth Ann?" Judy asked. "Nobody would think about looking there."

John pulled down a side street off Main and made another quick turn to my ranch style home. It was only two blocks off Main and I found myself longing to go inside and crawl into my bed, hoping when I woke up that this was just another horrible dream, but that wasn't to be.

"Nothing," I said, looking at the lack of cars in my driveway. "No car in my driveway. We can check the garage, but I highly doubt they'd be there anyway." John pulled into the driveway and hopped out of the car while the rest of us stayed put. He walked up to the garage door, punched in my code to open the door. It slowly started to rise…my car was the only car in there. "I didn't think so."

John backed out and headed over to Main. "I'm going to drive toward the station. We can see if there's been any news," John said. He took the side street down to the end where the school grounds began.

"Why did you go this way?" I asked him. "I thought you'd drive down Main Street to see the other businesses?"

"I thought I'd check out the school's three parking lots, too."

"What for? There's no school on a Sunday."

"Just to have a look around," he said, pulling into the grade school parking lot. "Empty." He drove past the football field, the soccer field, the baseball diamond, and the tennis courts. We entered the middle school lot that was also vacant. "High school lot is last," he said, winding around the newly constructed playground with swings and jungle gym apparatus.

"Look," I shouted out. "There's Nancy's car!"

"Why would Nancy be here on a Sunday?" John quickly asked.

"Maybe she's doing some work for her history class. Lynne said she's been really busy grading papers."

"We'd better check it out," he said, pulling up next to Nancy's bright red bug. He left the car running, but opened his door and peeked inside her car. "Nothing looks amiss in there," he said. "Maybe I'll just run inside and see if she's in there."

"You wouldn't know where to look, John. I should go with you."

"Wait," Inga interrupted. "We should stay together. If you two go, we all go."

"Fine," John snapped. "But let's get going. We're burning daylight here!"

Chapter 16

We hurried out of the police cruiser and headed for the front doors of the high school. "They're locked," John said, pulling on each of the door handles. "Do you know if Nancy has a key to the school or maybe she went inside a side door?"

"I have no idea, John," I said, frustrated. "Let's just go around the school until we find an unlocked door. We need to hurry, something doesn't feel right."

"Why?" Judy asked. "I'm sure Nancy comes here often to work on off days."

"Possibly, but that's not what's bothering me. I just can't shake the feeling that my daughters are involved in this mess somehow." I followed John and the rest of them as we took a corner around the side of the high school. "Oh, no," I cried out.

"What's the matter, Ruth Ann?" John asked stopping suddenly.

"What if Axel took my daughters hostage and that's why Prunella left me out of whatever she's doing?"

"Don't jump to conclusions, Ruth Ann," John said. "I'm sure Nancy's just here working."

We tried the first side door we came upon. "Locked," Judy said letting go of the metal handle. "Let's keep going, I bet there's more doors in the back of the school."

"Yes, there are," I answered. "That's where I've pulled up to pick up Nancy now and again when her car's been in the shop or she just needed help carrying stuff to her classroom."

"Great," John exclaimed. "Hopefully one of those doors will be unlocked."

We hurried around the back of the square shaped school and made our way to the first of three back doors. "Locked, what's the deal with this school?" Judy asked.

"It's Sunday, why would it be open?" Inga proclaimed.

Judy ignored Inga's comment and hurried over to the middle door. "AHA!" She yelled out to us just as we caught up to her. "It's open."

John gave Judy a little shove so he could be in front of the door and not her. I had to admit it made me giggle a little. "Let me go first," he said, grabbing the handle and slowly prying the door open. "There's no light on in here," he said turning back to us. "I wonder if Nancy came in this way?"

"If she did, she would've parked back here instead of in the front lot," I said. "Unless she didn't have a choice."

"What do you mean by that, Ruth Ann?" John asked.

"What if she was forced by Axel or one his men? He might've made her walk around or maybe she actually does have a key to the school."

"Let's not get too far ahead of ourselves, Ruth Ann. There's no evidence Axel's here or that he has contacted your girls," John said. "Plus, I don't see the black sedan, do any of you?"

"Hey, that's right," Inga stated. "They must not be here. So, why are we even bothering going inside?"

I glared at her and said, "To make sure my daughter's safe."

"I'm sorry, I didn't mean it like that."

"Enough," John stammered. "I'm going in and if the coast is clear I'll call out for you to join me."

"NO!" I bellowed. "It's my daughter and I'll go in with you."

"Not this time, Ruth Ann. There's a killer on the loose just in case you've forgotten."

"But, John…"

"Not this time," he said commandingly, but with a sympathetic tone. "Just give me a minute, and then I'll be back." John took off inside and shut the door leaving Inga, Judy, and me standing outside.

"I don't like this," I declared. "I have a strong feeling Nancy isn't in there on her own accord."

"Ruth Ann," Judy said, exasperated. "There's no evidence to show that Nancy's under any sort of duress. Give John a second and he'll confirm that."

The door flew open and John told us he didn't see anything out of the ordinary in the back kitchen of the school. That's the room he entered from the unlocked door. "Good, let's get over to the classrooms so I can check on Nancy."

"I go first," John said. "Do you understand my directions?" He particularly glanced over in my direction to make sure I understood not to going running ahead.

"Got it," I replied.

We entered into the spotless, stainless steel kitchen. The refrigerators were stainless, the several long counters were stainless, and the microwaves and stoves were stainless. There were no lights on except for the glow from the appliances along the wall. John pushed his way to the other side of the kitchen and exited through a set of double doors that opened into the school's cafeteria. "I already checked this room out briefly and there was no sign of any recent activity."

"Where do we go from here?" Judy inquired.

"Her classroom's on the east end of the school on the second floor," I announced. "I'd like to check in there first, please."

"Sounds good" John said. "If it checks out okay in your daughter's classroom then I think we should leave the school. We're wasting time here if Nancy's just working or by chance she just left her car here."

"I agree," I said. We hurried out of the cafeteria and hung a left down the main hallway of the high school. There weren't too many students registered here since Deer Creek is a small town. I don't recall the exact count, but I believe there are about three hundred students here ranging from ninth grade through twelfth. "We need to head up those stairs," I said pointing ahead to the staircase.

"Me first," John demanded, taking the lead. "If I tell you to go back or run…what will you do, except for Judy, of course?"

"Yeah, we run, John. I get it. Just hurry up," I said itching to get up those stairs and down the hall to Nancy's classroom.

We made it up to the second floor hallway and there were no lights on in the hall. It was still easy to see since it was afternoon and the sun was shining in from the windows inside each of the classrooms. "Here it is, John," I said showing him her room on the left side of the hall.

"Wait here." John disappeared into Nancy's classroom. You'd think I would know if Nancy was in there or not, but Judy blocked my way several feet before the door to her room. "Hey," I said to her. "Let me go."

"No," she said, holding her arms out so Inga and I were motionless. "Wait for the Chief."

A minute later, John came out of the classroom and shrugged his shoulders. "She's not in there. Are you sure this is the only room she teaches from?"

"Yes, John," I said, confused. "Where could she be?"

"Well, is there any way she could've just left her car here from Friday and walked home?" Judy asked.

I gave her a disgusted look and replied; "Now why would she do that?" I added, "She had her car at her sister's bakery yesterday before the Halloween party. I was helping them work in the bakery for their order for the party at the resort. Nancy was there, and so was her car."

"I don't know, Ruth Ann," John said, running his hands through his thick, graying head of hair. "Maybe we should take a quick run through the school and see if she appears."

"And if not?" I asked worried.

"Then we'll call Lynne and see if she knows where Nancy is," John answered. "Hey, why don't you just call her anyway? Then we might not have to search this school."

"No way, John," I said. "I don't want to alarm Lynne just yet. She'll ask all sorts of questions about last night and even about what happened to Helena this morning."

"Good point," he said. "Why don't we split up and search the school?" We agreed since it would be faster. John took Inga and I got stuck with Judy. I had no idea why John paired us up that way, but I didn't complain since I just wanted to make sure Nancy was safe.

Judy grabbed my arm and dragged me through each and every classroom on the second floor while John took Inga down toward the administrative offices. There was not a soul in sight on the second floor and I was beginning to wonder if Judy was right. Maybe, just maybe, Nancy's car was left here and she took off in someone else's car. But why, and who, is the question running through my mind?

"Second floor's clear, Ruth Ann," Judy stated. "Let's head back down and check those classrooms."

"I don't know if we need to check them since those are the under- classmen rooms." Judy looked at me and I explained that the first floor classrooms were for freshmen and sophomore students and Nancy taught the upper classmen.

"Oh, I get it, but I'd still feel better if we checked it out quickly." We hurried back down the stairs and went through each of the classrooms on the first floor. Nothing, except a science room filled with glass containers of frogs on the first floor. "Let's find John and Inga, maybe they came up with something."

Judy and I went back down the hall that opened into the main lobby. It was a two-story room filled with awards, trophies in glass cases, banners, and your basic rah-rah stuff high school kids love. "Which way to the offices?" asked Judy.

"Down the hall on the other side of the entrance," I said, pointing to another hallway opposite from where we were standing. "The large set of doors in the middle off to the right leads into the gymnasium and cafeteria."

Judy looked toward the doors to the gym but decided to find John and Inga first. "We can check that out on our way out since we already came through there when we entered the school from the back."

I shrugged my shoulders and told her I didn't care. I didn't think this was helping us any and we should've left here a while ago. Time was ticking, and I wanted to find Prunella and Sherman. They obviously weren't here because their car wasn't here either. I was sorely mistaken!

Chapter 17

Judy and I crossed the lobby to get to the other hallway. As we walked across the large room Judy looked down at the massive, painted emblem of a grizzly bear. "Why's a painted bear on the floor, Ruth Ann?"

"Seriously?" I asked, looking at her strangely. Judy didn't understand my question so I added, "It's their school mascot, you know, a grizzly bear?"

"Oh, I get it now. Deer Creek Grizzlies, right?"

"Yes, Judy, that's what it means." Really? I thought this woman came from the city, and I assume she went to a high school where there were mascots. Even I was aware of that!

"Ease up on me, Ruth Ann," Judy snapped. "You really have a serious problem with me, don't you?"

"Me?" I asked innocently. "I have zero problems with you *working* in Deer Creek." What a load of bull! Of course I had a problem with her, but there's no way I'm ever going to say that to her.

"Oh," Judy replied. "It sure seems you don't like me very much."

"Judy, I have no reason not to like you." I waited for her to reply, but she stood unmoving over the snout of the bear and stared at me. "We should get over to the offices, right?"

"Yes," I said, shaking off her confusion. "Let's go."

We hurried to the other hall and entered the Main Office where students, parents, and faculty go when they have administrative needs. "I don't see John," Judy said, walking around the long, high front desk. "Where else can we look?"

"There are several offices in this part of school. Let's keep checking…" We left the main office before checking the Principal and Vice Principal's offices. They were dark and locked anyway. The next office was tech services where the media, computers, and AV equipment were stored and used by students and faculty. "Empty," I said, closing the door and heading to the next office. "Counselor's offices are next," I said, pointing to those doors. "We can only go into a small waiting area because the two school counselor's offices will be locked."

"Where else, Ruth Ann? Something's wrong."

"Why do you say that?" I asked curiously.

"Because there's no sign of John and Inga down this way. Where else could they have gone?"

"Back through the gym and cafeteria possibly?"

"I think we should go back that way," Judy said, worried. "Hurry."

Once again, Judy grabbed my arm and dragged me down the hall and through the lobby until we stood in front of the large sets of doors that would open to the gym. "Let me go first," Judy declared.

"No way," I replied furious. "You're not leaving me alone out here. This place is giving me the creeps all of a sudden."

"Fine," she snapped. "Stay right behind me and don't do or say anything until I know it's clear."

Judy pushed on the metal bar attached to one of the doors and very carefully opened it up. She stuck her head into the darkened gym and said, "Looks empty."

"Great, let's get out of here. Maybe they're waiting for us outside."

"Maybe," Judy answered. "We need to walk through the cafeteria first, and then the kitchen. If there's no sign of them, we'll head outside."

"About time," I mumbled. "I bet they finished ages ago and are wondering where *we* are."

"We'll see," she said as we walked quietly across the gym. Every step we took echoed throughout the room and made me very jumpy. I was happy when we pushed through the doors into the cafeteria. "Looks pretty empty in here, too," Judy said, eyeing the room carefully. "On to the kitchen."

Once we entered the kitchen, I had a strange feeling that there had been a change in the atmosphere. "What's going on in here?" I asked, suddenly smelling a horrible stench in the air. "I don't remember smelling this when we came in here."

"You're right, Ruth Ann," Judy said, holding her gun in her hand tightly. "What's that odor anyway?"

"It's coming from the ovens on the wall over there," I said, pointing to the far right of the large kitchen. "Was the oven on when we came in here earlier?"

"I don't think it was, Ruth Ann," Judy replied slowly walking over to the ovens. "Stay here, let me have a look first." Judy walked away from me while I leaned against a stainless steel counter that was in the middle of the kitchen. This area, from what I would guess, had to be used to prep food since it was a long, shiny surface that would be perfect for that purpose.

The kitchen was still dark, but the light from the thin windows up high, and the appliances, made it possible to see inside pretty well. Judy walked up to one of the ovens, put her hand on the handle and slowly opened it up. "Oh my God," She cried out. "Stay over there, Ruth Ann, there's something or should I say some 'part' of someone being fried!

"WHAT?" I screamed, my voice bouncing off the walls.

"Shhh," Judy hollered over to me. "We don't know if the person responsible is still hanging around. Where's John?" Judy slammed the oven door shut, turned it off, and came back to me. "We need to call this in ASAP," she said, pulling out her cell phone.

"You have to go outside to get service. There's no service in many parts of the building."

"You're right," she said, holding her phone up high as if service would suddenly appear. "Come with me."

Judy and I opened the back door we came through. The sunlight momentarily blinded us. Once we regained our vision, Judy called the station, but it was that moment I noticed something else. "Look, Judy," I said, with shaking hands pointing to the ground right outside of the door.

"What's that?" she asked, bending over the numerous drops of a red liquid.

"It's blood!"

Judy waved me back and said, "Hold on, Ruth Ann. We don't know that for sure."

"Really, Judy?" I asked desperately. "Someone's been hurt. It could've been John or Inga and that's why we can't find them. They may have left in a hurry to get to the hospital!"

"Or it could be whatever's in that oven to scare us."

"Huh?" I asked, perplexed.

"Hear me out Ruth Ann," Judy said, putting her cell in her front pants pocket. "Lou and Dave are on their way, but in the meantime listen to my theory." I nodded for her to continue. "What if John and Inga were led somewhere else and didn't have time to tell us." She held up her hand for me not to interrupt. "Yes, they knew there was no cell service to contact us wherever we were at that time. Once they exited the building, whoever is playing this sick game snuck in the kitchen and placed a part of a body into the oven and cranked it up."

"Whose part is in that oven?" I asked disgusted. "And why?"

"I don't know, but it wasn't John or Inga. Part of a sleeve wasn't burned all the way and it wasn't what either of them was wearing. So take a deep breath and relax. It wasn't John."

"Or Inga," I added. "But where'd they go?" I asked, looking around the back parking lot. "We need to check out front for their car."

"As soon as Lou and Dave get here. We can't leave this spot until then. I have my gun so you're safe with me."

"I'm not worried about my safety, Judy," I shouted. "I'm worried about my daughters, Prunella, Sherman, Inga, and John!"

"I'm sure they're fine," Judy said, keeping a close lookout around us. "Now that I have cell service I'll just call him."

"Yes, that's right, do it, Judy."

Judy pulled her phone out of her pocket and dialed John's number. That was fast, I thought. She must have it memorized, but before I could comment she added, "Speed dial."

"Well?" I questioned her after several seconds. "Any answer?"

"Voicemail," she answered waving her phone in the air as if she was about to throw it.

"Don't," I said. "He may try and call you on it."

"What about your cell, Ruth Ann? Have you checked it for any messages?"

"It's in John's car," I said, remembering I left my purse with my phone and everything else in it.

"Wait…I hear sirens coming," Judy said quickly. "I think Dave and Lou are almost here."

"Good, we need to see if John's car is out front."

"Dave knows to look for it," she informed me. "Here they come!" We watched as the police cruiser whipped around the curve to the back of the school where we waited. They hopped out of the car and rushed over to Judy.

Dave said, "We called the hospital and coroner like you asked. There's been no one brought in to either."

I was astonished by Dave's announcement and asked, "Wait, you told them to check with the coroner?"

"There's a burned piece of a human body inside the high school's ovens. Maybe the rest of this individual was brought into either the hospital or coroner's office." Judy turned her back on me open-mouthed and quietly spat out orders to Dave and Lou. The two of them ran into the building and Judy pulled me toward the front of the school.

"So that's it?" I asked, wondering why we were leaving. "What about that poor man inside?"

"Nothing we can do about him, Ruth Ann. Dave and Lou have their orders. We have to find John and Inga. The guys haven't heard a word from them."

Judy took off in a run, and I tried to follow. Of course she would show off since she knows she's in way better shape than I am. I'm in my fifties, what does she expect? She's in her mid-thirties. At her age I would've easily beaten her to the front of the school, but now, not so much. I ran and caught up to her as she stood in the front of the school looking at the empty parking lot, except for Nancy's car. "Oh, no," I cried, out of breath. "Where'd they go?"

"More importantly, why'd they leave without us?" Judy inquired.

"What do we do now?" I demanded. "We have no way of knowing where they went and no vehicle to get there."

Judy stood dumbfounded. "I have an idea, Ruth Ann." She kept me in suspense a little too long before she said, "How far do you live from here?"

"Not far. Maybe six blocks or so."

"Let's get over to your house and get your car. We'll figure out where to go while we're on way over to your house."

"But…" I had no words. I didn't know what to say or do so I followed Judy as she marched down the long drive back to Main Street.

We made it to my house in about ten minutes, not bad, but still too much time was wasted. Judy asked me to hurry up and open my house. "I don't have a key to get in," I declared. "But I have the key code for the garage and I can get in through there."

"Fine, hurry up!"

I punched in my code and the garage squeaked open. My yellow, SUV shone brightly in the garage. "Phew, it's still here," I mentioned.

"Why wouldn't it be?" Judy asked. "And really, Ruth Ann…a bright yellow SUV? We won't exactly be discreet will we?"

"Sorry, Judy, I didn't know my truck would be used for a police chase. Maybe we could trade it in for one of those cars over at the police station with the sirens, logos, and cages blocking the front from the back seats."

Judy glared at me and said, "Yeah, funny, Ruth Ann."

I left Judy by my truck and ran inside. I felt a shiver run up my spine as I entered the mudroom. Was I safe entering my own home? It's happened before, I said to myself. Axel drugged me in my own bed a few short weeks ago, and when I awoke I was in Stockholm, Sweden. No, don't think too much. Just go and get my extra set of keys in the drawer of my beautiful antique cabinet; that my grandfather bought for my grandmother in the early 1920's. He carried that cabinet all the way home on a trolley car that ran in the city of Chicago, Illinois. They were the happiest couple I had ever met. Full of friends, love, and a wonderful family!

Every time I see that piece I think of my grandparents. I was named after my grandmother, Ruth Ann. She was the kindest person I ever knew, and if I could be a fraction as nice as she was I would lead a blessed life. A life I care to extend by many, many years. That's why I will not let Axel hurt anybody else in my family or someone else's. I opened the top drawer and pulled out the extra set of car keys and ran back to the garage where Judy was impatiently waiting.

"What took you so long, Ruth Ann?"

"I was only in there a minute. I'm not going to argue with you, let's go…but where are we going?"

"I'm not sure yet," Judy answered. "I was thinking about that while you were inside getting your keys."

"What about Prunella's estate up on the mountain? Maybe they hurried back there?"

"Why? I mean that seems like the obvious place, don't you think?"

"I guess so, but I can't think where else they would go."

Judy added, "Not just where they went, but who were they following? The person who stuck body parts in the high school ovens or did they spot Prunella and Inga?"

"Well, I'm not going to sit in my garage contemplating it. I'm going back on Main Street and driving in and out of every business up and down the street."

"I only wish your car was a bit more discreet. The bright yellow will give our identity a mile away?"

"If you have such a problem with my car why don't we go pick up your car?"

"I don't currently have a car, Ruth Ann," Judy admitted. "Mine's still in the shop. It's been in there a whole week now. I can't figure out what's taking Roger Jenkins so long."

"It's a small town and only two people work at the gas station. Roger and his son, Ricky. It takes longer to fix cars here than in a big city station."

"That's ridiculous! They should hire more help if they're that behind all the time."

"Get used to a small town, Judy." I added, "I'm taking off, any more complaints before I do?"

Judy said nothing, but her expression said it all. She obviously didn't like my attitude, and to be honest, I really didn't care. I headed onto Main Street and took another look around the school's parking lot. No Prunella and Sherman, and no John and Inga. There were cars in the back of the building, but they were the ones dealing with the tragedy inside the kitchen, and of course, Nancy's car.

"I'm going to go down the street and the alleys behind the buildings. After that, we can come up with another solution. They have to be around here somewhere," I stated.

Judy nodded and kept a watch out the truck window. First, we went through the hospital lot and that was clear. We headed back onto Main and went by the Village offices, the lawyer's offices, the bank, and then we hit the resort. "I'm going to have a look in there," I said, as I turned into the long drive that led back into the lot and resort. "Wow, that is a full lot," I noted.

"Tourist season's in full blast, Ruth Ann," Judy announced.

"Obviously," I responded rudely. "I do live in this town, I'm aware of the tourist season, Judy."

Judy turned her head toward me as I slowly drove up and down each aisle. "Knock it off, Ruth Ann," she barked. "I'm just as worried as you are. And to be perfectly honest, your attitude is really ticking me off."

I was being rude and obnoxious towards her. I just didn't like her very much. Even without our situation with John, there was something about her I couldn't stand. However, she was right, I needed to focus on the task at hand and knock off the rude remarks. "Sorry," I said to her. "Let's just find the group."

"Agreed," she said, turning her attention back to the parking lot. We were three-fourths of our way done with the parking lot with no luck when a woman came running down the middle of the aisle we were just leaving. I could see the woman in my rear view mirror waving her arms up and down. "What the…"

Judy whipped her head around and shouted for me to stop. I slammed on the breaks without alerting Judy and she flew forward toward the front windshield. If she didn't have her seatbelt on she would've gone sailing through it. "I'm sorry," I said, reaching out for her to help her sit back in her seat. I truly didn't mean that to happen, please believe me."

She shook it off and said, "I'm the one who yelled for you to stop and that's exactly what you did. No sorry necessary."

"Thank you," I said, pulling slowly to the side so the woman behind us could catch up. I couldn't tell who it was until she was almost upon us. "It's Carol, the owner of the resort," I said to Judy, surprised. "What's she doing running after us?"

"She must've seen your *yellow* SUV and needed to speak with you."

"Good thing it's yellow, because she might not have spotted us otherwise."

"Touché, Ruth Ann," she snapped.

I parked the car and hurried over to Carol as she leaned on the back of the trunk trying to regain her breath. "I'm so glad you stopped, Ruth Ann," she said, gasping. "I need you to come inside, quick."

Judy asked curtly, "What's this about, Carol? Is something happening inside the resort?"

"Yes, yes, John's inside on some kind of chase. He needs your help, now!"

I told Judy to go ahead and I'd catch up as soon as I parked my car in an open spot. Carol waited for me, which I was happy about, because she could fill me in on what was actually going on inside her resort. "I have no idea what's going on, Ruth Ann," Carol said, finally catching her breath.

"Is John alone or with Inga?" I had to remind her who Inga was, but she shook her head.

"He was alone when I saw him running through the lobby toward the staircase."

"Who was he chasing?"

"I have no idea, Ruth Ann. He flew inside the front doors waving his badge and yelling at people to move aside. He found Richard, they talked for a few seconds, and then he high-tailed it to the stairs and disappeared."

"What did Richard ask him?"

"He asked him if there was an older gentleman that might've come in a week ago to stay here at the resort. He gave Richard a description of who he was looking for then took off."

"I don't believe it!" I said, stunned.

"What...what?" Carol pleaded.

"Axel Eklund's been staying in plain sight at your resort all along." I ignored Carol for a moment longer and said out loud, "How could we miss that?"

"What...who's Axel Eklund again?" Carol took my arm and stopped me abruptly. "Tell me, what's happening in my resort?"

"I'm sorry, Carol, Axel's the man that had me kidnapped, killed people, probably even killed that poor man that was at your Halloween party last night."

"I thought you told me he was murdered back in Sweden!"

"We thought so until very recently. He staged his death and escaped from police custody back in Stockholm."

"And you're telling me he's here, in Deer Creek, at *my resort*?"

"Possibly," I answered just as shocked as she was. "We need to get inside and see if Prunella, Sherman, and Inga are there, too."

"I didn't see them, but that doesn't mean they're not there. I'm not always at the front desk."

"Let's hurry, Carol. I need to get inside and see what's happening."

Finally, we made it inside the massive, wood framed lobby. Dick was standing behind the front desk helping new arrivals. He had a terrified look on his face when he spotted Carol and me. He waved us over and handed over the young couple checking in to another resort employee. Dick disappeared into a door behind the counter and reappeared from a side door. "There you are," he said, worried. "I didn't know where you ran off to, Carol."

"I spotted Ruth Ann's yellow truck in the parking lot and knew something was up. I ran out of the lobby and chased her and that female cop down."

"Judy," I said to the both of them. "The female cop's name is Judy."

Richard said, "Well, that Judy came busting in here yelling at me to tell her where John went running off to." Richard glared at me and added, "We can't have this kind of behavior around here. It's horrible for business. We're doing all we can do to keep what happened last night away from our guests."

"I'm sorry, Richard, I don't know what's going on either. I just want to find out where John went. Once I find John, I'll bet the others will be around, too."

"Others? What others?" Richard asked, perplexed.

"Judy, you already know about, and then there's Prunella, Sherman, her butler, and Inga, her housekeeper."

"They're all here, too?" Richard asked, surprised.

"I don't know, Richard," I admitted. "I hope they're all here."

Suddenly, it hit me. I was alone; none of those I started with were around me anymore. Prunella and Sherman took off on a wild goose chase. Then John and Inga took off from the high school without telling Judy or me. Now, Judy took off inside the resort, and I had no idea where she went. All I'm aware of is that John and Judy went toward the staircase. "Hey," I said, turning back to Richard. "What floor did you tell John to go to?"

Richard looked at Carol trying to get a feel whether he should tell me or not. "C'mon, Richard. I'll go floor to floor and disturb every guest in here if you don't tell me."

"Fine, but you'd better tell John you forced me to tell you."

"Yes…please tell me…" I pleaded.

"Top floor," he mumbled hoping I wouldn't hear him.

"5th floor, thanks," I said, running over to the elevator. I wasn't going to take the stairs if the elevator got me there quicker.

Richard called out to me, "Wait, Ruth Ann, let me go with you…"

Too late, the door to the elevator slowly shut and I was on my way to the 5th floor or at least I thought I was. The door stopped on the 3rd floor, and when the elevator door opened up, Ben, the resort's handyman, was staring at my face. "Hi, Ruth Ann," Ben said humbly. "What are you doing up here?"

"Hi, Ben, I'm in a bit of a hurry. Are you going up?" Ben nodded and slowly walked inside the elevator.

Ben was new to the resort. Richard hired him on the spot because he felt sorry for him. Ben was in his late forties, I believe, and was a man ridden with fear and anxiety. I had heard he was abused as a child and at a very young age set out on his own. He never lived anywhere too long. He would do odd jobs from town to town and was always paid in cash. John and I encountered Ben when he innocently, became involved with Axel's men. Ben was up on the second floor of the resort and ran into one of Axel's main men, Finn. Finn was a horrible creature. He had a Viking ship tattoo on his neck and, long story short, met a nasty death back in Stockholm by being blown up on a pier.

Ben also had his fair share of Axel's wrath, He had been tied and gagged in his own, sparse, apartment a couple weeks ago because Finn and his men thought Ben knew where I was, and the whereabouts of the infamous necklace Axel Eklund was after. Ben and I became friends mainly because I was nice to him and not accusatory like John was with him. John became frustrated with Ben when he couldn't (or wouldn't) answer his questions. Ben had some type of disability that kept his intellect at around age 10 if I had to guess. He was an innocent soul, but hard working, and that's why Richard hired him to help out around the resort. Ben never questioned any of the work he was instructed to complete, and was always on time. It was the best job he'd ever had and told me he never wanted to leave the resort. Richard and Carol trusted him and would never do anything to hurt him.

"Are you going to the 4th or 5th floor Ben?" I asked, waiting for him to hopefully push the 4th floor button. I didn't want to involve the poor guy again.

"5th floor, Ruth Ann," he said, leaning back against the wall of the elevator as it crept shut.

"What 'ya got going on up there?" I asked curiously.

Ben smiled at me and pointed to a small device hooked on to his jean pocket. "Mr. Dickson just texted me to stay by your side until you came back down to the lobby. He was worried for you, and that's all he told me."

"Oh, no," I muttered. "Ben, I'm just fine, really. Why don't you head back down once we get to the 5th floor?"

"No, ma'am," he replied courteously. "Mr. Dickson told me to stay by your side and that's exactly what I'm going to do." He was observant enough to notice my exasperated look when he added, "He told me you wouldn't be happy and that you would try and trick me to go away."

"Fine," I said, admitting defeat. Ben was the type of individual that would shut down or panic if he noticed anything out of the ordinary. And let's just say...my mission was out of the ordinary!

Chapter 18

The elevator beeped as we arrived on the 5th floor of the resort. "We're here, Ruth Ann," Ben said. "What exactly are you doing up here anyway?"

"I'm trying to find my friends, Ben. Do you have any close friends?"

He stared at the door that was slowly opening and answered, "Not really. Just Mr. and Mrs. Dickson here at the resort, the chief, and you."

"Well, when things calm down, the first goal I'll have is to get you lots of friends here in town. Would you like that Ben?"

"Oh, yes, very much."

The elevator door fully opened and we headed into a small corridor and looked both ways down the hallway. "Are you looking for the chief?" he asked.

"Yes, he's one of the people I'm looking for, but also my cousin, Prunella, and some people that work for her." I wanted Ben to stop talking so I could listen closely for any voices because I wasn't given a room number. Ben must've sensed my apprehension and stopped talking.

We walked to the right down a long hall and I put my head up to each and every door down this way. "Nothing out of the ordinary," I said to Ben.

"I didn't hear anyone either, Ruth Ann." Ben put his arm straight out in front of me to block my way. "Wait, are you in some kind of danger?"

"Oh, no, Ben," I replied. "I'm just looking for the room where all my friends, and John, your friend, went to. They ran off without me."

"Then why did Mr. Dickson tell me to stick to you like glue?"

"Because he thinks trouble follows me, I guess."

"Does it?" he asked me, worried.

"It seems that way lately, Ben. But I'm hoping not right now."

"Good, then let's keep checking the rooms for your friends."

We headed toward the other end of the hall and I thought Richard sent me on a wild goose chase when I heard a loud thump coming from the last room on the right. "Did you hear that?" I asked Ben.

"It sounded like someone fell inside that room," he replied with his eyes wide opened. "Maybe we should knock and see if whoever's inside is okay."

"Let's wait a minute and see if we can hear voices coming from in there," I said curiously. Ben nodded and we put our heads close to room 525. "I don't hear any voices," I said, confused. "I clearly heard a noise coming from inside there." I looked over at Ben and he nodded his head in agreement. He stood up, stepped back a few feet and reached into his jeans pocket.

"You have keys?" I asked as he pulled out a large metal ring filled with keys.

"Yes, Mr. Dickson gave me a set to keep while I'm working. I have to turn it into him each time I leave. I can't go home with these keys, Ruth Ann."

"That's terrific, Ben!"

"But, I was told to *never* enter a guest's room without their permission."

"But whoever's in there could be injured, Ben. We need to check it out just in case."

"I don't know, Ruth Ann," he said, rocking back and forth.

"Don't get worried, Ben. I'm sure Richard, I mean Mr. Dickson, would want you to go into this room and see if there's somebody in there who needs help."

"Maybe I should call him first on my phone that he gave me?"

"Ben, we don't have time. Please…we need to open that door."

He hesitated for just a second longer and then found the old-fashioned room key that Carol and Richard still used to open their doors.

"You made the right decision, Ben."

"I hope so."

"If you get in any trouble for this I will take all the blame for you, okay?"

"That would help, Ruth Ann," he said as he stuck the key into the lock and turned it. "Here we go…" he turned the doorknob slowly and I felt my hands and neck clam up. I had no idea what we would find when we entered the room.

"Just open the door all the way," I asked. "Whoever's in there will know by now that someone's trying to get in here.

Ben threw open the door, but blocked my body from going in. He was trying to put himself first in case there was any danger inside. I'll have to remember to tell Richard how brave Ben was after we get back downstairs.

"Wait, Ruth Ann," he cried out. "There's a body on the floor!"

I pushed Ben aside with rushing adrenaline after he said he found a body. "No, Ruth Ann, let me go first," he yelled.

I didn't wait for Ben to lead the way. I ran over to the white robe that was laying over a body on the floor next to the king size bed in the middle of the room. "Oh, no," I called out. "It's a woman."

"Do you know who it is?" he asked, terrified.

"I think it's Judy, the detective who works for the chief."

"What's she doing on the floor?" he asked me, completely oblivious that she could be hurt or dead.

"Stay back a second, Ben," I said, hurrying over to her. I carefully pulled the white terry robe that was thrown over her and felt her neck for a pulse. "Thank God," I muttered.

"What...what's wrong with her?" Ben asked.

"She's okay," I said.

"Is she alive?"

"Yes, Ben, but I need you to call Richard and tell him to call for an ambulance." I stood up and looked him straight in his eyes and asked if he could help me out and do that.

"Yes, I'm going right now," he said and ran out of the room. Wait, where's he going? I asked him to *call* Richard, not go get him.

I went back to Judy just as she started moving around and moaning. "Judy?" I called out to her as I knelt beside her body. "Are you able to sit up?"

She took her arm and moved it from under her body and felt for her head. "I'm okay, Ruth Ann," she said painfully. "I was hit on my head."

"Who hit you?" I asked frantically. "Did you see John and the others?"

"I'm not sure," she answered.

"What?"

"Give me a moment," she said, trying to sit up. I helped her to her feet and she sat on the edge of the bed. Before she could say anymore, Richard flew in the room with Ben standing in the hall just outside the door.

"What happened in here?" Richard demanded.

"I have no idea, Richard," I said truthfully. "Ben and I were listening for voices when we heard a loud thump coming from this room. We stood outside the door and I finally convinced Ben to unlock the door. I thought someone was hurt inside and I was right."

"It's the new lady detective John hired recently, right?" he asked close to me.

"Yes, It's Judy Welch, she works for John. We were trying to find them, but Judy took off without me and this is where I found her. Wait," I said, confused about something. I turned to her and asked, "If Ben and I heard a thump, and you said someone hit you over the head…where are they?"

"Who, Ruth Ann," Richard asked.

"The person or persons who hit her?" I asked, wondering where the criminal was.

Judy looked confused and said, "It was a man, tall, blonde, in a suit."

"Did you know who he was?" I asked her.

"Never seen him before," she said, getting her wits back. "It wasn't Axel Eklund, if that's what you want to know."

Richard looked confused and said, "The man isn't who I saw check in the other day. He wasn't blonde, but gray and tall. Very distinguished looking."

"That sounds like Axel," I added. "Maybe the guy who knocked Judy out was one of his men?"

"Could be," Judy said. "It happened so fast. I arrived on the 5th floor and heard a lot of noise coming from this room.

I pounded on the door and heard voices clearly from inside this very room. But, if Ruth Ann and that other man were outside the door when I got hit, where'd everybody go?"

"So when you entered this room, who was in here?" I asked, baffled.

"Just the man I described. But where did the others go? I was on the other side of the door so no one could've gotten by me."

"Richard, is there another way out of this room?" I looked around the large room and noticed a couple doors. "Where do those go?"

"One is the closet, and one to the bathroom. Wait a minute…this is the end room and we have a staircase out of that balcony," he exclaimed.

The three of us ran over to the sliding glass door and found it wasn't locked. Judy pulled open the door with one hand while holding the back of her head with the other. It glided wide open and we stepped onto a large, wooden balcony with a staircase off to the left. "I can't believe I forgot about the stairs, Ruth Ann. I'm so sorry, but this has to be how the others left the room."

Judy carefully shook her head back and forth and mumbled, "This has to stop happening to me. I keep getting hit in the head."

"Judy, you had no idea who was actually in this room," I said, shocking myself. She was the last person I actually wanted to feel better. Not that I wanted any serious harm to come upon her, but a little wouldn't be too bad!

"I should know better to not come barging into a situation that might be dangerous."

"Too late," Richard said, looking down the long winding staircase that led to the back of the ski resort. "It's a fire escape for the upper floor rooms."

"Now what?" I asked, aiming my question at Judy.

"We go down the stairs and see if someone left any clues. Eklund must've contacted your cousin and conned her into meeting them here. John and Inga found out about it and couldn't contact us back in the school. We followed them here, and they were able to get away, again."

"What are we waiting for?" I asked. "Let's get down these stairs."

Richard called out for Ben who was still standing in the doorway of the room. "Come with us, Ben," he said, waving him over. Ben reluctantly obeyed Richard and the four of us set off down the stairs. The cold air felt good. I needed to clear my head and see if John, Prunella, Inga or Sherman dropped anything that could help us find them.

"Keep a sharp eye out for any object that they could've dropped," Judy called back to us. I noticed Judy held onto the railing until her balance returned to normal from her head injury. I told her to be careful because we didn't want her to fall off the staircase. I think she was beginning to believe I actually liked her. I still didn't, but didn't want anything to be blamed on me if something happened to her.

We made it past the fourth floor…third floor…second floor… "Nothing so far," I said, discouraged. "They had to leave us something." I was about to hit the bottom few stairs when I spotted a hairpin. "Wait," I cried out to Judy who was already on the ground looking around for clues. I held out the hairpin and said, "It's from Inga. I knew it!"

"How?" Judy asked skeptically.

"Because she's used them with me before when trying to break into locks. It's something that she knew I would find."

"Where'd you find it?" Judy asked quickly. "Maybe there's something else near there."

We went to the step where I discovered the hairpin and carefully searched around the area. "Here," I exclaimed. "In between one of the planks in the wood."

"What...what did you find?" she inquired looking down at the step.

"It's a folded piece of paper stuffed inside this plank," I answered pointing down at the wood step. Judy carefully knelt down and pulled out the paper without putting on gloves or anything. "What about fingerprints, Judy?"

"No time for that, Ruth Ann. We need to see if this is even related or just garbage."

"It's perfectly folded and stuffed inside the plank right where I found the hairpin. It has to be related. Inga planted it, I just know it!"

Judy unfolded the piece of paper, which ended up being a coffee filter from inside the hotel room. "Ingenious," Judy murmured.

"C'mon, what does it say?" Richard asked from behind me. I had forgotten Richard and Ben were even with us.

Judy read the coffee filter to herself. "Judy," I snapped. "What does it say?"

"It's written in pen and it says: M. Svenson and A. Eklund."

"Is that all? Not where they went?" I asked impatiently.

"There's something else scribbled on it, but I can't make it out," Judy said handing the coffee filter over to me. "Maybe you can make it out. My head's a little fuzzy still."

"I think it says...house??"

"House?" Judy questioned.

"Yes, but the ink's smeared. I would have to say my best guess is house. OH MY..." I bellowed. "I know who it is and where they're going."

"Where?" Judy pleaded trying to hurry me up. "We're burning daylight, Ruth Ann."

"It's Axel Eklund and Steven Svenson."

"Who's this Steven Svenson?" Judy inquired.

"The lawyer from Sweden who worked with Bertha's brothers to steal the necklace from the bank here in town and then back in Sweden."

"Why would he be with Eklund?"

"They must be working together to get back his assets, mainly the necklace," I answered. "And I think they headed back to the house up the mountain."

"Are you sure, Ruth Ann?" Judy asked. "I don't want to drive all the way up the mountain if they're somewhere in town here."

"Where would they go in town? I doubt my house. Unless, they went to my store."

"Why would store be confused with house?" Richard chimed in.

"Because, Richard, don't you remember, my store was built to represent an antique house?"

"Oh, that's right, but I doubt they would go there. It's too obvious. Meme or your daughter, Lynne, would spot cars there and go over."

"We need to get there right away!" I yelled heading around the back of the resort toward the parking lot. "Hurry, Judy, if they're at my store my daughter may walk right into a trap."

Chapter 19

We ran through the crowded resort parking lot and finally, with the four of us totally out of breath, made it to my bright yellow, SUV. "Ruth Ann," Judy said, regaining her breath before me. "Would you mind letting me drive?"

"Why?" I asked her. "I know the way."

"But I can get us there faster."

"Fine," I said, letting her feel superior. She was the cop, but I was the one who had lived in this town longer. Richard stayed back, but sent Ben with us and told him to do whatever it took to keep us safe. I didn't think we needed him, and to be perfectly honest, thought he might just get in the way.

Judy got behind the wheel and I sat in the front next to her. Ben climbed into the back seat and immediately put on his seatbelt. "We're not going very far, Ben," I said. "We're going to check my antique store out first. It's less than a mile away."

"I'm just a little nervous, that's all."

Judy eyed him in the rearview mirror and smiled. "Don't worry, Ben, I've driven many times before. I'm a police officer so I've been trained to drive fast."

"Oh, okay," he said tightening his seatbelt.

We hurried down Main Street and pulled down the last entrance to the alley in between the hardware store and the gas station. I could see my store and there were no cars parked in the street near it. "Hurry, Judy, I have a bad feeling we're missing something, but I can't figure out what."

"I agree with you, Ruth Ann," Judy said, pulling behind my store. "There are no cars back here. We should head up the mountain. If Eklund's back and he wants all his assets returned to him they would go to his estate, not your store."

"I just want to check to make sure before we drive up the mountain."

"Do you want to go in your store and have a look alone?" Judy asked.

"I don't know," I admitted. "I doubt we'll get anywhere here, but if they were here I'd hate to have missed something they might've left behind."

"We should go in together," Ben said from the backseat. I almost forgot he was back there.

"Why?" I asked him curiously.

"To be sure. We're already here and wasting time. If you pass this opportunity and miss something, you'll be mad at yourselves."

"Good point, Ben," I called back to him. For Ben, the statement was well thought out. He never received a proper education, and I don't believe he's as handicapped as he protests. Hopefully in time, he can gain more confidence and improve his lifestyle.

I grabbed the extra set of store keys I kept in my glove compartment and we exited the truck. "Anyone could find those, Ruth Ann," Judy spat out. "It's the first place a thief would look."

"I've never felt the need to hide them here in town. We normally live in a safe town."

"Not anymore," she mumbled.

"I won't do it anymore, but it sure helped us out at the moment."

I hurried over to the back door and unlocked the door. I was worried what we would find after we entered. The first room was my storage room. It's where deliveries are dropped off before they're put out on the floor. My office was also off the back room. We went inside the storage room and found it untouched. "Nobody's been in here," I said. "Let's look inside my office."

Judy went in first and said, "Empty."

"The showroom's through those swinging doors," I said, pointing to the double doors. I was so happy with myself for putting in swinging double doors because some of the items we passed through the back storeroom into the showroom were large pieces of furniture.

"Let me go first, Ruth Ann," Judy said again, pushing through the doors. "Stay close behind me."

Ben and I followed Judy into my showroom. The ample sized room was dark because the front awnings I had installed last year toned down the light that usually shone in from the windows. The sunlight can be quite intense and it fades items near the window. I couldn't see anything out of the ordinary until we headed up the extra wide staircase that led to another showroom on the second floor. Judy went up the stairs first, with Ben and I going up side by side. "Hmmm," I said out loud.

"What'd you say that for?" Judy asked.

"Something's not right," I said. "I see the light coming from one of the crystal chandeliers up here."

"Do you normally turn all the lights off?" She asked quickly.

"Yes, they're old and I don't want them to burn out or break."

"You two stay back," she ordered. "I'll call you over when it's clear."

Ben and I waited on the top step while Judy walked to the back of the second floor showroom. "How long should we wait for her?" Ben asked quietly.

"I have no idea, Ben," I answered truthfully. "But in a second or two I think we should go find her anyway."

"I don't like this, Ruth Ann," Ben said stiffly. "Maybe we should just leave here."

"It's okay, Ben, we're with a police detective. She'll protect both of us." I know the words came out of my mouth, but I didn't exactly believe them. Judy had been duped one too many times in my book.

"Okay, Ben, I think it's been long enough. Let's go have a look." We grabbed onto each other's hand and I pulled Ben along. "Really, it'll be alright," I whispered, trying to believe the words myself.

We made it past a large display of Oriental rugs that were standing upright. I lost sight of Judy when she went on the other side of the rugs. I was reprimanding myself for standing the rugs up when one of them moved slightly. "Ben, did you see that?"

"Yes…that rug wiggled, Ruth Ann. Do rugs do that?"

"No, Ben, they don't," I said inching closer to the moving rug. "What's going on here?" I asked out loud.

"Ruth Ann, where's Judy?" Ben asked staring directly at the rug. He sure looked like a man that wanted to turn and run as fast as he could.

Out from behind us, Judy appeared and caused Ben to trip and fall into the standing rugs. They toppled over on top of one another with Ben on top. "Ben," I called out. "Are you okay?"

"NO! The rug underneath me is moving and it feels like a hard object is inside of it!"

"Get up!" Judy demanded. She held her gun out aimed at the rug. "Who's in there? Tell me immediately before I shoot!"

A muffled voice came from inside of the rolled rugs. "Wait," I cried out. "There's someone in there!"

We hurried and grabbed the top rug and tried to unroll it. It was too heavy to handle when out of the top of the rug a hand appeared. "LOOK," Ben screamed. "A hand!" Ben turned and ran towards the stairs and disappeared. I was torn and wanted to go after him, but we had to figure out who was inside this rug. They were clearly alive since the hand and body was wriggling incessantly.

"Can you talk?" Judy called out. No answer.

"Ruth Ann, you take the top part and I'll be down here on the bottom of the rug. When I say 3 we use all our might to unroll this rug off the pile. Got it?" I nodded. "Okay, here we go…1…2…3!" We grunted, but we were able to move the rug and it rolled off the pile and onto the wood floor. It thumped hard on the floor, and when we unrolled the last bit of rug, we saw who was forced inside.

"INGA!" I bellowed. "Judy, is she okay?"

I fell to the ground beside Inga and took her by the shoulders and rolled her over so her face was aiming towards the ceiling. "Inga, can you answer me?"

Inga's eyes popped open and she wanted to speak, but her mouth was covered with duct tape. Judy knelt over and ripped it off leaving Inga to scream out in pain. "What did you do that for?" I snapped.

"It's the easiest way to pull the tape off. Quick, painful, but done in an instant."

"Gee, thanks," Inga said, rubbing her mouth with her hand. "Where am I?" she asked, baffled by her surroundings.

"You're in my store, Inga," I replied. "Do you remember how you got here?" I asked, helping her to a sitting position.

"No, wait…yes!"

Judy didn't wait for Inga to answer my question, but asked her, "Is John here with you somewhere?"

"No, I don't think so, but I don't know for sure," she replied. "We were at the school when your chief pulled me so hard I almost fell to the floor. I asked him what was wrong when he yanked me into the kitchen."

"Did you hear something from in there? Where were you when John pulled you into the kitchen?" Judy questioned.

"We were in the gymnasium. We were checking out the bleachers that were folded up against the wall when we heard a loud slam coming from the kitchen."

"The door to the outside or the door to the ovens?" Judy asked.

"Huh?" Inga asked confused. "Oh, yes, the back door that led to where we entered the school earlier. Chief John heard the door slam shut and he dragged me over to the entrance to the kitchen from the gymnasium. He put his finger to his mouth so I wouldn't say anything."

"Did he go through the door and leave you waiting?" I asked impatiently.

"No, he and I peeked through the door and we saw two men carrying a black plastic garbage bag. They went to the oven and turned it on."

"Who were the two men?" Judy asked. "Was one of the Axel Eklund?"

"No, no," she insisted. "These two were dressed in holey jeans and t-shirts. They spoke with a Swedish accent and laughed as they pulled out…" she stopped and put her hand to her mouth to stop herself from gagging.

"It's okay, Inga," I said, patting her shoulder. "Take your time. We know that there were body parts in the oven. The smell was horrendous and…" I saw Inga's pale face turn green and said, "Sorry, we know what was in there, so go on without talking about that."

Inga took a few deep breaths and said, "The two men waited until the ovens were super-hot, and then took off through the back door. All the while laughing! Can you believe that? They were laughing at what they just did."

"What did John do then, Inga?" Judy asked eagerly.

"He ran over to the oven, looked inside…" she let out a large burp and held her stomach. "Sorry, I can't talk about that part anymore."

"Skip it," Judy said irritably. "What did John do after he saw what was in the ovens?"

"He told me to follow him. We rushed over to the outside doors and your chief opened the back door just a tiny bit. He said that the men were outside walking over to a large black SUV."

"Was it still just the two men?" Judy asked.

"No, he said there were two men standing next to the car waiting for them."

"Did he know who they were?" I asked before Judy could.

"Yes, he said one of them was Mr. Eklund. The other man he didn't know, yet."

"What do you mean, yet?" Judy inquired.

"Let me finish and you'll understand," Inga said, frustrated by our interruptions.

"Fine, we won't say a word until you're done," I said, getting Judy to agree also.

"Okay, once they got inside their truck, John grabbed my arm and we ran around to his police cruiser. We followed the black truck to the resort. John parked away from the truck and we very carefully followed the four men inside the resort." Judy was about to ask a question when Inga raised her hand to stop her.

"The owner of the resort was in the lobby and spotted the chief and me enter. The two of them had a quick conversation then Chief John and I took off to the staircase." Inga took a deep breath in and said, "Before you ask me, the other two men seemed to disappear. It was just two men in business suits who went up to the 5th floor of the resort."

"Where'd they go?" I asked, then said, "Sorry, didn't mean to interrupt."

"That's okay. I have no idea where the two other men disappeared. Maybe they went to another room?" Inga waited for Judy to ask a question, but she stayed silent. "So, we went up all five flights of stairs. Your chief went much faster than me, but he waited for me at the top of the fifth floor. He didn't want to go ahead and have me blow it by calling out for him or barreling into a room." Inga stopped talking for a second to stand up. "I need to move around a little. Being trapped in that rug made it hard to breath and I got really stiff in there, too."

"I bet, Inga. I feel horrible you had to be rolled up in that rug. Hopefully it wasn't for too long?" I asked.

"No, just a short time, and then you showed up. Thank God you did!"

"What happened after you got to the fifth floor?" Judy asked anxiously.

"Your chief found the room he was looking for immediately. Richard told him what room to go to. He held me back while he put his ear up against the door. He had his gun out and told me he was going to knock on the door and pretend to be someone from the hotel staff."

"All they had to do was look through the peephole and they would've seen it was a cop," Judy replied.

"He had me step forward because I looked more like an employee than he did. I didn't have much a choice so I did as he asked. He knocked and then stepped away. I turned my back to the door and said what the chief told me to say."

"What?" I asked eagerly.

"He told me to say it was housekeeping and I had fresh towels for the room."

"And they bought that?" asked Judy, surprised.

"We thought they did, but once the door opened, my arm was immediately grabbed and I was dragged inside the room. Chief John had no choice but to give up his gun once he saw me with a gun planted against my back."

"They held you at gunpoint?" I asked, worried.

"Yes, and it made me very angry, Ruth Ann. You know me, I don't take any crap from anyone and I very much wanted to turn and bash this man in the face."

"Who was holding the gun at your back?" Judy questioned.

"That lawyer, Steven Svenson."

"Steven Svenson?" I asked, shocked. "That's Prunella's lawyer, why would he be here working with Axel?"

"No, Ruth Ann," Inga said walking over to a chocolate colored, leather, wingback chair and leaning against the high back of it. "Ms. Prunella's lawyer that helped her back in Sweden, and sent you the necklace was Steven Svenson."

"That's right! Steven was the corrupt cousin of Michael."

"Exactly," Inga said. "He was here working with Mr. Eklund, but why?"

"Even I can figure that one out," Judy declared.

"Do tell, Judy," I responded brusquely.

"Well, Steven was betrayed by Bertha's brothers, right?" Inga and I nodded. "It's obvious, Eklund knew that and contacted Steven Svenson when he escaped from jail after pretending to be stabbed. Steven wants to get his hands on that gem, too."

"But Axel knows that. Why would he ask Steven Svenson to help retrieve a necklace they *both* want?" I questioned.

"Eklund doesn't care who he uses and then back stabs, literally. I bet this Steven Svenson works the same way. They probably both believe they'll end up with the necklace once they get it away from Prunella."

"Makes sense," Inga commented.

"That's why Prunella was contacted earlier back at her estate," I stated. "Axel or Steven Svenson contacted her and said if she didn't want more people to die that she had to bring the necklace to them. She confided in Sherman only because he could drive her to their meeting place."

"Very good, Ruth Ann," Judy exclaimed.

"I knew she was acting strangely when John asked her to show him the new safe where she kept the necklace."

"She did what?" Judy asked.

"Prunella started acting funny not long before she and Sherman took off to meet Axel and that lawyer." I added, "I wonder if she knew it was the corrupt cousin or did she believe she was meeting Steven?"

Inga said, "So you think Ms. Prunella thought she was speaking with Steven Svenson, and she went off to meet him?"

"Possibly," I answered. "She might not have known Axel was involved."

"She must have hoped that Eklund was really dead and Steven was here to help her," Judy stated.

I looked over at Inga who was still leaning heavily against the chair and said, "The question is…where did they go now?"

"Yeah, Inga," Judy chimed in. "Where did they go?"

"Back to the house," she replied.

"I knew it!" Judy cried out. "Let's get going we're wasting time here." Judy started for the staircase when Inga told her to stop.

"I didn't tell you everything," she said slowly.

Judy and I stopped and turned around toward Inga. "What? Is there something else you left out?"

Inga looked over at Judy then me. "There's someone else they took with them."

I panicked and asked, "Who?"

"I'm sorry to tell you this, Ruth Ann, but it's your daughter."

"MY DAUGHTER!" I screamed and the room went spinning.

"Ruth Ann…are you alright?" Inga hurried to my side and held me up before I fell to the ground in shock.

I got myself together and asked Inga, "Which daughter, Lynne or Nancy?"

"Lynne, the baker."

"Why? How?" I asked Inga, knowing she might not have the answers I was looking for.

"They came into your store to drop your chief and me off," Judy quickly interrupted Inga. "Wait, are you saying John was supposed to be here? Or is he here somewhere?" Judy anxiously glanced around the room.

"Yes! Chief John was supposed to be dumped here, too. That was their plan. Then when we arrived here at your store, Mr. Eklund had Chief John open up your back door."

"He knows where the spare key is hidden out back," I mumbled.

"Yes, you might want to change that hiding place now, Ruth Ann," Inga stated. "When we were inside the showroom on the first floor a loud knock occurred from the front door area."

"Lynne," I said.

"Yes, your daughter was standing at the front door banging on the window next to the door."

"She probably noticed the people and didn't see me. But did she see John?"

"Not at first," Inga replied. "John was being dragged up the stairs with me. I just happened to see when Mr. Eklund demanded Steven Svenson open the door."

"They *let* her in willingly?" Judy inquired confused.

"Yes, they didn't want any witnesses so Svenson unlocked the front door and Lynne stomped in just as stubbornly as you would, Ruth Ann."

"I believe that," I declared. "Then what did they do to her?" I didn't want to hear, but knew I needed to hear every single detail.

"What did she do?" Judy asked, egging Inga to go on with her account.

"Lynne's eyes glowed a deep, chilling, brown and she demanded to know who they were and where her mother was."

"Oh, boy, I've seen her that mad and upset only one other time in her life."

"When's that?" Inga asked curiously.

"After she and her twin, Nancy, were told that their father had died in a plane crash."

"I'm so sorry, Ruth Ann," Inga said sincerely.

"It's her strong constitution that got her through that tragic ordeal, and will with this, too."

"What happened after Lynne demanded to know where her mother was?" Judy asked, trying to get us back on track.

"Mr. Eklund told Svenson to tie her up in a chair and make sure he gagged her. He didn't want anyone to hear her screaming. She was making quite a scene, Ruth Ann," Inga explained. "Then, Mr. Eklund told me to go over to your pile of Oriental rugs. He made Chief John unroll one and I had to lie down."

"John did that?" Judy questioned.

"He didn't have a choice. Mr. Eklund was pointing a gun at the both of us. So he told me to go along with him and he whispered that he would try and make it as loose as possible so I could still breath."

"That's good, at least," I replied.

"But then Mr. Eklund told him to tape my mouth shut."

"We did have to pull that off," I said, sorry for her.

Judy asked, "What happened to John after you got rolled up in the rug?"

"I heard Mr. Eklund and him argue, but I was wrapped in the rug so I didn't hear what they said. Their voices were raised and then I heard a loud thump."

"Thump as in Eklund hit him with something or something fell?" Judy questioned.

"I heard John yelp in pain and I'm pretty sure Chief John fell to the floor, unconscious."

"How did you know all that?" she asked curiously.

"I could only hear muffled voices, and after that thump and loud cry, I knew it came from your chief. Eklund then yelled at him to get up."

"Did he?" I asked, worried about John's condition.

"I don't think so," she answered looking directly in my eyes. "Eklund yelled for the lawyer to come up to help move him."

"Move him where?" Judy asked.

"*Oh my God!*" Inga cried out. "I think he's still here somewhere."

"What?" I asked, looking around the second floor showroom.

"So you heard Eklund yell up for Svenson to help him with John. Lynne was downstairs tied and gagged to a chair. Where were Prunella and Sherman?"

"I think the other two men took Ms. Prunella and Sherman back to Mr. Eklund's estate up the mountain," Inga replied confused. "I don't even know if Lynne was left down there or taken with Ms. Prunella."

"You don't think they would hurt them, do you?" I asked, terrified for their safety.

"Not until Mr. Eklund has that necklace in his hands."

"Judy, enough questions for now. We need to search up here to see if John's still around."

The three of us searched my upstairs showroom. Ben was still missing so I stood by the top of the stairs and called out for him. He slowly came up the stairs and asked me if it was safe. "Yes, Inga's here, and we need to find Chief John. He may be injured up here somewhere and I need your help. Can you help me, Ben?"

"Yes, yes, I will help you find the chief. He's my friend, too."

Judy and Inga went towards the back of the showroom and searched every cabinet, sofa, and other furniture displayed to see if he was lying behind or under the items. Ben and I took off toward the sidewall where I knew there were large armoires on exhibit. I walked up to a dark, walnut armoire dating back to mid-1800 and put my hand on the handle of the large double door. "Here goes, Ben, maybe John's inside this cabinet."

I was petrified and just couldn't bring myself to open the cabinet. I had the fiercest sensation that John was stuffed inside here. I just hoped he was still alive. Ben caught my reticence and put his hand over mine and said, "I'll help you." His words calmed me down and we slowly opened the door.

"Empty," I said, exhaling in relief, but disgusted in myself for believing the worst.

Inga's voice from back of the showroom called out to us. "I found him, hurry!"

Ben, Judy, and I hurried over to where Inga was standing. She was looking behind a black velvet chaise with cherry wood arms and legs. "Look under this piece, Ruth Ann," she said, pointing a shaky hand to the bottom of the chaise.

"Is he alive?" Judy asked quickly.

"I couldn't look," Inga said. "I just saw his legs sticking out the other end and I called you over."

I bent over and sure enough, John was gagged and tied up with ropes from my storage room. His eyes were open wide and staring straight at me. He started to violently shake his head for us to free him.

"We're coming, John," I said as Ben and Judy lifted the chaise off to the side. "Are you hurt?" I asked him as I carefully pulled off the duct tape over his mouth.

"Quickly, Ruth Ann," Judy exclaimed. "It hurts more when you go too slow." Fine, I ripped it off and John yelped, but he was able to take a deep breath in and wait until Ben cut the ropes away from him.

"I thought you were going to leave me here," were his first words. "I could hear everything you were saying over there when you freed Inga."

"I'm sorry, John," Inga started to say. "I almost forgot you were knocked unconscious in here."

"I'm glad you did remember, Inga. Good job," John said, jumping to his feet. "We need to get moving."

"To the mountain home, right?" Judy inquired. "Do you need to get more guns before we go up there? I've only got the one gun."

"Good idea, Judy," he said. "We're going to quickly run over to the station and grab me a gun. Ruth Ann, Inga, and Ben can stay there while you and I head up the mountain."

"NO WAY!" Inga and I shouted together.

"No choice," John ordered. "These guys could care less if they kill you or not."

"John," I said, trying to remain calm, even though I was ready to blow. "They took Lynne, and there's NO WAY I'm not going up there. If I don't go with you and Judy, then I'll get there myself. Do *you* hear me this time?"

"Fine," he said conceding. "But you and Inga will follow my direct orders, got it?" John looked over at Ben and said, "You don't have to go. I'll have someone drop you off back at the resort after we get to the station."

"I want to go," Ben replied. "Mr. Dickson told me to protect Ms. Ruth Ann, and that's what I'm going to do."

John, mumbling to himself, said, "This is a complete circus. All these people trying to get in my way."

"I'm no cop," Ben said. "Just a man who knows it's the right thing to do. I'm not afraid anymore."

"I hope not because we can't afford any more slip-ups, got it?" John said, glaring over at me. I knew he thought I'd mess this up because Lynne was now involved. I felt sure Lynne could take care of herself. Plus, Prunella and Sherman were with her.

Chapter 20

We made it to the station in no time. John turned in my SUV for one of the other police cruisers. Judy and John stocked themselves with new guns and ammunition. Ben tried to get John to give him a gun, but he shot him down immediately. "I've hunted before, I know how to handle a gun," he said to John.

"Not this time, Ben," John replied. "Maybe sometime soon I'll take you shooting and see how you handle a gun. Who knows, Ben, maybe you have a future as a cop?"

"Nah," Ben answered. "I'm too old now."

"Maybe there's something else we could come up with."

"I'm happy working at the resort for Mr. and Mrs. Dickson."

"They love having you work for them, Ben," I interrupted trying to get John off the track of Ben handling a gun. I didn't really think that was in Ben's or any of our best interests.

"Let's head out," John said, with the rest of us trailing behind him. "I'm glad you called in the school incident, Judy," John said, referring to Judy calling Lou and Dave over to the school to handle the body parts in the ovens.

"They got it handled. We can be filled in later about what the coroner thinks."

"I really don't want to talk about that," I said as my stomach ache returned. "If you don't mind."

"No," John said, smiling sympathetically at me. "We should be there in twenty."

The next fifteen minutes or so, John and Judy, talked quietly amongst themselves. Ben, Inga, and I remained quiet in the back. I wasn't sure how I would react if I saw Lynne being mistreated. Would I just stand back and let John do his work? Or would I run in and make a bigger mess of the situation? John must've sensed my uneasiness and said, "Ruth Ann, I know you're upset about Lynne being taken hostage. I promise you I'll get her out of this unharmed. But," he said and hesitated for a second. "But, you have to let me handle it. I really need you to hear me this time. I don't want any mistakes when it comes to your daughter or the others. Understand?"

"Yes, John," I said, resigned. "I'm not qualified and I know that, but if I see any of them lay a hand on her, I only hope I don't just react."

"You won't, not when lives are at risk." John added, "We're almost there. I need you all to hang back in the truck until I know where we need to go. I may park the cruiser away from the house so they don't see us coming."

"But they know we *will* be coming?" Inga asked. "They'll be waiting for us."

"Yes, but they don't know *when* we'll be showing up," Judy answered for John. "We're not leaving you alone long. Just enough time to sneak up to the house and see where we can enter safely."

John made a right onto Lookout Mountain Road. He didn't have much room on the side of the road and it was only about a quarter mile to the estate. "Hang on," he said.

"It's gonna be a little bumpy while I try and put the truck as close to the tree line as possible." John swerved off the gravel drive and we bounced up and down until we were safely under some large trees and imbedded between a couple pines. "Here we are," John said, putting the truck into park.

"How long do we wait?" I asked.

"If we don't come back in an hour, you get this truck out of here and get more help at the station."

"An hour?" Inga protested. "That's too long."

"I'm just giving you a limit. Judy and I plan on being back here in a few minutes." Ben, Inga, and I agreed, and Judy and John exited the truck. He tapped on the back seat window and said, "Ruth Ann, I think you should sit in the driver's seat. If you hear any loud noises such as gunfire, leave immediately."

"Not without my daughter, John," I replied. "I will not leave without her."

John didn't respond, but took off with Judy, following the tree line closely. They wanted to sneak up to the estate without being noticed. But who knows how many men Axel had guarding his place. I just hoped Prunella and Lynne were giving them hell!

It didn't take long before they were out of our sight. Sunset was occurring and it was getting darker outside. "I don't like just sitting here," Inga said. "I wish we could've stuck together."

"Me, too," I said, shivering a little. "But I see their point. It's only the two of them and they're trained for this. If you, Ben, and I were with them, one of us could easily slip up and it could make things worse for Prunella, Lynne, and Sherman."

For the next several minutes we sat in silence. I was listening for any noise coming from outside the truck. I turned the key enough so the windows could be rolled down even though the temperatures were diving. I didn't want to be surprised by anyone. "I can't take this much more," Inga said anxiously. "How long's it been, Ruth Ann?"

I looked at the display on the dashboard and it was 4:30 p.m. "It's been twenty minutes since they left."

"I sure don't plan on leaving if they don't come back, do you?" Inga questioned.

"No way," I replied. "The three of us can do the same thing as John and Judy did. We can sneak around the tree line and take a peek. Maybe they're just being cautious, but if they got caught, then they'll need us to help them."

Ben finally spoke up. He cleared his throat a little then asked, "Didn't the chief tell us to leave and not go rushing in to save them?"

"He knows me," I said to Ben. "The chief knows I would never leave without my daughter, Prunella, and Sherman."

"Oh, I just don't know what we can do without any weapons."

"We don't need weapons, Ben," Inga said.

"Ben," I started to say. "If you're more comfortable staying here in the truck, that's okay, too. I don't want you to do anything that you feel is wrong."

"I'm okay. I just wanted to make sure you weren't scared. I'm here to protect you"

"Thanks, Ben, I really appreciate you being here and helping us."

Inga smiled at Ben and he lowered his head. I believe he was actually embarrassed. I don't think he's received too many compliments in his past.

We waited until John and Judy were gone thirty minutes before making our final decision to go in after them. "I think we'll be okay if we stay hidden until we get up to the house," I said.

"Unless they have surveillance cameras we didn't know about around the estate. Then they'll detect us before we get anywhere near them," Ben added.

Inga eyed me curiously. I turned to Ben and asked him, "How do you know about surveillance cameras?"

Ben fidgeted in the back seat for a second then answered, "I've worked people's homes before who have had them installed."

"Doing what?" Inga asked quickly.

"Odd jobs," he seemed nervous and started stuttering his words. "Ah…I told the…chief all this before. I did this and that for people to make enough cash to get my food and shelter."

"That's right, Ben, you did tell John and Richard that," I said cheerily. I didn't want him to fall apart now when we needed him to remain strong and ready to help us if needed.

"Oh," Inga said, not as jolly as I was. I could tell by Inga's expression that she was skeptical about Ben's past. Was he truly as innocent as he claimed to be?

"Let's get going," I said, opening up the driver's side door. "Be careful and head over to the farthest part of the ground where the bushes or trees meet the grass. We'll go in and out until we get near Prunella's house."

"If Mr. Eklund's still alive, it's his house isn't it, Ruth Ann?" Inga questioned.

"I don't know the legalities, but as far as I'm concerned it's Prunella's."

The three of us made our way out of the truck and into thick clumps of bushes. It was freezing outside. The temperature had dropped significantly, and I wouldn't be surprised if we saw some snowflakes beginning to fall. "I'm not going to be able to stay out here for long," I said, looking at the lightweight coat I had on.

"You'll be fine," Inga said, wearing nothing more than the cardigan she had on over her housekeeping uniform. She was a much larger woman than me and was used to the cold climate back in Stockholm. I know I live in Colorado, but I never seem to adjust to cold weather that well. And poor Ben only had on a flannel shirt and jeans. I could tell he was already shivering a bit, and it made me wonder, like Inga, if he was telling everyone the truth about his past.

"If you hear any sounds, don't panic. We need to stay calm, and as hidden as we can. Once we get within eyesight of the house, we'll decide on our next move."

Chapter 21

John Wilkinson's narrative

Judy and I took off from the police cruiser and left Ruth Ann with Inga and Ben. I didn't want to leave her behind, but Judy and I needed to investigate the house and see who was actually in there. If anyone believed that I would trust Ruth Ann, they would be sorely mistaken. Ruth Ann's word when it comes to investigating is worse than any criminal I've seen before. Not that she's totally untrustworthy, just that if I give her a direct order, she will, nine times out of ten, disobey me. However, she will be the first one to assert that she was usually right in disobeying me. I would never tell her she was right or what would be the point in trying to contain her crazy behavior?

"John," Judy whispered over to me. "Are you okay?"

I shook my head to get back in the game and replied, "Yeah, why?"

"You seem to be deep in thought, that's all."

"I'm just going over our next move," I admitted, lying. Judy was the last person I would talk to about Ruth Ann. For some unknown reason they didn't like each other very much. I'm aware that I may be to blame for that. Judy and I knew each other from years back because I was a friend of her parents. She was too young for me to be personally involved, but Ruth Ann didn't think so. She was jealous, not that she ever used those words to my face, but her actions towards Judy made it pretty obvious. Judy, on the other hand, has flirted a little with me. I paid zero attention to her moves, and in time, she ceased trying. She was resolved to that fact that Ruth Ann and I were together and she couldn't stop it.

"John!" Judy called out a little louder. "What's going on with you?"

"Nothing, chill out, Judy," I said, a little perturbed. "We're almost in sight of the house. Keep your voice down."

"Fine," she snapped.

"Do you see any sign of surveillance cameras or any of Eklund's men looming around?"

"Not so far," she answered.

"Good," I said. "I think we should head around to the back of the house. We've been there before and know where Eklund used to have cameras. Maybe he hasn't had the time to change them."

"We don't even know if they're here, John," Judy stated.

"They're here," I said.

"How do you know that?"

"That's how," I said, pointing to the black sedan that Sherman and Prunella took off in earlier that day.

"It's parked right out front, John," Judy declared, stunned.

"Obviously, they didn't want to be hidden from us. They knew we'd be after them eventually. Once you and Ruth Ann found Inga and me in Ruth Ann's store, we'd be up here right away."

"That's what worries me," Judy said, grabbing her gun a little closer to her body.

"I agree. They must be waiting for us, and I'm hoping they're looking for *all* of us and not just you and me."

"Oh, they think that Ruth Ann, Inga, Ben, you and I would come raging up to the front of the house with sirens blaring?"

"Exactly. Now with just you and me, we can sneak in there a little quieter."

"We'll soon find out," Judy said.

We were as close to the house as was comfortable without being spotted. There were no men roaming the grounds from what we could see. "Let's head over to the side of the house. Just stay low in case the curtains from Eklund's office are open and they see us running around the place."

"Got it," she replied as we took off as low as we could around the side of the house. I was happy to see the large set of curtains that were on the side of Eklund's office were drawn close. "That helps," Judy said.

We made it around to the back where the kitchen entrance was located. "We've used this door several times. I'm just not sure who'll be in there if we enter."

"I'm going to peek over the window ledge. Give me a second," Judy said, crawling on the ground to a bay window where the kitchen table was placed. She put her hands on the ledge and ever so carefully peered over. "I don't see anybody from this view. It looks fairly bright in there."

"Maybe someone's in there working in the kitchen," I said, making my way to the back door. "I'm going in."

Judy hurried back to my side, and with our guns out and aimed, I carefully grabbed the door handle and gave it a slight turn. "It's unlocked."

"Be careful, John," Judy whispered. "I've got your back."

I pushed the door open slowly, and once it was opened enough for me to look in I said, "I don't think anyone's in there at the moment. Let's get in there while we can."

I went inside with Judy on my heels. The second I entered the kitchen an arm from behind the door grabbed me and a hand was shoved over my mouth. Judy was about to get in on the altercation when the body appeared. "Don't shout," a voice called out quietly. "It's me, Sherman."

Judy backed off and Sherman let go of my mouth. "Sherman?" I exclaimed, furious at what he just did. "What are you doing here by yourself?"

"Where's Eklund?" Judy asked.

"And Prunella, don't forget about her?" I asked him.

"Hold on," Sherman started to say nervously. "I need you two to hide before one of them comes back in here."

"Who?" Judy asked.

"One of Mr. Eklund's men," Sherman replied. "Mr. Eklund hired two crooked cops from Sweden and they keep coming in here to check on me. So, let me put you in the pantry and keep the door closed. They won't go in there if they see me working in the kitchen."

"Fine, let's get in there. You need to fill us in on everything that's going on, quickly," I said, following Sherman to a door that opened into a large walk-in pantry.

"In…quick," he said, giving Judy a little shove.

"I'm in, I'm in," she said, checking out the pantry. "This room's huge."

"Yes, it's a large estate, we always have a full supply of food and other supplies on hand. Anyone can stay here for months on the food in there."

"Sherman, where's Prunella and Ruth Ann's daughter, Lynne?" I asked.

"I don't know," he answered with strained nerves. "When we got here she was being so resistant, Mr. Eklund had to restrain her by putting tape over her mouth. I didn't see her daughter at all. I overheard Mr. Eklund say he dropped Lynne off back at her bakery. He didn't want to involve her. Something about a promise to Ruth Ann that he would never involve her kids, but I don't know if that's what they did or not."

"Hopefully, that's what they did and Lynne's safe and sound back in town. He didn't put Prunella in the basement, did he?" I asked.

"No, I don't know where she is or Mr. Eklund."

"Sherman, you're confusing us, tell us from the beginning what happened!" I demanded. "If you hear anyone coming, just shut the door and pretend you're going about your normal routine. We'll understand if you shut the door abruptly."

Sherman grabbed a package of dry pasta in case he had to have an alibi in his hand if they showed up. "Okay, the last we saw any of you we were at the resort. Ms. Prunella and I were up in that room you discovered with Inga. But they took us down the outside staircase once you showed up at the door."

"Who took you away from there?" I asked.

"The two goons he hired to be his brute force," Sherman replied curtly. "They hurried us back to the sedan and shoved us into the back seat. They held a gun to each of us and told us not to move."

"Didn't anyone see you in the parking lot?" Judy asked.

"No, I don't think so."

"Go on, Sherman," I insisted, knowing we were short on time.

"We waited for several minutes before Mr. Eklund showed up with that awful lawyer, Steven Svenson."

"How did Svenson get involved with Eklund?" I asked.

"I'll get to that. It's a long story and I'm not sure when they'll be back."

"Fine."

"They drove us back here and pulled up to the front of the house. Ms. Prunella and Ms. Lynne's mouths were still taped shut. I tried to get Ms. Prunella to cooperate until you all got here, but she was a wild woman. She wouldn't calm herself down, which is so unlike her."

"She's been through alot, Sherman," Judy explained.

"But she should know better when it comes to dealing with Mr. Eklund. She did it for months and months."

"Maybe she just snapped," I tried to suggest.

"Whatever, we were brought inside the house and Eklund had me wait in the foyer while the two men took the women into the library. Once the doors of the library closed Mr. Eklund told me to get into the kitchen and resume my normal activities. If I didn't want anything to happen to Ms. Prunella or Ms. Lynne, I wouldn't try any funny stuff."

"So that's it?" Judy asked, frustrated. "You just started up your butler duties?"

"What choice did I have?" he eyed me desperately. "I couldn't let anything happen to them. Do what they want with me, I'm old and worthless."

"You're not worthless, Sherman," I told him. "I get why you did as you were told. You knew we would come eventually."

"Yes, yes," he said with renewing energy. "I knew you and Detective Judy would show up. But," he said looking around as if he was going to get surprised by others. "Where are Ruth Ann and Inga?"

"They're hopefully still back in my police truck waiting for us to come back to them," I said doubting my own words.

"Okay, okay," Judy, said. "What happened after you went about your *duties* and the two women were dragged into the library?"

"I tried to come up with excuses to leave the kitchen and head into the foyer near the library, but the doors were guarded by those two goons. Every time I pretended to be busy around there they shooed me away."

"Then what?" I asked.

"That's the strange thing," he said, confused. "The last time I tried to sneak over to the library doors, there was nobody guarding it."

"Where'd they go?" Judy asked impatiently.

"I don't know. I put my ear to the door and I couldn't hear Mr. Eklund, Ms. Prunella or Ms. Lynne. I hoped they took Ruth Ann's daughter and left."

"Did you go into the library?" I asked.

"Yes, I knocked, then waited for an answer. When nobody called out, I grabbed the handle and turned it. It wasn't locked or anything. I just didn't want someone to shoot me for going in."

"Was Eklund in there with them?" I inquired.

"No, it was empty!"

"What?" Judy cried out loudly.

"Shhh," Sherman snapped. "Keep it down or we'll get caught."

"Ya, ya, I got it. So go on, where'd they disappear to?" she grilled.

"I ran back out into the foyer and over to the front door. I opened the door and Mr. Eklund's two men came running out from the dining room and grabbed my arms. I protested, telling them I was just having a look out front. I wasn't going anywhere."

"They didn't believe you, did they?" I asked.

"No, they dragged me back into the kitchen and told me not to leave this room until I get permission. They haven't given me permission yet."

"So you didn't see anything when you looked out front?" I asked.

"Ah, yes, I noticed the sedan was still parked out front. I figured Ms. Prunella's still somewhere around here."

"But where?" I inquired.

"John," Judy interrupted. "We need to look around this place for her. What if they brought her down to that torture room in the basement?"

"No, no they didn't," Sherman, bellowed. "They would've had to come through here to get into the basement. They haven't."

"That's good," I said.

"So, maybe they brought her to her bedroom on the second floor?" Judy asked.

"Maybe, we'll go have a look around." I looked at Sherman, nervous as can be, and told him, "We'll be fine. You stay here and do as they say. We'll be back soon."

We left Sherman, holding the dry pasta, watching as Judy and I snuck through the butler's pantry and up the back staircase. As I walked up to the second floor I couldn't help but wonder if Ruth Ann was still in my truck anymore.

Chapter 22

Ruth Ann's Narrative

We were standing in the bushes near the estate. I couldn't see any sign of life except for the empty sedan parked out front. At least I knew Prunella, Lynne and Sherman were here, too.

"Let's take a peek in the car?" Inga asked. "Maybe someone's in there lying down tied up."

"That's too risky, Inga," I answered. "We'd be standing right out front for anyone to see us. We don't know who's in there or not."

"Then where are we going? We can't stand here the whole time."

"I think we should go around to the back and see if we can sneak into the kitchen," I suggested.

"What if we get caught, too?" Inga asked. "Chief John will be furious with you for not waiting in the truck."

"He knew I wouldn't stay put long, Inga."

"I think we should go and see if the chief and Judy are safe," Ben said out of the blue. "We'll be fine if we stick together."

"Yes, Ben, you're right. Let's go," I replied, heading toward the right side of the estate and peeking around the side of the building. "We need to make sure the library's clear. The windows on the side of the house are huge and we'd be a target walking by them."

"Hopefully they'll be closed so nobody could look in," Inga said.

"Stay low, just in case," I suggested. We slowly went along the landscaping on the side of the house and noticed the curtains were drawn shut. "It's pretty dark out so they probably shut them anyway."

"*Who* shut them is the question?" I asked.

"Are you implying Sherman's in there and did it?" asked Inga, surprised.

"I have no idea, Inga," I answered. "I'm hoping Sherman is in there in his role as butler. Then he could help us."

"Or Sherman, Ms. Prunella, and your daughter are held prisoner down in the basement."

"Let's hope not," I stated terrified. "C'mon, let's get back to the kitchen door. I'll peek in there and see if anyone's in the kitchen."

"No, let me," Inga ordered and pushed me aside. "I've worked in that kitchen and know where to look." I agreed and let Inga glance into the back door side windows."

"Well?" Ben inquired anxiously. "Is anyone in there?"

"No, I don't think so. Let's get in, quick."

Inga opened the unlocked door and stepped inside. Ben and I followed her in and we took an immediate look around. "I think it's all clear," she said.

"No, it's not," a voice called out from the pantry.

"Sherman!" I exclaimed. "What are you doing in here?"

"Me? What are you three doing in here?"

"We waited for John and Judy to return to his truck, but they never did. We got worried and came in here to find out what's going on."

"He was right," Sherman muttered.

"Right about what?" I asked curiously.

"That you couldn't wait for them to return."

"They've been gone a long time, and we *all* got concerned." I looked over at Ben and Inga and their blank faces. Thanks for backing me up. "Right?" I said to them.

"Uh, yeah, sure," Ben said, lowering his head toward the kitchen floor.

"Ben, this is Sherman, he's worked for my cousin, Prunella, for a long time and will do anything to protect her."

"Ben is...who?" Sherman asked, wondering who this stranger was.

"Ben works over at the resort," I said. "He's completely trustworthy and will help us find Lynne, Prunella and..." I looked around the kitchen and asked, "Where's John and Judy?"

"Right before you walked in here they took off up the back stairs to look in Ms. Prunella's bedroom."

"Is that where the girls are?" I asked, shocked that she would go back there.

"I have no idea," Sherman replied.

"You were with her, Sherman," Inga exclaimed. "Shhh," Sherman asserted. "You don't know what happened."

"Then tell us, quickly," I demanded. Sherman insisted we enter into the pantry in case one of Axel's men came to check on Sherman in the kitchen. We learned about what happened up until we arrived. I was completely relieved when Sherman told me he heard Lynne was dropped off back at her bakery. That was one person safely back in town. (At least that's what I thought!)

"Wow, so you have no idea what happened to Prunella after you went into the library and found her missing?"

"Yes, it was empty. I figured Mr. Eklund took her back up to her bedroom and one of his men's guarding the room. That's where John and Judy took off to."

"Let's go," I said, trying to get past Sherman to leave the pantry.

"NO," Sherman cried out barring me from leaving the pantry.

"We need to see where they went, Sherman. What's the problem?"

"You'll get caught, Ruth Ann. If Ms. Prunella's up there, and that's a big if, then there'll be a guard watching over her. We need to let your chief do his job. He knows to come back down here to the kitchen if Ms. Prunella's not there."

"And if she's in there, and John and Judy get hurt, then what do we do?" I asked.

"You think *you* can get by a guard and not the Chief of Police?" Sherman questioned.

I thought about it for a moment and backed off leaving the pantry. "What are we supposed to do in here?"

"We wait," Ben said, siding with Sherman. "Wait for Chief John and Judy to come back for us."

"I'm not very good at waiting," I muttered.

All together they said, "We know."

Chapter 23

John Wilkinson's Narrative

We hurried up the back stairs and didn't encounter any of Eklund's men or Eklund himself. I wondered where that lawyer, Svenson, went also. Judy and I made it to the second floor landing and quietly looked around the hall to see if we could spot a guard outside any of the bedrooms up there.

"Coast is clear," I said to Judy. "If she's up here I would think her room would be guarded."

"Strange, that's for sure," Judy whispered. "Should we try all the doors?"

"You listen at each of the doors on this side," I said, pointing to the rooms on the right. "And I'll listen on the other side." Judy and I stayed parallel to each other as we made our way down the wide, dark hall. The minimal lighting came from the sconces next to each of the bedroom doors. "It's dead silent up here."

"She might not be on this floor," Judy stated. "There's a third floor. Looks like we should check up there, too."

"Let's go," I said, walking back to the staircase and making sure there wasn't anybody lurking around the stairs. "Hurry, let's get up to the next floor."

We rushed up the stairs since we could now be seen from the grand foyer. Once we landed on the third floor we decided to check each of the doors again since we didn't see any sign of men guarding a particular door. "I don't get it," Judy said, not having any luck finding Prunella. "If she's not up here, where did they take her?"

"The basement," I stated. "But Sherman said that was impossible since he would've seen them come through the kitchen to get to the basement door."

"What if Sherman wasn't in the kitchen when they took her that way?"

"He insists he was always in there until he went to the library to check on them. That's when he discovered the room empty."

"Maybe they snuck her out when he was in the library and put her down in the basement."

"It won't hurt to look just in case," I said, heading back down the main staircase with Judy. "I can't believe there's been no sign of any guards, Eklund or that lawyer. We're walking down the main staircase and nobody's around!"

Judy shook her shoulders and continued down the stairs. "John," Judy called out to him once they were on the second floor landing about to head down the back staircase into the butler's pantry. "There's always the slight chance that Eklund took Prunella off the property."

"I don't see how, and that would raise a terrifying point."

"What are you talking about, John?" "Ruth Ann, Inga, and Ben are still in my truck. If Eklund drove out of the property, he would've driven right by them. That could be disastrous if they were spotted."

"We better hurry and get back into the kitchen and see what Sherman's been up to first. Then we'll check out the basement quickly."

Judy and I went into the butler's pantry. There were two choices once in there. One door led into the dining room. We slowly opened up the swinging door. There was no sign of anyone recently having been in there. The other door went back into the kitchen. We headed in there next.

"Sherman," I called out startling him. He was standing next to the pantry still holding the dry pasta. The box flew out of his hands and strings of dry spaghetti went sailing into the air.

"What the..." Sherman exclaimed, slamming the pantry door shut. "Why did you do that?" he asked, furious.

Judy replied, "All we did was call out your name, *Sherman*."

"You scared me half to death."

I rushed over to him and eyed him suspiciously. "Why'd you slam that door?"

"What...oh, the pantry door?" Sherman asked frantically. "You startled me, that's all. My first reaction was to slam the door."

"And throw the pasta up in the air," Judy added.

"I didn't mean to do that," he snapped at her.

"Enough," I demanded. "What's been going on since we left?"

"Uh..." Sherman couldn't speak.

"Has Eklund or *anyone* been in here recently?"

"Uh..."

"John," Judy said to me, but eyeing Sherman suspiciously. "What's wrong with him?"

"I don't know. Something's got him riled up. It couldn't be us surprising him when we came in here."

Sherman regained his composure and asked, "Did you find anything out when you went upstairs?"

"No, both floors were empty," Judy answered.

"We're going to double check the basement," I said, and rose my hand to stop Sherman's adamant response. "I know you said they couldn't have gone by you. Just give me this one, I'm going down there anyway and the longer you keep us here the longer it'll take us to check it out."

"Fine, go ahead," Sherman, replied coolly. "You won't find anyone down there, though."

I ignored Sherman's remarks and Judy and I took off down into the basement.

Chapter 24

Ruth Ann's Narrative

"John and Judy are in the kitchen," I said, worried he'd catch us. "Let's see if we can hear them."

"Well, that explains why Sherman slammed the door on us," Inga spat out.

"*Shhh*," I said quietly to Inga. "They'll hear us."

"Excuse me," Ben whispered. "Why don't we just open the door and let them know we're here and safe?"

"Not just yet, Ben," I said. "The chief might not be happy with us for disobeying him when we left the truck."

"Then why'd we do it?" he asked, worried. "I don't want the chief to be mad at me!"

"Oh, Ben, he won't be upset with you. It's *me* he'll be furious with."

"Then tell him you're in here and get it over with," Inga added. "What's the big deal? It's safer for us to stick together anyway."

"Could we stop talking and listen to what they're saying to Sherman?" Ben and Inga snapped their mouths shut, and the three of us leaned against the closed door, and tried to listen.

"The basement?" I questioned out loud after hearing where they were disappearing.

"Sherman didn't give us away," Inga said, surprised. "I wonder why?"

"He'll wait to see why we didn't come out of the pantry first," I replied. "He'll be mad that we didn't."

"Because he knows, as I do, that we should've come clean with John and Judy," Inga said.

We waited until it was quiet. I scratched on the door from the inside hoping to get Sherman's attention. I wanted him to open the door once John and Judy left the kitchen, if they left the kitchen. We waited patiently as the muffled voices faded and Sherman opened the pantry door. "About time," Inga snapped.

Sherman glared at Inga inside the pantry and said, "Try saying thank you instead, Inga."

"Thank you for what?"

"Not blowing your cover. I presume that's why the three of you didn't come out of the pantry while they were here." Sherman's anger grew deeper; "I almost had a heart attack when they walked in here. The spaghetti I was holding went flying in the air."

"That was kind of funny," Ben interjected.

"For someone I don't know at all, I don't think you should be saying my actions were *kind of* funny!"

"Easy, Sherman," I said, watching Ben carefully, hoping he wouldn't get troubled again. "Ben was just trying to lighten up the situation, Sherman. He meant no harm." Ben nodded frantically.

"It's not a situation we should be taking light heartedly, Ruth Ann," Sherman stated. "People have been murdered, horribly, murdered."

"You're right, Sherman," I said regretfully. "Bert, Helena, and that poor person who was put in the school ovens. That's horrific!"

"So, let me ask you again," Sherman started to say. "Why didn't you let John and Judy know you were in the pantry?"

"I wanted to hear what they knew so far," I admitted. "I couldn't make out too much of what they said to you. But, I did hear that they were going into the basement?"

"Yes, but they'll be back any minute, Ruth Ann," Sherman declared. "She's not down there."

"We can also assume that they didn't find Prunella upstairs either?" I inquired.

"No," Sherman answered. "If she's not down in the basement or anywhere else in this house...where'd she disappear to?"

Our little group stood just outside the pantry when I had to make a quick decision. Should I announce to John that we were inside the house? I didn't know what to do when we heard footsteps coming up from the basement. "Hurry," I said. "Back into the pantry."

"But, why?" Sherman begged. "This isn't helping any of us if we're lying to one another."

"Just shut the door, Sherman," I ordered from inside the pantry. "I'll figure out our next move after we hear what they say. Why don't you leave the door opened an inch so we can hear better?"

"But..." Sherman spat out.

"They won't catch us," I said, not so sure of my own actions.

Chapter 25

John Wilkinson's Narrative

"It's dark on these stairs, John," Judy mentioned pulling out her cell phone. "I'm turning the flashlight on my phone."

"No, wait until we make sure it's clear at the bottom," I demanded.

The stairs were hard to see in the dark so we had to carefully make our way to the bottom in complete darkness. "I don't think anyone's down here, Judy."

"Pull the light string and I'll be ready, just in case," Judy whispered close to my face.

"You'll have to either turn on your flashlight or give me a second to find the string." She didn't turn on her light so I raised my arms in the air and deliberately waved them around searching for the string that would turn on the light bulb hanging from the rafters. "Got it, Judy," I said slowly pulling the string and waiting for the light to go on. "Be ready." The low wattage bulb shone dimly in the empty cement room.

"Somebody must've replaced the bulb, because the last time I was down here it didn't work. However, it looks like nobody's down here now, Judy," I said walking around the room. "We need to find that button on the wall that'll open up into the secret room." Judy ran her fingers along the flat cement wall and struck out.

"You're not in the right area," I said, helping her out. I went about three feet to the left and ran my hand along the rougher part of the wall where there were bumps in the cement anyway. "Here it is," I said, rubbing a bigger bump on the wall. "Stay back." We watched as the heavy cement piece opened up into the ceiling. "There's still police tape down here from Helena," I said. "I don't want to disturb the scene down here so be careful."

"We don't have to bother going in because nobody's been down here since earlier today." Nothing was amiss from the last time I was down here. "Let's get back up and figure out what we need to do next."

Judy and I rushed back up the stairs and found Sherman, once again, standing against the pantry door. "What's with that pantry, Sherman?" I asked.

"Well," Sherman started to say, but was interrupted with a thumping sound from inside the pantry.

"Who's in there Sherman?" Judy demanded from Sherman.

Chapter 26

Ruth Ann's Narrative

I knew it was time to get out of the pantry and confront John and Judy. "I tried to open the door when I heard them talking to Sherman, but when I opened the door I was blocked from exiting by Ben. "What are you doing, Ben?" I whispered angrily. "I need to let John know we're in here." "We need to make sure it's safe out there first, Ruth Ann," Ben said. "What if that bad man's also in the kitchen?"

"He's not, we'd have heard him," I said, trying to move Ben aside. "It doesn't matter anymore because the noise we just made will let them know someone's in this pantry. So, let me open the door, now."

Ben stepped aside and I put my hand back on the doorknob to open it up. Sherman was standing with his back to me on the other side of the door as it opened. He turned to face me and I could see his skin turn a pale shade of white. "Sherman," I called out, "Are you okay?"

"No, Ruth Ann, I'm not," he snapped. "I didn't want to be a part of any of this." Sherman took a deep breath, bent over and started picking up the dropped spaghetti from the floor. "You all figure out what we need to do and stop backstabbing each other. We should be working together on this. We have to find Ms. Prunella!"

John stayed silent for the first couple seconds, and when I looked up at him his face took on that familiar reddish hue that was growing deeper in color. "John," I said cautiously. "Before you blow you temper; please remember we have to be quiet. We don't want any of Axel's men coming in here and finding us."

He rolled his head to loosen the muscles in his neck, took a deep breath and glared into my light brown eyes. "Ruth Ann," he said through gritted teeth. "I thought I made it perfectly clear that you, Inga, and Ben were to remain in my vehicle until we returned."

"Yes…but," I was stopped immediately.

"No buts, Ruth Ann!" John said, trying to calm himself down. "You have to stop running into situations you aren't able to control. If any of Eklund's men would've seen you three tramping through the woods up to this house they would've shot first, asked second. Do you understand that?"

"Yes, but," John interrupted me again.

"No buts, Ruth Ann," he repeated himself. "This is an official police investigation. You will follow my orders or I *will* lock you and anyone else who disobey my direct instructions up. Do you *all* understand what I'm telling you? I'm not asking, I'm telling…" John stare left my eyes burning and landed on Inga and poor Ben. I thought Ben was going to turn and high tail it out the back door, but before he could, Sherman grabbed his arm and reeled him back next to him.

"Ben," John said, noticing Ben's urge to escape, said, "I'm *not* blaming you."

Once again my mouth said, "But…" John still wouldn't let me speak. "Ben, do you understand what I'm telling you?"

He stood straight up and replied, "Yes, Chief, even I can tell your anger's directed at Ruth Ann. But, sir, if you'll let me say one thing?" John nodded. "We *all* agreed to leave your police truck and follow you and Judy into the house. You had been gone a while and we were worried for your safety."

"With all due respect, Ben," John spoke slowly and clearly. "Judy and I are trained for these and many other situations. You, Inga, and even Ruth Ann, aren't."

Ben's face turned toward the floor and he mumbled, "Yes, Sir, you're right. We should've stayed in the police vehicle."

"Thank you, Ben." John grinned in my direction, but I chose to ignore it. "Now, can we get to the matter at hand? Any moment, one of Eklund's men or Eklund himself, may enter the kitchen. We need to get to a safe place and discuss what our next move will be. Any suggestions, Inga or Sherman?"

The two of them looked surprised that John asked for their advice. "Hey, I've lived here, too," I exclaimed.

"Us?" Inga still asked.

"Yes, you and Sherman know this place up and down. Tell me where we can *all* go to talk safely?"

Sherman blurted out unexpectedly, "The guest house."

"Excuse me?" I asked, stunned. "What guest house?"

"Yeah, Sherman, what guest house? And why haven't we heard about this place before now?" John asked exasperated.

"It's rarely used," Sherman replied.

"How did you know about this place?" I asked curiously. "You haven't been here that long."

"Bert told me about it."

"Bert? He despised you," Inga snapped. "Why would someone who wanted you gone tell you about a hidden guest house?"

"It slipped one day when Bert ordered Helena to go out back and clean the guest house. I asked him what he was talking about, but he just ignored me."

"Did you get him to tell you more?" I asked quickly.

"Yes, eventually he did. He said he wanted the guesthouse cleaned. It had been a while since anyone had been down there to clean it."

"Are you serious?" John asked. "That's a HUGE detail to have left out, Sherman. I bet Eklund contacted Bert and had him fix up the guesthouse for them to hide out in. Did Bert say anyone else knew about this place?"

"Helena, and Bertha, when she worked here, and now me."

"Why on earth didn't you tell anyone about this? It has to be where Helena and Bert went to meet Eklund. It all fits now."

"To be perfectly honest, I forgot about the place until right now. I'm not twenty-five anymore, my memory isn't the sharpest."

"Sherman," I started to say as calmly as I could. "I'm not young either, but this is a huge sign." I turned to John and said, "Shouldn't we hurry up and check the place out?"

"Since we're sitting ducks in this kitchen right now I suggest we get out fast. Those men will be coming back soon and I don't want them to know we're here."

"Unless they already do, John," Judy stated.

"Why would you say that?" I asked her.

"Our police truck's parked down the road."

"Oh, yeah, that might be a problem unless they haven't gone that direction yet." John grabbed Sherman by the arm and turned him to face him. "Sherman, is there another road out of here or just the one my truck is parked on from the main road?"

"That's the only one I know of. Look, I haven't even seen this guesthouse. I forgot all about it. Maybe we should get down there right away."

John would've made us wait it out here in the kitchen, but he didn't feel it was safe to leave us alone. He suggested Sherman stay behind because that's what Eklund and his men already thought. Sherman argued and wanted to go with us, but John promised him we'd come back for him and assured him he wasn't in danger if he played nice with the men.

Sherman reluctantly agreed so we headed out the back kitchen door down a gravel path that led first, to the large garage. "Sherman told us to follow the gravel path to the driveway and then at the edge of the drive the path will continue into the woods." We followed the path around the side of the garage and arrived at the front of the garage with several large closed doors. How many cars does he have?" John asked, bewildered. "There are five garage doors!"

"No wonder we didn't see another path," Inga said. "The building is massive and we can't see the front of it from the house. You have to walk all the way around the brick structure to get to the front of it."

"Look," I called out. "I can see where the path picks up again."

"Should we take a look inside the garage first?" Judy inquired. "There's definitely a second floor in there, too." We looked up and noticed the windows on the second floor.

"Maybe there's an office or guest quarters up in the garage," I replied.

"Okay, let's take a look before we go on down the path. It should be safe in here," John stated, leading the way to a door off the side of the large garage doors. "Judy, you stay at the back of our group, and I'll go in first. If Judy or I yell for you to run or take cover, do as we say."

We entered a large, spotless garage with three of the spaces filled with cars. There was a small, red, sports car in one space, then a large, silver truck in another. The black sedan must've come from one of the empty spaces. The other filled space had a gold, luxury car with an impressive hood ornament. It appeared to be…no, it couldn't be…it was a small gold Viking ship!

"Do you see that?" I cried out to the group. "That hood ornament on the gold car is of a miniature Viking ship."

John walked over to the car and touched the hood ornament. "What this guy won't do to make himself stand out."

Inga said, "He had just as many cars back in Sweden, too."

Ben added, "This man must be very rich."

"And very evil," I told him. "He's a dangerous man that would do anything to get what he wants."

"Even murder?" Ben asked.

"Yes, Ben, even murder," John answered for me.

"What gets me is that these cars are spotless. Someone must come in here and clean them regularly or they would be dusty, but who?" Judy asked curiously.

"Had to be Bert," Inga said. "Sherman never came down here and Bert was Eklund's right hand man. He defended him up till he was murdered at the Halloween party."

"Nobody's been in here recently so let me run upstairs and see what's up there," John said, turning and taking off to a wooden staircase that was off a sidewall.

I followed him without asking permission. The rest of the group stayed behind checking out each of the cars. John was halfway up the stairs when he noticed me following him. "Go back, Ruth Ann," he ordered.

"Nope," I'm coming. "I doubt we're going to find anything up here. I think the guesthouse is where we might run into something that'll help us find Prunella."

"Fine, just stay behind me."

We landed upon a large opening that overlooked the garage below. "This place is huge," John muttered. "It's just a big loft that overlooks below. We can rule out anyone being up here. It's just storage from what I can see."

"Yeah, let's head back down and find that guesthouse."

We walked down the driveway and picked up the gravel path that led away from the garage and the house. "I wonder how far down this place is?" John asked curiously walking on the path as it narrowed. "Stay together."

We walked from a small, open grass area into the woods. "It's dark in here," I said. "Do you have a flashlight?"

"I do," Inga replied, whipping one out from her coat pocket. "I grabbed it from the garage. "I figured it was getting dark out now and we could use it."

"Perfect," John said, reaching his hand out and taking the flashlight from her. "I'll lead, and be careful of anyone following us."

Judy stayed at the back of the group while I followed John, then Inga and Ben in the middle. We must've walked ten minutes when John suddenly held his arm out to stop me. "Shhh," he whispered. "I think there's a clearing ahead. It's so dark in here I can't tell for sure. I'm going to turn my light off in a second so tell the rest of them behind you."

I passed the information to the others and we kept close together as we carefully took each step. The path was descending so we must be going down the mountain a little. I could barely make out John's back in front of me when he stopped. "Look ahead, I can see some light coming through the trees."

We stopped and squinted our eyes to focus. "I do see a dim light ahead," I said. "It's got to be the house!"

"If there's a light on we could be confronting some dangerous men," John said. "I thought we were going to find a safe place to talk, but this is turning into more than we bargained for." He asked Judy if she had her gun ready.

"Of course," she answered. "Maybe you and I should go forward and the rest of you stay here until we see if it's safe."

"No," I exclaimed. "We can't see a thing out here and you said we should stick together."

"She's right, Judy," John said. "You and I will lead the group and when we see the guesthouse I'll decide what's safe or not."

John picked up his step and I found it difficult to keep up. "Slow down, John," I whispered. "I can't see where I'm going and the path is so uneven." Just as I said that, a body fell into me and knocked me to my knees. "Ouch," I cried out too loud.

"Shhh, Ruth Ann," John said, as he turned and saw me on the ground. "Are you alright, Ruth Ann?" John asked quietly, grabbing my arms and helping me to my feet. "What happened?"

"I tripped over a rock and fell into Ruth Ann," Inga admitted. "I can't see a thing! Are we almost there?"

"Yes, in about fifty feet we'll be in an open area. Be quiet and try not fall into each other again." John made sure I was ready before he turned and continued forward. I was thankful I had pants on because it prevented me from scraping my knees when I fell.

Judy was getting anxious and started passing each of us to get to John. "Judy," I spat out. "I already was knocked down once, do you have to push us to get in front?"

"I didn't mean to fall into you, Ruth Ann," Inga said to me.

"I know that, Inga," I said regretfully. "I didn't mean anything towards you, just that Judy was shoving her way up to the front of the group and it's still pitch black in here."

"Not anymore," John said, halting again abruptly. "I can see by the lights from that house," he said pointing toward a two-story log cabin.

"Wow, that's quite the guesthouse," Inga called out. "It's huge."

"It's bigger than all the houses in Deer Creek," I agreed. "Well, except the mayor's."

We stood at the edge of the gravel path and the woods in a small grassy area that was obviously the back yard to the cabin. "I think the only way to go forward is on foot through the back yard, and that could be dangerous," John said, looking around the grounds. "I don't see a garage, driveway or even a small road to get here."

"It's totally hidden," Judy said. "How perfect to hideaway in, don't you think, John?"

"Considering this is the first I've heard about the place…I think they succeeded."

The wide log cabin boasted massive windows in the back. "Anyone could see us coming," Ben said nervously.

"Not really, Ben," John answered. "The lights from inside will make it difficult for anyone inside to see anything outside."

"I don't get it," Ben said, confused. "But as long as we're safe, I'll just believe you."

"Good idea," I said, patting Ben on his shoulder. "We'll follow John's orders and then we'll be safe."

John turned to me with a funny grin on his face. "Seriously…did I just hear you say *follow my orders*?"

"Ha ha, John," I said, sticking my tongue out at him. "I always follow your orders when our impending safety is on the line."

"Whatever, Ruth Ann," he said, returning his gaze to the cabin. "I'm trying to think of the best way to go about this. On the one hand, it could be totally empty and we're standing here debating what to do for no reason. But…it could also be more dangerous than any of us can imagine."

"How's that?" Inga questioned.

"If Eklund, Svenson, and his men are in there, we're outnumbered."

"Don't forget Prunella," I exclaimed.

"I'm not worried about Prunella," John replied. "She's not going to harm any of you."

"She must be so scared right now," I said, worried. I can't imagine what's happening to her. If Eklund has harmed her, I won't be responsible for my actions.

"Prunella's tough stock, Ruth Ann," John said, grabbing my hand and giving it a squeeze. "She's part of your family you know."

"True," I said, smiling at him. "But Eklund and that Svenson guy have done some horrible things lately. At least before, he was kind of a gentleman and didn't murder anyone."

"You're forgetting that appraiser he had murdered at the bank, Ruth Ann," John reminded me.

"Oh, yeah, what was his name again?"

"Jeffrey Toggles," Judy answered for John who looked like he couldn't remember.

"He was a weak man. Not that he deserved to be killed, but he should've never agreed to help Eklund in the first place. He should've contacted the police and we could've prevented most of what happened back in Sweden."

We stood in silence for a few minutes when John blurted out loudly, "Okay, this is what we're going to do."

"Geez, John, you scared me to death," I said, getting my heart rate back to normal.

"What?"

"It was totally silent when you startled us by announcing your idea."

He ignored my comment. "I'm going to have a look around the cabin. You all stay here; I won't be gone long."

"But, John," Judy began to say. He held his hand up to halt her. "Look, I won't be seen, but if all of you come with me, there's a higher chance of being noticed by anyone inside that place. So stay here, I'll be back in a few minutes." With that he took off around the perimeter of the property. We lost sight of him as he ventured closer to the house.

"He'd better not get himself caught," Inga declared.

Judy turned to Inga and stated, "He's a police chief, Inga, and I highly doubt he would get caught just taking a quick look."

"We'll see," I mumbled. I stood by patiently, looking for any sign of John near the cabin. He had only been gone a couple minutes when Judy started pacing back and forth. "I should be following him," she kept repeating. She didn't wait too long when she declared, "I'm going after him."

"He ordered us to stay put," I snapped at her. "If you go chasing after him he may accidentally shoot you!"

"Get real, Ruth Ann," she said mockingly. "I'll give him plenty of warning."

"Fine, go ahead," I barked. Deep down inside of me I was hoping he'd accidentally injure her...not seriously of course, but getting her out of my sight would be okay, too.

Judy left Ben, Inga, and me. She took the same route John did when she disappeared into the darkness of the wooded area. "Now what?" Inga asked. "We just sit here waiting to be seen by one of Mr. Eklund's men?"

"We don't have a choice," I said. "John told us to stay put."

"And *you're* going to listen to him?" she inquired, flashing her yellowed teeth in a taunting grin.

"Yes, I am, Inga." I added, a moment later, "At least for the time being."

Ben, watching the surrounding area closely said, "I think we should listen."

"Listen to what?" Inga asked rudely.

"Voices."

Inga and I looked at each other wondering what he meant when I asked, "Do you hear voices, Ben?"

"Yes, I do."

"From where?" I asked, looking to see if John and Judy were returning. I couldn't see them, but maybe they were coming back through the woods or was he hearing *other* kinds of voices?

Ben stood frozen but was able to raise his arm slowly and point in the direction of the cabin. "There are two men walking around the side of the log cabin. They're on the opposite side of the house from where Chief John and Detective Judy disappeared."

I spun my head back toward the cabin and grabbed Inga and Ben's arms to bring them to the ground. "Hurry," I said, panicking. "Drop to the ground before they see us."

"Who are they?" Ben asked lying on his stomach, but lifting his head to watch the men.

"They're Mr. Eklund's men. They must be guarding the guesthouse," Inga replied.

"You know what that means, Inga, don't you?" I asked excitedly.

"That Ms. Prunella must be inside there."

"Yes."

Ben interrupted Inga and said, "So, we let Chief John and Detective Judy go in and get her."

"Maybe, Ben, maybe," I said, wondering if that would be the case.

"Maybe?" Inga asked surprised at my comment.

"They may not know there are two men walking around the cabin right now. We need to warn them."

"But if we warn them, we'll be caught!" Inga proclaimed.

"Maybe that's the best thing to happen," I announced.

Ben and Inga desperately tried to understand what I meant by my statement. "Look, if I get myself caught there's a better chance I'll be reunited with Prunella." "You must've hit your head before, Ruth Ann," Inga said, furious. "There's no way I'll let you get yourself caught."

"They could shoot you first," Ben added.

"Not if I announce who I am before they see me coming."

"No way, Ruth Ann," Inga said. "I'll hold you down myself until Chief John returns before I let you go."

"Hear me out first, Inga, please," I begged. Inga stayed silent so I took my cue and explained my thinking. "If I get taken inside the cabin, we know I'll find Prunella in there, too."

"And that maniac Svenson, Ruth Ann," Inga interrupted. "Don't forget about him, he's a cold-blooded, ruthless, murderer."

"Yes, but in my dealings with Axel, until the very end back in Sweden, he was a complete gentleman with me."

"Oh, so kidnapping, drugging, dragging you to Sweden and locking you up in his estate back there is gentlemanly?" Inga questioned. "Oh, don't forget murdering people."

"He didn't actually commit murder, Inga," I said. "He did have his people do it, but he wouldn't hurt me."

"He's desperate now," Inga said.

"Listen, let me go on before you completely rule this out." Inga nodded while Ben looked on, stupefied. "So, I go inside the cabin and Axel realizes I was being my reckless self and got caught. He won't know I did it on purpose." I took a moment to make sure no one was sneaking up on us. "Then Axel reunites me with Prunella. Why wouldn't he?" I asked. "He thinks we're two helpless females waiting to be rescued."

"Go on," Inga said slowly. I think she was beginning to understand.

"Prunella fills me in on what's been happening with Axel and Svenson, and then we plan our escape."

"How do you plan on doing that?" she snapped, pulling up to sitting position and putting her hands on her waist.

"I…I don't know exactly," I stuttered. "Prunella and I can figure that out once I'm in there and see what we're facing."

Ben lifted his head off the ground and asked, "Why did this man kidnap Prunella in the first place?"

"It's a very long story, but mainly he wants a particular necklace that Prunella and I have, and all his other assets."

"Oh, like his house and money?"

"Yes, Ben," I said. "He's an evil man who tried to have us killed before. But he was caught and supposed to be living out the rest of his life in jail. He escaped and came to Deer Creek to seek his revenge."

"Wow, sounds complicated."

"Hopefully, we won't have to worry about him too much longer. Chief John will catch him and this time he'll go away for a very, very long time."

"I sure hope so," he said, dropping his head back to the ground and covering his head with his hands.

"Ben, it's pretty dark over here, those men have passed through the back of the house now and went around the side. I think we're in the clear."

"They didn't even look out this way, Ruth Ann," Inga mentioned. "They just laughed and didn't look like they were guarding much of anything."

"Just Axel's hired thugs. Until Axel needs them to finish someone off I doubt they're any help."

"So, what are you going to do, Ruth Ann?" Inga inquired. "I don't agree with your plan, but sitting here waiting is driving me bonkers. Why haven't Chief John or Judy returned? Where could they be this long?"

"They left us alone out here haven't they?" I asked curiously. "I hope they haven't gone and gotten themselves captured!"

"That would be horrible," Ben mumbled from the ground. "What are we going to do now?"

"I'm going in," I announced. "You two stay here and wait for John and Judy. If they come back, tell them what my plans are. He'll be furious at first, but hopefully he'll calm down enough to see that Prunella and I working together will be better than Prunella alone."

"We'll see about that," Inga said with a lack of confidence I wasn't willing to admit I also had.

"Okay, the coast's clear right now. I'm going to walk straight down the middle of this back yard and basically knock on the back sliding door. I'm assuming someone will come and grab me immediately." I stood up, wiped the grass and dirt off my slacks, turned, and took off. "See you soon, I hope."

I could swear I heard Inga say, "You're nuts," but I wasn't going to let her dissuade me.

Chapter 27

John Wilkinson's Narrative

I took off and walked toward the cabin, but I didn't see anybody guarding the place yet. It was early in the evening, but pitch black outside. The temperature had to be nearing freezing. I was wearing my police leather jacket, but even that didn't keep me from shivering.

I wasn't gone more than a few minutes and about to head closer to the cabin when I heard a rustling come from behind me. I spun around and aimed my gun towards the trees. "Who's there?" I questioned with authority. "Show yourself, I'm the Chief of Police."

"John, it's me, Judy," a voice called out from the trees. "Put your gun down."

"Judy?" I questioned, starting to make out a figure walking out of the trees. "What are you doing here?"

"Backing you up," she stated bluntly.

"But I specifically ordered you to stay with the others. They're not to be trusted. You know Ruth Ann; she'll probably won't be far behind you."

"No, I told them to stay put until we came back."

"And you think that'll stop her?"

"They seemed scared so yes, I do."

"We'll see," I said, waving her near to me and heading toward an arrangement of bushes closer to the cabin. "I'm trying to get as close as I can so I can take a peek inside. I want to see if anyone's in there."

"I'll follow behind you."

We got on our hands and knees and crawled through the wet, cold, dewy grass and into the hard mulch that enclosed the small yews and pines that surrounded the corner of the cabin. "I'm able to get right under the window. Stay there for a second while I take a look." I crawled over to the other side of the bushes and came upon a corner window. I held onto a wooden ledge while I peered inside. "Wow, this is quite the guesthouse."

"Why? What do you see?"

"Nobody's in this enormous room at the moment, but I can only describe it as a fancy ski chalet. The walls are made of wooden logs; several massive antler chandeliers are hanging with their lights blazing away. They weren't trying to be inconspicuous at all."

"You don't see Prunella or Eklund and that lawyer?"

"No, not yet. Somebody's definitely been living in there. There's a fire burning in the floor to ceiling stone fireplace, and some loose newspapers sprawled out on a coffee table in front of a large, brown leather sectional."

"Can we get in there without being seen?"

"I don't know yet. I'm going to sit here and wait a few minutes to see if anyone comes in this room."

"Are there other rooms you can make out?"

"There's a large staircase that leads to a second floor. The walkway on the second floor goes to at least four doors so maybe a few bedrooms up there? I can see a doorway to a kitchen, but can't see much more than that."

"What if we went around to the front? Maybe we can see more from there and also if anyone's hanging around."

"Good idea, let's do that," I said, crawling backwards out of the cramped bushes. "You haven't seen anyone outside have you?"

"No, not yet," Judy answered.

We made our way to the side of the cabin. The only window was the bay window in the kitchen. "Be careful, there's a light on in there."

As we approached the kitchen area we fell to our hands and knees again. The window would reveal our identity immediately since it started at about my waist. "Lower, Judy," I whispered. "I think I saw some movement in there."

"Can you see from whom?"

"Hold on, I think there's a table in the bay window. I don't want to stick my head up and have someone sitting right there."

"Be careful, John."

I put my hands on the wooden ledge and slowly, deliberately raised my head high enough to look inside. It was clearly a kitchen. A heavy, wooden, round table was set in the bay window opening. I was happy the table would block my head looking in as long as nobody was sitting at the table, which there wasn't.

"What do you see, John," Judy asked impatiently.

"The table in the window, and…an island with a marble top and pot rack hanging above it. Let's see, there's the typical stuff in the kitchen, but wait…no," I stopped, closed my eyes and tried to re-focus them.

"What…what?" Judy demanded again.

"Prunella's in the kitchen!"

"What?" Judy exclaimed.

"Shhh," I said, irritated. "Keep it down."

"Sorry, I thought you said Prunella was in the kitchen."

"I did!"

"Why, how? Is she chained to a chair…a wall or something?"

"No, she's just standing in front of the refrigerator grabbing something out of there…a water bottle. What's happening here?" I was momentarily confused. Why would Prunella be alone in the kitchen when all she had to do was run out the back door that was not more than ten feet away from me? Something wasn't right.

"Judy, we need to get inside…Judy?" I turned around and Judy was gone. "Judy?" I called out a little louder. I turned to make sure nobody else was in the kitchen, but it was still just Prunella leaning against the island drinking her water from a bottle as if nothing was wrong.

"What's going on around here?" I asked myself. I crawled around the bushes and there was definitely no Judy. Where'd she disappear? I frantically retraced my steps to the tree line and didn't find her. I went around the side of the house and just as I was about to round the corner to the front I felt an unbearable pain in my head. All went black.

Chapter 28

Ruth Ann's Narrative

I made my way through the damp, cold grass onto a brick-paved, peanut shaped patio that ran along the backside of the cabin. The lights were shining through the sets of sliding glass doors, leading my way so I didn't trip. There was no patio furniture outside since the seasons were changing and winter was fast approaching. Most people stored their furniture indoors due to the harsh winters in Deer Creek.

I didn't try to conceal myself as I walked up to the middle sliding glass door. There were two other sets of sliders, one to my right and the other to my left. It would make a beautiful view from inside during the daytime. I put my head up against the glass door and peeked inside. "Nobody," I said thinking how strange that was.

I gazed around the massive living area starting from the left side of the room to the right. The first showpiece was the massive stone fireplace with a fire blazing. Somebody had to be in there. In the middle of the room was a brown, leather sectional and a few chairs spread throughout. The ceiling boasted the highly used (in Colorado, that is) antler chandeliers to illuminate the room. The right side of the room veered off into a kitchen and I would guess a dining area.

I still didn't spot any people hanging around. It wasn't late in the evening so I made a quick decision to start pounding on the glass hoping I would get a response. I know it doesn't sound like I'm thinking clearly, but I can assure each and every one of you that I am. I didn't want Prunella to go through this alone. She must be terrified by now wondering what happened to us and what was going to happen to her.

I made a few gentle taps to see if I would get a response. I didn't want anyone to be overly surprised and get a little trigger happy, but I did want someone to come and find me. Nothing. I tried a little harder tap and still nobody came around. I reached my hand out and grabbed the long, cold handle and gave it a little shove. The door was unlocked so I slowly slid it open a few inches. I felt a surge of warm air hit my face and longed to be in there with my hands and body in front of that fireplace. I was freezing and I wasn't dressed in enough warm clothes to be able to handle the night air.

I stuck my head inside and looked around. There were signs people had been in the room. Newspapers and an empty mug sat on the coffee table in front of the sofa. I slid the door a little further and stepped inside. The last thing I wanted to do was surprise someone with a gun and be the next victim. "Hello?" I called out quietly. There was no response so I walked into the middle of the room to get a better look of the cabin's first floor. There was a floating staircase in the middle of the room just behind the sectional sofa. I looked up and could see a number of closed doors because the hallway was opened to the below.

I walked toward the right and went down a hall that led to a dining room off to my right and a kitchen straight ahead. Once again, I called out, "Hello?" But this time I was rewarded, if you could say that, with a response.

"Who's there?" Was the immediate response from a female voice? If I didn't know any better, I would've said it sounded like Prunella's voice. But why would she be in the kitchen asking who's there? Suddenly, I felt a shiver run up my spine. I was afraid to find out what was really going on here.

The voice definitely came from the kitchen. I carefully, slowly walked toward the doorway into the kitchen. "I'm coming in," I said cautiously. "I'm not armed, it's just Ruth Ann."

"Ruth Ann?" the woman's voice called out.

I entered the kitchen and looked past the massive marble island with a copper pot rack full of expensive looking pots and pans hanging over it. There stood Prunella, holding a bottle of water as if nothing was wrong. "Prunella," I cried out running over to her. "What? How?"

"Ruth Ann," she said with a panicked crack of her voice. "What on earth are you doing here?"

"I came to find *you!*"

"Me or your friend *John* and his bumbling partner, Judy?"

I stood frozen on one side of the island while Prunella stood on the other side. "I'm very confused, Prunella. Why are you just standing here as if you're not being held prisoner by Axel?" I quickly added, "And that evil lawyer, Svenson?"

She took a slow, deliberate swig of her water and smiled. "Because I'm not his prisoner, Ruth Ann. I'm his wife."

What? I was stunned by her response and didn't know what to say. Was I in some horrible nightmare or even better…maybe I froze outside and this is some kind of traumatic event I'm imagining in my mind? Prunella didn't speak, she stood still waiting for me to speak, but I couldn't respond. My mind was reeling, and in my head my mouth was talking a mile a minute, but the words weren't materializing.

"Ruth Ann?" Prunella said sweetly. "Did you hear me? I'm here of my own volition."

Finally, I exclaimed, "NO! You can't be."

She walked to the side closest to me and put her hand on my shoulder. "Yes, Ruth Ann, I'm here because I want to be. I know you must be confused, but I can't talk to you for long. Axel will be back and the last person he should see is you."

"Me?" I questioned. "Why, what did *I* do to him? It's you he's been after!"

Prunella got fidgety and said, "You need to leave, now."

"But you just asked me if I'm looking for John and Judy, too. Are they here somewhere?" I asked, not thinking clearly. My head was spinning. What was happening?

"Go, Ruth Ann, just go."

"Where am I supposed to go to, Prunella? You'd better start explaining, and quick," I demanded. "I'm not moving an inch until you do."

"I can't be seen with you right now, Ruth Ann," Prunella responded. "If Axel, Steven or any of his men catch me talking casually with you they will kill you."

"Why would they want to kill me? I didn't do anything to him. Axel was actually decent to me until the very end back in Sweden."

"Not any more. He blames you for everything."

"Why?" I didn't understand what was happening. Prunella was the one who hid the necklace from Axel and took his entire fortune. He should hate her!

"He said that if it wasn't for you none of what happened here or back in Sweden would've taken place. It was because you got involved with trying to swindle the necklace from him and turned me against him."

"But none of that's true, Prunella. You believe me and not him, right?" I must be having a nightmare. "Wait, *you're the one who sent me the necklace in the first place.*"

"I did."

"And…that's all you're going to say? I didn't kidnap myself and kill those people. Axel and his men did. Plus, you're the only one who was going to benefit from Axel being sent to prison."

"True," she said with a grin on her face.

I couldn't believe what I was hearing. Prunella turned on me and was now on Axel's side. She wasn't even willing to listen to me. Wait…maybe she's been drugged somehow. Axel could've given her something that would make her believe him and his lies?

"No, Ruth Ann," Prunella said curtly. "I was not and have not been drugged by my husband."

I tried to explain she might not know if he slipped her a pill or two. "No, he loves me Ruth Ann, and I love him back. That's it, nothing else. So why don't you turn around and just leave."

"There's no way I'm leaving here without you, John, and even Judy."

Prunella put her hands on her hips and gave me an insulting glare and asked, "What about Ben and Inga, Ruth Ann? You deserted them back on the ground near the cabin. They could be frozen to death by now."

"I'm sure they're fine, Prunella," I said, realizing one important problem. "Wait a minute, how did you know where Inga and Ben were?"

"Seriously?" she asked mockingly. "Axel's grounds are well equipped with surveillance equipment."

"But…we were able to get around his cameras before," I cried out.

"How do you think we were able to?" Prunella asked me. "Sherman and I know exactly where they are, and when I want to come and go without being seen I can."

"Sherman?"

"Sherman. He's been by my side for a long time. He does whatever I tell him."

"So, when we were back at the big house a little while ago and he told us about the guesthouse he knew more than he proclaimed?"

"Yes. He knew I was hiding back here with Axel."

"But why?" I asked, more and more confused. "He tried to kill you and you were forced to fake a terminal illness back in Sweden."

"That did happen, Ruth Ann. We worked it out once he contacted me back here in Deer Creek."

"When did he contact you? Before or after he had Bert and Helena horribly murdered?"

"After, of course," she pronounced. "I just heard from him this morning, and when I disappeared after lunch I met up with him here in the guesthouse."

"But that's only a few hours, Prunella. How on earth did he redeem himself and everything he's done in such a short amount of time?"

"That's not really any of your business. It's time for you to   leave   before   he   returns." I looked around my back to check the hall into the great room. I didn't want Axel or Steven Svenson sneaking up on me. "What's happened to you? You're not acting like your normal self, Prunella."

"Go."

"No, not until you tell me where John and Judy are. Are they being held here against their will or did they make it out of here?" I added, "You owe me at least that."

"I don't owe you anything."

"Just a short time ago you offered me half your estate or have you forgotten about that?" I snapped bitterly.

"I'm back with Axel now and that won't happen anymore."

"But you'll never be able to be free. Axel's wanted for murder and I'm sure a number of other offenses. How will you live? On the run all the time?"

"He's got that figured out and you don't have to worry about it. Now leave!" she demanded and pounded a fist down on the marble island.

"No, not until you tell me where John and Judy have been taken."

"Fine, but after I tell you I *need* you to get out of here."

Chapter 29

John Wilkinson's Narrative

I awoke in a dark, freezing cold room. My head was throbbing as I tried to sit up from the cot I was shoved onto. Wherever I was, there was no heat in the room. I reached into my pocket and found the flashlight I put in my front coat pocket. I turned on the light and flashed it around the small room. My eyes immediately focused on another cot on the other side of the small, empty room. "Judy, is that you?" I called out quietly. I grabbed the back of my head with my other hand and rubbed the spot I was hit. There was a large lump on my head, but it didn't bleed from what I could feel. I hurried over to Judy who was still unconscious on her cot. I grabbed her shoulders and gently shook her. After several tries, and several breaks to rub my head from pain, she started to stir. "Finally."

Judy tried to pop up to a sitting position, but realized she was still dizzy. "What happened?" she asked groggily.

"You were clobbered back in those bushes. When I realized you weren't still with me I went to look for you and someone bashed me on the back of my head. How's your head?"

"My head?" she questioned. "It's fine. I never got hit. I got chloroformed."

"That's why I didn't hear you get hit over the head. I couldn't figure out how you were taken away without me hearing a thing."

"I was back in the bushes and the last thing I remember you were peeking into the windows and then someone reached around my face and put a cloth around my mouth. I couldn't yell, and the next thing I know I'm waking up here."

"I wonder how long we've been up here."

"I have no idea. I can't see anything in here. Where are we anyway?"

I stood up from the edge of the cot and walked around the very square, small room. I made my way to a door and grabbed the handle. "Locked."

"I would think so."

"It'll be easy to break out, though. Can you go and look out the window?"

Judy stood up, wobbled a little, then made her way to a small window that was on the wall in between the two cots. "It's pitch black out there, I can't see anything."

"I'm going to try and pick the lock, but we have to be prepared if there's a guard outside the door."

Judy reached into her coat and pants pockets. "They took my gun, how about you?"

"Yep," I said, figuring that out a little sooner when I looked for the flashlight. "I'm surprised they left my flashlight on me." I said, opening up the base of the light and pulling out a little kit. "My knife's in here."

"Clever, John," Judy said.

I walked over to the door and put my ear against it. "I don't hear any movement out there, but that doesn't mean there's not a guard there.

Judy came closer, and while I tried to stick the knife in the lock she kept a listen with her ear against the door. "Still quiet."

It didn't take long before I broke the lock. It was louder than I wanted, but there was no other option. We needed to get out of here and see where we were and, most importantly, find Ruth Ann. "I'm opening the door, be ready." Since I broke the lock the knob wouldn't turn. I pulled it gently and the door opened an inch. "There's light on the other side, but I still can't see where we are."

"Be careful," Judy whispered as I pulled the door toward me another inch or so.

"Wait a minute," I protested. "We're in the garage!"

"What?" Judy cried. "How did we get back here?"

"We're on the second floor. Ruth Ann and I looked up here briefly, but thought it was just a storage space." I walked into the large upstairs room and noticed we were in a closet shoved back into the corner of the room. "I didn't see this door earlier."

"You probably didn't think much of it. It's just car parts and tools up here."

"Nobody's in here, let's get downstairs and have a look around."

"We need to see if Ruth Ann, Ben, and Inga are in here."

I hurried down the stairs feeling less dizzy from the blow to my head. Judy checked the cars and I walked around the entire floor. "Nothing," Judy stated.

"Did you check the trunks?" I asked, terrified of what we could discover.

"No, I'll do that now." Judy popped each one of the vehicles in the garage and came up empty. "They wouldn't still be out in the cold would they?"

"No way, they'd be frozen. I just hope they didn't get caught by Eklund and his men because they could be anywhere."

"If they did get caught, they're probably somewhere in that cabin we were trying to get into."

"Let's get out of here and back to the cabin."

We zipped up our coats and grabbed a couple blankets from a storage rack near the door. "Just in case," I said to Judy.

"Good idea. We don't know if they're inside or out anymore."

We followed the pitch-black gravel path back down to the log cabin guesthouse. "No sign of anyone along the way, John," Judy stated. "Without a flashlight they could never make it back."

"I'm aware of that, Judy," I said, worried. "Nothing looks any different than before."

"Except one huge mistake we made last time."

I turned around to look at Judy in the dark and asked, "What would that be? Getting knocked out and thrown in a storage closet?"

"No, look," Judy said, pointing up in the trees. "We missed this last time."

I looked and carefully aimed the flashlight up toward the tree Judy was pointing at. "You've got to be kidding. It's a surveillance camera. How could we not see that?" I took a rock and threw it up to knock the camera down. It took only two throws when the camera cracked and fell to the ground. "That should cover that one, but how many others are there?"

"That's why they caught us in the bushes. They saw us coming all along."

"If they saw you and me, then they saw Ruth Ann, Inga, and Ben!"

Judy nodded, but didn't say a word. I looked around our surroundings and thought about taking another way in toward the cabin. "Let's head to the left this time instead of the right. Keep a close eye out for cameras." We took off to the left and no sooner than we started I halted. "Look," I said, pointing to the ground.

"I don't see anything. What's up?"

"The grass is matted down here; can't you see it?"

"Oh, yeah, kind of like someone was lying down on the ground." Judy noticed there was two other spots close by that were also matted down. "I bet Inga, Ben, and Ruth Ann were the culprits who made the three spots, John."

"But where'd they go?" I said, frantically searching in the nearest grove of trees and bushes. "I don't see any sign of them anymore."

"It doesn't look good, John. Maybe we should assume they've been captured and are inside the cabin with Prunella."

"No," a different voice called out from a distant bush.

I twirled my body around and tried to focus on the area the sound came from. "Who's there?" I asked immediately. "Come out!"

Ben rose from his hands and knees and pleaded for us not to shoot him. "Ben," I said, thrilled to see him. "What are you doing in those bushes?"

"Hiding out," he replied shivering.

"Judy, give him a blanket to wrap up in." Judy hurried over to Ben and enrobed him in the thick wool blanket. "Good, that'll warm you up a little." Then I asked, "Where are the other two?"

Ben violently started to shake his head back and forth. He couldn't speak out of fear so I grabbed him by the shoulders to keep him from moving. "Ben, please, tell me where Inga and Ruth Ann are." I quickly added, "I'm not mad at you. I just need to know what happened to them."

He stopped shaking his head and stared into my eyes and replied, "Inga, went back to the estate to get Sherman. She wanted to get us some supplies and warmer coats." He shivered a little and added, "She told me she didn't know how long we'd be out here, and when Ruth Ann would come back to us."

"Wait, what did you just say?" I asked alarmed.

"I said...Inga..." I interrupted him and re-phrased my question carefully. "No, Ben, what do you mean when Ruth Ann would come back to us? Where did Ruth Ann go?"

"She...she..." he stopped, panicked again, regained his composure and said, "She went to the cabin to get herself caught." Ben backed away as if I was going to slug him. "Please don't be mad at me. I, I mean, we tried to stop her, but you know Miss Ruth Ann, she doesn't listen very well."

I calmed down and released my grip from Ben's shoulders. "You're right, Ben. Ruth Ann makes up her mind and there's no dissuading her. It's not your fault. I'm not mad at you."

"Thank you."

"So you've been waiting here all this time? How long has Inga been gone?" Judy chimed in.

"A very long time. I got scared and hid in those bushes. Plus, it was a little bit warmer in there."

I glanced over at Judy who was eyeing me strangely and said, "Something's not right."

"I agree. Why isn't Inga back yet?" Judy asked.

"And now we know Ruth Ann's been taken prisoner again by Eklund."

Chapter 30

Ruth Ann's Narrative

Prunella told me that some of Axel's men caught John and Judy in the bushes trying to look inside the cabin. They were disabled and thrown into a closet back in the garage. "Why?" I asked, horrified. "Were they badly hurt?"

"No," she stated. "Just temporarily indisposed. Knowing them, they're probably out and trying to get to you. I don't need them interfering anymore either. Just gather them and go back to the estate and leave. Just leave and never come back!"

"You're losing it, Prunella. I would never do that. Something's happened and you need to tell me what. You would never kick me out like this…please, I'm begging you to come clean with me."

"Go or I'll call Axel's men myself and have them throw you out."

"But, where am I supposed to go?"

"Go grab Inga and Ben and head back to the garage and let John and Judy outta the closet up on the second floor. Then get back to the estate and get into John's truck and leave…forever."

"No."

"This is my last warning, Ruth Ann," Prunella threatened. "I will give you ONE MINUTE to leave or I'm pushing the button on the intercom." I looked in the direction Prunella was pointing, and sure enough there was an intercom planted on the wall next to the hallway leading to the dining room.

"Fine," I exclaimed. "I'll leave, but this isn't over. Do you understand me? I don't believe you feel this way about Axel. I *believe* you're being forced into doing this and I *will* prove it, Prunella."

"You're wrong, Ruth Ann. We're through, I've made up my mind and I'm sticking behind Axel. I'm not drugged or out of my mind. I love him and I will stay married to him. We'll share everything and live happily ever after."

I tried to comprehend what she was saying, but I didn't see in her eyes that she was as passionate about her relationship as she was claiming. I absolutely knew she was putting on an act, and I will concede for now, but this isn't and will not be over as easily as she thinks.

I turned and headed out the side kitchen door that led to a small walkway around to the back patio. I passed a number of small bushes along the way and wondered if these were the bushes where John and Judy were captured. I couldn't see a thing once I made it back to where I left Inga and Ben. They were gone. I needed them to come with me to find John and Judy. I was about to give up when I heard a rustling close by. I couldn't tell if an animal or a human being caused it. I hurried over toward the gravel path about to run back toward the garage. I stopped and waited when I suddenly spotted a group of people walking in the middle of the grassy backyard area. I was able to see a little better now that they were in the path of the cabin's lights. I couldn't believe my eyes!

"John?" I called out from a distance. "John, it's me, Ruth Ann!!"

The three of them turned their bodies in my direction and John aimed his flashlight toward me. "Ruth Ann?"

"Yes, it's me, I'm coming over so don't tackle me or anything, okay?"

"Why would I do that?" John asked.

"Just in case you don't think it's me."

"I know that voice anywhere," John said rushing over to me and taking my shoulders in his hands and checking out every inch of me. "I'm fine, John, really."

"What…how…are you here?"

"It's a long story and it's freezing out here." I turned to Ben and said, "Have you been out here this whole time?"

"Yes, until Chief John and Judy found me."

I looked around and wondered where Inga was. "Where's Inga?"

"She went back to the main house to get Sherman's help," Judy answered.

"I was just on my way to rescue you two from the garage closet."

"How did you know we were in there?" John asked me.

"I just left Prunella."

"Why?" Judy asked stunned and confused.

"Can we go somewhere warm and I'll explain. Maybe back to the main house and we can meet up with Inga, if she's still okay."

"Wait, why wouldn't Inga be okay, Ruth Ann?" John questioned. "She's back there with Sherman."

"You won't believe what I just found out."

"So, you were inside this cabin with Prunella, Eklund, Svenson, and his men and you just walked out?" Judy asked curiously. "Something doesn't sound right about that."

"You're right, Judy, it isn't right. Let's go so I can fill you all in at one time. But, I have to tell you we need to get Inga away from Sherman first. He can't be included anymore."

"Why?" John exclaimed. "He's on our side."

"Not exactly." I refused to answer any more questions until we arrived back at Axel and Prunella's main house. Yes, I said it as if they were a couple. I wasn't completely convinced either way yet, but I had to make sure everyone else agreed with me that Prunella was putting on an extravagant act.

With the help of John's flashlight and the fact that we were freezing, we made it back to the house in no time. Before we headed inside I stopped everyone. "I need you to pretend that Sherman's still with us and we have no idea he's betraying us with Prunella. Can you trust me until we get somewhere safe and quiet?"

"It makes no sense, Ruth Ann, but we don't have a choice," John replied. "What if Inga's not with Sherman?"

"Inga, as far as I know, doesn't know what I know so she'll still be on friendly terms with Sherman … unless … Sherman detained Inga."

"But…this makes no sense!" Judy stammered. "Let's get inside and see what we find. We understand what you're telling us so it'll be good unless Sherman tries to pull a fast one."

"He's not a problem," John said. "I don't think an aging butler is anything to worry about."

John led the way to the back door that led to the estate's massive kitchen. As soon as we entered, Sherman was there to greet us with a large smile on his face. "Oh, I'm so relieved to see all of you. You mustn't have found Ms. Prunella or Mr. Eklund?"

"No, Sherman, we didn't get close enough to get in. We didn't want to make the situation worse by barreling in. One of us could've been shot," I answered quickly.

"Oh, that's smart. What do we do now?" he asked nervously.

"We warm up and come up with another plan," John said, looking around the kitchen for Inga. "Where's Inga?"

Sherman shrugged his shoulders and said, "She's around here somewhere."

"I thought she came back here to get your help?" Ben asked.

"She did, she went looking for supplies and I told her I would go back down to the cabin when she's ready."

John helped us out so we could get a little time without Sherman. "Hey, Sherman, could you whip up some hot chocolate for us frozen folks while we warm up in the library?"

Sherman looked surprised at John's request. "You want *me* to make you hot chocolate when Ms. Prunella's a prisoner down in that cabin?"

"We've been out in the cold a long time and could use something hot. Oh, and throw in some of those biscotti in that jar on the corner. Those sound pretty good, too." I figured out what John was doing. He was trying to throw Sherman off track and keep him confused about our plans.

LYNNE'S FAVORITE ALMOND BISCOTTI
(Time for a break from this grueling mystery!)

- **½ Cup Sugar** (I always cut a little bit of the sugar out when I can! But you can add ¼ cup

more if you'd like. You won't miss it
though!)

- **2 Large Eggs** (Beat them in a little bowl
  before adding to mixer)
- **1 Teaspoon Almond Extract** (I add a
  smidgen more)
- **1 ¾ Cups Flour**
- **1 Teaspoon Baking powder**
- **Dash of salt (no more than ¼ teaspoon)**
- **1 Cup sliced or slivered almonds (can
  roast first if you like because it brings out
  the flavor of the almonds. Put the almonds
  on cookie sheet and place in 350-degree
  oven 5-7 minutes.)**

**Beat the sugar and eggs until thoroughly
mixed (3-5 minutes). Add almond extract.**

In separate bowl combine dry ingredients.

**Add dry to wet mixture and combine
thoroughly. Fold in almonds.**

**Form dough into one long log or 2 short logs
and place on a parchment covered cookie sheet.
They won't expand too much so pick the size you
would like for your biscotti.**

**Bake 25 minutes then remove and let cool for
a few minutes. Many recipes say 10 minutes up
to 20 minutes. I find it doesn't make too much of
a difference with the final outcome. However, the
logs are hot and may hurt to touch too soon.**

> **Lower oven to 325 degrees.**
>
> **Slice diagonally (You pick desired thickness, but usually ½ inch to 1 inch), and place cut side down onto cookie sheet. Bake another 10 minutes, flip biscotti over and bake another 10 minutes until both sides are a nice golden brown color.**
>
> **Let cool and store in glass container (or plastic bag, but they may not stay as hard in there). Enjoy! They last a long time unless you eat them all right away. Unfortunately, that's what I do because I can't stop eating them since they're so yummy!**

"Ah, sure," he said, trying to figure out what to do. "I'll prepare it immediately so we can go and rescue Ms. Prunella."

John motioned for us to follow him out of the kitchen. We hurried to the library and didn't see any sign of Inga along the way. "What do we do about Inga?" I asked, worried.

"We need to find her. Sherman must've done something with her, but what?"

"There's no way Inga could be overpowered by that old man," Judy snapped. "Inga's such a strong female and Sherman's, well, he's kind of puffy and slow."

"I agree, Judy," John said. "Unless he blindsided her and she didn't see him did coming."

"Even if he did drug her or knock her unconscious, he could never have lifted her and dropped her somewhere else."

"Could he have had some help?" Ben suggested.

"From whom?" I asked. "Axel, Svenson, and his two men are down in the cabin. Unless he has others around here we haven't seen?"

"Maybe we can get that information out of Sherman," John said. "We need a plan." John plopped down on one of the chairs in front of the desk. He rubbed his head with intensity until he sat upright and said, "Okay, we'll get Sherman back in here and I'll demand he tells us what he did with Inga. We confess we know he's betrayed us for Prunella and Eklund and see his reaction."

"Then what?" I asked angrily. "Tie him up and gag him? We can't do that. I don't believe Sherman or Prunella have truly   betrayed   us."
"But Ruth Ann," John said. "You just told us they have. You need to fill us in on *everything* that transpired while you were in the cabin...quickly"

We moved our group over to the couch and chairs in front of the fireplace. There was already a burning fire going so we huddled around it for a short time while I explained, in detail, what happened to me inside the kitchen with Prunella.

"Amazing," Judy declared.

"No way do I believe her," John stated. "She must've been drugged or brainwashed."

"She was only with Axel for a few hours," I said, frustrated. "How could he have turned her so fast? And Sherman, too?"

"The only explanation I can come up with is that he has something on her," John suggested. "It's too quick for me to believe she's back in love with the guy and stabbing you in the back."

"I agree," I said, finally getting somewhere. "But what can he have on her?"

"It's obvious to me," John declared. "*You.*"

"*Me?*"

"That makes sense," Judy agreed. "Eklund threatened your life so Prunella would agree to anything he says."

"I never thought of that," I admitted. "What can we do now?"

"First, we find Inga," Ben intervened. "We need to find her."

I looked over at Ben and said, "Ben, you can get out of this now. It's me they're after and I don't want anything bad to happen to you. Why don't we arrange to get you back into town and safely at home?"

"Good idea, Ruth Ann," John said standing to go over to the desk to call his office. "I'm going to call Lou and have him drive up here and pick you up."

"No, sir, please don't. I want to stay and help."

"But, it's dangerous, Ben," I said.

"I really want to help you, Ruth Ann. You and the chief have been very kind to me and it's the best I can do to repay you for all your kindness. I don't have any money to buy you a nice gift so I'll offer you my protection."

"How could I say no to that, Ben. Thank you."

"Okay, fine, I guess," John conceded tentatively. "When Sherman gets in here, I'm going to put him in the chair by the desk and he won't be able to move until he tells us everything he knows about Prunella, and where Inga is." John looked at me directly and added, "I don't want anyone else interrupting my interrogation, clear?"

Everyone nodded even though John's gaze was still aiming in my, and only my, direction. "Fine," I replied. "I'll do my best."

"That's all I can ask for, Ruth Ann."

It must've been twenty minutes when John started pacing around the library. He looked over at Judy who was leaning against the stones surrounding the fireplace. "We might've just made a crucial mistake, Judy."

"I know exactly what you're about to say."

"He's not coming in here with hot chocolate or anything!"

"What?" I exclaimed. "Why?"

"He's onto us. He must've done something to Inga and he knew we'd find out. We need to see if Sherman's still in the kitchen. If not, we'll split up and search the place for Inga."

"This place is massive," Judy said. "She could be anywhere."

"We don't have a choice, Judy," John stated. "Then we get back down to that cabin and find a way to get to the bottom of this."

John stomped out of the library and headed straight for the kitchen. The rest of us followed a short distance behind. He flew open the swinging door that led into the kitchen and stopped just as he entered. "Gone!" he bellowed. "I knew it. I waited too long."

"We had no idea Sherman was on to us, John," I said.

"Yeah, John," Judy said. "Let's split up and search this place."

"You're both right," he admitted. "I'll go down into the basement. Judy, you and Ben take the third floor. Ruth Ann, you come with me."

It just figures! I always get stuck going into the basement. I hate it down there. It's dark, damp, and has that secret room of torture. If I walk down there and find Inga…no, I won't go there. I shook it off and hurried to catch up to John since he was already halfway down the rickety, wooden steps. "Wait up," I called out to him. John stopped at the bottom of the stairs and told me he was just going down so he could turn on the light at the bottom of the stairs. I hit the last step as he pulled the string to lighten up the room.

"Looks clear down here," John said. "I'm gonna go check that other room. You wait here." I didn't argue because the last time I was down here I saw Helena, stabbed and killed against a wall full of shackles. I leaned against the wall as John easily found the little button that opens up the secret entrance (we've had too much practice opening that wall!). The cement wall slowly creaked up into the ceiling as John disappeared inside, and I found I was holding my breath. I was happy John stuck his head out immediately and told me that Inga was not in there. Phew, I thought as I let out a long exhale.

"Now where?" I asked him.

"We go up to the second floor and check all the rooms up there. Hopefully, Judy and Ben came up with something while they were up on the third floor."

"What if we don't find her?"

"We'll find her or at least a clue as to where they took her. I'm sure of it." We headed back upstairs and into the kitchen. There was still no sign of Sherman, so we headed out into the foyer and up the main staircase. This staircase was nothing like the one that just took us down into the basement. The grand staircase, as I would call it, was at least three times as wide and covered with a thick, red runner that showed no wear. The stairs continued to another floor, but I noticed the stairs narrowed as you went higher and higher. "John, Axel's bedroom is on this floor. Inga's old room was up on the third. Do you really think we need to check each of these rooms?"

"Yes," he replied.

We went down the second floor hall and made our way to Prunella's bedroom or should I now declare it, Axel and Prunella's bedroom? Nonsense!

"Prunella took over this room since she's been here, but I don't think she's had time to redecorate. I'll suggest she do so when this nightmare is over."

"I sure hope it ends the way you want it to, Ruth Ann."

"How else could it? There's no way she's staying with Axel. I just won't believe that...ever!"

We went through each of the rooms on the second floor and came up empty. Inga had to be somewhere on the third floor. Where else would she be? "Let's meet up with Judy and Ben. Hopefully they found her or at least a clue as to where she is."

I agreed with John and just as we were heading up to the third floor, Judy and Ben were descending toward us. "Any luck?" I asked desperately.

"No," Judy answered. "Where on earth is that woman? She's not exactly a small, quiet person who they can shove in a closet."

"I'm not sure what we should do," John said, rubbing his head in frustration. "Let's get back downstairs and check back in the kitchen. Maybe Sherman came back."

We rushed back into the kitchen to find Sherman still missing. "I bet he went down to the cabin to warn Prunella that we're on to them. Maybe he brought Inga with him?" I asked.

"How?" Judy questioned. "We were all over this house."

"Easy, Judy," John chimed in. "Sherman must've had Inga held up somewhere close by and while we were in the library he took her and threatened her to follow him."

"That's the only way she would've left with him," I snapped. "I bet she was tied up, gagged, and he held a gun to her. Otherwise, she would've fought him off easily."

"Unless one of Eklund's men helped Sherman out," John corrected me.

"That would be bad. Inga thinks she can fight off anyone. I hope she didn't do anything that would've forced them to hurt her."

"We didn't hear any gunfire, Ruth Ann," John said, trying to reassure me.

"There's other means of hurting or killing people, John," I answered.

"Just don't go there too quickly. Let's get out back and hurry over to the cabin. It's pitch black out and freezing. We need to grab a few supplies in case we're stuck outside for any length of time." John went into the front hall and opened a huge closet.

"Look, there's a bunch of coats in here. Load up and I'll search some drawers in the kitchen for extra flashlights."

John took off and left Ben, Judy, and me to grab coats. I grabbed a long, black mink fur that was stuffed off to the side of the closet. It must've been a female's coat at one point, but whose? Judy grabbed a man's long down coat and took another one for John. Ben was stuck with a long, brown wool coat. He put it one and found it too tight to button. "It'll be okay," I reassured him. "It's just in case we're outside for a long time. Grab another short coat and put that on too." Ben pulled out a fleece waist length coat and put in on and zipped it up. "Perfect."

We grabbed whatever gloves and hats we could find and headed into the kitchen. John had every drawer in the kitchen open and he held up two flashlights and a gun. "Looky what I found in one of the drawers."

"That's great," Judy declared. "Any ammo?"

John held up a box of bullets and stuffed them inside the down coat Judy handed him. He put on the long, navy blue puffy coat and we headed out into the dark, frigid night.

"Brrr…it's freezing out here," I said, wrapping the mink a little closer to my body.

"You shouldn't complain, Ruth Ann," John said. "Look what you're wearing."

"I've always secretly wanted one of these, but with the whole campaign against killing animals for these I never would buy one."

"I would never wear an animal product," Judy declared righteously.

"I'm doing it just for warmth, Judy," I said curtly. "I didn't buy it."

John stopped our bickering and led us down the path toward the garage. "It's snowing!" he announced.

"They'll see our footprints coming down the path," Judy said alarmed.

"I believe everyone's already down at the cabin so it really doesn't matter anymore," John responded, surprised at Judy's ignorance.

I was impatient and said, "Let's hurry."

"We can hurry up to a certain point. Once I spot those cameras we need to go off into the woods and wind around. I broke a couple of them, but I don't want them to sit and watch us coming this time. Eklund must've had a good laugh at us last time," John said, obviously reprimanding himself for his ignorance and for being so complacent.

Once we reached the garage, Ben asked John if we were going to check inside there, but he said no, flatly.

"Maybe there are more flashlights in there. Then we can all have one," I suggested.

"We're just wasting time if we stop in there. In fact, we've wasted so much time they might've left the cabin by now."

"How?" I asked curiously. "The only driveway out is around the front of the cabin back in the woods toward the garage. We would've heard them or seen the tire tracks in the snow, don't you think?"

"Hopefully," he replied. "But we did spend a lot of time in the house searching rooms."

"I still think one of us would've noticed, but if they did, we're in trouble."

"How so, Ruth Ann?" asked Ben, who was walking so close on my heels I almost tripped over an object on the path just past the garage.

"Be careful, Ben," I said, irritated. "I almost fell on something on the ground."

John halted and turned around, causing me to bump into him now.

"Would you two give me a little space, please?"

"Ruth Ann," John began to say. "What did you trip on? There's just gravel on the path." He bent down to where I stood and had Judy shine the flashlight so he could see a little better. "Wait…"

"What'd you find?" Judy asked, excited.

"It's a wad of paper around something, hold on…I can't see what it is," John replied, picking up the object and standing up.

"Paper? We didn't see any paper before?" I remarked.

"It could've easily been missed, Ruth Ann, it's dark out here," Judy retorted.

"Stop, both of you!" John bellowed. "It's a piece of paper rubber banded around a coffee mug. That's why you almost tripped over it."

"That had to be placed there," I exclaimed. "I bet Inga did it to warn us."

Judy asked eagerly, "Is it a note? Is there handwriting on the paper, John?"

"I'm carefully taking off the rubber band so it doesn't tear. This could be a significant clue." John worked on the rubber band while Judy and I held a flashlight next to him.

"Hurry, John, is it from Inga?" I asked impatiently.

"It's a note!" he proclaimed.

"Read it!" I demanded.

"It says...*taking me to guesthouse. Go to basement. Follow to secret tunnel. Hurry, they're going to kill me next*, the note was signed and I'm pretty sure it was from Inga." John handed the note to me next so I could look at the signature.

"It's her alright," I said, handing it to Judy.

"Basement," Judy said slowly while reading the note. "What's with these homes and their basements having secret rooms, and now a tunnel?"

John turned to me and asked me, "Did you know there was a basement in the guesthouse? You were the only one in there."

"No, I only made it through the back sliders into the great room and the kitchen."

"How would Inga know where they were taking her?" Judy asked suspiciously. "You don't think she's in on it, too?"

"No way!" I declared.

"If she's part of this then we might be walking straight into a trap," Judy continued on. "John, what do you think?"

"I don't think Inga's working with Eklund and the others. She's definitely on our side."

"Thank you, John," I said, glaring over at Judy. "You always think the worst of people, don't you?" I grumbled at her.

Judy didn't respond, but suggested to John that we hurry up and get over to the guesthouse before they take off and we're back at the beginning trying to find them and figure what was going on!

Chapter 31

We hurried down the gravel path until we could see a dim light in the distance. "Stop," John said, abruptly stopping himself, and then having me, once again, bump into him.

"I think you do that on purpose, John," I asserted.

John ignored my comment and went on. "We're going to head off to the right this time. I know it might be rough on a couple of you, but it's the safest way to approach the cabin. Just in case a couple of men were left behind."

"So you think they're already gone?" I asked, surprised. "Maybe it's taking time to get them down in the tunnel, if it even exists."

Ben grabbed my arm and said, "You don't think Inga told the truth?"

"Oh, no, no, that's not what I meant," I said reassuring him. "I just wondered if they just told her there was one hoping she'd throw us off the track somehow."

"So, Ruth Ann," John started to say. "You think they *purposely* told Inga that information and hoped she'd find a way to leave a clue behind? Or should I say an inaccurate clue?"

"You never know, John," I replied, wondering if I should be the one wearing a police badge!

"Hmm, well, nonetheless, we need to get over to the cabin and check it out." He made a quick exit into the woods. If I thought it was dark on the gravel path, this was complete blackness. I asked John if he would turn on his flashlight, but he said, "I'm going to, but I'm going to filter it with my hands and keep it aimed straight at the ground. I want no chance of them picking us out from a camera."

"But I can't see a thing," I protested as I kept as close as I could to him and holding onto the bottom of his down coat.

"If we hold on to each other's backs, we can follow my lead."

John slowed his pace while moving branches and bushes aside as we trudged through the pitch black forest. Each time a branch was about to snap back and hit one of us he tried, not always successfully, to warn us. One time I got hit in the head from a brittle, empty branch. After that, John was better at warning us. I made it clear, from a loud yelp that he had to inform us of anything that was coming up that could trip, hit or bump into us.

It took much longer to get near the cabin than the path would've taken. Once we were within eyesight of the lights shining from inside the guesthouse we stopped. "Okay, this is what we're going to do," John said, but I quickly stopped him. "If you're about to tell us that you and Judy are going in without Ben and me it won't work. I will not get separated anymore. Look what's happened before. Inga's now captured. Prunella and Sherman have gone rogue, and my daughter was captured then released by Axel. No more abandoning each other!"

"Geez, Ruth Ann," John said, exasperated. "I wasn't even going to suggest that this time."

"Oh, sorry, go on," I said, embarrassed at my outburst.

"As I was saying…this is what we're going to do." He looked around the darkened patch of bushes surrounding us and said, "Once we approach the cabin I'm going to check out the side kitchen door."

"You just said we weren't separating," I bellowed.

"We aren't, Ruth Ann, just stop talking until I'm finished. If it's not acceptable enough for you by then, you can complain at that time. But, to go on, I am, alone, crouching down and making my way to the kitchen door that's on the side of the cabin. I'll peek inside, then, and only then, if it's clear, I'll wave for you, Judy, and Ben to head over to me."

"Then what?" Ben asked, excited.

"We'll enter the kitchen and make our way to the basement door. I'm hoping the door's off the kitchen like his other houses."

John waited for us to agree, even though there were no other options, and handed the flashlight to me. He took off in the dark while Judy, Ben, and I watched silently. "He'll be fine," Ben said, patting me gently on my back. "He's used to this kind of stuff, he's a policeman."

"He's the chief, Ben," Judy corrected. "And he's perfectly capable of handling the situation."

"Except last time he went to look inside he got bashed on the head if I do recall, and ended up in a closet with you in the garage."

"He won't make that mistake again."

"Okay," I said. "It looks like he's being guided by the light from the cabin so that should help."

We watched as John made it to the side of the house and over to the door that I knew from experience, led to the kitchen. Once he turned around to make sure there was nobody lurking behind him. Judy kept a close eye out for

John, too. Within a few minutes, John's armed slowly raised and he motioned us to come over to him.

"Follow me," Judy ordered. "And stay low."

We turned our flashlights off and Judy led the way through the thick foliage out into the wide open frozen, grassy grounds. I was happy the light snow ended so we didn't have to worry about leaving footsteps. Judy went quickly, I had a difficult time following her until we were in the open. I felt vulnerable out in the open until we made it over to where John was waiting next to the guesthouse. "Good, I think we did it this time."

"I looked around, too," Judy said. "The cameras are on the back side of the guesthouse, the front and in the woods, but not the side we came from."

"I noticed that, too," John said.

"Now what?" I asked quietly.

"I'm going to slowly, deliberately turn the handle on the door and check to see if it's locked. If it's not, I will push it inch by inch until I can fit inside."

"So, you didn't see anyone when you looked inside?" I asked curiously.

"No, it was empty as far as I can see." John continued, "Once I'm in and make sure it truly is empty, you three will follow me in. Got it?"

"Yes," Judy, Ben, and I said in unison.

Very carefully, John lifted his hand to the round, frozen brass door knob and gave it a turn. "Locked." He pulled a tool out of his pocket that he must've grabbed from the kitchen and put a metal pick into the lock. Judy, who has claimed to be the best at picking locks, whispered, asking if she could help him. John twirled his head and glared at her. "I'm perfectly capable." Ooh, he didn't appreciate that, and I couldn't help but crack a little smile as he snapped back at her.

Within a few seconds, John broke the lock and he turned the knob again and pushed the door in slightly. "Nobody make any noise." John only opened the door enough to enable himself to get in. I took a step back and watched as John disappeared into the kitchen. I was suddenly aware of a strange sensation streaming up from my legs into my head. I sensed doom overcoming me and I almost fell to the ground. Ben noticed I was behaving strangely and grabbed one of my arms and kept me steady. He whispered, "Ruth Ann, are you okay? I could've sworn you were about to pass out."

Whatever happened was over as quickly as it started. "No, I'm alright, Ben," I said giving my body a slight shake. "I just felt this horrible sensation in my body like something terrible was going to happen. I couldn't control myself for a moment."

"Anxiety," he replied.

"Anxiety?" I questioned him. "I can't believe I would have a sudden onset of anxiety."

"It can happen to anyone, even someone as strong as you, at any time."

"He's right," Judy chimed in. "A lot of good cops have gone down because they were unexpectedly attacked by severe anxiety."

"Well, I don't think that was my case. I just haven't eaten anything in a long time. I don't do well if I'm not eating something every couple of hours, at least."

"Whatever, Ruth Ann," Judy mumbled.

"It's okay, Ruth Ann," Ben said. "I've had a long history of anxiety issues and it's hard to overcome in the beginning, but after time, you learn ways of controlling it."

I looked at Ben and remembered how upset he's gotten when he's been questioned about his past. Ben had been known to get hysterical and shut people off when he felt threatened, even when the threat was only in his mind. "Thanks, Ben," I said. "I'll be okay, now. I just had a bad feeling something's about to happen that will change us all."

"Really?" Judy asked curiously. "And what would that be?"

"I have no idea, Judy," I said curtly. "I just said it was a strange feeling, and it made me dizzy."

Judy ignored my comment and turned away from me and looked inside. John was all the way over by the island where Prunella had dumped on me, telling me that she was now on team Axel. I wished I never let her talk me into leaving. I was just so confused and, at the time, hurt by her revelations. But now that I'd had time to think about it, I knew it had to be a lie.

"John's waving for us to come in," Judy said, opening the door and stepping inside. Ben waited for me to go in then joined me in the warm, bright kitchen.

"It feels good in here," I said, opening up the front of the mink coat.

John put his finger up to his mouth. "No talking until I know how safe it is in here." He walked toward the doorway that led to a dining room. We followed him and stepped inside a rustic, medium sized dining room. The other end of the dining room flowed directly into the great room that I was in earlier. The lights were on, but nobody was in sight. John whirled around and headed back into the kitchen and went out another door that led back into the great room where we were waiting for him. "Nothing, not a sign of anybody."

We followed him back into the kitchen and John walked over to a couple doors. The first set of doors opened into a large pantry stocked with food and small appliances. He walked around the island and to a small powder room.

There was another door with a bolt on the top of the door, but it wasn't locked. "They could lock anyone down there with that," he said, pointing to the lock.

"But it's unlocked, let's get down there," I said, hurrying over to John.

"I really wish there was another way, but I can't leave any of you up here."

"You promised we'd stick together this time," I said.

"We don't have a choice," he said. "If this is the basement, I'll go down and see if it's clear. You guys stay up here for a second."

John opened the door and it surely was the basement. I couldn't see the bottom from where I was looking because it was so dark. I was just hoping this basement wasn't like the previous ones. The basement in Sweden was a large, cement walled and floored room where we held Bertha's brothers prisoner until they escaped. The basement here at the large house had a secret room where I've been held shackled to a wall, and recently where we found Helena, murdered.

It didn't take long before John flicked on a light. "C'mon down," he called up to us.

Judy motioned for Ben and me to go first while she went last. I noticed, once the light was on, these stairs were in much better shape than in the other houses. They were carpeted and plush while the other houses' basement stairs were old, wooden, and dangerous to step on with loose boards. I couldn't see the actual basement until I was at the bottom because the wall went all the way up to the ceiling as I descended. Once at the bottom I was stunned at what I saw.

"Isn't what you expected, is it Ruth Ann?" John asked me first.

"No, this is amazing."

"What?" Judy asked when she was just halfway down the stairs. "What's amazing?"

"Get down here and you'll see," I responded.

Once the four of us were together at the base of the staircase, Judy and Ben saw what John and I did. "This is a basement?" Ben asked, surprised. "It's so nice!"

"I know, really," I replied. "It's a nice change from the other ones."

The large open basement was fully carpeted with a high piled carpet. It wasn't just a cement room. This room was dry walled, painted a beautiful, cheery, yellow and furnished with warm weather styled furniture. "What is this place?" I asked, walking over to a rattan loveseat and chair.

"Are we in Colorado still?" Judy asked, stunned. "Whoever decorated this place had a woman's touch for sure."

"*Who* is that woman is my question?" John asked curiously.

"I know what you're getting at John," I answered. "It can't be Prunella because she's only been in Colorado a short time. Not enough to do all this." I waved my arm around the rest of the room that was furnished from top to bottom. There were tropical paintings of palm trees, beautiful flowers and birds, and water scenes staged around the room. Even the entertainment center, which was gigantic, against the far wall was constructed of rattan. "That television is monstrous, too."

"It's gotta be at least a 60-inch screen on that thing!" Ben expressed. "And look at all the speakers around the top of the walls!"

"It's surround sound," John replied unimpressed. "Not that big of a deal with all the money Eklund has."

"It's not the money, John," I said. "Why's it down here, who's been hanging out here? And who furnished it?"

"And look at that bar over there," Judy called out pointing to a long, white wood stained bar along the back sidewall. There were six tall stools on one side and a fully stocked bar, from what I could tell, as well as a mirrored wall on the other side of the bar.

"Whoever planned this layout definitely intended on spending some serious time down here," John said. "But was it built for *someone* else to hang out down here or for themselves?"

"What are you getting at, John?" I asked, confused.

"Look, it's definitely decorated for a female, except for that bar. But the bar is white and not very masculine."

"So what you're saying is that it's possible Axel had this done up to keep someone down here for an extended length of time?"

"Possibly," he said, walking over to the couch and looking underneath the cushions. "Pull-out."

"I've never seen a rattan couch made into a pullout bed," I replied as I inspected the brightly cushioned couch. "Hmm, clever, isn't it?" I held up one of the cherry red cushions with yellow, periwinkle blue, and lavender colored flowers. "If I had a place down in say, Florida, this would be perfect!"

"Not the issue, Ruth Ann," John said, taking the cushion and putting it back on the couch. "It appears someone's used this to sleep on."

"How do you know that, Chief?" Ben inquired.

"The sheets are still on the mattress underneath, and not neatly placed, but messed up like it's been used." He bent over, lifted the cushion for a moment, smelled the sheets and stood back up. "It even smells like a female."

"And how's that?" I asked stiffly.

"I'm not being sexist, Ruth Ann, bend over and smell."

I did as he asked and I hated to disclose there was clearly a scent of perfumed soap on the sheets. "You're right," I admitted. "Hey, maybe it was Prunella, and she was staying down here instead of her story about being back with Axel?"

"How do you mean?" asked John.

"She's insisting that Axel and she are a couple again, right?" The three of them nodded. "Well, that could be part of her lie. She tells me one thing, because she's being threatened by Axel and Svenson, but actually is his prisoner and he put her down in the basement to stay."

"That could work, in fact," John said, pausing. "I hope that's the truth versus the one where she's back with Eklund."

"That will never happen," I declared.

"Okay, we know this basement has been recently occupied. Has anyone noticed a bathroom or other door?" Judy asked impatiently.

We split up and walked around the basement. There was a door next to the bar that led into a small, but luxurious bathroom. There was a jetted tub, clear glassed in shower, a double sink and a separate toilet area. The style in this bathroom was less tropical and more modern. The shower had multiple jets sticking out the front and back and even a rainforest showerhead hanging from the ceiling. The tiling was a darker taupe, much more masculine looking in my opinion. The dual glass bowl sinks were set on a black granite counter and dark cherry cabinets. It was tastefully done, but completely opposite of the adjoining room.

"Nothing strange in here," I said, looking around the spotless bathroom.

"Towels are wet," Judy noticed grabbing a hold of the towel on a rack closet to the shower.

"The shower was also recently used. It still has water drips on the walls and floor."

"Hey, what kind of product is inside the shower?" I asked curiously.

"Who cares?" Judy sarcastically requested.

"And you're a big city detective?" I snapped back. "Look, I know what kind of hair product Prunella uses, and maybe it's in that shower!"

"Great thinking, Ruth Ann," John commended me, sticking his head into the bathroom. Judy glared and I hurried inside the shower grabbing a bottle of Prunella's favorite shampoo and conditioner. "I knew it!" I yelled excited.

"Well, well," John said smiling. "It's looking a lot more like Prunella and Eklund *aren't* back together."

"I knew that wasn't the truth," I stated, feeling happier than I had in a while.

"But, that doesn't mean she's safe," John said, plummeting my hopes for the moment.

"Then let's find this supposed tunnel and go after them!" I said, leaving the bathroom and searching the room for another door. "Hey, there are no other doors down here? Where's this tunnel?"

"If this tunnel exists, it's probably not an obvious opening," John said, walking over to the bar area. "It could be something we're missing," he replied, bending over the inside of the bar area looking at each item near the floor. "Maybe there's a button somewhere on this bar that opens a door or a portion of the wall or something." John and Ben took the inside of the bar while Judy and I searched around the outside of the bar.

"There's nothing I can see here," John said, discouraged. "Maybe it's somewhere else down here." John stood up and headed back to the bottom of the stairs and searched every inch of the wall. He was almost done with the first wall when I pulled out one of the bar stools to sit and rest a second that a loud, screeching noise began.

I yelled out, "What's happening?" I jumped away from the stool as it disappeared into the floor of the basement. "The stool just flipped over and there's a big hole in the floor!" John ran over to where I was standing and pulled me further away so I didn't fall in.

"I don't believe it!" he hollered. "Look, there are stairs that lead into this hole." I took a few steps closer and glanced inside the hole. A light was on the bottom of the stool that was now upside down in the hole hanging there. "It's the tunnel! Ruth Ann, you found it."

It's not like I *intentionally* discovered the tunnel, but I was willing to take the credit for it. "I knew there had to be a trick to getting into the tunnel," I said, gloating a little. Judy gave me a cynical glance revealing that she knew I found it out of sheer dumb luck.

"Stand back," John ordered. "I don't want one of us falling down there. I can see the bottom and it's about ten steps down, but the steps are steep so it would be a nasty spill." I backed away allowing Judy and Ben to take a peek. "Okay, we have one gun, and a couple of flashlights. I don't think that's enough. Check the bar drawers and cabinets to see if there's anything else we can use before we head into the tunnel."

I hurried over to the bar before Judy and opened drawer after drawer. Judy hit the upper cabinets attached to the mirrored wall. "Nothing in here but booze," she said.

"Aha!" I cried out. "I had a little better luck. There are knives, all sizes, in this drawer." I held out a small, paring knife in one hand, and a large, chopping knife in the other.

"Bring both, Ruth Ann," John asked. The only other item I grabbed, but didn't mention, was a lighter that could be stuffed inside my pocket. You never know when it could come in handy as either a light source or if I needed to burn something or someone.

Ben was standing with John as he descended the steep stairs. The light from the backside of the stool only showed the steps, not what was waiting at the bottom. John was fully aware of this and demanded that we wait until he hit the bottom and looked ahead. It didn't take him more than a few seconds before he told us to come down in the order he requested. First, I went with the help of Ben following me and holding on to one of my arms to keep me steady. I didn't think that was necessary until I went down one of the steps. It was quite a large, steep drop and I was thankful for Ben's assistance once I made the plunge down the stairs.

Once at the bottom, I shrugged Ben's hand off my arm and looked at my surroundings. I didn't mean to hurt Ben's feelings, and I thanked him for his help. He didn't seem put out by my actions because he was also gazing down the long, cold, dimly lit hall constructed of cement. "Wow," I said listening to my voice echo in the institutional environment. "I feel like I'm in some kind of bunker used for emergencies years ago."

"It was well constructed, that's for sure," John stated. "Let's head down and see where it takes us." He added, "Try not to make any noises. Everything echoes in here."

We trudged forward and I noticed the upward inclination as we pressed on. "We're going uphill a little," I mentioned.

"I noticed," John said, walking up to one of the electric torches that dimly lit the tunnel. "It had to be used recently," he said looking under the torch and opening up the back of it. "They got juice down here." He pointed to a cord that ran from torch to torch.

"I'm just grateful for some light. I don't want any surprises while we're down here. There's nowhere to run to escape."

"Just where we came from and wherever we heading to," Judy said, beginning to walk ahead of John who was replacing the torch. He let her lead for a short time when he took a hold of her arm and stopped her. "Shhh," he whispered. "I think I hear something ahead."

My heart started to pound and the walls were beginning to close in on me. I told myself to keep it together and that I could handle whatever would happen to us. Breath, Ruth Ann, just keep breathing.

John gave Judy a slight shove to the side so he could step in front of her. She let him slowly go forward, the one gun we had was in his hand aiming straight ahead. Judy held the large, chopping knife and Ben and I had nothing. Except, the lighter I grabbed inside my pants pocket. "Do you hear that?" he murmured to us. "I hear some kind of muffled noise ahead, like voices."

"I don't hear anything," Judy replied anxiously. "You think someone's just ahead of us?"

"Maybe, we're going to take this slowly," he said, starting to walk again.

Judy was right on John's heels. Ben and I were two steps behind her. Ben was walking next to me because the tunnel was wide enough for two or three people to walk side by side, and about seven feet high. We made it another minute when John turned around and put his finger to his mouth. "Someone's just ahead of us." He put his hand up now and had us stay behind while he went on. Judy didn't follow his order and followed him anyway. John didn't want to make any noise so he let her, but the scowl he gave her was priceless.

If anything, this will show John that Judy wasn't the big city detective he had hoped to hire. I looked over at Ben and his wide-open eyes appeared to be popping out of his head. "It's okay, Ben," I whispered as softly as I could. "John will handle this. I'm sure it's okay."

He nodded his head to agree with me, but I could tell he was nervous. So was I! We waited until John and Judy disappeared around a slight curve in the tunnel. "I'm not staying back here," I said to Ben grabbing his arm and leading him forward. "Let's get up a little closer to them so we don't get separated." We took tiny, soft steps trying not to be heard until we made it around the curve. John had made a left turn into the side of the wall. It looked like he disappeared into the cement wall! "What the…" I started to say when Judy put her finger to her mouth and waved us forward.

Ben stood solid in his stance until I grabbed his hand and gave it a little a squeeze. "C'mon, it'll be okay." He nodded and we moved forward to where Judy was and what I saw brought me to my knees.

I make no excuse for my next reaction. I crawled over to the cubbyhole that was carved into the tunnel. I couldn't find my voice at the moment, but my body went right up to the individual tied and gagged in a metal chair. John took my hands and heaved me to a standing position as I threw my arms around my daughter, Lynne. John backed up for a moment once he removed the gag from my daughter's mouth.

"Mom, thank God you found me in here," she said with a dry, brittle voice.

"What on earth are you doing in here?" I summoned somehow, completely stunned.

"I was never brought back to my store like you were told," she said, regaining her speech. "I was brought down here and thrown into this chair and tied up"

"That's horrible," I cried out. "They didn't hurt you, did they?" I looked her from head to toe to make sure she was truly unharmed.

Lynne shook her head while accepting a mint from Ben who held one out in his trembling hand. "Thanks," she said kindly to him. "This will help."

John asked, "Who exactly is *they*?"

"Mr. Eklund and his henchmen." She chewed the mint and Ben handed her one more. "And that lawyer, what's his name?"

"Svenson," John answered.

"That's it!" she exclaimed. "He's seriously disturbed, Mom. That isn't the lawyer Prunella uses is it?"

"It's his cousin, Steven Svenson."

"Before we get you out of here, tell me exactly what happened." John ordered politely.

"I was dragged out to Prunella's estate from your store." She stopped, hesitated a minute and added, "Prunella's in on it, Mom. She was with Mr. Eklund and they were definitely not estranged."

"I've heard," I said, not going into my theory about them yet.

"They forced some kind of liquid down my throat and the next thing I knew I was sitting in this chair in this tunnel."

"They drugged you!" I yelled.

"Ruth Ann," John said, glaring at me. "Do you want them to come back and finish all of us off? Keep your voice down. I know you want revenge now that Lynne's been involved again, but let's get everyone out of this safely, please." I calmed down and let Lynne continue.

"I don't know how I got in here and how long I've been here." She looked at John and me and said, "I'm sorry, I'm not being much help."

"Nothing to be sorry for," John stated. "None of this is your fault."

"How did they force the liquid in you?" I asked, knowing I'd be sorry I asked the question.

"When I was thrown into their limousine, Eklund motioned for one of his men to hold my arms down and the other to hold my legs. I was fighting pretty hard, Mom."

I wanted to scream and find Axel myself, and then I'd shoot him! But instead, I said, "You're tough, just like your mother!"

Lynne smiled dryly and continued. "Mr. Eklund told me to settle down or they would have to hurt me. I forced myself to cool down a little when one of his men forced my mouth open and shoved a small bottle in my mouth and poured whatever liquid was inside down my throat. I gagged and spit out some, but there must've been just enough in my system to knock me out."

"That's all you remember?" John inquired.

"Yes. Until I woke up here." Lynne looked around her surroundings and asked. "Where are we anyway?"

"In a tunnel off of the guesthouse on the property," I answered.

"What guesthouse?"

"If you look out the back of the kitchen you'll see a large garage in the distance. There's a path that leads down the mountain a little and stepping out of the forest a huge, log cabin appears out of nowhere."

"So they brought me all the way to this cabin?"

"Unless," John said, backing into the middle of the tunnel and looking toward the direction we came from.

"What're you thinking John?" Judy asked him.

"This tunnel must be to and from the large house to the cabin. Where else would it lead to?"

"I guess I thought it would come out into the night air somewhere near here," Judy replied. "Where would there be a tunnel entrance in the big house?"

"We're about to find out," John said, walking over to Lynne and asking her if she was strong enough to walk.

"I feel fine," she answered. "I don't like it in here anyway. Let's get going." John helped Lynne stand and outside of a slight wobble or two she appeared quite herself.

We headed down the tunnel, which was gradually ascending. I was anxious to find out where this tunnel led. John and Judy walked side by side with Lynne and me behind them. Ben was at the back end of our group constantly whipping his head around making sure nobody would sneak up on us. We must've walked for several minutes when we came upon a few wooden steps that led up to a wooden door. It was the end of the tunnel.

"This is either going to open up to the outside, which I highly doubt, or to somewhere in Eklund's estate," John declared.

"I don't know which one I'd rather have it be," I said. "If we end up outside, we can find a way to get Lynne back into town safely. However, if we end up somewhere inside the house, we can search for Prunella and get her, Inga, and Sherman out of there."

"Wait!" Lynne exclaimed holding my arm to stop me.

"What's the problem?" I asked her, knowing well enough that she would fight going back into town without me.

"Why would we take Prunella and Sherman out of here? They've betrayed you. I get that we have to save Inga, they kidnapped her!"

"I don't believe that's true, Lynne," I said steadily. I watched as Lynne's shocked face turned red. "Don't be angry, Prunella's been forced to take Axel's side so he doesn't hurt me. I believe that's the truth."

"I don't believe that!" Lynne argued. "First, I saw how Prunella and Axel were acting with each other. Either Prunella's a really good actor or he's drugged her with something, too. Second, didn't you just tell me that Prunella kicked you out of her life? Told you to go away and never come back? And what about Sherman, he lied to all of you!"

"Maybe he had no choice," John interrupted. "I think Ruth Ann's theory could be accurate. Prunella must be threatened to go along with them or they'll kill Ruth Ann and possibly even you."

"Exactly," I agreed. "She didn't have any choice. We have to find out where they have her, Inga, and even Sherman, quickly."

Judy had made her way to the wooden door and was examining it closely. She was about to reach for the long, metal handle when John brushed her hand away. "No!"

"I was just going to see if it's unlocked, John." Judy stepped back and let John take the lead. "Go ahead, the door's all yours," she said tersely.

"Once I open this door, I want all of you to be ready for what may or may not be on the other side."

"What're you expecting to find, John?" I asked. "I doubt whatever we walk into will be where Axel and the rest of them are."

"I agree, but you never know if he's got one of his men standing guard at the entrance to the tunnel. I want you, Lynne, and Ben to stand back until I see where we've ended up." John waited for the three of us to respond and then he reached for the handle and pushed it open. The door squeaked as it moved, and I couldn't help but step a little closer so I could see. "Judy, be ready." John stepped inside a black hole and Judy followed him in.

Lynne was holding onto my shoulders while standing behind me trying to get her own look at what was going on. "Do we just stay here?" she asked.

"I'm not going to for long," I replied. "It looks pitch black inside there," I said, only a few feet away from the doorway. I looked for Ben and he was standing next to Lynne not looking in the direction of the newly opened door, but behind us making sure nobody was going to sneak up from behind.

A minute later John waved us in. "It's dark so watch your footing," he said, reaching for my hand.

"Why's it so dark in there?" Ben asked, terrified.

"It's a cellar off the basement," John answered. "When I stepped inside there were only a couple of feet then I hit a dead end."

"But we didn't see you or Miss Judy so where'd you go if there wasn't much room?" Ben inquired curiously.

"You see, Ben, in front of me was the back of some kind of shelving. I grabbed one of the ends of it and it slid off to the side. Once inside, I noticed the shelves were full of wine bottles."

"So it's a wine cellar," I said, making sense of it. "How'd you move such a heavy portion of it?"

"It was only a few feet wide and there were only a few bottles on this particular shelf. It must've been set up so the tunnel door was accessible."

"Makes sense," I said. "If it was too heavy you wouldn't have been able to move it."

"Or anyone else," Lynne added.

"Yes, Lynne," John said. "I don't think it was because of us. I'm sure it's always fairly empty so whoever needs to escape into the tunnels can do so quickly."

I stepped inside the cellar and noticed hundreds of bottles of wine. There was a temperature-controlled thermostat in between one of the shelving units to keep it at an exact temperature for the wine. "I didn't know this room existed," I said looking around the large, dusty cellar.

"Where does it go?" Lynne asked, walking over to the door on the other side of the room.

"I'm assuming we're in the basement," John answered her.

"How many secret rooms does this man have?" Lynne inquired. "He's got his torture room, cellars, that nicely done one back at the cabin." She quickly added, "And I didn't even see the one back in Sweden. What was in that basement?"

"Nothing but a large, cement room," I said, remembering when Inga, Inga's cousins, and I held Bertha's brothers hostage down there. They were able to escape, but met a horrible death in the end due to their greediness.

"How boring," Lynne joked, but I reminded her what happened in the Sweden house basement, and she said she was sorry. She was just trying to lighten up the darkened mood we were in. "Maybe we should try and get out of here?"

"I'm going to open the next door. If I'm right, there probably won't be anybody down here. I'm sure they've already made their way upstairs and possibly fled entirely."

"No, they wouldn't leave, would they?" I asked. "Where would they go now?"

"Let's cross that bridge when it comes up," Judy replied for him. She turned to John and whispered something.

"Hey, no secrets," I cried out. "Tell us what Judy just told you," I demanded.

"She said, Ruth Ann, that we need to check the other secret room down here."

"I figured that," I said, irritated. "I still have Helena's death fresh in my head. It hasn't even been twenty-four hours since we found her down here."

John walked over to the door and put his head up to it. "I can't hear anything so I'm going to open this door now." He grabbed the door handle and pulled it toward him. He stuck his head out into the next room and told us it was the basement, but not where he thought it would be. "It's in the room with the hole and wall with shackles, Ruth Ann." He was warning me because I really didn't want to go back in there ever.

"Please tell me there's not anyone hanging from the wall or thrown into that hole?" The hole I was referring to was where Paul, the hired security guard, was thrown a number of weeks ago. I was shackled to the wall and even though we both got out without serious injury, it was still a place I didn't care to revisit. Especially since Helena was just found dead in here earlier that day. Or was it Monday now?

Chapter 32

"It's okay, Ruth Ann," John said, after sticking his head into the secret room. "Nobody's in here, and it doesn't look like anyone's been in here recently."

"How do you know nobody's been in here?" Lynne asked John.

"The police tape is still up and I can't see any signs other than the fact they must've come through here with Inga and Prunella."

"So where'd they go?" I asked, frustrated with all the dead ends.

"They could still be upstairs or they left."

"They better not have," I declared. "If they think we're going back to Sweden they're sadly mistaken."

"If they did are you just going to let them go?" Lynne asked me. "I mean, it's your cousin and you haven't known her *that* long, Mom."

"I feel like I've known her my entire life, and I can't imagine never seeing her or Inga again."

What would I do if I found out Prunella willingly left the country and went back to Sweden with her evil husband, Axel? I didn't want to think about it until I knew for sure they weren't somewhere in the house. But why would they stay? Surely they knew we were after them and Axel would be sent right back to prison.

"Are you okay, Mom?" Lynne asked.

"Oh, sorry, I was just thinking about what I would do if they did indeed leave the country."

"And?" John asked me curiously.

"I don't know." I truly didn't know at the moment. "Can we just get out of this room, please? I hate it in here and the dried blood of Helena is still all over the walls."

John hurried the group into the main section of the basement. He made sure nobody was waiting for us, and then we headed toward the stairs that will take us into the kitchen. "This is where we really have to be careful."

"Sherman may be up there," Ben added. "Maybe he can help us."

"Sherman?" Judy exclaimed. "He's betrayed us. Why would he help us now?"

"Maybe he didn't have a choice, Judy," I said. "Just like Prunella, he may have had to go along with Axel."

"Possibly," she said. "That surely didn't happen with Inga. I bet she fought them the whole time, and still fighting them."

"That's what worries me," John mentioned.

"They better not have hurt her," I cried out.

"Or worse," Judy added.

"Thanks a lot, Judy," I said, ticked off at her for even implying what she was. "They won't kill her. Prunella won't let them!"

"I sure hope not," Judy mumbled softly, but I still heard her.

We followed John over to the stairs. "I'm going up. You stay put for just a minute. I'll wave you up when it's safe."

"Want me to come with?" Judy asked.

"Not this time. I want to be as quiet as I can and these stairs are old and unsteady. They'll make too much noise with the both of us tramping up them."

He left us at the base of the stairs. There was no light in the basement because John didn't want to alert anyone to our presence. He turned on his flashlight that he was using and put it under his long-sleeved, navy police chief t-shirt. He was dimming any light that was coming from his flashlight. Once the wall closed from the secret room, the darkness surrounded us.

I could only make out John's form as he made his way to the top landing that was only about two feet by two feet. I wasn't sure how long he was going to take before trying to open the door. It felt like hours when I noticed the light from a crack in the door. He must've opened it up an inch or two to peek into the kitchen. I noticed Judy had already walked up a step or two when John opened the door all the way and disappeared into the kitchen.

"Hey," I whispered to the others. "Where'd he go?"

"He must be alone or possibly confronting Sherman," Judy replied. "Give him a couple of minutes, and then I'll go up after him."

However, it didn't take that long. The door opened up temporarily blinding Judy, Ben, Lynne, and me. I grabbed Judy's arm, as she was about to run up the stairs. "Hold on, make sure it's John, would you!"

She halted and I took my hand off her. Ben and Lynne were right behind me as we made our way half way up the stairs before we caught sight of John standing at the top. "It's okay, c'mon up."

Judy hurried up first with me close behind her. Lynne and Ben trailed behind me. "Is it all clear?" Judy asked.

"Not quite," John said, rolling his eyes to the side as if we were able to see what he was motioning at.

"What's the problem?" Judy asked.

John stepped away from the door and we immediately saw what the problem was. "Do what they say," John said as I observed a gun pressed against his back.

"All right," a deep, stern voice called out. "All of you, up here, now. And don't try any funny stuff."

Judy was the first to get off the landing into the kitchen. I was still on the top step when I saw an arm roughly grab Judy and pat her down. "She's clean," a male voice called out after finding the knife Judy had shoved in her sock under her pants.

I was next entering the kitchen. I slowly stepped one foot off the landing and a hand took my arm and pulled me the rest of the way in. "Hey, go easy with her," John ordered, but the man holding the gun in his back shoved it into his back a little harder.

"Shut up!" The voice snapped back. I looked at the person who grabbed my arm and didn't recognize him.

"Who are you?" I demanded.

"Ah, we haven't met, have we?" I looked at this tall, medium build man who had blonde hair, but graying at the temples. He didn't look like one of the goons Axel usually hired. "You're Svenson, aren't you?"

"You figured it out, Ruth Ann," he said mockingly. "Yes, I'm *Steven* Svenson. You've only heard about my good little cousin, Michael Svenson."

"Actually," I said, trying to release my arm from his too tight grip. "I haven't met him either. I know both your names and yours isn't the one I care to know."

"Easy, Ruth Ann," John said. "Do what he wants."

"You'd better listen to your police chief or you could end up like that maid."

"Helena!" I bellowed. "You murdered her?"

"Me? No, I just stood and watched my men carry out my order."

"But why would you kill an innocent young girl? She didn't do anything to *you*!"

"You have no idea what she did."

I wanted to waste more time hoping somebody could come up with a plan. Lynne and Ben were inside the kitchen now staring at what was happening. I was hoping they'd make a run for it back into the basement and through the tunnel, but that could put them at risk for being chased and shot. "Why don't you tell me what a twenty-something, homeless girl did to you?" I asked cynically.

He took the bait and pulled me over to the large marble island that separated the kitchen in the middle. He pulled out a stool and took me under the arms from behind and planted me it. "Wait here," he ordered as he went back to Lynne and Ben. "You two follow me." Lynne and Ben walked behind Svenson and he took them over to the kitchen table that was not far from where I sat on the stool. "Stay here. Any movement from either of you will force me to put you in much less comfortable positions, got it?" They nodded and sat down in the chairs he pulled out for them. He walked back over to where John and Judy were being held by gunpoint. "Keep them still," he ordered the armed man. He nodded and I watched as John and Judy's backs were against the wall as the armed man stood in front of them with the gun aimed at the two of them.

"Okay, we're all here, now explain to me what Helena did?" I said with authority. Svenson slowly walked back to me and sat down on the stool very close to me. I eyed John and knew he'd be willing to risk his life to get this creepy lawyer away from me.

"Are you in the position to be giving orders to me?" he asked, his face inches from mine. His breath smelled of whiskey and cigars.

"Of course not," I stated. "You're the ones with the gun."

"Good, as long as we got that straightened out I will tell you what that young, not so innocent maid did."

"STEVEN," a sudden loud voice came from the doorway that led to the butler's pantry. "What on earth do you think you're doing?"

It was Axel! I hadn't seen him since we were back in Sweden. Steven swiftly backed away from me and stood up. "What? I was just about to explain to our guests what Helena did to deserve her punishment."

"Punishment?" I cried out. "You just admitted to killing her."

"Correction, Ruth Ann, I admitted to watching her be killed."

"ENOUGH!" Axel yelled from across the room. He walked over to where John and Judy were being held and hesitated for only a second. He made his way to the island where I still sat. "Ruth Ann," he began to say. "I'm sorry for this man's rude behavior. It won't happen again."

"Huh?" Steven and I said at the same time.

"Steven, take our other guests and put them in the library. Keep them safe, but unharmed, in there until I come." He looked over at me and said, "Ruth Ann and I will have a little chat first."

"No way," John hollered. "She stays with us."

"Ah, Chief Wilkinson, you don't seem to be in the position to tell me where to keep anyone at the moment. But, I will give you my word, which you may or may not believe, that I won't harm her. I just want to have a little chat with her."

"Your word?" John remarked.

"I know you may not take my word, but I believe you don't have any choice but to accept it." He sat down on the stool next to me, but not as close as Steven Svenson was. He waited for his armed guard and Svenson to leave with Ben, Lynne, Judy, and a reluctant John. "I'll be fine," I said to him as he resisted too much with his guard. "Axel won't hurt me."

"Of course not," Axel replied in a calm, kind tone. Just as he was when I first encountered him, and then he turned around and kidnapped me and brought me to Sweden. Even then, he remained a perfect gentleman with me until the very end when his back was up against the wall and he thought he lost everything, including the precious necklace.

Once we were alone, I found I wasn't nervous at all. I had so many questions that my mind didn't know where to begin, but Axel started for me. "I assume you have a lot you want to know, Ruth Ann."

"Yes, but there's so much, I don't know where to begin."

"Why don't you let me do the talking at first, and then you can ask me whatever I don't cover. Sound like a plan?"

"Sure, I guess," confused at how kind he was being, again.

"First, let me answer your most pertinent question, I believe. Prunella's safe, happy, and willingly here with me." He held up his hand to stop my protesting. "Let me finish, please." I nodded shutting my mouth. "Inga's also here, but she's been a bit more difficult to deal with. I'm afraid she had to be sedated for the time being. Inga's very loyal to Prunella and she doesn't believe me when I tell her Prunella's here of her own volition."

He let me speak for a moment. "Are you telling me Inga hasn't even seen Prunella?"

"Not yet," he answered. "She put up such a, what do you call it, stink? Yes, that's it. She put up such a stink that I had no choice but to calm her down first. She's resting nicely upstairs on the third floor in her old room."

"Seriously?" was all I could mutter because I was too stunned by what he was saying.

"Yes, it's her room, why not let her be comfortable? I will add that she does have a man standing guard at her door. So don't let your friend, Chief Wilkinson, get any ideas."

"Where's Prunella, why can't I see her?"

"She's left you to me for the time being."

"*She* told you to do that?"

"Yes, Ruth Ann. Prunella's not the mean, spiteful person you are thinking she's turned into. She does care about you, but you won't let her live her life with me without interfering. That's why I'm having this talk with you."

"But you'll go straight to jail. You won't be able to live freely because you've broken so many laws and even murder."

"Oh, that's where you're wrong, Ruth Ann," he said, perfectly sanely.

"You had Helena killed, for some reason. Then there's Bert, why would you kill Bert? Oh, and we found some disturbing pictures in Bert's luggage." Axel looked strangely at me. "Are you his *son?*"

"I'll get to that."

"Fine, but please do, I don't like being separated from my daughter and the rest of them."

He stood up and walked over to the kitchen stove and grabbed the teakettle. Once he filled the kettle with water and turned it on he came to the opposite side of the island and said, "I'm making us a cup of tea then I'll continue."

Did he do that on purpose because I asked him to hurry up and tell me what was going on?

I sat quietly until the teakettle whistled loudly and he grabbed it and poured two cups of hot, steaming tea. "Here," he said, sliding a full cup over to me. "And you watched me the entire time. I didn't slip anything in it."

"I've thought that before and somehow you managed to slip stuff in my drink."

"Not this time, I want to you listen very carefully to everything I say."

I didn't say anything, but sipped my tea slowly and listened closely to what he told me, and then I'd be able to tell John. We could figure out what to do once I returned to them.

"So, let me see, what else am I able to tell you," he said, drinking his tea. "Ah, you first need to know how I came back to Deer Creek from the jail in Sweden."

"How did you pretend to be dead, but then end up here?"

"That was carefully planned back in Stockholm when I was stuck inside that filthy, tiny cell. Once I was thrown in the cell, I requested a call to my lawyer. I called Steven Svenson."

"So that's why he's here," I said.

"Kind of. He's been after my, oops excuse me, our necklace for a long time, too. Ever since his cousin, Michael, found out about it. I know he's a dirty lawyer, but I needed someone like him to get me out of jail."

"I thought you were stabbed and died on the way to the hospital."

"That was just a ruse, Ruth Ann. I pretended to be stabbed so they would transport me to the hospital. Once in the ambulance, I had Steven arrange for me to escape. He and I both had connections inside the police station so it wasn't hard to arrange."

"So they transported you in an ambulance and said you died along the way, right?"

"Yes, exactly."

"But didn't the authorities need a body?"

"The cops in my pay took care of that."

"So, case closed right?"

"Exactly, again! I was able to get to one of my planes and follow your little group back to Deer Creek."

"How could the police let you take off and land here?"

"They thought Axel Eklund was dead, but Steven Svenson wasn't and he was my lawyer so he was able to utilize my plane to get here for my other properties and assets."

"So you used him just as much as he used you?"

"Yes, I was well aware he was after the necklace, and he knew Prunella and you were here in Deer Creek."

"Okay, I get how you came here, but what happened once you arrived?"

"Well, I obviously couldn't stay here in the house. You were living here. That's when my two men, Svenson, and I put ourselves up in the guesthouse."

"And we didn't know about that place, but Bert did, right?"

"Now we're getting to Bert. Yes, he and I were in close contact. He was my eyes and ears back at the big house. I know you came to the conclusion that he was my father. You are seriously mistaken. Bert was never my father. He was my father's brother. He turned on my parents when I was still quite young. I, being the fair-minded person I am, gave him another chance later on in his years. He became my butler, that's all."

"So, Bert's your uncle, but he betrayed your father somehow and your parents disowned him?" Axel nodded. "Then, after your parents died you took him back into your life, but as your butler?" Axel nodded again. "So, if he was on your side why did you murder him?"

"Bert, believe it or not, was changing loyalties once again. He started having feelings for Prunella."

"He was falling in love with her?"

"No, not those kind of feelings, but he started to respect her and he couldn't believe how nasty he had been and she still didn't kick him out. His mistake was telling me this. I couldn't risk Bert telling Prunella that I was here, not yet."

"So you had him killed? And were you aware of how he was killed?" I asked, shocked at his nonchalant attitude about killing, burning, and hanging a man from a ceiling for everyone in town to see.

"That wasn't supposed to happen."

"But you ordered it!"

"No, I told Steven to handle Bert, but I never would've agreed with what he did. That's when I realized just how ruthless this man really is."

"And now you're in too deep with him and owe him too much, right?"

"I will admit I wasn't aware of how far this man would go to get what he wanted. But now that I'm cognizant of it, I won't let him pull a stunt like that again."

"I wouldn't call what he did a stunt. Why don't you just turn him in?"

"Because then *I'd* have to go to jail, too."

"What about Helena? Did Steven do that, too?"

"Yes, but her situation was a little different."

"How so?" I questioned him.

"I'm going to tell you something that may shock you." He smiled and added, "Even more than what's happened already."

"I can't imagine that."

"Helena did come back to my estate because she had nowhere else to go. She's been lying all along. She was never homeless or brought here because I gave her a second chance at a good living."

"Oh, don't tell me she was in your pay, too? I'm confused at who is and isn't on your side." Before he could answer me I added, "So, who is this woman and how did she get involved in your life?"

"Helena wasn't as young as she told you. She was in her early thirties, but looked like a woman ten years younger. I've known Helena for over ten years."

"Wait a minute! Are you telling me Helena and you were involved? As in a *relationship*?"

"Not like I was with Prunella. Prunella and I worked together, and we had a real relationship. My late wife and I had no relationship at all. She was only good at threatening me."

"Taking over your companies and all your assets, right?"

"Yes."

"Because you didn't have her sign a prenup, but she made you sign one?"

"Yes, let's not go down that path again. I'm painfully aware of my stupidity back then."

"Okay, I think I understand. Prunella was more on your level, intellectually, while Helena's was more of a physical thing?"

"You make me sound horrible, but yes, Helena and I became involved in a less than proper way."

"Why did she lie to John and all of us?"

"She only came back to the estate on my request. I contacted her the minute I landed in Colorado and told her what to do."

"Which was to get her old job back by saying she had nowhere else to go and then spy on us, correct?"

"Yes."

"But I thought Judy was caring for her well-being while we were in Sweden."

"She went along with that pain of a detective, if that's what you want to call her."

I couldn't help myself, but I laughed. Axel joined in and for a moment (slight), I forgot our troubles. "Okay, so what happened to her then?"

"She got in some other kind of trouble," he said lowering his head. "She wasn't supposed to die, but when the news came to me, I had to try and get rid of her."

"Couldn't you have just sent her back to Mexico or wherever she came from? Why did you have to kill her, and again, stab and hang her up in shackles in that secret room of yours down in the basement?"

"Once again, you're correct. She was just supposed to overdose and it would've looked like an attempted suicide, but Svenson took it a step too far, again." He waited for my reaction, but I wanted him to continue. "She was pregnant and claimed it was mine. I didn't believe her at first, but she swore she only slept with me."

"And you believed her?"

"Not at first, but once I saw the pregnancy tests I didn't think she was lying. I was scared, believe it or not, I didn't need this complication so I asked her to get it taken care of."

"You wanted her to end her pregnancy?"

"No, no, I wanted her to go back to her hometown in Mexico and have the baby and live the rest of her life down there. She flatly refused and said she deserved the money and possessions that Prunella had access to."

"Oh, I get it. Since Prunella didn't give you an heir and she could?"

"Yes, and she was getting greedy and threatening to expose me."

"I assume you're not just talking about the pregnancy, but your plans here in Deer Creek? Which, of course, you haven't really told me."

"Yes, Helena turned on me. She wasn't innocent and easy to manipulate. She threatened that if I didn't make her my wife, with the money and grand lifestyle, she would tell Prunella what I was up to and that she was having my baby."

"So, what were your plans been anyway?"

"Let me finish with Helena first."

"It's obvious, you forced a bottle of pills down her, then Steven took her down to the basement and stabbed her several times after hanging her in the shackles."

"Yes, but I told him to only give her enough pills to temporarily knock her out. Then he was to send her back to Mexico and take away any documentation she had to enter your country so she couldn't come back here. She could live her life down there and have the baby. I was even willing to give her all the money she would ever need, but he didn't listen. He told me that she would've come back and exposed the both of us."

"And you believed him? After what he did to Bert?"

"Look, you don't understand. There's a lot going on here, and I didn't need Helena ruining it. I'm sorry for what happened to her, but I truly didn't plan on her being murdered, plus my baby, don't forget that too."

"Were you ever planning on acknowledging your child even if she lived back in Mexico?"

"I don't know," he said, visually upset. "I would love to have a son or a daughter, but I'm too old for that stuff now. I would've taken care of the both of them though."

"As long as she stayed away from here, right?"

"Unfortunately, yes."

"So, you only claim responsibility for drugging Helena, not for her murder?"

"Yes, Ruth Ann, you can believe me or not. I know we have an up and down relationship. I've always tried to treat you with respect and even when I've forced you to stay with me I gave you a nice place to stay and as much freedom as I could. But you betrayed me with Prunella."

"Do you blame me? You did kidnap me and have me transported to Sweden just to get a necklace back that I never even owned. Of course when I heard about Prunella's circumstances back there and the fact we're cousins, we bonded and I took her side. You got greedy and broke the law several times over. Once you felt trapped your personality changed. You turned evil. I think you would've killed us yourself a short time ago."

"I admit I was horrible back in Sweden when I got caught. I try to pride myself on my calm thinking and manners, but when my boats blew up and I felt my businesses were doomed, I flipped out."

"I'll say. You held us by gunpoint in your office at Eklund Industries, and if Bertha didn't lunge at you I don't know how it would've turned out."

"I agree, Ruth Ann. I disarmed John and that detective, and Bertha's brothers were stashed away in my walk-in safe. Bertha thought she and I would live happily ever after, and when I told her I didn't love her she went mad and came after me. That gave John his moment to attack me. I have to say I'm not that sad over Bertha's or her brothers' deaths. They were more evil than I was at that time." He picked up his teacup, took a swig, placed it gently down on the island and said, "But I do feel horrible about Helena and my unborn child."

"I do believe you about Helena," I admitted, feeling sorry for this man. I know he's done horrible things, but I truly felt he didn't mean for Helena and his child to be harmed.

"Thank you." He perked up a bit and said, "So, let's get back to the matter at hand." He looked at me straight in the eyes with all sincerity, "As long as you're satisfied with what happened to Bert and Helena that is?"

"I guess so. At least I know *you* weren't the one who murdered those two so horrifically. I can't believe anyone would be that sick."

"Svenson is ruthless, I know that now."

"But why are you still working with him? He's a loose canon and now he's in the library with my friends. Can you trust him enough to leave him alone with anyone else that's against him?"

"My other men are with him and they've been filled in on Svenson. They're not to let them know that he's to be watched carefully, but if Svenson tries to harm anyone else, I'm to be warned immediately."

"Okay, as long as your men can control him."

"They can. Remember, Svenson's just a lawyer. He hasn't had a long past of criminal activity. He's been a crooked lawyer for years and years, but physically harming and killing people is fairly new to the guy."

"So, tell me what your plans have been once you got back to Deer Creek?"

"Yes, I'm willing to divulge my plans because I feel you and I have a bond, whether you want to admit that or not, we do." He waited for my response, but I didn't give one. I didn't want to admit to him that I agreed. For some very strange reason this man and I can talk things through. It's not that I trusted him, but on the other hand, I didn't distrust him either.

"When I arrived here with Svenson, the plans were to retrieve the necklace. Svenson only cared about the necklace. I lied to him and told him if he helped get it and my other assets back, I would give him the necklace."

"And he believed you?"

"He's so full of greed he had no idea I was playing him."

"Not such a great lawyer."

"Nope. He's a crooked, dirty lawyer. He didn't even have me sign a contract agreeing to the exchange with the necklace."

"From what Prunella told me, he would defend rather seedy clients."

"You're being nice, Ruth Ann. I'll just say it…mobsters."

"Yes, that's what I heard to."

"From Prunella, right?"

"Yes, because his cousin, Michael, was on the up and up, and couldn't stand Steven."

"Prunella and I haven't always agreed lately, but this one I'll give her. She's right."

"Okay, so you both came here to get back your life?"

"And the necklace, don't forget that."

"Yes, yes, I'm a little tired of the necklace. It's caused more harm than it's worth, Axel."

"Oh, never say that, Ruth Ann. That necklace is all I have from my past. It means more than money. It stands for everything I was raised to fight for. My family, my money, my pride…"

"To be frank, Axel, that makes no sense. It's a material item and you can't take it with you. Let go of this obsession with material things such as the necklace and your money, homes, and businesses."

"Easier said than done. This is all I've known for about seventy years. My life revolves around my father and grandfather's business, and this necklace. To just say give it up isn't possible for me."

"I don't understand it, but I'm not you. Go on."

"So, since the police would arrest me immediately, I had to hide my existence. You understand that so far?"

"Yes."

"Svenson, two of my loyal men for years, who worked undercover as cops, and I hid out in the guesthouse. The plan was to contact Prunella and convince her to hand over the necklace. Then we could split up some of my assets so she would live a wealthy, comfortable life. I told her she could even keep the Deer Creek estate since you and she were growing closer."

"She didn't agree, did she?"

"Oh, no, she blew up when she heard my voice. She still wanted to believe that I was killed back in Sweden."

"How did you contact her?"

"It was right after Helena was discovered yesterday morning."

"Prunella was acting strangely toward lunchtime."

"Yes, I'm about to upset you, Ruth Ann. I told her that if she told you or anyone that I contacted her that I would kill you."

"Me?"

"I had to hit her hard so she would take me seriously and do what I requested."

"So I was right!"

"Right about what?"

"I knew Prunella didn't go back to you because she fell back in love with you."

"No, she did, Ruth Ann."

"No way! You're lying."

He stood up and walked around to my side of the island and sat on the stool next to me. "How about I tell the whole story then you can ask questions? We keep getting sidetracked and I'm not that comfortable leaving your friends, and Lynne, in the library with Svenson."

"But you said your men would warn you if there's any trouble with him."

"They will, but for how long?"

"Okay, I won't interrupt you."

"Thank you. Prunella turned me down flat, at first. I told her to think about what I said and I would contact her again." He knew I was dying to ask a question, but he continued. "I know she must've been distracted with you, but I warned her not to tell you. Don't blame Prunella, she was protecting you." What I really wanted to ask was how he contacted her or who did use to he contact her?

"I bet you're wondering how I contacted her?" I nodded enthusiastically. "I texted her. That simple." Really? I didn't even think to look at her cell phone. Not that I would snoop on somebody's phone unless I really, really had to.

"I told her that after she read it to delete it immediately. I don't even know if she did that. I never checked her cell phone. She did respond to me, and I won't even tell you what she typed because it wasn't very ladylike!"

"Of course not!"

"Hold on, Ruth Ann. I know you're always going to jump to her side. Yes, I did threaten your life, but I needed her to listen and quickly. So, I waited fifteen minutes and texted her to go somewhere in the house where no one could hear her. I wanted to talk to her not text." He saw my brain going back in time and wondering when Prunella was alone. She did storm off and even used the excuse that she put the necklace in a different hiding place, and she was planning on taking me to it, but we never made it. That's when Prunella and Sherman took off.

"Yes, I can tell you're replaying yesterday when Prunella took off with Sherman. She went to the garage and we talked for a few minutes. Then she met me back at the guesthouse."

"Did Sherman know anything?" I asked out of turn, but I needed to know. Was Sherman in on this from the beginning?

He didn't complain about my question and answered, "No, Ruth Ann, Sherman only does what Prunella wants him to do. He's totally faithful to her, and only her." I nodded my approval and he went on. "I told her on the phone that she needed to comply with my demands. I wasn't asking her permission or her opinion. I said I would leave her plenty of money, and the house here, but she had to hand over the necklace and let me take control of my company."

"But, you were supposed to be dead or worst case on the run after you were discovered alive."

"Yes, my original plan was to have everything in Prunella's name, but she agreed to have me run it all. I had enough on her that she would have to agree."

"What are you talking about?" What did he have on Prunella?

"I'm only going to tell you that she has had her share of troubles." He saw my stunned reaction and quickly said, "I'm not telling you, Ruth Ann, you'll have to get that information out of her."

"But, that's not fair."

"Fair isn't playing into this scenario anymore. I'm just telling you once she heard what I said, and what I threatened to do, she complied with my demands."

"Are you talking about threatening to kill me or exposing her?"

"Both." Okay, so he still had to use me to put her over the top and make her go along with him and his crazy plan. I don't know how he thought he'd get away with any of this, but I hadn't heard everything yet.

"Prunella and Sherman made their way down to the guesthouse where I was waiting for her. She was surprised that Steven was there, but she agreed to go along with my plans. What she didn't realize was that we still had feelings for each other."

"That's crazy. You tried having her killed not so long ago."

"We both were in a bad place with each other. I blamed her for stealing the necklace from me once my first wife died, which she did if you recall."

"She told me you started acting strangely with her, and she was still in love with you back then. Then you grew colder and angry. That's when she decided to take the necklace and protect herself. Remember, she felt that necklace was hers, too?"

"Yes, we've rehashed that many times. I get that we all think the necklace belongs to us. I'm willing to let that go now. Prunella wants to stay with me and you have to accept that."

"I'm confused." How did she go to being threatened by him to willingly staying with him?

"Yes, it's awfully fast, I know. She came to the guesthouse, we hashed it out for hours and we both came to the conclusion that if the necklace didn't exist we would still be together."

"So, the necklace *is* cursed if you ask me."

"In many ways, yes. There have been several murders, and one side stealing it and the other stealing it back for so many years that we've grown greedy and bitter. Once we came to the same realization, Prunella asked if I still loved her. I told her I did, and she told me she did, too."

"Wow! Okay, I'm following you so far even though I'm not totally convinced that you're telling me the truth. But why, when I ran into her in the guesthouse did she send me away? She was mean and told me to go away and never come back. Why would she do that?"

"She wasn't totally convinced that I meant what I said. She didn't want to put you in danger. I told her to come clean to you. I knew you snuck into my guesthouse. I saw you on the cameras, but Prunella made her own decision to turn hateful toward you."

"So, she told you she loved you and you told her you loved her, but she wasn't sure if you were playing her or not, right?"

"Yes, and I do believe that she was worried you'd find out about her past and why I originally used that to threaten her to go along with my plans too."

"Why can't you just tell me?"

"Not my story to tell. I'm sure if you confront her she'll be forthright. If not, that's up to you how to handle. You can tell her I gave you some information about her past that she must tell you about or you can leave it alone. Somehow, knowing you as well as I do now, I don't think you can handle the latter."

"I'll give you that one," I replied, wondering what on earth Prunella could've done that was so bad Axel could use it to blackmail her.

"So, I talked to her after your meeting in the guesthouse kitchen. She felt horrible for the way she treated you, but felt she needed you as far away from this mess as possible. She did confide in me and I told her she didn't have to push you away. That's when she made the decision to believe my feelings for her. We've been moving forward since that conversation. I have to give you the credit for that."

"Me?"

"Yes, it was after I told her not to push you away she realized I wanted the best for her and you!"

"Okay, you're making me feel like I'm the bad guy and you're some kind of saint."

"Not quite, but I'm hoping you'll see I'm not as horrible as you thought. I did get caught up in the greed and the chase after the necklace. But now I just want to get back to a somewhat normal life."

"I hear you, but I don't know how you'll be able to do that. You've committed several crimes, and you and Prunella will always be on the run from the police. Is that fair for her?"

"I need time to come up with another solution, Ruth Ann. This is where I need your help."

"What can I do?"

"I need to find a way to pin *everything* on Steven Svenson."

"Wait, what?"

"I want my freedom, and with everything I've done to you, Prunella, and the others, I need to come up with a plan to pin it all on Svenson."

"But that's impossible!" Was he kidding? I didn't think so.

"Not exactly. I can say he forced me to do his dirty work. I'll admit to fighting for the necklace, but the murders, plotting, and kidnapping have to fall on him, not me."

"But John knows *you* kidnapped me weeks ago and brought me to Sweden?"

"That's where you can help. If you don't press any charges, then I won't be charged with the kidnapping."

"But even if I do go along with you, what about Jeffrey Toggles, the jewelry store owner that you admitted to killing?

"I didn't personally kill him. I wanted him out of the way and I'll admit to only you that one of my men killed him."

"Was it Finn?" Finn was Axel's right hand man and nephew. He was an evil, sick young man with a large Viking ship tattoo burned into his neck. Fortunately, and I do mean fortunately, he was blown up when a bomb blew up Axel's docks back in Sweden.

"Yes."

"Can you prove that?"

"Yes, I can. I recorded every planning session on my cell phone. I have back-ups and have Finn admitting to firing and hitting his target, Jeffrey Toggles."

"Okay, what about Bertha and her brothers? They were killed when you kept us prisoner in your office back in Sweden."

"I didn't kill any of them. Bertha got shot after she lunged at me and the gun went off. Her brothers did a murder-suicide in my vault."

"Bert and Helena were killed by Svenson. Hey, what about over at the High School? A body was put into the ovens and you were involved in that."

"Ruth Ann, that was just a ruse to throw you off our trail."

"You mean there *wasn't* a real body in there?"

"Nope, it was a dummy. Once your chief makes a call back to his office, he'll find out that it was just a rubber dummy."

"I don't believe it!" I exclaimed.

"What? You think I'm lying to you?"

"No, no, that's not what I meant. I'm just stunned with everything and don't know what to say or think."

"Do you think I can live freely after all this?"

"And Prunella truly wants to be with you after everything?"

"She says she does. I believe her and once you talk with her maybe you will, too."

"So you need me to back off all charges. Even if I do, what about holding John, Judy, Inga, and me at gunpoint at your office in Sweden? I don't think John will be so forgiving."

"If you plead my case he might."

"Wow, that's a lot to ask, and even if I did side with you, he still might not agree, no matter what I say." Plus, I added, "Wait, you also took my daughter, Lynne, hostage. How do I forgive you for that?"

"I didn't take her, Steven did. He grabbed her back at your store and wanted her as leverage. He knew you would do anything to protect her, and I was stupid to go along with him. I would never let him hurt her."

"You're asking an awful lot, Axel. I don't know what I'm going to do or say. You make a good case, but seriously, you've hurt a lot of people and done a lot of damage."

"I know," he said, lowering his head and leaning against his hands on the island. "I really want your forgiveness."

"I need some time to think about it and speak with Prunella. Can you arrange that?"

"She still insists that you leave here. I haven't told her I'm talking to you, and she doesn't know who we have stashed in the library."

"Where is she?"

"She took a walk and went back to the guesthouse. She wanted to get away and not see anybody for a little while.

She said she was going to rest in the basement there. I had a nice little area set up for her per her request."

"We saw that, and I figured it was Prunella's area."

"Yes. Why don't we go into the library and make sure everyone's still okay, and then I'll get Sherman to go get her."

"I haven't seen Sherman, where is he?"

"He was ashamed at his behavior with you, Inga, John and the rest of the group. He's hiding out on the third floor in his room."

"Hey, what about Inga? She's got a guard outside her room. Why?"

"She didn't want me talking with you. She doesn't want you to believe me. She wants your chief to overtake me and my men and throw us all in jail."

"And what if she's correct?" I asked, wondering the same thing.

"That's up to you, Ruth Ann. I'm not going to force you to do anything. I just wanted time to beg for your forgiveness and explain it to you. Inga's not so forgiving. She wants blood."

"That would be Inga," I admitted. "But, how is she?"

"She was given a mild sedative and last I heard she was resting comfortably in her bed."

"The last you heard? From who?"

"Not Steven, so don't worry. I stopped listening to him a while back. I know he's not trustworthy so I had one of my men stand guard with her. Svenson had nothing to do with her."

"That's good, I think," I said. "Let's get back into the library. I don't trust that lawyer with any of my friends and especially with my daughter." We hopped off the stools and Axel led the way into the grand foyer.

"That's strange," he mumbled, looking around the room.

"What?"

"The library doors are wide-open."

"Why would that be strange?" I asked curiously.

"Usually when people are being held against their will the door wouldn't be wide open for them to escape." He grabbed my hand and hurried me into the library. "I had a feeling something wasn't right."

I looked around the empty library and panicked. "Where are they?" I demanded of Axel.

"I…I don't know, Ruth Ann."

"Axel, you weren't lying to me and just wasting time while they got away, were you?"

Axel looked as stunned as I was. "NO," he shouted. "We need to find them, quickly."

"Wait," I cried, as I went around the room making sure there wasn't any clue left behind. "Look," I pointed toward the floor by the massive stone fireplace.

Axel rushed over to me and we bent over an unconscious body on the floor. "It's one of my men," he admitted. He put his finger on his neck and said, "He's dead."

"WHAT?" I jumped back and fell over the coffee table onto the couch. "He's dead? How?"

"Be careful, Ruth Ann! He's had a severe blow to the head, Ruth Ann. Stay back and I'll cover him up." I threw him the afghan that was lying over the back of the couch. "Thanks, we need to find the others, and fast."

"John must've been subdued or he would never have left a dead man just lying on the ground," I said, terrified. "Why would Svenson do this?"

"I don't know," he said, worried. "We need to get to the guesthouse immediately. I'm worried about what he'll do to Prunella."

"The necklace!" I exclaimed. "He's after the necklace." I turned to Axel and asked, "Where is it right now?"

"Prunella has it. I don't know exactly where she's put it either."

"Hold on. Were you using her until she turned over the whereabouts of the necklace or are you truly back in love with her?"

"At this very moment, I don't care about that necklace at all!" Axel threw his arms up in the air in exasperation and added, "I can't believe I involved that maniac. What was I thinking?"

"You were desperate."

"I've made mistake after mistake and it's costing people their lives. I deserve whatever punishment your chief wants to lay upon me."

"Let's just get out of this then worry about that," I said, finally realizing this was a man who truly was sorry for everything that he's done to get back this necklace.

"I think we could use extra manpower. Let's go get Inga and the guard outside her door."

We took off up the main front staircase and wound up to the third floor. "He's gone," Axel yelled from the top of the third floor landing. "What happened to him?"

"Inga! We need to see if she's alright, hurry." We flew down the hall to Inga's door. Axel hesitated before grabbing the doorknob. "Hurry up, Axel," I cried out anxiously. "Open it up."

"It's locked, hold on, I have a set of keys in my pocket." He pulled out a small round silver ring with several keys dangling. His hands were trembling fiercely as he searched for the right key. "Here," he said, putting the key into the lock.

He flew open the door and thankfully, Inga was laying on her bed with her hands tied to the iron rails on the headboard, and a gag tied around her mouth. I ran over to her and first pulled off the gag. Her eyes were wide open and furious. "Inga," I said, throwing the rag on the floor. "Are you okay?"

She coughed and swallowed a few times before she demanded, "Free my hands!" Axel was already working on it as Inga stared in shock at who was trying to help her. "What is *he* doing here, Ruth Ann?"

"It's too long of a story. We need to get you free and go after the others."

"What others? Where'd they go?" She asked, confused.

I explained about Steven Svenson, the lawyer, who now has John, Judy, Ben, Lynne, and soon Prunella. "Wait, where's Prunella?"

"She's at my guesthouse resting, but Svenson's after her," Axel spoke. "We need to get to her fast."

"I'm so confused. Last I knew Ms. Prunella was pushing me away telling me she was back with this man," Inga stopped talking and pointed at Axel. "That can't be true, is it Ruth Ann?"

"We don't have time to go into everything. Right now you need to just believe me, and we need to get to the guesthouse to stop this maniac, Svenson."

"Fine," she said roughly as she swung her legs off the bed and hopped up. Axel tried to help her but she pushed him away professing she was perfectly capable of getting up and walking. "Let's get out of here."

We hurried down the hall looking to see if we could figure out where Axel's other guard disappeared. "I hope he didn't kill him, too," I said.

"Kill him?" Inga questioned.

"Steven and one of Axel's guards were keeping everyone in the library while Axel talked to me back in the kitchen. When we finished, we went into the library and it was empty, and his guard dead on the floor."

"This is horrible, what's happening around here? One murder after another."

We made it down to the foyer and headed through the hall that led into the kitchen. Axel went in there first making sure we were safe from Svenson. Just in case. Inga stood still in the middle of the room. "C'mon, we gotta go," Axel demanded, standing by the back door that led to the back of the estate.

"NO," Inga bellowed loudly. "Where's Sherman?"

"I forgot about him," I admitted, feeling terrible that I didn't even think about him. I turned to Axel before he took a step outside. "Axel, where is Sherman hiding out again?"

"Oh, no, he was next to Inga's room on the third floor."

"We have to go back," Inga commanded. "He could be hurt."

"You're right, we do," I said.

"Even though he was mixed up in this too," Inga said, turning around and heading back into the hall. "He lied to us, and if he was just honest with us, this wouldn't have gone this far."

"Sherman isn't to blame, Inga," Axel stated. "He was following Prunella's orders, and you know Sherman, he's a loyal chap."

Inga ignored Axel's words and flew up the stairs leaving Axel and me way behind. I was terribly winded by the time I reached the third floor. Inga was already standing in front of the room next to hers. "I can't get in," she cried out. "It's locked."

Axel made it over to her and pulled out his keys and when he held up the correct key, Inga snatched it from him and stuck it into the lock. "No, it's not opening!" She tried key after key until finally she got the correct one. "Here," she said, opening the door and forcing her way in.

"He's not here!" She called out to us both as we made our way into the room. "Where is he?"

We were about to turn and leave when we heard a loud thump coming from the direction of the closet. "Did you hear that?" I asked nervously.

"Shhh," Axel said, tiptoeing over to the closed closet door. "Someone's in there, I'm sure of it." He put his ear to the door and nodded his head.

"Wait," I said. "You should have a weapon in case someone lunges out at you." I walked over to the side table next to the couch and grabbed a couple brass candlesticks. "Here," I whispered, handing one to him and one to Inga.

He shakily grabbed one of the doorknobs to the double door closet and gently turned it. "Here goes," he said quietly. He opened the door part way and tried to look in. "It's pitch dark in here. I can't see a thing," he whispered after turning his head back to us.

"Be careful," I tried to say, but before I could get all the words out of my mouth, Inga shoved Axel out of the way and flew open the closet door. She held the candlestick high over her head ready to whack whoever was inside with it. "Inga," I yelled loudly. "Stop!"

Axel gained his footing back and followed Inga inside the large, walk-in closet. I stood about two steps outside of the closet when Axel stuck his head out and said, "It's okay, Sherman's in here and…"

"And who? Not Prunella is it?" I asked, scared of what and whom they found.

"No, it's my other guard, he's been killed, too." Before I could respond Axel clarified, "The guard's dead, not Sherman. He's just been tied up and gagged."

"I got him freed," Inga called out from deep inside the closet. "He's okay, just a little stiff from being stuffed into the back corner of the closet."

I waited until Inga came out with Sherman. He looked fine, but his eyes were large and terrified. "I've been stuck in that closet for hours with a dead body!"

"Bring him over to the couch and sit him down, Inga," Axel said.

Inga listened and held tightly onto Sherman's arm and guided him over to the plush navy blue couch. He plopped down in one fell swoop and went immediately into his account of what happened.

"I was in here because…" he looked from Axel to me, but Axel interrupted him and said, "She knows, Sherman, I told her everything."

He looked me straight in the eyes and said, "Ruth Ann, I'm so sorry the way I lied to you and your friends. I didn't have a choice at the time and I only did what I did to protect Ms. Prunella. She was confusing me with her back and forth relationship with Mr. Eklund, I had no other choice but follow her orders. I've always followed her orders. Can you forgive me?"

"Sherman, I understand what you thought you were doing was right. So, yes, just go on and tell us what happened to you in here."

"Thank you. I was resting on the couch waiting for word from Ms. Prunella or Mr. Eklund that it was safe downstairs. I didn't want to risk ruining any of their plans by my presence so I chose to stay up here. That was a mistake I came to find out."

"Who did this to you, Sherman?" Axel inquired.

He gave his boss a bit of a glare and said, "Please, let me tell you my version as it happened." Axel nodded slowly so Sherman continued. "I was sitting on the couch reading a book when there was a knock at the door. It was the guard that was standing over Inga's room." He stopped, looked over to Inga and added, "Inga, I'm sorry they had to sedate you. I had nothing to do with that. I wanted to stay with you, but Ms. Prunella told me to stay in my room alone. Again, I'm very sorry." Inga didn't nod her acceptance with his apology, but instead gave him a disapproving look. Sherman chose to ignore her for the time being.

"I opened the door and he asked if he could come in and do a room check. I didn't think much of it so I obliged. He walked around the room, my bathroom, and then went into my closet. I couldn't figure out what he was doing in there when all of a sudden another man flew into my room and into the closet. I heard loud bangs and thumps, and then the strange man came out and pulled me off the couch, rather roughly I might add, and threw me into the corner in the closet. I had to step over the first guard who was lying on the floor in the middle. I couldn't see much because there was no light on in there. I didn't know at the time he was dead, but I did notice he wasn't moving. I assumed the stranger knocked him unconscious and he would be waking up eventually, which he didn't."

"Sherman, who was this stranger?" I asked, enthralled in his story.

"Hold on, let me finish then I'll answer your questions." We nodded. "So, I was thrown into the corner and the man took out a piece of rope and some kind of cloth. He rolled me over onto my stomach and tied my hands behind my back with the rope. Then he whipped me back around and stuffed some smelly cloth in my mouth. All went black."

"Chloroform," Axel announced. "He drugged you."

"Yes, he did."

"So, that's all you remember?"

"No, I don't know how long I was out, but when I awoke I was able to scoot myself over to the unconscious man. When I tried to kick him he didn't move. I was so terrified that I scooted myself back into the corner and waited for someone to find me. That's it, that's all I remember."

"Wow," I said. "That's horrible, Sherman."

"Yes, it was."

Axel stepped up and started asking questions. "First, I'm very sorry this happened to you, Sherman. I can assure you we will do whatever we can to make it up to you. However, you need to tell me what this stranger looked like. You said he was a man, correct?"

"Yes, it was definitely a man."

"How was he dressed? Did you recognize him?"

"He was dressed in black from his jeans to a hooded sweatshirt to a black knit face mask that covered his entire head. All I saw was a deep set of blue eyes staring back at me. Nothing else on him was visible."

"What about his hands?" I asked. "Did you see his hands?"

"Why would that matter?" Inga questioned me strangely.

"Maybe he had a ring on that we could identify or any other kind of markings?"

"Oh, like the tattoo that was on my nephew, Finn?" Axel asked me.

"I guess so. I was thinking more like a particular kind of ring."

Sherman didn't respond for a few seconds when he blurted out, "Wait, he did have on a ring on his right hand. I couldn't make out what it was, but it was big and clunky."

"Kind of like a class ring men wear?" I asked him.

"I guess so," he replied. "I noticed because when he was picking up the rope to tie my hands I observed his hands."

"How so?" Axel asked curiously.

"His fingers were so long and lean, just like his body. He was tall and slim, and moved very quickly."

"Did he speak?"

"Not really, just when he grabbed me off the couch. He told me not to fight him and do what he says so he wouldn't have to kill me."

"You didn't mention that in your account, Sherman." Axel said coolly. "That's a big thing to forget."

"Sorry," Sherman snapped. "I've just been through a terrible ordeal."

"Axel, let him be." I turned to Sherman and asked what the rest of us wanted to know also. "Sherman, did he have any kind of accent?"

"Of course he did," Sherman cried out. "He's Swedish."

"Not again," I said to myself. "Now who's involved?"

Chapter 33

Axel couldn't believe what Sherman was telling us. Sherman was shoved into a closet after he stepped over one of Axel's dead guards. The man who killed the guard, and threw Sherman into the corner, and gagged and tied him up, was a tall, lean, blue-eyed man who was dressed in black except for his eyes and hands. On his hand he wore a bulky ring and when he spoke he had a Swedish accent. I didn't know what to say. Who was this new stranger and did he have anything to do with Axel or Steven Svenson?

"Axel, do you know who this man is?" I asked him.

"He's not one of my men. They've been killed, possibly by this new person."

"Could he be someone Steven brought in to overtake you?" I inquired.

"That's my take on it. I bet he knew he'd need more help to pull this one off. My question is was this stranger here all along staying in the background until Svenson called him up to help?"

Sherman was filled in on what had happened with us up to this point. "I can't believe what's going on around here! Who's working with whom?"

"Don't ask me," Inga snapped. "I don't care anymore. We need to find Ms. Prunella and end this once and for all."

"I agree," I added. "The person we need to stop is Steven Svenson. He's the maniac who's having people murdered left and right."

"Don't forget this new stranger who's just come into the picture," Sherman said. "We don't even know for sure if this guy's working with Svenson."

"We can't speculate any longer. We need to get over to my guesthouse and see who's there…if they're still there."

"Axel, you don't think Steven would take them to Sweden again, do you?"

"Unless he has another plane, I don't see how he could. He's got Prunella, your daughter, Lynne, Chief John, Detective Judy, and Ben. Too many hostages for him to fly without a private plane."

"Can't he steal your plane since it's near hear?" Sherman asked him.

"Not without my permission."

"Let's hope that's the case," I muttered.

Inga helped Sherman stand and we took off back down the stairs into the kitchen. "Well, we shouldn't come across anybody else along the way," Inga said. "What do we have to defend ourselves with?"

"We need a gun," I exclaimed. I turned to Axel and asked him, "Do you have a gun stashed away here somewhere?"

"Yes, I have a whole collection hidden away in the library. Let's grab them before we head out."

"We've had too many distractions. We'll never get over to the guesthouse at this rate," Inga thundered.

"We have to protect ourselves, too," I said to her as we turned around for what seemed like the millionth time. "Let Axel grab what he can and hopefully we won't need to use any of them."

Axel rushed into the library and went over to one of the massive bookshelves that lined the wall behind his executive desk. He went to a specific area and pulled out a book. A group of books popped out from the wall as if on a sliding shelf. "Here," he said reaching in and grabbing two small pistols from inside the exposed shelf. "They're loaded and ready to go."

"Axel, you hold one and give the other to…" I looked at Inga and Sherman. "Inga."

"Hey," Sherman protested. "Why her?"

"She wasn't knocked unconscious like you were, Sherman," I quickly responded. "You seem a little shaky still. Inga's alert and ready to go."

"Fine," he agreed and Inga took the gun from Axel and expertly eyed the weapon.

"Okay, we're ready, let's get out of here, finally," Inga said eagerly.

Inga wasn't going to let us get sidetracked again. She led the way through the foyer and into the kitchen. Once we exited through the back door of the kitchen the cold morning air hit me square in the face.

"Do you realize we haven't eaten or slept at all?" I asked feeling exhausted, but invigorated by the cold, now November, air.

"Once we get Svenson captured and sent off to jail we can sit down and have a warm meal and then fall into our warm beds," Sherman said, shivering from the cold. I was glad that we had grabbed the same coats we had used before from the bench in the foyer. I slipped on the full-length fur and wrapped it close to my body.

Inga and Axel fought for the lead as we made our way past the large garage and down the gravel path toward the guesthouse.

"Once we get close I know where to go to avoid being seen by my own cameras. Steven knows them, too, so I'd like to stay clear of detection."

It only took a few minutes when Axel led us off the gravel path onto a hidden, grassy path. "I never saw this path before," I said.

"It's pretty hard to find. I just happen to know because I had it made." We followed Axel single file as we wound through some leafless barren woods until we came around the side of the guesthouse opposite the kitchen.

"Where does this take us to?" I asked him.

"I think you'll be surprised," Axel replied. We continued following him until he bent over and brushed a light layer of snow off of the ground.

"Hey, it's a manhole!" Inga exclaimed.

"Don't tell me that you have *another* secret tunnel into your house?" I questioned him.

"Kind of. It's actually part of the same tunnel you discovered earlier. This is another opening that we use to climb down and it takes us into the tunnel not far from the basement entrance."

Axel pulled off a round, metal cover from the ground and climbed inside. "Be careful, this is just a ladder." I peered over the edge and he was right, a metal ladder went down into the ground.

I entered after Axel and found my footing on the first rung. I had Sherman holding me until I was sure I wasn't going to fall. Once I stepped down a couple rungs, it was easy going until I reached the bottom. Sherman and Inga followed after me until we were all standing in a small area, and I mean small. The room was only big enough to fit the four of us. Axel did a little maneuvering and a door popped open and I found us stepping back into the original, dimly lit tunnel. "Wow, we never saw this opening from the other side," I said.

"It's pretty well disguised. Plus, it's not that bright in here so it's hard to see a slight crack in the wall."

"How far are we from the opening into your guesthouse's basement?" I asked him.

"Only a few steps away," he said, leading on. "We'll be in the basement in a jiffy."

Axel had walked less than thirty seconds when he opened up the end of the tunnel and stepped inside the warm basement. "Let me check it out before you come in here."

We waited only a minute when Axel stuck his head back in the tunnel and said, "Come in, but be quiet."

I went in first, then Inga and Sherman. I didn't see anyone around, just the couch where Prunella had slept. "Looks like nobody's been here since we were here earlier."

"Hard to tell. We need to go upstairs and check the place out thoroughly," Axel said, walking around the entire basement while I walked over to the bottom of the stairs leading up to the main floor. "Don't go up yet, Ruth Ann."

I wasn't planning on going up. I only wanted to come over and see if I heard any noises coming from upstairs. I sat on the bottom stair starting to really feel the exhaustion kick in. Inga and Sherman have had time to rest and even sleep, I haven't. Axel noticed me on the stairs and put his hand on my shoulder looking down at me. "It's been a long forty-eight hours or so, Ruth Ann. You look tired. Maybe you should stay back and let me handle this. It's my doing in the first place."

"No way," I said, hopping right up. "I'm okay, just frustrated at all these twists and turns."

"I'm hoping we can finish this nonsense soon."

Axel walked around me and headed up the stairs. He had a gun ready just in case he confronted Steven. He thought it best that we wait at the bottom just in case we made too much noise going up. Inga, Sherman, and I waited while Axel made it up to the top of the carpeted stairs without making a sound.

He tried opening the door at the top of the stairs, but it wouldn't budge. "I think someone put something in front of the door, it won't move." Inga took this as her cue to come up and help him. She hurried up the stairs and gave Axel a little shove to the side and tried to open the door.

"Nope, it won't move."

"What are we going to do from down here?" I asked, exasperated.

"The only thing we can do is go out one of the window wells," he said. "We don't have any other choice. I'm not going back inside the tunnel to risk getting caught with one of the cameras."

"Won't it be obvious? Us climbing out of a window well?" Sherman asked, annoyed.

"No, the cameras are directly above the window wells attached to the house or further out near the woods. We'd be directly below the camera so as long as we hover along the outside walls, we'll be good."

Axel and Inga came back down the stairs and we followed them toward the bar. "This one's closest to the side of the cabin. If we go out here," he pointed to a large window well about five feet off the floor. "We'll end up near the kitchen entrance. I'm not sure if they're even still in there, but it's the safest entry back inside the house."

Axel took a couple of his sturdy bar stools and placed them under the window well opening. He climbed up the stool while Inga held it in place. "I just have to get these unlocked," he said, reaching up high to the top of the window and unlatching the lock. "Got it." He slid the window open just enough for human bodies to get out.

"Ruth Ann, let Inga go first, then Sherman, and then you. I'll go last and shut the window just in case someone notices it open."

I moved away from the stool and let Inga get up on it. She's a large woman, but quite strong. She didn't need any help from Axel or Sherman. She kneeled on the stool and pushed her robust body through the window opening. We decided to leave our coats behind since the opening was fairly small and we planned on getting inside the guesthouse quickly. Axel stuffed the fur I was wearing and the other coats underneath the bar in an empty cabinet. We didn't want to leave any clues behind just in case Svenson or one of his hit men made it into the basement. Once Inga was inside the well on the other side of the window she put her hands on the top of the metal frame and pulled herself up. She was kneeling on the frozen ground underneath the large bay window of the kitchen. Sherman was next. He wasn't as strong or agile as Inga. It took both Axel and me to heave him from behind to get him out of the window. I watched closely as he tried to pull himself up out of the window well, but failed. Inga reached down and grabbed his arms and hoisted him up as if he was a sack of potatoes. I wondered if I was going to be able to handle this without help? I was about to find out.

"Okay, Ruth Ann, your turn. Need any help getting on the stool?"

"No," I proclaimed as I hopped myself up onto the stool, balanced on my knees (I watched Inga closely so I knew how to do it), then climbed into the well and stood up. I grabbed the metal sides to lift myself up and out of the well. I managed it with little to no problem (well kind of, I faked how difficult it really was!) at all.

"Great job, Ruth Ann," Axel called out to me from inside. He was up and into the well in two seconds, and then pulled himself out onto the ground. He was in terrific shape for a man almost twenty years older than me.

"Everyone stay down just in case someone's in the kitchen. We don't want to be spotted after everything we've done to get this far," Axel remarked. "I'll just take a peek inside the window above us and see what's going on in there"

I watched as he took his hands, rubbed them together and blew some warm air from his mouth. It was still morning, the Monday after the Halloween party at the resort. I can't believe it's been less than 48 hours. He raised himself up just high enough to grab onto the ledge of the window and take a quick look inside. However, it wasn't a quick look. He was taking a long time looking inside when he said, "I don't see anyone. I think we can get inside fairly safely, so follow me." Axel stood to his height of over six feet and casually walked over to the side door of the guesthouse that led into the kitchen. I've also been here before, I thought to myself.

The last time I was in this kitchen, Prunella banished me from her and their estate. She told me to never come back. Well, I knew that wasn't going to happen, but she was definitely convincing at the time. I didn't wait long before I stood up and followed Axel over to the door. Inga and Sherman were close behind me.

"Okay, I didn't see anybody in there, but that doesn't mean the place is empty. No talking, and walk softly. I don't want to alert anyone to our presence just yet." He took the gun he was carrying and pulled it out of the back of his pants. He held it up in one hand as he opened the door with the other. The door wasn't locked so he didn't hesitate to open the door enough to squeeze in. I went in right away to get out of the freezing cold November air. Inga let Sherman go in before her as she held the gun and watched from other directions.

"We're in," Axel said, as we gathered around the island. "I can tell there've been people in here recently."

"I see the dishes in the sink and crumbs all over the island," I commented.

"Plus, the stove's still warm," Inga said, resting her hand on the stove.

"Maybe they're resting up in the bedrooms, sir," Sherman suggested. "Nobody's really had any sleep, and that Svenson chap may need some time to make his plans, whatever they could be."

"Possible, but I find it highly unlikely. They have to know we'd be right behind them."

"Maybe they left one of the others behind," I hoped. "Why do they need my daughter, Lynne? Or Ben, for that matter?"

"Sorry, Ruth Ann, if I were taking hostages I would definitely keep your daughter. She's worth more to you than any of them."

"Of course, she's my daughter! However, that doesn't mean I would care any less for the others."

"Even Detective Judy?" Inga asked me, knowing I was lying.

I ignored her question and said, "With Prunella, Lynne, John, Judy, and Ben…that's five hostages."

"I agree, too many hostages with only two men guarding them does leave room for them to take over Svenson and his hit man," Inga said. "Chief John must've tried to get away a number of times by now."

"I hope they didn't hurt him," I said, worried about John's temper when dealing with someone as vicious as Steven or the other man that just killed Axel's guards.

"I have a strong feeling they're not in this place anymore," Axel started to say. "However, Ruth Ann brings up a good point. Five hostages are too many for those two men, unless Svenson has more men I didn't know about. Any case, we should search the main floor and upper floor to check for any clues or if one of them were left behind."

"Sounds good, let's get moving," I said, anxiously hoping beyond hope that Lynne was left somewhere upstairs unharmed.

We stayed together as a group because there's safety in numbers, especially when dealing with a killer on the loose. We left the kitchen and checked the dining room off to the left. It was empty, but a mess. "These people were slobs," Inga said, disgusted at the dirty plates, glasses, and utensils sprawled over the beautiful mahogany table.

The next room we entered off the hall from the kitchen was the great room. A massive room with antler chandeliers still lit even though the sun was shining through the floor to ceiling windows and sliders. Axel walked around the room and checked behind every chair, table, and couch. "Looks clear in here," he said, as he flipped off the main switch for the lights. We waited at the bottom of the stairs while Axel peeked inside the powder room located near the front door.

"Okay, I sure hope we find something," he said, traipsing up the wooden stairs. "There are six bedrooms up here and two baths. We stay together the entire search." That's quite the guesthouse, I thought to myself. Who has six bedrooms in a guesthouse? A very wealthy person does!

As we stood in the upper floor hall, we could overlook the great room. Axel opened the first door that was to the left of the stairs. "It's just one of the bathrooms," he said, opening the door.

"Look in the shower, too," Inga called out.

"I am," he said, walking inside the bathroom. I peeked inside the narrow room and there wasn't anywhere to hide in here. The double sink vanity was on the right, a toilet next to that. On the opposite side there was a large, clear glass shower stall. Nobody could hide in there. The bath was nicely decorated with a marble vanity top and the shower was surrounded with beautiful white and gray swirled marble.

"Next room is the first bedroom," he said, grabbing the handle and opening the door. He did have his gun ready and so did Inga. Sherman and I stayed a step or two back just in case we were confronted once the door opened, but that didn't happen.

We went from one room to the next until we hit another bathroom halfway down the hall. There was no sign of activity until we entered a much larger bathroom. The four of us went in and had plenty of room to spare. The square room consisted of two separate vanities on opposite sides of the room surrounded by tons of storage cabinets. The mirrors above the vanities were oval and ornate. On the far end of the bath was a large jetted whirlpool tub and next to that was the clear glass shower stall. There was a separate door for the toilet area and when I went in to check I was about to turn to leave when from behind the door I felt a slight push.

I froze. Have you ever had that nightmare when you're scared, and try and open a door, but it's being pushed from the opposite side? It's a terrifying feeling that I hoped would never come to life, but it just did. I couldn't move or speak. Axel noticed my resistance to move and hurried over to me. "What's wrong, Ruth Ann? Is someone in there?" he asked as he looked inside the small toilet area.

"I think the door just moved, Axel," I said, shaking from head to foot. "Someone's behind the door," I whispered to him.

"Stand back, Ruth Ann," he ordered as he gave me a slight shove to get me out of the way.

By now Inga was right by us and she had her gun ready. Sherman was ready to bolt. He was halfway out of the bathroom into the hall. "What's there?" Inga inquired urgently.

Axel pulled the door toward him as he took a step further inside the small room. "Oh, no," he cried out loudly.

"What? Who's back there, Axel? Is it Lynne?" I asked frantically as my nerves took over and I buckled to the ground.

"No," he said, going down to his knees. "It's that friend of yours…what's his name?"

"Ben?" I asked. "Is he hurt?"

"No, he's just been subdued. Let me get the gag out of his mouth and get him up and out of here."

"Finally," I said out loud. "We've got someone who might be able to fill us in on what's going on."

Axel asked Inga for help getting Ben to stand up. He was so scared he couldn't move a muscle. I peeked inside the toilet room and once he saw my face he relaxed a tiny bit. "Ben, it's okay, let them help you."

Ben's wide open eyes revealed his distress, but he was able to wiggle out a nod. Axel and Inga got him to his feet and brought him into the large open space in the bathroom. The first thing Axel asked Ben was if he was hurt.

"No," he replied with a shaky, hoarse voice. "I'm alright."

"Good," Axel said in a reassuring voice. "Can you tell me how you got in here?"

He suddenly awoke from his trance and rambled so fast none of us understood a word he was saying. "Ben," I shouted. He stopped, snapped his mouth shut and waited for me to talk. "Please, Ben, being scared is normal. You've been taken hostage, but we need you to pull yourself together and tell us where the others are and what happened to you. Why were you thrown into the bathroom?"

Before Ben could answer, Inga threw in one more obvious question. "You weren't tied up in there, why didn't you escape?"

Ben looked from me to Inga to Axel and back to me. "Just tell us what you can, Ben," I said, smiling gently at him to see if that would have a calming effect.

"Take a deep breath, Ben," Axel added. "Then you'll find you can speak more slowly and clearly."

Ben took an exaggerated inhale in and held it for a moment or two. Then he blew the air out and started his version of what happened to him. "We were in the library back in that big house up the mountain. Your chief told me to do what they wanted and I wouldn't get hurt. Why'd they hurt me?" Ben asked, looking at me pathetically. I must remind the readers that Ben was a special case. He's been on his own since he was just a young teen and never finished any schooling. He made his money by moving from town to town doing odd jobs for whoever would pay cash. Ben's mental condition was evaluated thoroughly by Doc Albert back in town, and he concluded Ben must've had a serious trauma when he was young. Ben was a simple man, uneducated, and fearful of just about everything. Richard and Carol Dickson own the ski resort in Deer Creek and hired him a few months back. At first, John was suspicious of him, but he's done nothing that would elude to him being anything else but a scared to death middle-aged fortyish man.

"I'm sorry you've been hurt, Ben," I said. "What did they do to you to hurt you?"

"They were very rough with me. The two men laughed at me and called me stupid. I'm not stupid, Ruth Ann, you know that."

"I know Ben, you're not, and they're not very nice men so don't listen to anything they say. Now, go on."

"They held us in the library for a long time. When you and..." I interrupted and said, "Axel." He nodded and continued. "Yes, Axel didn't come back I saw the man with the suit panic. He and the other man whispered back and forth to each other. The next thing I knew he took the other man over by the fireplace and bashed him in the head. The man fell to the ground and I think he killed him."

"Yes, he did," I said solemnly.

"Well, it made the man in the suit very angry especially when Chief John tried to go and help the man on the floor."

"What happened to John?" I asked, worried about what Ben was going to tell me.

"He warned the chief to not make any moves or else he'd be shot."

"What did John do?" I asked him.

"He backed off and stood by the rest of us. He whispered something to Judy, but I couldn't hear him."

"Then what, Ben?" Axel asked, urging him on so we could get moving.

"He pulled out a cell phone and made a call. Within a couple minutes another man rushed inside the library."

"That must be the man who killed my guards," Axel said to me.

"He was really tall, and wore black clothes. He was a scary looking man with deep blue eyes that stared at you like he wanted to hurt you."

"Did Svenson call him anything?" Axel asked.

"Svenson, oh, he's the man in the suit. Yes, he called him Jimmy."

"That's good Ben, keep going. What happened after Jimmy showed up?" Axel asked steadily so not to upset him.

"The two men told us we were going to be leaving."

"Leaving? Svenson planned on leaving without Axel and me coming back into the library?"

"Sounds like it, Ruth Ann," Axel said. "I knew I couldn't trust him. He must've had this planned a long time now. I let him in this country and now look what he's done."

"I can't believe I'm going to say this, but you didn't have any choice. If you wanted to get back your life and your wife, you needed someone to go along with you, and that person was Steven Svenson."

"Poor choices seem to be what I've made lately. But that stops now," he said.

"I'm glad, Axel," I said thankfully.

"Can we get back to what happened?" Inga asked, reminding us of the urgency here.

Ben took this as his cue to talk. "The man said we were going to take a walk to get one more person. Your chief knew exactly who he was talking about."

"Prunella?" I asked, knowing the answer.

"Yes, Ms. Prunella. She was here, in this huge place."

"How'd you get out of my house without the chief or Judy overtaking Svenson?" Axel asked.

"They both had guns. That Svenson man said not to make any fast moves or we'd be shot. The chief didn't want any of us to get shot so he followed their orders."

"So, you made it down to the guesthouse. Then what?" Inga asked.

"This man laughed when he talked about you, Ruth Ann, and…and Axel."

"Why?" I asked.

"Because he said you two would probably still be talking to each other and wouldn't find us until we're long gone from this place."

"We did talk a long time, Axel," I said.

"We had a lot to talk about," he replied.

"Yes, so, Ben, what did you do in the guesthouse?"

"The tall man, Jimmy, said he was hungry and ordered Prunella and Lynne to make food."

"Did he threaten them to do it?" I asked, worried for both of them.

"No, he just told them to do it and they did. They made eggs and toast with sausages. Jimmy brought the rest of us into the dining room and told us to sit and not move. Svenson stayed in the kitchen watching over the two women while they cooked."

"So you all ate?" I asked, thinking this was getting weirder and weirder.

"No, well, they told us to eat because it was going to be the only time we'd be able to eat for a long time."

I didn't like the sound of that. Please don't tell me they're about to take a long trip!

"Why, Ben?" Axel asked quickly to keep his train of thought going.

"I didn't know. They just told us to eat and I did. Lynne and Prunella didn't eat anything, but Judy and John did. I heard John say to the others to eat because we needed to stay strong so I ate."

"But Prunella and Lynne didn't eat anything?" I inquired.

"No, I overheard Prunella whisper to Lynne that they could've slipped something in it."

"Drug them?" Axel questioned.

"I guess so, but I listened to the chief."

"Okay, you ate in the dining room. What did Svenson and Jimmy do after that?" I asked, trying to stay as patient as I could with Ben.

"That's just it, I don't remember anything else."

"Why?" Axel asked.

"I must've fallen asleep and then I woke up in the bathroom."

"You *fell* asleep?" Inga asked, dumbstruck.

"I don't think he fell asleep Inga," Axel said. "It sounds like Ben was drugged and they transported him into this bathroom."

"Maybe the others are up here too, somewhere," I said, hopeful.

Axel turned away from Ben and whispered to me, "I think they had no use for Ben and didn't want too many hostages so they left him here."

"Hey," Ben cried out. "I could've helped them escape, too, if I had the chance. I followed Chief John's orders and didn't make any quick moves against those two bad men."

"You did the right thing, Ben," I said, glaring over at Axel. "He didn't have any choice but to follow their orders. Ben might not be the only one left behind, Axel."

"Then we'd better look a little further," he said, walking out of the bathroom and heading toward the next door on the left.

We left Sherman with Ben in the hall leaning over the rail that overlooked the great room. "Don't go anywhere," I called out.

There were three doors left to check. Axel grabbed the first handle and tried to open it up. "Locked." He put his ear on the wooden door and tried to hear inside. He didn't say a word, but walked to the next door. "It's also locked." I didn't have to guess what he would do next because he quickly went to the last door at the end of the hall. He grabbed the knob and again, it was locked.

"Aren't we going to open them up?" Inga asked anxiously. "We've done that many times before."

"I'm aware of that Inga," he said, "I don't hear anything in those rooms, but it's suspicious that the doors are locked."

"I think someone could be injured or tied up like Ben. We need to get inside and look," I said worried.

"We will. I just have a couple questions for Ben first," Axel said, walking back toward where we left Ben and Sherman. Ben was sitting on the floor rubbing his head while Sherman stood and leaned on the railing. When Ben saw Axel coming toward them he popped up.

"I noticed you didn't go in any of the rooms," Sherman said interestedly. "Why didn't you break in?"

"I will. I just need to make sure it's safe. But first, Ben can I ask you a few things." Axel looked over at Ben who looked scared but nodded his head slowly.

"My head's pounding a bit, but I'll try and answer what I can."

"Your head probably hurts from the drug they slipped you. I'll go in the bathroom and see if there's anything you can take for that," I said, heading back into the bathroom. I was only a few feet from them as I opened a large medicine cabinet located on the side of the wall next to the light switch. I immediately located an unopened bottle of a pain reliever and grabbed it. I picked up the cup on the counter and filled it with some water. I walked back out to find Axel waited for me to return before he started asking Ben questions.

"Here," I said, handing two tablets to Ben. "This should help."

He took the tablets and popped them in his mouth and swigged the water to help them go down. If anything positive came out of this, it was Ben trusting me with whatever I handed him. It does show Ben's come a long way from when I first met him.

"Ben," Axel began. "You need to think really hard and tell me if they said anything about where they were going and who they were taking with them. Can you do that?"

"I'll try, but I don't remember much after I ate the eggs."

"Try, were Steven and Jimmy at the table with you?"

"I was sitting at the table with Chief John and Judy. Lynne and Prunella were in the kitchen with Steven. Jimmy was standing by the buffet holding a gun on us. The chief and Judy were sitting on one side of the table and I was opposite them." He rubbed his head as if that would help him remember more. "I remember when Lynne came in with a large plate of eggs and sausage."

"Did she seem okay, Ben? I just want to know if she was scared," I said, devastated that my daughter was involved.

"No, ma'am. I would have to say she was quite strong and very angry. I think she's a lot like you, Ruth Ann." He quickly added, "Not that you're angry, I mean. I meant you're a very strong, smart person."

"Thanks, Ben, go on."

"After your daughter came in she dropped the platter of eggs and sausage onto the table. A lot fell off and that made Jimmy mad. He poked her in the back and told her to clean it up. She started to say no when Chief John told her to do it."

"She does sound like you, Ruth Ann," Axel commented with a hint of a smile. I gave him a grin back because I took this as a compliment.

"Right after Lynne sat down at the table next to me, Prunella entered with Steven and a plate full of toast. She didn't drop the plate, but gently put it in the middle of the table and sat next to Lynne."

"Who ate first?" Axel asked, but I didn't think it mattered.

"Steven had his own plate of eggs when he came in. He sat at the head of the table with Prunella on one side and Judy on the other."

"Ah, so he didn't eat from the platter?" Axel asked curiously.

"No, sir, he didn't."

"What about that Jimmy? Did he eat off the platter?" Inga quickly asked before Axel or I could ask the same questions.

"I don't remember," he said at first. "Wait, he didn't!"

"That's why Prunella told Lynne not to eat the food. She knew it was spiked with something. She couldn't get the information to the others, but Lynne was right next to her."

"I was next to Lynne, she didn't say anything to me," Ben complained. "Why would she let me eat that stuff?"

"I don't think she did it intentionally, Ben," I said. "She probably thought she'd get caught."

"Oh, okay."

"So, you're saying that man named, Jimmy, didn't eat anything?" Axel asked oddly.

"No, he did eat, just nothing from the table. He never sat down, but he disappeared once into the kitchen and that's when I noticed him eating. He had his own plate when he returned into the dining room."

"They were very sneaky, weren't they?" I asked Axel.

"What did you talk about while you were in the dining room, Ben? Any mention of their plans?"

"That's where it gets foggy, sorry."

"Try really hard, Ben," I said, pleading with him. "You may remember more than you think if you place yourself back at the table and go over in your head what was said." I put my hand on his shoulder and he flinched a tad. "It's okay, nobody's mad at you. Just close your eyes and recall the scene." He nodded and closed his eyes so hard that his face was wrinkled.

"I remember the Chief telling me to eat to keep my strength. I ate a large plate of eggs and only one sausage. I don't like sausage very much. It gives me a sharp pain in my stomach if I eat too much of it." I wanted to say it was probably just gas, but I really wanted him to get moving with his version. "Oh, the man in the suit, Steven, told Prunella she'd better cough it up. I didn't know at first what he meant, but then Prunella mentioned she didn't have it. It was safely hidden away."

"The *necklace*," Axel mumbled.

"I guess so," Ben replied. "Steven was very angry and said she didn't have much time to give it to him. That he needed to leave the country as soon as he has his hands on it."

"BEN," I cried out loudly. "That's terrific!"

"Ruth Ann," Inga interrupted frustrated. "What's so good about that? He'll murder them if they don't cooperate."

"No, don't you get it?" I said, excited.

"I do," Axel said, smiling at me. "Inga, if Prunella gives up the necklace to Svenson then he has no reason to keep any of them alive."

"Oh, that makes sense."

"Oh, no," I blurted out. "He only has to keep *Prunella* alive."

Axel understood my implication and explained to Ben, Inga, and Sherman. "Svenson could threaten each of their lives if Prunella doesn't cooperate with him. If she doesn't hand over the necklace he could kill each one until she does."

"That's terrible," Sherman exclaimed. "Ms. Prunella would never risk any of their lives. I'm sure she either hasn't thought of that or is planning her own escape for them."

"I sure hope so," I said. "If he hurts a hair on my daughter's head, I'll kill him myself!"

"Easy, Ruth Ann," Axel said, squeezing my shoulder. "They won't harm Lynne either. I can't say the same for John or Judy, though."

"Why do you say that?" I demanded.

"They'll keep Lynne alive because of you. You're the other connection to the necklace. If Prunella refuses to cooperate, then they'll want you."

"Oh, they think I know where it is?" I said, feeling a tad relieved. I didn't want Lynne to be behind one of those doors injured *or...* I won't let myself go there!

"You know what that means, right?" Axel said, amused.

"What?"

"They're not leaving town until they have the bloody necklace."

"That's right!" I said, thrilled that we weren't going to be taking a trip back to Sweden. Not that I wouldn't love to visit Sweden, but not because I was kidnapped or chasing my daughter because she was kidnapped.

"Axel," I started to say, but hesitated.

"What, Ruth Ann?"

"Will you honestly tell me if you know where the necklace is at this moment?"

"I would tell you if I knew," he admitted. "Whatever she told you, Prunella has kept the secret whereabouts of the necklace from me...actually, from anybody, even you."

"Why?" I begged the question. "Why'd she do this? Everything was fine with us sharing the piece. Out of the blue, she told John and me that she moved the necklace from the original safe in your office to a secret safe she had installed. I just can't figure out why she did that and didn't tell me."

"Maybe she had a feeling something bad was going to happen to it," Inga added.

I realized Sherman was fidgeting a bit. He knew something about this and I needed to confront him. "Sherman," I looked directly into his eyes but he didn't reciprocate. "Look at me, Sherman," I demanded.

"What's up, Ruth Ann?" Axel inquired.

"Sherman, please," I begged. "You and Prunella are closer than anybody. You must've known about the new safe and why she did it?" A light bulb went off in my head. "Wait a minute. Prunella wouldn't know who to call or how to put in a new safe, but..." Inga and Axel now got it and stared at Sherman who was rocking back and forth against the railing looking guilty. "You would!"

"Me?" He replied with a question. "I...I don't know what you're accusing me of."

"C'mon, Sherman. You and Prunella were always together. She trusts you more than anyone else on this earth. You *know* about the new safe and why she did it!"

"Fine, I did help her. Of course I would help her. Ms. Prunella's the only one I would risk my life for."

"But why did she need a new location for the necklace?" I asked, turning my attention to Axel. "Did you contact her before yesterday?"

"Me, no," Axel stated. "I was hiding out here, but I didn't threaten her or anything until yesterday."

"Then who did?" I asked, directing my question to Sherman.

"That lawyer, Svenson." He held his head low in shame. "He called the estate last week before the Halloween party. Ms. Prunella wasn't supposed to tell anyone, but she confided in me. She needed my help."

"That snake," Axel growled. "He went off on his own before I was aware of it. He must've called and told her to hand over the necklace or people would start dying."

"Prunella would never let anyone die over it!" I bellowed.

"Shhh," Axel said to me. "Just in case someone's still in here we don't want to be found."

"Sorry, I just don't believe Steven Svenson would tell Prunella he would have Bert and Helena killed and she would let him."

"Maybe she didn't believe he meant it," Sherman mentioned. "That's what she told me."

"Why don't you tell me exactly what Prunella confided in you?" Axel ordered.

"Shouldn't we check those rooms first?" Sherman asked, suddenly impatient. "We're wasting tons of time here. I can tell you all about it after we check the rooms."

"No, I need to know everything, Sherman, so spill it," Axel demanded once again.

"Fine, but it'll be quick. Last week, Wednesday, I believe, Ms. Prunella grabbed me in the kitchen and said to meet her in the library. She said to come in with some tea, so that I would appear to act normally. She was afraid you, Ruth Ann, would be suspicious."

"*Me*? I wouldn't think anything of you two talking, but go ahead."

"She closed the door right after I entered with the tea service. I almost dropped the whole tray because she startled me so. She hid behind one of the library doors and when I walked in she jumped out and slammed the door shut."

"So much for being discreet," Inga mumbled.

"Nobody came running, but I did mention to her that if she wanted to keep something from Inga and Ruth Ann, that she best be a little quieter."

"Very funny, Sherman," Inga stated.

An aggravated Axel said, "What did she tell you, *exactly*?"

"She told me to listen and not ask any questions until she was done telling me her problem. She said I wouldn't approve if I didn't let her explain everything."

"So?" Inga asked impatiently. "That's why Ruth Ann and I were excluded. She knew we'd never go along with her scheme to hand over the necklace to Svenson."

Sherman pleaded, "At the time, I didn't know the lawyer contacted her. A lot has happened since then and you don't know for sure how you would've handled it either, Inga. You're just as loyal to her as I am."

"Possibly, but I would've never followed Svenson's orders."

"You can't say that," I said to Inga. "We weren't there when Prunella was first contacted by Steven Svenson."

"Let me go on," Sherman protested. "She started by telling me not to react too loudly when she told me that she was contacted by her lawyer's cousin, Steven Svenson. He was the crooked lawyer that her own lawyer, Michael, wouldn't work with. He started by telling her that people would die if she didn't follow exactly what he requested. She said she didn't think he was serious, at first. What could he possibly do to her with people surrounding her?"

"She didn't think he was a cold-blooded killer, just a crooked lawyer, right?" I asked him.

"Yes, exactly, Ruth Ann. That's why she let it go for a couple days until the night of the Halloween party at your friend's resort."

"When Bert was murdered so viciously," I muttered.

"Yes. She panicked and I did whatever I could to calm her down. She said Steven Svenson left his number with her and when she realized he was serious to call him."

"So, let me get this straight," Axel, said thinking out loud. "Svenson contacted her and made his threats about people dying unless Prunella handed over the necklace."

"Yes," Sherman answered.

"Then she grabbed you, only you, and confided this to you?"

"Yes."

"Then she decided, by herself, to ignore his threats and go about as if nothing's happened. In the meantime, I was making my own plans to confront Prunella and give my own set of rules about giving back the necklace."

"Yes, Ms. Prunella did tell me about your call, too. But that was the day after Bert's demise and the same morning we found Helena murdered."

"Yes, yes, but I had nothing to do with their murders. I think you believe me about that. We now know that Svenson's the disturbed maniac here and even though I did make threats to Prunella, they weren't about murdering people."

"She couldn't make the distinction between you and Svenson at first, sir," Sherman explained. "When Bert was killed she was beside herself and was going to confess everything the next morning, but that's when we found Helena murdered."

"So, she kept quiet?" I asked. "That doesn't make any sense. She should've immediately come clean especially after John and I discovered Helena stabbed in the basement."

"I agree," Sherman acknowledged. "I tried to tell her to confess, but that's when Mr. Eklund contacted her with new threats."

"I didn't know about Svenson's previous threats though," Axel said.

"She didn't know that at the time. I truly think she thought you and Svenson were working together and she was terrified."

"I would never hurt her," Axel said guiltily. "I know I've been horrid to her, but I would never hurt her. I'm a reformed man, and I intend to prove it."

"Then what happened, Sherman?" I asked, trying to get back on track. Time was ticking away and we've done too much talking and not enough acting.

"She told me that she was going to go to the guesthouse and hand over the necklace to Svenson, and, Mr. Eklund."

"But I wasn't in on this part," Axel said.

"No, she didn't know that until you and she met up and talked it out. She left out the part about Svenson because she started to believe you."

"She did?" he asked, surprised.

"I thought you and Prunella did work it out and you two were back together?" I asked, confused.

"Yes, but until Sherman said that those were Prunella's words, I wasn't fully aware she was willing to give me another chance."

"So, you and Prunella were together at the guesthouse and that's where we came in the picture, right?" I asked.

"Yes, too much happened too fast. The next thing I knew we had a bunch of hostages and Prunella closed up about the whereabouts of her necklace. Hey, Sherman, I thought you were going to tell us where the new safe was installed?"

"I almost forgot about that. Yes, it's somewhere nobody would ever think of looking for it."

"C'mon, Sherman, spill it?" Inga insisted.

"I promise I'll take you to it after we check those three, locked rooms."

"Fine," Axel said and stormed down the hall and pulled out a set of keys from his pants pockets.

"Don't be mad, Axel," I said, catching up with him. "Sherman gave us a lot of information. We now understand her motives much better."

"I needed Sherman to come clean about a few things before we moved on. Now that I understand how Prunella feels and how ruthless Steven is, we need to hurry and find the rest of them before Steven kills them, too."

"Let's go, we're talking about my daughter!"

Axel opened the door next to the bathroom first. I was anxious to find out why the door was locked; from the outside I might add. "Okay, here I go," he said, holding the gun in his hand. He slowly opened the door and the room was pitch black even though it was a sunny, late Monday morning.

"I can't see if anyone's in there," I said, frustrated. "Turn on the light. I think we're safe. If someone's in there they must be hurt or unconscious."

Axel flipped on the switch`and it took a second for my eyes to adjust. What I saw was an average sized bedroom. Not the massive ones that were up at his large estate house. There was a queen size bed with a large quilt covering the mattress and pine bed frame. The two nightstands next to the bed were also made of pine. Bears and pinecones covered the quilt on the bed and even the closed curtains and loveseat were covered with bears, mountains, and pine trees. It was a cozy, comfortable room, but that's not why we were in here. We needed to see why that door was locked. "I don't see anyone," I called out.

"I'll check the closet," Axel said, walking over to the door on the left side of the room. "They seem to put their hostages in closets." He grabbed the handle on the door and pulled it open.

"Stay back," Axel cried out as he was taken to the ground by a large object. "What the?" Axel said, lying on the ground on his back after a large, brown-blanketed wrapped object fell on top of him. "Get it off!" He demanded, and Sherman and Ben ran over to help him.

"It's a body," I screamed as the object in the brown blanket rolled off to the side. "Unwrap it, hurry," I demanded, worried that Lynne, Prunella, John or Judy were inside of it.

"Ruth Ann, don't look until we know who's in there," Axel said, sitting up and crawling up to the wrapped body.

"Inga, help me," he said, as she kneeled beside him.

I couldn't turn away, but Sherman came beside me and turned my body so I faced the door to the hall. "Give them a minute, Ruth Ann. I don't want you to see until we know what we're dealing with."

It didn't take long once Inga cut away the duct tape that kept the blanket over the body wound so tightly. "It's okay, Ruth Ann," Inga called out to me. "They're not dead, I found a pulse."

I still couldn't turn around. My feet were frozen to the ground. "Just tell me who's inside the blanket?"

"It's that detective, Judy," Axel told me "She's not dead, just unconscious."

"How?" I asked, still not turning around.

Inga and Axel checked Judy to see if they could find where she was hurt. They said there was no lump on her head or any cuts. "She must've been drugged like Ben, but they made her look as if she was dead," Axel said. "Or they expected her to suffocate under here, and when we did finally find her she would've been dead."

"Can you wake her up?" I asked as Sherman slowly turned my shoulders and my body followed. "I'm okay now, thanks Sherman."

"We just freed her," Inga said. "She's coming around."

"Judy," Inga said, taking her muscular shoulders in her hands and giving her a hard shake. "Judy, can you hear me?"

I went by Inga's side and waited until Judy's eyes slightly opened and rolled around a bit trying to gain consciousness. "Judy, it's Ruth Ann, can you talk?"

Judy's eyes adjusted and she licked her lips trying to get some moisture to them. She hoarsely said, "I'm so thirsty, can you get me some water?" I looked over at Sherman and he nodded. He hurried back to the bathroom and grabbed the cup from the sink counter and brought back some cool water. "Here," he said, handing it to me.

"Okay, Judy, can you sit up?" I asked her.

"Yes, yes, I'm just groggy, that's all."

Once Judy was in a sitting up position, I handed her the glass and she took it with a trembling hand. "I'm still a little shaky, can you steady my hand, Ruth Ann?" I grabbed her hand with the glass and helped her bring it to her lips.

"Drink it slowly," I suggested. Judy ignored my suggestion and downed the entire glass of water. "More," she begged, looking over at Sherman.

He begrudgingly took the glass from Judy's hand and disappeared back to the bathroom. After Judy downed not two, but three glasses of the water was she able to tell us what happened to her. "I see Ben's here, and okay, so I guess he told you what happened up until he passed out at the dining room table, right?"

"I passed out?" Ben asked.

"That's when John and I realized the food had been drugged and we didn't have much time before we'd be out, too."

"So, Ben fell into his plate of food?" Axel asked.

"No, his plate was empty and he fell back against the chair. This lunatic, Jimmy, picked him up as if he was as light as a feather and took him out of the room."

"Then what? It was just Svenson against the rest of you?" Axel asked, surprised. My thoughts were the same as his. How could John and Judy, being police officials, keep getting caught?

Judy suddenly realized Axel was with us and asked, confused, "Wait, why's *he* here?"

"Too long of a story for now. Just trust me that he's on our side trying to help us get Lynne, Prunella, and John back, alive."

Judy looked confused, but after a moment she shrugged it off. "You can fill me in on this after I tell you my version." I nodded and told her to go on. "Ben was gone, it was Prunella, Lynne, John, and me. I knew John and I were about to be knocked out. There wasn't much time, but I did notice Lynne and Prunella didn't eat any of the food."

"I wondered if Prunella knew Svenson drugged the food and she warned Lynne, but not John and Judy," Axel proposed. "Maybe it was their way of disposing of too many hostages?"

"Oh, I see what you're saying," Judy said, getting to her feet slightly unsteadily, but she recovered nicely. "Svenson only wanted Prunella and possibly your daughter, Lynne. He drugged us to get rid of us. Makes sense," Judy said, putting it together out loud.

"Why do they need Lynne? That's where I'm still foggy."

"Obviously to keep Ruth Ann willing to negotiate," Axel said. "Svenson assumes Ruth Ann knows where the necklace is, but the truth is she doesn't."

Judy looked at me amazed. "You *don't* know where your precious necklace is?"

"No, Prunella had a new safe installed because Svenson contacted her during the week. She was afraid for *my* life, Judy."

"Why didn't she tell anybody? All this could've been avoided. The murders of Bert and Helena, the incident over at the high school, and everything." She threw her arms up in the air and wound them around indicating the guest and estate houses.

"I don't know, Judy," I admitted. "I'm not happy either, and as soon as we get Prunella and Lynne back I'm planning on talking with her. She should've trusted me and not just Sherman." I looked over at him as he formed an unhappy frown on his face. "Nothing personal, Sherman." He relaxed a little and shrugged his shoulders.

"She could find herself arrested for that," Judy announced.

"Nonsense," I snapped.

"Can we get over to the next door?" Axel asked impatiently. "I have a strange feeling we know who's in there."

"John!" I cried out and hurried over to the next locked door. "Hurry, Axel, unlock the door." He was right behind me ready with the key in hand.

"Stand back, Ruth Ann. We don't know positively that John is in here."

"Or what shape he's in," Judy answered, walking a little wobbly trying to catch up to us.

"Why would they do anything more to him than what they did to Ben and you?" I questioned her. "You think they hurt him?"

"No, I don't know, though."

"We'll find out in a second," Axel said, opening the door and peeking in. "Whoa, it's bright in here."

"They don't have it closed up like the last room?" Inga inquired shoving Judy aside so she could take a look.

"Hey," she snapped back at Inga. "I'm the police officer. You stay back yourself."

"Really, you and the police chief *eat* food that's more than likely spiked and you expect me to respect that?"

"If you don't want to find yourself locked up in a cell when this is over you will!" Judy barked back at her.

"Enough!" Axel ordered. "I don't see anybody in here so far. Maybe this room's empty." We followed Axel in and searched the sunny, yellow themed room. It was such a cheery room Svenson probably had a hard time even walking in here.

Axel took a look in the closet a little more carefully this time, but nobody fell out of this one. "He's not in here."

"There's one more room up here, maybe he's in there," I said, walking out of the room and down to the last room at the end of the hall.

Axel opened the door and instead of glancing in he went in full speed ahead. Unfortunately, that didn't work out so well for him. We heard a crack then a thump. Axel's body was on the floor. "What the..." I cried out loud stepping away from the door.

"Somebody's in there and just whacked Axel on the back of his head," Judy announced, grabbing the gun from Inga's hand and rushing into the room screaming to whoever was in there to put their hands up in the air. "It's no use, you're surrounded, put whatever weapon you have down on the ground." We waited in the hall as Judy shouted her orders when we saw a leg from the nightstand fall on the floor right next to Judy. "Step out in the open," she ordered. It didn't take long for the person to step near Judy.

"Stop, it's me, John," the voice called out.

"John!" I bellowed and ran into the room and threw my arms around his neck.

"Ruth Ann, thank God, you're okay," he said, returning my grasping hug.

"John, are you hurt?" I asked, looking him over from head to toe.

"I'm good, just stupid," he said. "I allowed myself to get drugged and they obviously threw me in this room." He pointed around the bedroom, but these curtains were drawn shut so it was fairly dark in there.

"Who's here?" he asked.

"Ben and Sherman are in the hall. Inga, Axel, and I are with you. That's all. Lynne and Prunella are still being held by Steven Svenson and Jimmy."

"Jimmy," John repeated rubbing his stomach. "He can throw a mean punch."

"He punched you?" I asked.

"Yes, but wait…" John looked over at Axel and was about to knock him down again when I yelled, "No!"

"Why not? He should be thrown in jail for the rest of his life. We need to subdue him until I can take him into the station."

"No, John," I said, trying to explain. "You've got it all wrong, Axel's on our side."

He looked at Axel then back to me. "You've got be kidding, Ruth Ann. He's lying to you, and you should know better than to believe a word that comes from his filthy, murderous mouth."

"Easy, John," Axel said, standing almost as tall as John, but about fifteen or so years his elder. "Ruth Ann's telling you the truth, actually, I'm telling her the truth. If you hear me out hopefully you'll believe me, too."

"I don't have time for your nonsense," John said, looking around the room for something to tie Axel up with. "We've got to find Prunella and Lynne and I don't have time for this right now." He looked over at Judy and demanded she find something to hold Axel until we get back here.

"Look," I hollered to get his attention. "You hear me out or I'll just let him go after you walk out of here. Do you understand *me?*"

John looked over at Judy who shrugged her shoulders. "John, Ruth Ann's got a point. I've heard the whole story and I have to say its got some truth to it. Let him tell you, quickly, and then we can figure out where they took off to."

"You didn't hear anything they planned?" Inga asked curiously to John.

"No. I was dazed, not knocked out, but I pretended to be unconscious. If I fought back, Jimmy was willing and ready to kill me."

"Well, I'm glad you were thinking rationally at *that* time," I spat out angry with him for thinking I was such a fool for believing Axel.

"Ruth Ann, I'm not even going to acknowledge your comments." He turned to Judy and Axel and demanded why he should trust Axel Eklund.

Within ten minutes Axel pleaded his case. He did a good job, not great, but we didn't have the time to go into serious detail about Axel's motives for his past crimes. "Look," Axel started to say. "After this is over I'm willing to face whatever consequences are placed upon me. Can we just move on and find my wife and Ruth Ann's daughter? I can't give Svenson much time before he gets too anxious and eliminates one or both of them. He's a maniac."

John wavered back and forth with his decision, but timing won out. "Fine, we'll move forward with you, but if you try anything to doubt my trust in you, it's over for you. Got it?"

"Completely," he replied. "Now, we need to figure out where Svenson took Prunella and Lynne."

"We know they won't leave town without the necklace. I'm convinced Prunella won't turn it over willingly. The problem is that it could go two ways. Svenson will either wait it out and keep threatening to kill people she cares about or he'll kill her out of pure hatred and impatience." I looked at the group waiting for their response to my theories.

"Possibly, Ruth Ann," Axel said. "Prunella had this new safe installed and only one other person knows about it." We looked over at Sherman who rested against the rail overlooking the great room below.

"I know, I know," he exclaimed. "I have to take you to it. Fine, let's go."

"Wait," Axel called out as we were heading back toward the stairs to the main floor. "Svenson might believe there's another person who knows the whereabouts of the safe."

"Ruth Ann," John said out loud. "Unless Prunella denied it. I doubt she would want Ruth Ann to be sought after, too."

"I don't know her state of mind. The last time I saw her she was cold and distant with me. She told me to go away and leave her and Axel alone."

"That was just her way of protecting you, Ruth Ann," Axel reminded me. "She felt horrible and full of guilt about that."

"So, there's no way Prunella would say Ruth Ann knows where the safe was?" Judy interjected.

"Unless he didn't ask Prunella, but assumes Ruth Ann's aware of it, too," John added.

Inga was getting impatient and asked, "Can we just go check the safe? Maybe she already gave it to him and Lynne and Prunella are somewhere, unhurt."

"I doubt it," Axel said. "But, I haven't known his plans for some time now."

"He fooled you, Axel," I said, feeling sorry for him. Not too much, but just a small part of me felt sad that Axel was being taken advantage of, too. "He used you like you used him to get back to Deer Creek. He knew all along that he was going to stomp all over you to get that necklace before you did."

"Quite true."

John turned to Sherman and told him to lead the way. "Where's this hidden safe anyway?"

"I'd rather not say just in case we're being listened in on."

"You think they can hear what we're saying?" I asked Sherman, but looked at Axel as if he would know the answer.

"No, Ruth Ann," Axel said, knowing what I was implying. "I don't have any sound devices in the guesthouse. Just the cameras on the outside."

John was behind Sherman as he headed back into the basement. "Are we using the tunnel again?"

"No, just grabbing the coats that we left down here earlier."

John followed Sherman down into the basement and left the rest of us in the kitchen. "Wait here," he demanded then disappeared.

Judy walked over to the refrigerator and opened it up. "Should you be doing that?" I asked her.

"Why not? I'm thirsty and looking for some water bottles. Aha," she said, as she grabbed a few and set them on the island. "I think we should drink some water and clear our heads and bodies from that drug we were slipped."

"Only Ben, John, and you were drugged, Judy," Inga reminded her. "But I'll take a bottle because I'm thirsty." Inga snatched one of the cold bottles and I decided it was a good idea, too. It's been a long day already and another meal has passed by. I spotted some donuts on the counter and walked over to the plastic covered, store bought donuts and carried them over to the island. "I'm starving," I said, prying open the container. "I think they're safe, don't you?"

Judy eyed them suspiciously then took one of the powdered sugar donuts and smelled it. "Smells fine," she said, then taking a huge bite. "Tastes alright, too."

"Good, because I'm eating a couple," I said, shoveling one of the donuts quickly in my mouth and reaching for another. "Lynne would cringe at us eating store bought baked items," I said, smiling and thinking about my daughter if she caught me. "But, I'm sure she'd understand my dilemma. I haven't eaten hardly anything in the last twenty-four hours."

Inga also grabbed a donut for each hand. "Don't know when we'll get a chance to eat next," she said, stuffing one of the chocolate glazed donuts in her mouth. "These taste pretty good for store bought."

"Probably because we're so hungry," Judy said, chugging her bottle of water.

"Ben, come on over here and eat one," I said to the shy man standing near the back door. "The last thing you ate was those eggs and sausage that were drugged. You should drink some water and have something else to eat."

He wandered over and grabbed a bottle of water off the island. "I'm not hungry," he stated. "I still feel a little sick to my stomach from those eggs."

"Maybe the donut will help replace the drugged foods in your stomach," Inga suggested to him. He reluctantly grabbed one of the jelly-filled donuts and popped the entire thing in his mouth. It took him a minute to chew it up when he said, "Those are good. Maybe I'll have one more." Ben grabbed another jelly-filled one but ate that one in two bites instead of one.

"Better?" I asked him as he guzzled his water. He was nodding when John and Sherman entered the kitchen with their arms full of coats. "Let's go," he said, eyeing the food we were eating and the bottles of water.

"I'm assuming you know that stuff is safe?" he questioned Judy.

"Store bought, sealed in the plastic container. Unless they have the store stickers that we had to break to open it I would say they were safe."

"Good," he said, reaching over my shoulder and grabbing one of the chocolate glazed donuts and a water bottle. "Get your coats and let's go," John said with a full mouth. Ben looked at him contemplating another donut when I told him to grab a coat because we're heading out into the freezing cold afternoon.

"Oh, okay" he replied, staring at John in amazement at how he was able to talk while an entire donut was shoved in his mouth.

We bundled ourselves up and I wrapped the fur coat around me and hugged it close to my body. I sometimes question why I chose to live in a state where there's almost more snow than in any other state in the country and the summer is so short. Ever since I was a young girl I thought I'd be living in the South. I've got a passion for swaying palm trees and the sounds of the Gulf. But with my daughters and life here in Deer Creek, I just don't see myself moving any time soon.

John led the way and surveyed the area before we followed him into the crisp, but very sunny, afternoon air. "Brrr," I said, holding the coat closed since I couldn't find the buttons to fasten under all the fur.

"It's freezing and it's not even Thanksgiving," Ben said, zipping his lightweight coat. "I'm not used to this kind of weather."

At the back of the pack, Judy grabbed onto Ben's comment. "So, Ben, where'd you live if you didn't have cold weather?"

Ben turned his head around and glared at Judy for revisiting his past once again. "Most of the odd jobs I did were in the South where the weather's much warmer."

"Then why did you come here?" Judy asked, puzzled. "In fact, if you normally do jobs in the warm weather what brought you up North at all, especially to this unheard of pokey little town?"

It was my turn to scowl at Judy for her rude comment. "Pokey?"

"Oh, I'm sorry. I didn't mean anything offensive. I was just curious what would make Ben come to a town that most people have never heard of?" Judy looked accusingly at Ben and added, "Unless that person could be running away from something or someone?"

"Judy," I snapped. "Stop this! Leave Ben alone. He's done nothing to make us suspicious of him." I thought Ben's past has been put behind us weeks ago. Judy keeps trying to stir things up.

John stopped and said, "Ben, you might as well just answer her. She won't stop with her questions until you do."

"John," I said. "We've already been down this road. Leave Ben alone."

Ben watched horrified. For what reason, I have no idea. His eyes zoomed from Judy to John back to me. "Ben, just answer Judy this one question, why did you come to Deer Creek?"

"I-I don't have a reason," he replied nervously. "I've always just wandered around, but this time I came further north than I usually did."

"So, you didn't have anyone you were trying to find for any reason?" Inquired Judy.

"No," he snapped and shut his mouth up tightly. He did what I asked him to do. He answered one question, but it opened the door to his past again, and even I was suddenly curious about what led him to our town.

John shrugged his shoulders and mumbled quietly, "Don't have time for this now, but it'll definitely come up when this is over." He trudged through the frozen, wet grass and headed for the path that led back to the garage and main house.

"Sherman," John bellowed. "Where exactly are we going?"

Sherman hurried to catch up with John and left Judy, Ben, Inga, Axel and me to follow. "Um, I'll tell you when we get closer," was Sherman's response. He was holding onto this secret for as long as he could get away with it.

"Why are we stopping here?" I asked Sherman curiously as we stopped by the garage.

"Yeah, Sherman," John snapped. "Do you think somebody's in there?"

"Who?" I hurried and asked before Sherman could speak. "You think Lynne might be in there?"

"No," John said, as he scowled over at me. "Ruth Ann, we've been down this path before. I don't think Svenson's going to let Prunella or Lynne go until he gets what he wants."

"But what if Prunella doesn't cooperate?" I asked him. "I can't bear to think what that Jimmy fellow could do to them."

"Nothing," John answered. "He won't hurt them; I'll give you my word on that. I've been doing this job for a long time, and Svenson won't hurt either one of them unless things get desperate."

"Don't you think this is all desperate? I mean we've been going back and forth from the guesthouse to the estate to the guesthouse and now back to the estate."

"If Sherman would've come clean earlier we might've had some better answers to your question, Ruth Ann," John said, his eyes burning daggers back at Sherman's bewildered look. "Yes, Sherman, don't give me that, 'I don't know what you mean' look," John stammered. "I've about reached my limit with anyone who's leaving out pertinent information. We should've checked that safe long ago."

Sherman didn't reply but walked into the garage door. "Wait, why are we going in here?" I begged. "I thought the safe was up at the main house."

"Nope," Sherman replied, without further comment. He was fuming that John's accusations were directed at him. I didn't blame Sherman, but I did agree with John that we'd wasted valuable time.

"Where is it in here?" Judy demanded as she made her way inside the garage. "In one of the cars in here?" she asked, walking up to each of the three luxury vehicles inside the immaculately clean space.

Sherman didn't speak a word. He walked over to the stairs that led to the second floor loft area. "Hey, we've been up here before," I said, climbing the familiar stairs.

"One too many times," John said unhappily.

"Let's just get this over with," I remarked. "I'm tired of going back and forth with twists and turns. I need to know if that necklace is still in the safe." I waited at the top of the stairs and watched as Sherman went over to a wall at the back of the loft.

"It's just a blank white wall, Sherman," Judy called out catching up to him.

"Just wait," he said, reaching down to the ground and picking up a small, red toolbox.

"That's the safe," Judy exclaimed.

"No," Sherman said, stepping on an item on the floor. "Here it is." I looked over his body just in time to see him step on a large button that was hidden under the toolbox. A piece of the floor popped up and disclosed a hole in the floor.

"Clever" I said, watching as John shoved Sherman aside to see better. Sherman nearly fell back into me, but I held him firmly and help steady him to his normal, hunched stance.

"I need light," John barked. Judy pulled out one of the flashlights she was still holding onto.

I noticed Axel was awfully quiet since we've left his guesthouse. He stayed in the background until now. This was his garage, his necklace (he believes), his wife, and his entire fault. He didn't want to push any of John's buttons, but now that we're about to discover whether the necklace was inside this small, square hole he wanted to be up front and center. "Back off a little, Eklund," John snarled at him. "I know you want to see if your precious necklace is in here."

"Of course I do," he remarked. "The implications either way are huge. If it's missing that means Svenson got it from Prunella, and what will he do to her and Lynne?"

"And if the necklace is still in here?" I asked him curiously. "Are you thinking of taking it and hiding it somewhere else just in case Svenson hasn't been here yet?"

"Yes," he stated, matter of factly. "Then we can wait for him, because we know at some point Svenson will be here unless he already has."

"Let's just see if it's in this hole first," John said, as Judy flashed the light inside the hole. "There's a metal box in here," he screeched reaching inside to grab it. "It's really heavy," he said, asking for Axel to give him a hand.

Axel bent down on his knees and they each took a hold of the box and hauled it to the surface and planted it down with a clunk onto the floor. "There's a digital display on the top, Sherman," John said. "How do you open the thing?"

Sherman, who was now standing behind us moved forward and stared down at the thing. "It requires a combination."

"We know that!" John yelled. "Tell me what it is, now!"

"But, I was told to never disclose the numbers."

John stood up, grabbed Sherman by his shoulders rather brusquely and shook him. "Do you really think this is the time to be discreet?" Sherman stared back at John's furious expression and shook his head.

"I'll whisper it to you," he agreed, looking over at Axel. Axel caught the look and said, "So, you still don't believe me, do you Sherman? You think I'll betray you and steal the necklace for myself?"

"Well, I-I just don't know what to believe, sir," Sherman said.

"I don't care about that, tell me the combination, Sherman," John ordered, directing Sherman's attention back to him. Sherman bent over towards John's right ear and murmured the information. John just muttered, "Uh-huh, hmm, okay." He told Axel to give him a little room or as I believe, he didn't want Axel to see what numbers he typed in. Not that it would ever matter because I doubt anyone would use the same combination again.

"Green light," Sherman said anxiously. "That means it's ready to open." John grabbed the small handle on the top of the metal box and gave it a lift. "It's unlocked." We huddled together as the lid slowly released.

"I can't take this much longer, John. Hurry it up!" I cried out.

"Yeah, hurry," Inga, stammered.

The lid was all the way open when I spotted a black velvet box inside. "It's the case for the necklace we had made," I exclaimed. "It's in there!"

John held the black box in his hand and said, "Not necessarily. It could be empty."

"Well, what are you waiting for? Open it up!" Axel said impatiently.

John forced open the tightly sealed box and inside revealed…NO necklace.

"We're too late," I wailed horrified. "They've already been here and Svenson took our necklace."

John stood up and put his hand upon my shoulder. "I'm sorry, Ruth Ann. I had a feeling they were already here. We've taken too much time to get to this place," John explained, sneering over at Sherman again.

"You think this is all *my fault*, don't you?"

"Well, if you would've told us the whereabouts of this safe a long time ago we might've had a chance, but now we're too late," Judy snapped at him. "It's not *all* your fault, Sherman, but this was a huge thing to hide from us."

"I promised Ms. Prunella that I would never, ever tell anyone about this." He looked over at me with a guilty, nervous expression and added, "Even to you, Ruth Ann. I wasn't even to tell you."

"I don't understand, why?" I questioned. "She didn't trust me?"

"No, I don't think that was the case at all," Axel replied for Sherman. "She didn't want you in any danger, but that happened anyway."

"Now what?" I asked, feeling completely useless.

"We need to find them before they leave the country," Axel answered. "Once Svenson gets what he wants he'll leave."

"But what about Lynne and Prunella?" I asked nervously.

"I don't know, Ruth Ann," he admitted. "Chief?"

"There's one thing we didn't mention yet," John said. "What if Prunella took the necklace out *before* getting captured by Svenson?"

"Yes!" I exclaimed with some newfound confidence. "She might've stashed it away somewhere when you, Axel, and she were supposedly getting back together."

"*Supposedly*?" Axel asked me. "Ruth Ann, we are together. I thought you believed me."

"That's not what I meant, sorry. I was thinking when you were closing in on her and she knew the location of the safe could be disclosed, she might've moved it. Once the both of you worked it out, she just didn't have time to retrieve it, and put it back in the safe."

"Oh, I see what you mean," he said thoughtfully. "You could be right. When I first contacted her, she thought I was threatening her, but once we hashed everything out, we realized that we still loved each other. I'm the one who closed her off and treated her like I didn't want anything to do with her."

"That's when she originally stole the necklace from you back in Sweden, right?" I asked.

"Yes, after my first wife died, Prunella and I married each other too fast. I was distraught, but madly in love with Prunella. I went in the wrong direction when dealing with my grief. Prunella tried and tried to get through to me, but I shut her out. I pushed her away and she didn't have any choice but to steal the necklace from me."

"Then you tried to kill her," I added.

"I wasn't thinking clearly, Ruth Ann. Remember, when she told me she was dying from some strange illness, I set her up and pampered her."

"She was a prisoner in your house back in Sweden," Inga snapped. "She had to pretend to be dying so you wouldn't kill her!"

"Not exactly accurate, Inga," Axel replied. "I could never hurt her. We were in a very bad place, but that's all in the past. We need to find out whether the necklace is still hidden or in Svenson's hand. That's the matter at hand."

"I agree," John chimed in. "Where do we go from here?"

"Is there anywhere they could be hiding out until Svenson convinces Prunella to hand over the necklace?" Judy inquired.

John looked at Axel and added, "Or should we be asking you if there's anywhere else you've had built that could hide them?"

"If Svenson thinks I'm working with you he wouldn't hide them anywhere I know about."

"Does Svenson know you're working with us now?" I asked him.

"The last Svenson knew was when Ruth Ann and I were talking back in the kitchen in the main house. They were in the library when he took matters into his own hands."

"So, he might not *assume* you're working with John yet?" I asked.

"Not sure. What else would he think now?"

"If he's been watching us or following us somehow he would know," Judy said. "But, if he took off he might think there's two groups after them."

"That's right!" I cried out. "Our group with John, Judy, Ben, Inga, Sherman, and me. Then there's Axel, and for all Svenson knows, Axel could have more men helping him to find him, too."

"I would have to assume the latter is what Svenson thinks," John replied. "Why would Axel work with us? Svenson knows he's on the run from the law and he believes Axel still despises us. Unless…" I took over and said, "Unless Prunella told him differently."

"She wouldn't do that!" Inga protested. "She wouldn't tell Svenson anything."

"We can only hope so," John stated.

"I know so," Inga retorted. "I think she hid the necklace before she left to meet with you and Svenson," Inga said looking at Axel. "She might've thought Sherman would tell someone about the new location of the safe so she hid it safely away somewhere."

"I wouldn't and didn't tell anyone where that new safe was." He looked at John and stated, "Until I was forced to."

"We know, Sherman," John replied. "But you waited too long to tell anyone and now we've wasted valuable time."

"Let's get back to the matter at hand, please," I begged. "I'm sure Svenson's getting impatient and who knows what desperate move he'll make. He has my daughter."

"So, if Prunella hid the necklace elsewhere, and is still making Svenson run around for it, then I bet they're close by," Inga suggested. "But where?"

"Where else could they be?" I asked. "Svenson doesn't know the town well and neither does Prunella."

"But your daughter does, Ruth Ann," Axel mentioned.

"You're right!" I cried out.

"Now we're getting somewhere," John said. "If Svenson's smart, and he is a lawyer, I bet he relied on Lynne's knowledge of Deer Creek." John and everyone looked over at me and asked, "So, if you were Lynne, where would you take us?"

"I know!" I bellowed. "Her bakery."

"Exactly," John answered. "Let's get out of here and head back into town."

John put the empty black velvet box back into the safe and lowered it back into the hole. "Just in case someone comes back, it won't look like we've been here."

"Good thinking," I said.

We rushed down the stairs and headed out of the garage and through the grass into the back kitchen door of the main estate. "I'm fairly confident they're not here, but we should do a quick check to make sure," John suggested. He looked at Judy and said, "You take Axel, Ben, and Sherman and check the second and third floors. I'll take Ruth Ann and Inga and hit the basement and first floor. Meet back in the foyer as fast as you can." With John's instructions we took off in our designated groups, and once again, I had to go into the basement.

"You're with me, Ruth Ann," John commented when I complained.

"But I'm tired of finding bodies in basements."

"There won't be any down here now. They've left, I'm sure of it. This is just a quick, cautious look around."

"Fine," I said, as I followed John down the rickety, wooden stairs. Inga was right behind me and just as I stood on the bottom stair I tripped over an object that John must've missed. He grabbed me, as I was about to fall flat on my face.

"What happened, Ruth Ann?"

"I stumbled over," I bent over and picked up a small object from the ground, "this." I held up a small piece of foil.

"What is it?" Inga asked, pushing her way in front of me from the bottom stair.

"It's garbage," John said, dismissing the object and starting to walk away.

"No, it's not," I said, unwrapping the tightly balled up piece. It took me a few seconds when I hit jackpot. "Look," I cried out. "It's a piece of donut!"

John hurried back to me and stated, "So what. It's probably from the guesthouse. We ate donuts there, too."

"Exactly," I declared. "Don't you get it?" John shrugged his shoulders so I explained. "It's a clue left here. Lynne did this on purpose."

"That's pushing it a little too far, don't you think?" John inquired.

"No, she did it on purpose. I know it."

"How, Ruth Ann?" Inga asked curiously.

"Think about it. We now know they came back through the tunnel. Lynne knows they would have to go somewhere outside of this house to waste time, but Prunella wouldn't know where to go. They have to stay close because of the necklace, so Lynne suggested her bakery."

"And her way of telling us where they went was putting a piece of a donut inside a rolled up ball of foil?" John asked. "Hmmm."

"There's another huge clue in this, too."

Inga and John looked at each other in confusion.

"What?" John replied baffled.

"If they came to the main house through the tunnel from the guesthouse, that means they passed up going to the garage!"

"That's right!" John hollered happily. "Prunella must not have disclosed the new safe's location."

"But, it doesn't really matter," Inga interjected.

"Why?" I asked.

"Because the necklace wasn't there anyway. Prunella knew that and figured it really didn't matter to tell them about it."

"That's a good point, Inga," John said. "But, I'm curious about where Prunella would've hidden it then."

"She must've found someplace in the last twenty-four hours or so. Axel didn't convince her to leave us until lunchtime on Sunday. That was only yesterday."

"It seems like days ago," Inga murmured.

"I agree," John said. "It's early evening now and getting dark outside. If they did actually go over to your daughter's bakery, then we can easily sneak up on them."

"I think we need to find the others and tell them what we found," I said, turning around and heading back upstairs. John took one last look around and headed up after Inga and me. We waited in the kitchen for him, and then hurried out into the hall towards the foyer. "They're not back yet," Inga, said.

"I'll run up the stairs and call out for them. They have to be either on the second or third floors. We weren't gone that long so they haven't had too long to search up there." John took off up the long, wide staircase and Inga and I watched as he stood on the top of the landing of the second floor. He yelled out, but shook his head down to us. "Not on this floor," he said, turning and heading back up the narrower staircase that led to the third floor. At this point the stairs turned and we lost sight of him.

"He should be right back," I said to Inga who was anxiously pacing back and forth in front of the staircase.

"I know," she snapped back at me. "I think we need to get going, that's all. We're wasting time looking upstairs. They won't be here."

"I agree, but best be sure," I responded.

It didn't take John long before we saw him bounding down the stairs two at a time. "They're finishing up on the floor. No sign of anyone, so we'll take off to the bakery."

"If they're not there then I have no idea where to search next," I said, worried about the safety of my daughter and Prunella.

Chapter 34

We piled into John's trooper that was parked down the road. Judy sat in the front with me in the middle hovering over the gearshift. Axel, Ben, Inga, and Sherman squeezed into the back. John told us to hold on for a fast, bumpy ride. I wasn't looking forward to this part since I was barely able to put part of my behind down on the armrest.

"Turn on your siren, John," Judy called out. "Just in case we come across any cars, they'll pull over."

"Not this time, Judy. I don't want any warning that we're coming into town. I'm not even going to park at the bakery. We'll use the back alley behind Ruth Ann's store again. Then we'll walk over to the bakery."

"It's only two stores away. It's just a minute's walk, if that," I added.

Normally, it would take about twenty minutes to reach town from Axel and Prunella's estate. Tonight, John did it in less than fifteen. "Easy," I said, falling into Judy's lap on one of John's wild turns around a bend. Judy caught a hold of me before my whole body landed on her.

"Hold on to the seats," John instructed. "We need to hurry."

After a few dicey turns and a slide or two, John made his way into town. We would have to pass by the bakery in order to get to my store. The entrance to the alley wasn't until after Sinful Sweets and John didn't want to make the turn there. He passed my store, Ruth Ann's Antiques, and entered at the next opening. He pulled into the spot I usually park behind my store. "Hold on," John said, as we started to unload out of the truck. "Not everyone's going over there."

"What?" I exclaimed. "Don't even think of banning me!"

John looked over at me, as I was about to crawl out of the truck. "I know I can't keep you away, Ruth Ann." He turned his head and looked in the back seat. "I think we're too big of a group."

"I agree, John," Judy chimed in. "But who's not going with us?"

"Ben, you go over to Doc Albert and tell him I sent you to get checked out."

Ben protested and told John he was perfectly fine, but John said it wasn't his fight to fight and please do as he asked. Ben was officially excused and left the truck sulking. I felt horrible for him, but John was right. We didn't need Ben getting hurt or in the way.

"Next," John began again as Axel, Inga, and Sherman spread out in the back seat. "Sherman, I don't think you're in good enough shape for a chase if it came to that. Why don't you follow Ben and have Doc check you out too?"

"Absolutely not," Sherman objected. "If you won't let me go, I'll wait here, in this vehicle."

John looked at me and I nodded. There was no way Sherman would leave with Prunella in such danger. He felt partially responsible for the position she and Lynne were in. "Fine," John agreed. "Sherman, you stay here and guard the police truck. I'll leave the keys in it so if you see Svenson or that Jimmy character coming your way, you take off." He looked back at Sherman in the rear view mirror and quickly asked, "You okay with that? I know it's not a limousine, but you can handle it, right?"

"Yes." Sherman replied, and sat back and relaxed a little when suddenly Inga, worried she was next with John, said immediately, "I'm going."

"Yes, Inga, you, Eklund, Ruth Ann, Judy, and I are heading over there now." John opened the door and made sure he had his gun and Judy had hers. Inga, Axel, and I were weaponless, but that was okay. I wasn't comfortable with a gun, and I bet John didn't give Axel one because he wasn't positive whether he could trust him.

John took us through the alley over to my daughter's bakery, Sinful Sweets. There were no windows on the backside of the bakery so we wouldn't be spotted as we got closer. "I hope this isn't a wild goose chase," John said, reaching the back door to the bakery. "Okay, I'm going to take Judy and go inside. If you hear any shots or if you hear anything that says we're in danger, go back to Sherman and head to the police station. Got that?" The three of us nodded even though I knew that's probably not what we would do.

John took hold of the long metal handle of the bakery back door. "It's locked," he said, pulling back frustrated. "Ruth Ann, by any chance do you have an extra key to the bakery?"

"Yes!" I exclaimed. "But it's back in my office at the store."

"Take Judy and go get it. Hurry back. We'll step aside and wait."

Judy didn't wait for my response, but grabbed my elbow and yanked me to go. "Geez, Judy, don't break my arm in the process," I snapped angrily. "I'm going." We took off and made it back to the antique store within a minute or so.

Judy went over to Sherman before he started the truck. "I thought you were running back here to have us take off," he said panicked, but appeared ready to go with his hands firmly on the steering wheel.

"No, we need Ruth Ann's key. The back door is locked at Lynne's bakery."

Sherman bobbed his head up and down and took his tightly gripped hands off the steering wheel. "Oh, do you need me to go back with you and Ruth Ann?"

"No, stay here and do exactly what you just did."

"What did I do?" he asked, confused.

"You were about to start the truck for us. That means you were paying attention and ready for action."

"Oh, yeah, it does," Sherman said, grinning from the compliment of a very difficult detective. Having Judy give a compliment, well that's practically unheard of.

I hurried and opened the back door of my store. I had already given Meme, my Assistant Manager, the day off so I knew she wouldn't be there. It was early evening and the store normally would've closed at five, but sometimes Meme's overly ambitious and I could see her coming in to redecorate the showroom while the store was closed. I entered my storage room. It was in a state of disarray with new merchandise we had recently received. The biggest holiday season for a store owner was approaching and I had been busy ordering several new items to fill the first and second floors. Meme will have a fit when she shows up Tuesday morning and sees the mess in here. I made my way around the boxes and rolled up rugs to get over to my office. The mess flowed into there, too.

"What a mess!" I yelled to myself. "I need to retire from this detective business and get back to my store!" I went around a new set of wingback chairs that had just arrived and made my way to the beautiful, mahogany desk I found a year ago. The large, smooth top was supposed to be bare. That was my promise to myself. I never wanted to leave the store unless the papers were cleared from there. However, after being kidnapped and flown to Sweden then back to Deer Creek with a new family, I just haven't spent the amount of time in here necessary to keep up. I collected the sprawled out papers into one neat pile. "Tomorrow," I mumbled, knowing it wasn't going to happen until this mess of a nightmare I got myself into was finished.

I opened the middle drawer that stored small accessories such as pens, scissors, and tape and grabbed a small box of staples. I slid open the cardboard box and inside was the spare key for the bakery. I hid it in a common item because I was told no burglar would look in a plain old staples box. "Here it is," I said, putting it into my pants pocket and heading back out of the office. I locked my back door and went to the police truck.

"About time," Judy snapped impatiently.

"I had to find it," I replied curtly. "Let's go," I said, not wanting anymore snide remarks from her. I waved to Sherman and we took off back to the bakery. John, Axel, and Inga were waiting against the brick wall in the back of the store.

"Got it?" John asked, not daring to mention how long it took us.

"Yep," I answered, pulling it out and handing it over to John.

"Great, stay back alongside the building. Judy, let's go." She stood right next to John as he gently put the key in and gave it a slight, slow turn so the click wouldn't be too loud. The door unlocked more loudly than he would've liked, but it was rusted a bit from the harsh weather here in Colorado. Maybe I'll just have her lock replaced for her, not that she isn't a successful bakery owner, but because she's so busy she'd never get around to doing it. Lynne's business was thriving. She was the only full service bakery in town and it just happened to be the main hub for gossip. Lynne was notorious for trying new baked items and either giving them away as samples or selling them for an absurdly low price. Her busiest time was morning and early afternoon. Townspeople and tourists, during ski season, would come in and eat their breakfast or afternoon dessert in there and gossip away. If they weren't at Lynne's bakery, then they were over at Wilma's Café.

SHE'S GOT BALLS
RECIPE #2 - OREO BALLS

- **1 package Neufchatel cheese (softened)**
- **1 package Oreo's**
- **1 bag semi sweet or white or milk chocolate chips**

Whip up the cheese in a large stand mixer (hand mixer or good old fashioned mixing bowl and wooden spoon will work, too!)

Crush cookies (use food processor or a plastic bag and rolling pin to smash cookies)

Add cookies to whipped cheese and mix just until combined. Put in bowl and freeze for 30-60 minutes. (Any longer cover with plastic wrap)

On lined waxed paper cookie sheet, roll into 1-2 inch balls (any size you'd like!). Place in freezer for 15-30 minutes.

**Melt chocolate in microwave until smooth.
Dip balls into chocolate and place back on lined
cookie sheet. Place back into freezer for 10-15
minutes.**

**Enjoy. Store in plastic bag or any other
container in the refrigerator**

Axel and I leaned against the back of the building while Inga paced back and forth around the back door. "Inga, you're making me nervous. Come over here," I said, getting dizzy watching her pace.

"I want to go in and see what's happening," she said eagerly. "We can help them."

"It's their job, Judy," Axel added. "They'll let us know what's going on as soon as they can." Inga stopped her pacing and stood right next to the back door. She glared at Axel when he spoke to her, and by the way she looked at him, I could see she just didn't trust him. I didn't blame her. She had been through so much with Prunella back in Sweden. I wasn't sure how I was able to get past it myself, but I had.

"It's okay, Inga," I said. "John and Judy are the only ones with guns so let them check it out." I looked at the back door hoping it would open when I added, "Don't you think I'd like to run in there myself? My daughter could be in danger inside there."

"Then why didn't you?" Inga asked, wondering why I was so calm.

"I have a tendency to make matters worse. I've put too many people's lives in danger as it is, so I'm doing what John ordered." I quickly added, "For the time being."

"Now that sounds more like you," Inga said chuckling. "We'll wait a few more minutes, then I'm going in."

"I agree," Axel said to Inga. "I know you don't like me very much, but why don't we put that aside for the moment and work together? What do you say?" Inga begrudgingly nodded and for a second I thought she even flashed him a teensy weensy smile. It would help if we could get along, but if they expected me to behave with Judy, well, that might not happen.

"How long's it been now?" Inga asked after a few more minutes passed.

"They've been in there seven minutes. I think it's long enough," Axel said, checking his watch. "Why don't we just have a look inside?"

"What's right inside the door, Ruth Ann?" Inga asked.

"It's the kitchen for the bakery. There's a storage room off to the right where the flour, sugar, and other non-perishables are stored. Then next to that is a large, walk-in frig and freezer area." I caught myself panicking and blurted out, "Oh, no, what if they threw them into the walk-in?"

"We'd better get in there right away," Axel said, reaching for the handle. "I'd ask if I could go in myself, but I'm pretty sure I'd get vetoed immediately, so let's go in together, eh?" Inga was about to pounce before Axel was finished explaining.

"Be ready for them to grab us," he said, implying Svenson and Jimmy, not John and Judy.

"As ready as I can be," I remarked standing right behind Axel.

He pulled the door toward him and opened it about six inches. He stuck his head around to peek inside. "Well, see anything?" Inga asked excitedly.

"It's really bright in there," he replied blinking his eyes to get used to the light.

"It's dark out here and Lynne's bakery's very sterile. Can you see anyone?"

"No, let's go in," he said opening the heavy, metal door just widely enough to fit through. I was right behind him, and then Inga behind me. She had to open the door just a bit more to fit her stout figure through the door.

We entered into the back of the bakery. As I mentioned, the storeroom closet and walk-in were to my right. Straight ahead were the stainless steel prep tables filled with bins of flour, sugar, rolling pins, and utensils. To the left was a wall of ovens. Lynne put in several ovens so she could always keep her customers happy without ever running out of any baked goods. The overhead lighting was intense with white walls and stainless appliances. It took a moment before our eyes adjusted and we were able to take a serious look around. Axel and Inga headed straight for the storeroom while I went to the walk-in.

I had an eerie feeling I would find someone in there and my intuition was accurate. "Over here," I yelled to Axel and Inga. "Someone's in the walk-in!"

Axel and Inga rushed over to me as I tried to see inside the smoky-glass opening. I couldn't make out if it was one person or several. "We need to get in there," I demanded trying to get a grip on the handle. I pulled and pulled, but the door wouldn't budge. "Why won't it open?" I begged.

Axel looked around frantically around and it was Inga who spotted the blockage. "There's a broom pulled through the handle on the inside. We won't be able to open it from out   here."

"Can't the person inside open it then?" Axel asked, confused.

"If they're able to," I said, banging on the glass door. "Why won't they get up? I can't make out who it is, can either of you?"

Axel put his hands up to his eyes as if he was shielding the sun and looked in. Inga was right next to him, also staring into the walk-in. I was pacing around the room trying to find something that could open up that door. "We're going to have to break it," I proclaimed. "Why can't we just do that?"

"It's really thick glass, Ruth Ann," Axel said, feeling the door. "I think I see movement from the back of the walk-in, why won't they get up and pull the broom out?"

"Maybe they're restrained back there and Svenson knew we wouldn't be able to save them," Inga said.

"Ridiculous," I cried. "We have to find a way to get in there, and quickly."

Axel backed away from the door and told Inga and me to keep banging on the door. "Keep whoever's in there alert."

I felt my hand throbbing with pain as I pounded on the glass door until Axel finally made his way over with a large, cast-iron pan. "I'll try this. It's the heaviest thing I could find." He held up the pan and ordered Inga and me to back away. "It could shatter so stay back," he said.

"Wait," I hollered. "You'll get hit with the glass if it shatters."

"I'll be fine, Ruth Ann. The only exposed skin I have is my hands and head. I'll duck away if I see it breaking."

Inga and I watched from one of the stainless prep counters as Axel raised his arm and give it an awkward blow. "I'm just trying to get a feel for how hard to hit the glass," he said. I wondered if Inga might not be better at whacking the glass with the skillet. She's got a ton of anger brewing inside her and maybe she'd be better at this than Axel. I watched as he put both hands on the skillet, lifted it about shoulder height, and he turned his body to give it the full force that was needed to break the thick glass. He whirled it straight into the glass, but nothing happened except a loud, high-pitched dinging sound. "It may take a few hits before it starts to loosen," he said, winding up and hitting it again.

It took several hits when finally, the glass cracked. "You did it," I cried out. "Do it again, quick!" Axel hit the glass harder than ever the next time and the skillet broke through the glass and, without shattering it, broke into several large chunks of thick glass.

"You did it!" Inga exclaimed excited.

"Hurry, clear the way so we can see who's in there," I yelled desperately wanting to run right inside to see who was in there. "Are you alright?" I asked Axel, as he stood unmoving.

He quickly shook his body as shards of glass fell to the floor. "Stay back for a second," he demanded, as he shook a few more times. He didn't want to brush the glass off his body because his hands would get cut.

Inga and I were still about ten feet back when I couldn't take it anymore. "Can you see who's in there?" I asked frantically.

"I haven't opened my eyes yet," he called back to me. "I've got glass on me everywhere."

Inga ran over to the massive, country style sink basin and looked around. "I've got gloves," she yelled. "Hold on, I'll get you cleaned up." Inga ran past me and over to Axel. She carefully stepped over many big pieces of glass and almost lost her footing, but caught herself before she tumbled into the dangerously sharp glass on the floor. I wasn't afraid of her stepping on the glass because Inga was always wearing heavy work shoes with soles as thick as my highest heels!

"How's Axel look?" I shouted over to her.

Inga didn't respond. She was carefully wiping the loose pieces of glass off his hair and face. While she was cleaning him up I noticed her head wasn't looking directly at Axel's face. She was looking inside the walk-in, but wasn't saying a word. "Inga?" I called to her again. "What do you see?" She looked like she was in a trance so I shouted, "Inga!"

She shook her head and went back to work on Axel. I still was clueless as to the identity of the person inside the walk-in. I couldn't take it any longer so I carefully took a few steps forward. "Stop!" Axel screamed at me, scaring me half to death.

"I need to see who's in there. Is it Lynne? Please don't avoid telling me, I have to know." I was worried Inga saw who was in there and whoever it was they weren't in good shape. "Please," I begged of them.

"Ruth Ann," Axel said, finally able to fully open his eyes. "It's not Lynne."

"Thank God," I muttered. "But who is it then?"

"It's John and Judy," Inga answered stepping into the walk-in and disappearing from my sight.

"Can I get any closer?" I asked Axel.

"Let me throw down a tarp, Ruth Ann," Axel said, hurrying over to the storage closet and grabbing a clear plastic sheet. He shook it open and laid it down on the ground over a large portion of the glass. "The glass may break through, but I think you can make it over if you step lightly and take notice if the glass starts to come through the plastic."

Axel grabbed my hand and led me over the plastic. Once or twice I heard a crack in the glass, but I made it to the opening of the walk-in without injury. I stood in the doorway and looked in horror at John and Judy who were thrown on the floor, tied, and gagged. They were awake and wide-eyed as Inga desperately tried to free them of their restraints. Axel hurried to help her, and I stood frozen inside the frigid space. "Are they okay?" I anxiously asked them.

"I think so," Axel said, getting Judy's hands freed, but still not taking the gag out of her mouth.

"I can't get John's ropes off," Inga said, frustrated. "It's so cold in here my hands aren't moving."

"Let me try," I said. "I'm still warm." I went into the back of the walk-in and John reached his tied wrists up to me in desperation. I pulled off the gag and he took a deep breath of frigid air. "I'm so glad you didn't listen to me and stay outside."

"Really?" I laughed even though I knew the moment didn't call for any humor. "When have I ever?"

John smiled and shivered while I hurried to untie the ropes from his wrists. "Got it," I said, rubbing my sore hands together. "Let's get you in the warm air," I said, reaching down and holding my hand out for him to grab. He took it eagerly and I heaved as hard as I could when he got his footing and stood up. I looked over at Axel as he helped Judy get to a standing position. Unfortunately, he had to take off her gag, too.

Judy left the freezer quickly and went into the warm kitchen. "Brrr," she said as she uncontrollably trembled. "I'm about to turn on one of those ovens just to stand by it and warm up."

"How long were you two in there?" Axel asked. "We weren't outside that long."

"Long enough," Judy snapped at his comment. "They put us in there to die!"

"WHO?" I demanded loudly as we were now out of the walk-in and standing away from the cold air that was spewing out. "Svenson and Jimmy," John admitted. "They were waiting for us the minute we entered the back door."

"Wait, were Lynne and Prunella with them?" I asked.

"No," Judy replied. "They weren't back here." I looked from John to Judy over to Axel and cried out in agony, "Then where are they?"

"Well, with all the noise we've made in here, I doubt they're still here," Judy remarked. "That glass breaking was really loud."

"Would you rather we left you in there?" I retorted.

"That's not what I meant, Ruth Ann," Judy answered exasperated. "Of course you guys had to rescue us. John and I would be dead pretty quickly in there."

"So, you didn't see my daughter or Prunella?" I asked John, ignoring Judy. "Did they *say* anything about them?"

John looked intently in my eyes and said, "Yes. They made a point of laughing in our faces and bragging about how stupid we were, and wondering how we ever got our badges."

"For getting caught and mislead so often?" I asked, even though the statement was rhetorical.

"Yes."

"What did they say, exactly?" Axel chimed in on the conversation. "Please tell me we don't have to go back up to my estate again."

"Not yet," Judy answered for John. John glared at her for answering, but Judy ignored him and kept going. "Svenson referred to this as a game, like a hunter when searching for his prey."

"A *game*?" Axel asked strangely. "He's doing this on purpose, isn't he?"

"Yes," John answered quickly. "Svenson has Prunella and Lynne. He won't hurt them, right now. Not while he's still waiting for Prunella to hand over the necklace." He looked at me irritated and added, "She's playing him, too."

"What do you mean, *right now*?" I questioned him instantly. "You think he'll hurt them soon, don't you?"

"Yes, I do, Ruth Ann," John replied solemnly. "Prunella should just hand over that ridiculous necklace of hers. It's the root of this entire position we're in."

"Are you sure about that, John?" Axel interjected. "There may be more to this than we're aware."

"Such as?" John asked Axel.

"Maybe Prunella doesn't have access to *our* necklace or let's just throw out there that she already gave it to him."

"That makes no sense, Eklund," John retorted. "If she already gave him the bloody necklace then why's he still hanging around? He would've taken off back to Sweden and stayed away from any attention."

"You already answered that yourself, John," Axel pointed out.

"Huh?"

"You and Judy just finished telling us Svenson's looking at this as a game. He wants all of us to suffer, and by keeping Prunella and Lynne away from their loved ones I 'd say he's playing a perfect game, don't you?"

"Ridiculous," John stammered.

"Hey," I interrupted them. "Axel, you mentioned that Prunella might not have access to the necklace. What did you mean by that?"

"Yeah, Eklund, the box in the safe was empty."

"We concluded Prunella took the necklace and hid it somewhere else before she ever saw you or Svenson," Sherman said out of the blue.

"Hey, where'd you come from?" I asked, turning around and seeing the butler standing just inside the back door from the alley.

"You took so long I was curious. I locked the truck and hauled myself over here. I heard the glass breaking, but didn't know if it was safe to come in here so I waited outside a little longer. Once it was quieter I poked my head in here just in time to hear your conversation. There's no way Ms. Prunella would be participating in Svenson's sick game," Sherman glared over at John for his accusations.

"I'm not saying Prunella's *willingly* playing his game. She's being forced to go along with him, but why?"

"So what's next with them?" I asked, worried. "Where can they go now?"

"Well, let's see, they've made an appearance at the Halloween party, all the back and forth up at my estate. They've been at the high school, and then back to the resort, and back to my estate. Now, we're back in town and in your daughter's bakery."

"Don't forget my store," I added. "John and Inga were held up in there, too. Plus, Lynne was taken from there."

"Yes, but I don't know this town well enough to figure out what their next move could possibly be."

"That's just it, the only one who would know is Lynne," I replied. "We need to look around and see if she left another clue for us. I thought for sure we'd find her here."

"I know," John replied feeling sorry that my hope for Lynne being here was dashed. "But Lynne's a smart cookie, she'll be okay."

I know he didn't mean the pun about the cookie, but he's right. Lynne's brave and intelligent. She wouldn't let Svenson and that Jimmy character get under her skin. Hopefully Prunella wouldn't either, but I wasn't so sure about that. Prunella might've done something to tick these men off, and who knows what they're threatening to do to her. Prunella was acting strangely the last time I saw her. I know she felt Axel was threatening her, but once those two figured out their own relationship, why did she still shut me out? The only conclusion I could come up with was she wasn't truly trusting Axel yet. We need to find them both and put an end to this disgusting 'game.'

Chapter 35

Before we headed out to the front of Lynne's bakery, we did a thorough search in the kitchen. We avoided the walk-in and broken glass, but we couldn't find any clues from Lynne or Prunella. "Let's go up front," I said, pushing through one of the swinging doors that Lynne used to go in and out of the kitchen to the front of her store.

"Me first," John said, pushing me gently aside. "I doubt they're waiting for us after all the noise and commotion we've made, but I want to be sure." John pushed his way through the door and instantly stuck his head back in the other swinging door. "All clear," he said, letting the door swing shut.

I went first, and then Axel, Sherman, Judy and Inga followed. We were a large group, but we were determined to find my daughter and Prunella safe. We split up and each checked an area of the bakery. John took charge and walked the perimeter of the front room. Inga and Sherman checked the dozen or so four person tables and chairs while Axel and I checked the long counter and underneath it. Judy double checked our work and just plainly got on my nerves. "Stop that," I snapped at her for walking right on my heels. "I'm perfectly capable of looking around the counter. It is my daughter's bakery," I said. "I'm the only one who knows how things should really look."

"That's a good point, Ruth Ann," Axel said, smiling over at me. He tried to get me back on track searching for clues instead of fighting with Judy, once again.

"Thank you," I said, going back to my own hunt. I was becoming more and more discouraged and I knew my feelings were being taken out on her. I decided I should apologize, but she really did need to back off.

"Ruth Ann," Judy said, after I reluctantly apologized for my rude behavior. "I know you're worried about Lynne and Prunella. I'm sure they're both completely fine and giving them hell."

"If she takes after her mother she will be," John said jokingly.

"Can we please finish here and figure out where we're going next," Sherman pleaded. "I haven't slept in two days!"

"None of us has, Sherman," John said to him. "If we don't find something in the bakery that tells us where they're going, I'm afraid we're at a dead end."

"Knowing my daughter, I'm sure she left a sign."

We continued our search and I concluded there was nothing on the counter that was of any use. I went on my hands and knees and searched every shelf and space underneath the counter. "I can't find anything," I said annoyed.

"I doubt Lynne would have time to leave a note under the counter, Ruth Ann," Judy said. "That would be too obvious."

"Has anyone found *anything*?" I begged. Sherman and Inga shook their heads, and Axel...hey, where was Axel? He was just with me searching the counter area a second ago and now he was nowhere in sight.

"Hey," I called out loudly. "Where's Axel?"

John, who was helping flip tables upside down to see if anything was taped to the bottom, popped up and anxiously looked over the room. "He's not in here. He must've gone back into the kitchen."

I was about to head back there when John stopped me. "Let me," he ordered, flying through the swinging door. He wasn't gone long when he rushed back in and said, "He's gone!"

"Gone?" I asked, stunned. "Where'd he go?"

John and Judy gave each other a fast look and I wondered what was going through their minds. I believe he was frustrated with our lack of progress so he took matters into his own hands. John and Judy, on the other hand, had a different viewpoint.

"You think he found something and didn't share it with the rest of us?" I asked them.

"That was my first thought," John admitted.

"Mine, too," Judy confirmed. "The minute he had a chance to ditch us I knew he would."

"But he's changed sides," I said, confused. "He said he wanted forgiveness for everything he's put us through."

"Especially you, Ruth Ann," John said sincerely. "He's put you through the most, besides Prunella."

"If he found something it had to be where I was searching too. I didn't see anything out of the ordinary," I said, wondering what he found.

"Think back, Ruth Ann," John said seriously. "You went over every inch of the counter above and below. Axel searched the exact area you did. Is there anything you can recall coming across that you thought was unimportant or trivial?"

I walked back to where I started looking and walked the entire counter up and down. I leaned against the end of the counter and put my elbows down and my hands in my head. Think, think, and think. All I came across was empty creamers, napkins, containers with an assortment of sugars, and…" I GOT IT!" I screamed as I popped up.

"What, what do you got?" Judy asked eagerly.

"There was a pamphlet on the counter advertising the school play over at the high school." I scooted over to where it was and I was right, it was missing.

"You're saying when you searched the counter you noticed a pamphlet about a high school play?" Judy asked. "And now it's not there?"

"Yes," I repeated. "It has to be what Axel took because it's not there anymore."

"Good, Ruth Ann," John said soothingly. "Why would he take that?"

"I don't know," I admitted. "I just passed by it and didn't look at it."

"Maybe something was written on there," Inga suggested. "Ms. Prunella or Lynne may have had a moment to scribble something down on it."

"Well, we don't have it anymore, and Axel does. The only thing we can do is head over to the high school and check it out," John said. "Ruth Ann, can you recall if the play was tonight or for a date in the future?"

"It's not tonight," I replied. "I know that for a fact. Nancy has been working with the students on that play for some time now. I think opening night's in three days."

"So, not until Thursday?" John asked, thinking out loud. "Hmmm, I doubt it's about the play then if it's not tonight."

"They may have dress rehearsals though," I said to him. "It's pretty late now so I doubt the students are still there."

"What time is it?" Inga asked curiously.

"It's 9:00 in the evening now," John replied looking at his watch. "On Monday," he added for us.

"I still can't believe it's only been 48 hours since we've started this nightmare," I said sadly. It was at 10:00 on Halloween night when the nightmare began with Bert falling from the ceiling, dead.

"Let's see if we can't put an end to it tonight," John stated, stomping back into the kitchen. "Let's get over to my truck and head to the high school. It may be a wild goose chase, but we need to check it out."

"Remember," Judy said. "It's Svenson playing his sick little game."

"Not so little," I murmured to myself.

Our not so little group headed out the back door and over to my store. John was first to arrive in the alley behind my store and shouted so loud he could've woken the dead. "What's your problem?" I asked, out of breath from running around the store to get to the alley. Before he could respond, I saw why John yelled.

"It's gone!" he bellowed. John slowly turned around and glowered over at Sherman who just arrived. "You didn't leave the keys in the ignition, did you?"

Sherman looked horrified and shook his head. "No?" John asked him, full of doubt and fury. "Are you telling me you have my keys on you?"

Sherman corrected himself and said, alarmed, "I, well, yes, I mean," John cut him off his rambling and said, "Yes, you did take the keys with you or yes, the keys were left in the ignition?"

Sherman shook then nodded his head confusing us. "Stop it, Sherman," John snapped at him. "Just tell me!"

"I did leave the keys in the truck. I thought that's what you'd want me to do."

"Great, just great," he muttered pacing back and forth. "Eklund stole my truck!"

"That's not going to help his case, is it?" I asked John. "He must've been desperate or he wouldn't have done it."

"Stop protecting him, Ruth Ann," John spat angrily at me. "He's done it again."

"We don't know that for sure."

"He must've found a clue that made him take off in a hurry," Inga interrupted.

"Now what're we supposed to do?" Sherman asked, worried. "How far is this high school from here?"

"Almost a mile away," I answered. "We can make it, let's just get going."

"We obviously don't have a choice," Judy said, pulling out her flashlight and aiming it down the alley opposite the bakery. "I think we should stay in the alley until we hit that resort here."

"Yes," John said. "Let's get outta here."

John stomped off with Judy on his heels. I grabbed Sherman's arm and whispered to him that it wasn't entirely his fault. John did tell him to leave the keys in case we had to take off quickly. Inga walked next to Sherman and didn't say a word. She was a tough woman and probably blamed Sherman for us having to walk a mile over to the high school on a cold, November 2nd night.

We passed through the alley without running into a soul. Nobody was out this late, and most local businesses closed by now. By the time we ran into the parking lot of the resort it was almost ten at night and the parking lot was full. "Tourist season has begun," I said to Sherman and Inga trying to talk about something else. "Lots of people come here to ski and stay in this beautiful lodge." John ignored my comment, but waited for us to catch up to him and Judy before cutting across the parking lot.

We were almost on the other side of the lot when Judy yelled, "Hey, isn't that your truck, John?" We turned our heads around to where Judy was standing. "How did it end up here?"

"You've got to be kidding," John said, hurrying over to his truck. "It is my truck, but what's it doing here and not at the high school?"

"Isn't that easy to figure out," Inga said with a sarcastic edge. "Just because Mr. Eklund grabbed the play pamphlet doesn't mean that's where he went hurrying off to."

"Ah," I said. "You think Lynne or Prunella did write something on it?"

"Yes, we don't know what it was because none of us saw it," Inga replied.

"Yes, one person here did see it," John said, looking over at me. "Ruth Ann did glance at it."

"But," I started to say frustrated. "I didn't think much of it. It was just a high school advertisement for their play."

"So you can't recall anything out of the ordinary with it? Like some kind of writing on it?" Judy asked me.

I stood still next to John's truck and closed my eyes. I knew if I opened my mind up I might be able to recall seeing the pamphlet. "Think hard," Inga told me.

"Take a deep breath, Ruth Ann," Sherman added. I popped open my eyes and snapped, "Could you all please be quiet!"

"Sorry," Sherman snarled back at me. "We're just trying to help you."

I realized I wasn't being fair and apologized. I just asked them to give me a minute so I could concentrate and see if my mind would bring something to the surface about the writing, if any. They backed off a little and leaned on the side of John's police truck. I closed my eyes and took a deep breath and took myself back to the bakery, walking along the counter. I passed by the sugars and creamers, a cardboard box full of napkins that Lynne would set out the next morning, a roll of paper towels and cleaning solution…a pen. Aha, I saw a pen, but was it next to the pamphlet? Think, Ruth Ann, think…yes, it was next to the clear plastic holder that held the play pamphlet. That's when I saw it in my head. "There was writing on it!" I yelled excitedly.

John held his hands out so nobody would interfere with my thinking. "Stay with it, Ruth Ann, can you make out what it says?"

"I'm trying," I answered with my eyes tightly squeezed shut. I put myself back in the bakery and glancing at the piece of paper, and the pen, the pen, the paper, the pen, the paper… "I got it!" I opened my eyes and said in a rush, "There were a few scribbled words written in blue ink. I didn't think much of it when we were searching the bakery, but now that I took myself back to the very moment I passed by it, I could see it clearly."

Judy anxiously asked, "C'mon, what was written?"

"Scribbled," I snapped. "It was scribbled so I didn't think much of it. I thought it was just someone's messy note to him or herself. I remember thinking briefly that whoever did that made a mess on the play pamphlet."

"That's good, now tell us what was scribbled?" John asked, getting irritated with me. "We need to find your daughter, remember?"

"And Ms. Prunella," Sherman added.

"Yes, yes, both of them," John corrected.

"Only three messy words were written on it, and now that I've thought about it, it all makes sense."

"WHAT?" John demanded.

"Halloween, skeletons, catwalk."

"Huh?" Inga asked, confused.

"I said, Halloween, skeletons, and catwalk." I waited for those words to dawn on them. "Don't you get it?"

Inga and Sherman shook their heads while John gave me a funny glance. "I think it was a clue left for us."

"Yes, but do you see why my mind ignored it?"

"You probably brushed it off because it was just Halloween and someone was scribbling about the play or the party," John replied back to me while the others were finally getting what those three little words could imply.

"Exactly," I called out excited.

"I get it!" Inga shouted.

"Shhh," John insisted. "We don't want to raise attention to us."

"Sorry, it finally hit me. The truck's here at the resort because that's where the party was when Bert was murdered."

"Yes, and remember when we found Bert it was right after a bunch of plastic skeletons dropped from the ceiling," I reminded them.

"Then, when one of Chief John's men went and searched the ceiling they found a large space where someone could've hidden out before dropping Bert on the crowd," Inga continued.

"The catwalk," Judy said out loud even though we understood what it was.

"So, you think Lynne and Prunella are being held in the catwalk?" I asked John, excited.

"What else could it mean?" he questioned. "We should get in there right away. Maybe Richard or Carol saw Eklund and the others come in their resort."

"You think they just walked in the lobby?" I asked John, curiously.

"Maybe," he answered me. "This lot's pretty full. Lots of people coming and going so they would have blended in."

"But how would they know how to get up above the ballroom's ceiling and find this catwalk?" I asked.

"I'm sure it's not that hard to figure out," Judy remarked. "They did it already with Bert."

"Oh, sorry, I forgot it was Svenson who did that," I responded, but quickly asked, terrified, "You don't think he and Jimmy would do anything like that to my daughter, do you?"

"No, Ruth Ann," John quickly said. "They have to get the necklace so killing Prunella or Lynne would make no sense right now."

"But what if Svenson already has the necklace?" Inga asked, horrified. "He could kill them both and add them as victims in this game he's playing with us."

"Prunella would not give him her necklace!" I declared. "Svenson's desperate and trying to threaten Prunella and Lynne, but he won't kill them until he gets what he wants."

"Then he'll get out of this town," John said. "He wouldn't risk getting caught so I'm not too worried about this catwalk thing. I do think we need to get up there, maybe he let Lynne go."

"Oh, I hope so," I exclaimed. "Let's get inside."

"I need to get out of this freezing night air, too," Sherman said, as we hurried through the parking lot toward the front entrance. "My arthritis is making me slow and very sore."

"Stay in the lobby, Sherman," John said, just as we made it outside of the revolving door that opened into the elaborate lobby.

"No way, sir," he declared. "I won't stop until we find Ms. Prunella and Lynne."

Sherman entered the space in the revolving door with me. "I'm okay, now," he said. "That cold air just slows me down a bit."

"I understand, Sherman," I said. "It's painful for me, too."

"How?" he asked curiously.

"I've got two knee caps that are tilted inward, and after years of exercise and overuse, I've developed arthritis in them. Also, when I was younger, my father and I were in a car accident and we were hit from behind and just at impact, I turned my head around to see if a car was behind us. Ever since then, my neck hurts and the doctors told me I have arthritis there, too. Whenever the weather changes, hot or cold, my neck acts out. It's very painful."

"So you do understand?" he asked compassionately.

"Yes, that's why I wanted to mention it to you. Don't let John bully you, Sherman. He's just impatient and tired of being fooled by Axel and Svenson."

"Yes, he's had a difficult time doing his job."

"Exactly, so give him a break, too."

We exited the revolving door and entered the ski resort's lobby. It always takes my breath away coming inside here. The log-framed walls, antelope chandeliers, and warm fireplaces made me feel safe and warm. Even though we were anything but safe and warm, yet. I searched the room for any sign of the owners, Richard and Carol. I spotted Carol behind the front desk and I headed over to her. John grabbed my arm to stop me. "No, Ruth Ann," he ordered. "Not Carol."

"But she may have seen Axel or the others come in here. She sees everything when it comes to their resort."

"I'd rather find Richard," he said, looking around the lobby full of people sitting and talking near one of the several fireplaces.

"There he is," Judy said, pointing to a table against the back wall of windows. "He's talking to that group of people." We turned around and saw Richard laughing and talking with two couples who were sitting and drinking a steaming beverage. Richard was pointing to the back of the resort. It was pitch black out there, but I could only guess he was referring to the gorgeous views of the mountain and the slopes that were behind the resort.

"Let me go over and have a talk with him first," John said, releasing my arm. "I like Carol, but you of all people know she likes to gossip."

I let him leave without any comment. I highly doubt Carol would chatter over something so dangerous as our situation. However, she may panic if she thinks her resort is in jeopardy again. Inga and Sherman plopped down on a nearby sofa. Judy was tempted to follow John, but stayed with us. We watched as John interrupted Richard and pulled him away from the two couples. At first, Richard appeared calm, but after John started waving his arms up in the air and talking extremely fast, I noticed Richard's smiling face change to anger. He stormed away from John and headed, not to the front desk where his wife was, but toward us.

"Ruth Ann," Richard said, trudging up to me ready for an argument. "Your chief tells me that those pack of lunatics may be inside my resort, again."

"Ah," I muttered just as John caught up with him. "John, what did you tell Richard that made him so angry?"

"I told him that there's a good chance your daughter and Prunella are being held hostage in the catwalk that's above the ceiling in the ballroom. And Richard told me that would be impossible."

"Why's that?" I asked Richard curiously.

"Because, after the incident a couple days ago we locked and barred anyone having access to it." He took a calming breath and said, "I am the only one who can open it up. I have the one and only key to the lock on the door."

"But," I started to say and stopped. I didn't know what to say to be honest. I wasn't sure how much John confided in him, and I wasn't about to spill what I knew, either.

John noticed my hesitance and started pleading with Richard. "Seriously, Richard, we have a strong piece of evidence that clearly states the women may be in danger above your ballroom. I asked you nicely to let me enter the area, but if you deny me again I will have to *order* you."

"Order me?" he asked, glaring at John with a beet red face. "And how can you order me to do that? It's my resort."

"It's a police matter, so I can trump anything you throw at me. So, can we do this peacefully?"

John waited for Richard to contemplate his order and calm down a little. He didn't wait too long before I noticed John growing extremely impatient. He was about to reiterate his demands when I interrupted. "Hey, did you ask Richard if he saw Axel come in here?" I looked from John to Richard and it was obvious from the dumbfounded look on Richard's face that John neglected to do so. "Ah, no, I was keyed in on Svenson, his henchman, and the two women."

"Are you saying Eklund's with them, too?" Richard asked, stunned.

"Yes," I answered quickly before John. "It isn't what you think, Richard. Axel has come clean to us, but he jumped the gun on us when he got this clue about his wife and my daughter being held up here. Instead of waiting for us to come over here he just left us until we figured it out, too."

"Oh, well, I didn't see him inside here," he answered. "But maybe Carol did. She seems to be the one who notices everyone who comes into our friendly, safe resort. I'd like to keep it that way, too."

"If we keep it down, nobody will notice us," John said, looking around the crowded lobby. "It appears you're doing great business, too."

"Yes, we're completely booked and if people start hearing about the murder a couple of days ago and the possibility they're back for more, I'll lose all my guests."

"You won't," I said reassuringly. "Just let John have a look above the ballroom. Can't you do that for him? Then we can be out of here and you can rest assured that your resort will remain safe."

"Yeah," Judy chimed in. "What if they're in there and you did nothing about it? You could be partially responsible for another two murders."

"Me?" Richard exclaimed. "It's not my fault these lunatics keep picking my resort to do their dirty work." Richard ceased talking and glared over at me. "If you didn't bring that cousin of yours over here none of this would be happening."

"You're blaming me?" I asked, shocked at Richard's accusations. "Prunella shouldn't be blamed either. That's really unfair of you. I understand you're upset about what's happening, but have you forgotten that my daughter's life's at stake right now?" I was so angry I added, "How dare you blame an innocent woman when we should be welcoming her. She can't help that she was married to a man who committed several crimes and tried to have her killed. Then, he hired a lunatic, as you called him, to come to our country and kidnap, rob, and possibly hurt her. You should be ashamed of yourself, Richard. You, of all people, should want this to be over as soon as possible so your resort's reputation won't be tarnished after the horrific events of Halloween."

"Event's caused because your cousin came to Deer Creek," he mumbled again.

"It's NOT her fault!" I cried a tad too loud.

"Shhh," John said, trying to calm *me* down now. "Richard's just frustrated that we keep ending up at his resort. Now," John said, turning back to Richard, "If you'll hand over the key we can get this over with and you can go on with your evening." Richard looked astonished at John's request, but reached into his pants pocket and pulled out a metal ring full of keys. He went through each one and then held up a large, silver key. "Here," he said, taking the single key off the ring. "Go, do it quickly and come back here to let me know if anyone's up there." He didn't give me a second look, but turned and stormed off back to the table with the two couples.

I watched Richard's demeanor drastically change as soon as he made his way to the table. He was once again smiling and laughing with his guests. "Wow, that didn't go like I expected," I said to John.

"He'll get over it," he replied moving on to our current dilemma.

"I'm going up there," he declared, about to walk away.

"Hey, what about us?" Inga asked him from the couch.

"Oh, yeah, you stay here. It'll be safe here with lots of people. Judy," John said, turning to her. "You come with me."

I wasn't going to argue because he was right on both accounts. First, Sherman, Inga, and I were safer in this crowded lobby than in an empty ballroom. Second, let Judy and John crawl into the tiny space above the room and search. From what Richard told us I doubt they're up there. How could they be? He had it locked and nobody could get up there without the key John was now holding in his hand.

Inga waited for John and Judy to be on their way down the hall toward the ballroom. "Are we *really* going to wait here?"

"Yeah?" Sherman asked. "I think we should at least go down to the entrance of the room. We can stay safe in the hallway."

"I guess so," I said, looking as John and Judy disappeared into the hallway off the side of the front desk. "And if they get into any danger we'll be able to hear them from the doorway of the ballroom."

"Let's go," Inga announced hopping off the couch. She grabbed Sherman's arm and then mine. She pulled us along until we were passing the front desk. "Uh-oh," I muttered. "Carol just spotted us."

"Hurry, we'll get away from her before she can get out from behind the desk," Inga said.

"She'll see where we're going and I'm pretty sure Richard hasn't said a word to her about what we're up to here."

"What are we supposed to do now?" Sherman anxiously asked.

"Just follow my lead," I said as Carol disappeared into a back door. I knew that door. Many times I've been at the resort when she was behind the front desk. When she sees me she usually goes through that exact door and comes out another door that opens directly into the lobby. "We can't get away from her because she'll meet up with us before we can get in the hallway."

"Fine, but get rid of her and fast," Inga snapped impatiently. "She'll panic and make a scene."

"No she won't," I said, just as Carol came through the door and stood directly in front of us.

"Hey, what are you three doing here so late?" she asked with a surprised, but worrisome look on her face.

"Oh, we're just here getting warm and wanted to walk around a little," I said, knowing that made zero sense even to me.

"Huh?" she asked, confused. "What are you doing out so late on a Monday night? Normally, Ruth Ann, you're long tucked away into your warm bed."

"Yes," I said, trying to get us out of this. "But, Prunella was here with us and she wandered off. I think she went back to the ballroom to get over what happened the other night. You know, like getting on a bike after you've had a bad fall?" I waited to see if she would understand me or laugh at my face.

"Oh, that makes sense," Carol said, shrugging her shoulders. "She did lose her butler." She quickly amended her comment after Sherman looked offended. "I'm sorry, Sherman, I mean *one* of her butlers. It was a horrible end to a great party, and I'm thankful we didn't lose any guests over it."

"Yeah," I said, quickly jumping on that angle of her conversation. "Your resort looks packed tonight so I'm glad to see Bert's murder was well covered up once the guests departed Saturday night."

"Thank God Sunday was a big departure day here. Many guests that were at the party or heard about it checked out yesterday. The new guests haven't caught wind of it, yet. I just hope they don't." She added, "We can't have that kind of publicity here, it'll kill the resort and the town's businesses."

"How's that?" Inga asked Carol curiously.

"If the resort doesn't do well, then many of the local businesses can't survive. Our town's built around this resort and the tourists that come here to ski in the winter or fish in the summer."

"She's right," I agreed. "Well, do you mind if we have a little looksee into the ballroom? I don't know if Prunella's in there, she could be in the bathroom, too. I just want to make sure she's not reliving that moment alone."

"Of course, Ruth Ann," Carol said, brightening up. "Go right ahead. There's nothing booked for that room until Thanksgiving."

"Thanksgiving?" I asked, wondering what she meant.

"We're going to serve a huge meal that day for any guests or residents that don't have family or plans. You should bring the girls and eat dinner here." Carol seemed so excited about her suggestion that I readily smiled and nodded.

"Sounds like a plan," I said.

Carol looked at Sherman and Inga and added, "Sherman, Inga, you two should come with Prunella, too."

"Great idea," Inga said, trying to crack a smile, but she was tired of this conversation and wanted to get moving. "It would be nice to not cook."

"But, Inga," Carol said, just as Inga was about to take off. "You just arrived from Sweden. You don't celebrate Thanksgiving over there, do you?"

Carol waited for Inga to answer her so Inga turned around slowly and said, "I meant, it would be nice not to cook at all for a day."

"Oh, I get you," Carol said chuckling. "Well, let me know if you need me. I've got to get back to the front desk. I'm on night duty tonight."

I nodded and smiled. Great, Carol will be in the lobby all night. I sure hoped we weren't going to get caught in our lie before the night ended. I couldn't worry about Carol. We took off down the hall and arrived at the entrance to the ballroom. The oversized sets of wooden double doors were closed. John must've closed the doors behind him to keep any noise or uninvited guests out of there. I didn't consider myself one of those uninvited people, but knew he wouldn't be happy with us for following them.

"Let's open it up," Inga said, shoving me to the side so she could do the honor. I didn't complain, but waited for her to grab one of the long, brass handles and give it a push. The door was heavy, and even with Inga's strength it moved slowly until we could fit our bodies inside. I hadn't been back since Bert's death so entering was making me uncomfortable. "Can you hear anything?" Sherman asked, standing behind Inga and me.

"No," Inga snapped, looking around the dimly lit room. "It's too dark in here." She looked around the wall for the set of switches to turn on the chandeliers that were spread throughout the room. I was first to hit the switch. The left side of the ballroom lit up brightly and momentarily blinded our eyes. "John may not want the room so bright," Inga added. I quickly dimmed the lights way down so they were still on, but not so bright that would attract too much attention. "Where'd they go anyway?" she asked me.

"I have no idea," I said, looking around the gigantic room. "There's gotta be some door that leads to the kitchen and an opening to get up to the ceiling." We walked into the room carefully. It was the first time we stood in the room since Bert's body was found hanging from the ceiling, burned to death. "It's eerie in here," I said quietly. "I've been in here for many occasions, but I don't think I'll ever get Bert's body out of my head."

"I know what you mean," Inga said.

"He still was a miserable pain," Sherman spat out. "But," he said before I could reprimand him. "But, he didn't deserve to die like that."

"Let's get out of here," Inga said, hurrying to the bar on the opposite side of the room. "This is where he fell," she said, crossing the spot on the floor where Bert landed.

"They've cleaned everything up so nobody would ever know it happened," I said sadly.

"We know," Inga said, hurrying past the spot. "Look, there's a door next to the bar. I bet it goes to the kitchen." We went over to the door and I stepped in front of it. "What're you doing, Ruth Ann? Let's go in there."

"I thought we were going to wait by the front entrance to the ballroom?"

"But, don't you think we should know where they went to get up above this room?" Inga questioned me.

"We're not going up the ladder or stairs, right?"

"No, but maybe we can listen and hear something," Inga said, pushing open one of the swinging doors. Sherman and I followed her and we entered into a medium sized room where we found numerous piles of chairs and tables. "Where's the kitchen?"

"Probably straight through those doors," I said, pointing to the other side of the room. "The kitchen just doesn't serve the ballroom. There's a couple of restaurants in the resort and there's always room service, too."

"And that door?" Sherman asked, pointing to another door on the side of the room to our left. "You think that goes upstairs?"

"Only one way to find out," Inga said, marching over to the door. "I'm going to just have a little look. Stay here," she said, pushing open a single door leaving Sherman and me in the middle of the room with our mouths hanging wide open.

"What's she doing?" I asked. "I think we should just wait here."

"I agree," Sherman replied. "However, we don't know exactly where that door leads. She's just having a peek and will come right back to us, right?" Sherman asked, alarmed. He wasn't getting younger, and I'd bet he would rather be working in a mansion serving out his last years with a gentle, normal boss.

We didn't move for quite some time. Where did Inga disappear? Should Sherman and I go have a look or wait a little longer? She knew better than to keep investigating without telling us what she was doing, right? All my questions were about to be answered, but not to my liking.

After my head kept filling up with numerous inquiries I told myself to stop. Inga was just seeing where and how John and Judy went to get up into the space above the ballroom's ceiling. I highly doubted Prunella and Lynne were being held up there as prisoners of Svenson's. Just because I remembered the words, Halloween, skeletons, catwalk, doesn't mean Svenson took the girls here to continue his cat and mouse game. I thought we were going over to the high school to make sure Svenson didn't end up there?

However, if there was a best case scenario in this, I wouldn't want to end up back at the high school when I knew Nancy could be there working on the play. One daughter involved in this was enough.

"Ruth Ann," I heard a voice calling out. I was lost in my thoughts when I heard Sherman calling out my name. His voice came across strangely, almost terrified, when I saw the reason why.

"What?" I snapped at him. "Inga, why are you standing in the doorway looking at us like that?" I broke out of my own thoughts and spotted Inga, frozen solid; in the doorway between the room Sherman and I were in and the door that we thought led to the ceiling.

Inga rolled her eyes to the side frantically. I couldn't figure out what she wanted us to see. The doorway wasn't wide and Inga took up most of it. I looked over at Sherman who had the same confused look on his face. I watched as Inga moved her head to the side and kept trying to communicate something to us, but I had no idea until...

"Move it forward," I heard a low voice demand. I couldn't help Inga until I knew what was happening. I started to panic when Inga took two steps forward and Sherman and I spotted the reason for Inga's stiff demeanor. "I said move it forward!" the voice demanded.

"I am!" Inga shouted back, but the unknown man didn't care for her tone and we saw Inga bend over in pain.

"What's going on here?" I hollered.

"No, Ruth Ann," Sherman murmured to me. "Don't yell, can't you see what just happened to Inga?"

I looked over at Inga as she slowly straightened the top half of her body. Before she stood all the way up, I saw what made her wince in pain. A gun was digging into the middle of her back, and the person holding it stepped into our sight.

"Who are you?" I demanded. "And why are you holding a gun in our friend's back?" I waited for his response, but I wasn't acknowledged. I looked at the man who was threatening Inga. He was very tall, blonde and blue-eyed. Aha! This must be Svenson's right-hand man, Jimmy. I wanted him to know we weren't afraid of him, but I also didn't want to risk Inga's life or Sherman's and my own for that fact.

He wore a black pair of tight jeans, and a black muscle t-shirt. He had a horrible, menacing grin on his face as he shoved Inga into the room a little further. "Go over to your *friends,*" he ordered with a thick, Swedish accent (what else?). Inga almost fell into Sherman after Jimmy shoved her, but Sherman was able to break her fall. He grabbed a hold of her shoulders and turned her around so that the three of us were now facing this killer.

"You must be Steven Svenson's hired man, Jimmy?" I questioned with a hint of sarcasm.

"Yes," he responded without hurting Inga for my mouth.

"What do you want with us?" I asked him bluntly. "Where are Prunella and my daughter?"

He let out a gurgling, horrifying sound that I believe was a laugh, but he didn't answer my question so I added, "And where are our other friends?"

He quickly stopped his laughing and looked dead serious. "What *other* friends?"

Inga elbowed me in my side and I cringed from how hard she knocked me. I turned a nasty stare on her when she motioned with her face curling up and eyeballs whipping side to side. She was trying to tell me John and Judy haven't been caught and I needed to keep my mouth shut. I nodded slightly and Jimmy, becoming agitated said, "Well?

"Uh, no one," I stumbled. "I, I only meant Prunella and Lynne. Where are you and Steven holding them?"

"Why would I tell you?" he asked mockingly.

"Because they're my family, you goon!" That did it. I knew I just blew it, and once again, my mouth didn't use a filter. He stormed to the middle of the room where we were standing and stood within inches of me. He smelled of cheap vodka and cigars. I wanted to turn my head away from him, but then he'd know I either was disgusted with him or afraid. I looked him straight in his deep blue eyes and noticed every freckle and the numerous pimples on his horribly leathery face. He was much older than I thought. He must be in his forties instead of his twenties like I imagined. This man looked like he's led a tough life with his worn skin and crooked, yellowed teeth. Must be from the tobacco, I said to myself silently.

"What did you just say to me?" He barked with the most disgusting stench spewing from his mouth.

"If you don't mind taking a step back I'll explain myself." I said with conviction, and waited until he growled and stepped back like I requested.

"Now, start apologizing," he ordered.

"Apologize?" I asked stupidly. Inga was about to jam my side again with her elbow when I said, "Oh, yes, I'm sorry for calling you a goon, but why won't you just tell me where my daughter and cousin are?"

"You'll find out soon enough," he roared, and then turned his head as if he was expecting somebody else to come through the door. Sherman, Inga, and I noticed his nervousness and reacted quickly. "Who're you looking for? Steven? Or is someone else after you?" I asked that question specifically hoping he would mention the cops.

"None of your business," he exclaimed. "Now, follow me." He quickly amended his order and said, "Follow me and don't try any funny stuff. You three aren't young, it wouldn't take much from me to finish the lot of you off."

"Finish us off?" I questioned him. "What good would that do?"

"Get you off our backs."

I realized there was someone else we had momentarily forgotten about, Axel. Where was he? Maybe he was the other person Jimmy was looking for? I wanted to ask this guy if he knew if Axel was around, but decided I shouldn't open my mouth just in case he's farther along in finding Prunella and Lynne. Once Jimmy turned to go toward the door that led into the next room, I quickly whispered to her, "Where does that room go to?"

"I didn't make it too far. It's another storage room, but I did notice it led into a huge kitchen. There's also a ladder that leads up to the ceiling. I know that because there's an opening in the ceiling where I thought your chief and detective disappeared into. But I haven't seen them."

"I wonder if they're up there or did they get caught too?" Sherman inquired softly.

Jimmy was ignoring our conversation or he was hard of hearing. He took it for granted that the three of us would follow him into the next room. "Whoa," I said, looking around the tiny, empty room. "I see the swinging doors and the ladder's in here."

"Be quiet!" Jimmy bellowed to me. "No talking between the three of you."

I snapped my mouth shut since he was aiming his pistol in my direction. I didn't know what we were waiting for when from the ceiling a pair of legs started to descend from above. They weren't John's or Judy's as far as I could tell, but who was coming down from the ceiling?

"Stand back," Jimmy ordered as he walked over to the ladder and held on to it to steady it.

"Jimmy, you have all of them?" a voice from above asked.

"I've got the help and that irritating woman you call, Ruth Ann."

"Hey," I cried. "I'm not irritating, I'm getting a little tired of being chased, kidnapped, and watching people die for no reason."

"No reason?" The voice called out from above. "I'll give you one really solid reason...that necklace your bitch of a cousin won't give up!"

So, we finally knew that Prunella hasn't handed over the necklace or told him where it was hidden. "Good!" I disrespectfully shouted back at him. I knew it had to be Steven Svenson coming down the ladder.

He made his way to the floor and Jimmy inquired, "What should I do to her? She's a royal pain, and if you give me the word, I'll make her sorry she's still breathing." Jimmy scowled at me as I threw him one of my sweetest, but taunting, smiles. He rushed over to me and raised his hand to whack me in the head when Steven hollered,

"STOP!" Jimmy lowered his hand that was just inches away from my face and turned back to his boss. "C'mon, she deserves it."

"No, leave her alone," he demanded. "Now, Ruth Ann, could you please, for a moment, shut that mouth of yours and follow my orders?" Before I could respond he added, "Unless you would rather I unleash Jimmy's fury on your daughter?"

That did it for me. I decided to concede in the best interests of Lynne, "Fine, we'll do what you ask. As long as you give me proof that Prunella and my daughter are still alive."

"You think *I* would kill two women?" he asked, stunned. "I'm no murderer."

"What?" I couldn't help myself. "You killed Bert, Helena, and whoever else has gotten in your way."

He looked strangely at me and over to Jimmy, who just grinned mockingly. "We didn't kill Bert or Helena. Did Eklund tell you that?"

I didn't know what to say. What was happening here? First, Axel tells us the physical violence came from Steven and Jimmy and he had nothing to do with it. Now Steven's shocked that he was accused of killing them. "Ruth Ann?" he called my name, waiting.

"I," I didn't know what to ask. I turned to Inga and Sherman who also had the same shocked expressions on their faces. "Well?" Steven asked again.

"I'm so confused," I admitted. "Axel told me you were responsible for those deaths. Are you telling me you and Jimmy didn't do any of that?" I hesitated a moment and said, "Wait a minute! You admitted to me back in the kitchen at Axel's estate you watched your men carry out *your* orders to kill Helena and Bert!"

"Well, firstly, we did 'slow' down your chief and that obnoxious detective of his, but we did not, and let me say again, did not, murder Bert or Helena. I was just goading you on back at the house." No way, I thought, he must be crazy and I had a strong feeling he was lying to me now.

"Then who did?" Inga chimed in even though she regretted doing so the minute the words left her mouth. "Sorry, Ruth Ann, you can do the talking."

Steven ignored Inga's request and said, "Look, I don't know what's going on around here except for the fact that we're here only for that necklace. I will stoop pretty low to get what I want, but murder isn't something I'll do." Maybe he suffered from a form of amnesia. He commits a horrific act and his mind shuts down?

"But you could have him do it," I said, pointing at Jimmy who still looked like he wanted to kill me. His gun was aimed at me, which made me think murder wasn't out of the question for him.

"He takes orders only from me," Steven stated, wiping some dust off his black dress pants. His crisp white collared shirt was wrinkled, but still clean. His top button or two were undone allowing the necktie to hang a little lower. From the dust on his pants I would guess he was on his hands and knees in the catwalk and not standing. Otherwise, his shirt would be dirtier than it was.

"I'm so confused," I said, rubbing my temples with my hands. "You're saying you only want the necklace, but you didn't kill anyone? Will you admit to kidnapping Prunella and Lynne?"

"Yes, I'll give you that much."

"Will you tell me where they are?"

"Maybe."

"What can I do to convince you to let me see them?" I asked, hoping he was softening towards me and dropping the confusion on the murders for now.

"You must promise to find out where Prunella has hidden the necklace. She's led us all over this godforsaken town. My patience is wearing thin, and even though I said *I* wouldn't kill a woman, I may severely injure her soon." He veered over at Jimmy who looked as though he was a dog being teased with a bone. His distorted grin grew broader exposing his disgusting yellowed teeth. It gave me such a chill that I felt it run down the back of my spine.

"So Prunella hasn't taken you to where she has the necklace?" I asked, verifying what I've learned so far.

"No! She's mocking Jimmy and me, and he's about to blow." He motioned his head in Jimmy's direction again with a slight tilt. "I don't know if I can even hold him off much longer."

"If I work on Prunella," I began, "You have to swear Jimmy won't touch any of us."

"Speaking of *all* of you," Steven said. "You haven't asked me about that bumbling chief of yours and his younger, female detective."

I was wondering what happened to them. I didn't know if they took off somewhere inside the resort or if Jimmy apprehended them too. "Are you going to tell me?" I asked, watching for any changes in his demeanor.

"Let's just say I didn't touch them, but we led them off in another direction," Steven said, grinning. "Let's say they're on, what do you call it? Oh, yes, a wild goose chase."

"So, they aren't being held prisoner up in that catwalk with Prunella and my daughter?" I asked, hoping he would slip and admit the two women were up there.

He gave me a slight twist of his mouth. "Ah, you're trying to trick me, Ruth Ann. I see why you have so much power in your little alliance."

"Power, me?" I questioned him innocently. "I'm just trying to get my daughter and Prunella back safely. John and Judy are the police officers."

"But they're not here protecting you three?" he said, looking at Sherman and Inga who stood still without speaking. I looked to see how Sherman was holding up and noticed his body was swaying a little. Inga was solid just itching to make her move.

"What can we do from here? Sherman's not young, and this is taking a toll on him. Why can't you let him go?"

Steven took a quick glance over at Sherman and said, "I wish I could, Ruth Ann, but he'll just go and get help from the police."

"No, I won't," Sherman belted out in a hurry. "I'll go straight to the estate and wait for you there."

"Unfortunately, Sherman, I don't trust you. You work for Prunella, and I know for a fact that you're devoted to her. I doubt you'd abandon her while she's in need."

"You're right!" he exclaimed without thinking and just blew any hope of being released! "I'd do anything for her."

"Sherman!" I bellowed. "That didn't help your case."

"He wouldn't have let me go anyway."

"Enough!" Steven shouted. "We're going to stay together, well, actually, Jimmy's going to stay with these two," he pointed at Sherman and Inga. "And you, Ruth Ann, are coming with me."

"Where are we going?" I asked anxiously. "Are you finally going to take me to Lynne and Prunella?"

"Yes, but we have an agreement. Do we not?" He waited for my response and I didn't hesitate even for a second.

"Of course." I wasn't happy about leaving Inga with this Jimmy character. Her temperament mixed with his could be volatile, but we didn't have a choice. Sherman wouldn't do anything to upset him, but I wasn't so sure about Inga. I turned to her and quietly said, "Please, listen to him and don't do anything that could get you or Sherman hurt."

Inga didn't verbally respond, but slightly nodded her head. I didn't feel overly confident with her answer, but it was all I got. It was time for me to get to Prunella and see my daughter. "Let's go," I said, leaving Inga and Sherman and walking over to Steven. "Where are we going?"

He didn't answer probably because he didn't want Inga to overhear. If there was any way she could escape from Jimmy's claws and find us she would definitely try. "I'll be back soon," I said as Steven led me not up the ladder, but through the doors that led into the kitchen of the resort. I halted a moment and asked him, "Isn't the kitchen staff in there? They'll see us coming."

"Ruth Ann, it's late and a Monday night. The kitchen's been pretty empty for some time now."

"But they have 24-hour room service," I said. "There have to be some workers in here."

"Don't worry about them," he said, entering the resorts massive, spotless kitchen.

"You paid them off, didn't you?" I asked him, wondering what Richard and Carol would think of their employees.

"I will tell you that the owners of the resort have retired for the evening and I hired a staff member or two myself."

"I thought Carol was on night duty tonight? She told me herself."

"She came down with a slight case of the flu."

"She was fine just a little while ago. What did you do to her?"

"I slipped a little something in her coffee." He saw the look of horror in my eyes and said, "Don't worry, it'll only last twelve hours. It's just a little drug that induces vomiting, but not severe."

"That's horrible!" I cried. "What about her staff?"

"The kitchen workers were given double their salary for the week if they let me borrow the kitchen for a few hours."

"So you bribed their night staff with a week's salary if you could come and go through the kitchen? They didn't think to ask their own boss if that was okay?"

"Would you if you were only making minimal wages? This gives them extra money for food or clothing. I think I did them a favor."

"But when their bosses find out they could lose their jobs."

"Not if you don't tell them," he replied.

"But if John and Judy found out, they would tell Richard and Carol."

"The chief and detective didn't go through the kitchen. I can tell you that much."

"Where'd they go then?" I asked, confused. "The last I saw them they came into the ballroom to check out the catwalk for Prunella and Lynne. What happened to them?"

"They never made it up to the catwalk."

"I don't understand," I said, worried about what Steven did to John and yes, Judy.

"I was waiting for them when they entered the ballroom. I was on the opposite side of the room before coming into the storage room."

"They saw *you*?" I asked curiously, wondering where he was going with this, and if I believed him.

"Yes, well, kind of. I was disguised at the time and when they saw a 'hooded' man in black they came running across the room. I set a bunch of clues that would take them out of the resort completely."

"They aren't even inside the resort?" I asked, stunned.

"Nope."

"Where then?"

"I carefully recorded a few loud screams on my cell and they thought it was your daughter or Prunella making the screams. They came flying after me, but of course, they weren't going to find me. They were going to find a piece of paper that your daughter supposedly dropped on the floor as they were being dragged out of the resort."

"What was written on the paper?" I asked, frustrated.

"Kind of like the clue that I left in the bakery that Axel got a hold of."

"So, you left some words on the paper that would lead John and Judy somewhere else?"

"Yes, that left me time to get you on my side, Ruth Ann, to help convince Prunella to disclose the location of the necklace. Let's just say it bought me some extra time. They won't be fooled for long, but right now I'm pretty sure they're over at the high school searching for your daughter."

"The high school?"

"Yes. I wrote three words on the paper that was crumpled up, but easy for your police friends to find."

"What were the three words?" I asked.

"Rehearsal, backstage, midnight."

"Well, that would definitely lead them to the school, but why midnight?"

"It gives them a time when I might have them at the school."

"But that's in an hour from now," I said, glancing up at the clock on the wall in the kitchen.

"Exactly. It gives me some time to get you to convince Prunella to give up the necklace."

"I get it now, but what about Axel? Isn't he somewhere around here, too?"

"He's safely tucked away, Ruth Ann," he answered. "Don't worry, I didn't hurt him."

"But Jimmy could!"

"No, I didn't allow Jimmy to touch him either. I believe I can now tell you that Eklund's the person you would've found in the catwalk." He waited for my response, but I didn't give one. I thought Prunella and Lynne were being held up there, but now I find out that Axel's up there.

"Why up there?" I asked curiously. "And if he's up there, where are Prunella and Lynne?"

"Well," he started to say. "You were expecting to find *someone* up there, so why not? He's not hurt, just a bit indisposed, that's all." Steven let out a low gurgle of laughter and coughed. I gave him a strange look for thinking it was funny to stuff a human up in a ceiling. "Sorry, he got what he deserved. Actually, he should've gotten worse." My eyes looked surprised and he said, "He used me, Ruth Ann. He was going to jail back in Sweden and contacted me for help. He knew my being a lawyer could get him out of jail somehow."

"Out of jail?" I questioned him. "He faked being stabbed and was supposedly being transferred to a hospital when he suddenly disappeared. We were told he was dead, but then you stepped in and illegally brought him here." I gave him an accusing look, "All to steal my necklace! Enough with the necklace," I bellowed. "That thing has been nothing but a nightmare."

"Then convince Prunella to give it to me and this goes away. Prunella can be reunited with her precious Axel, and the rest of you can go free."

"But, two people I knew have been murdered, and Axel's guards! How can this be over? You say you or Jimmy didn't do it." I watched his eyes and they didn't show any change of emotion. "If you didn't then who did?" That's the big question, I thought to myself. I needed to figure out who was playing me for a fool, Steven or Axel?

"You don't believe me do you?" he asked angrily. "I told you I didn't do it so why can't you let me have the necklace you think is cursed, and then I'll leave and you'll never see my face again."

"But it's not only my decision, Steven. Prunella's the one who has possession of the necklace, and she's not letting it go!"

"Maybe once she sees you she'll change her mind."

"I told you I would try. Take me to her," I requested. "Are they here in the resort?"

"Yes."

"Then it should be simple."

"We do have to hurry, so I'll take you to them." He held out his arm for me to hold. I walked right past him and into the middle of the kitchen. I was standing next to a long, stainless steel counter full of spotless pots and pans and turned to see if he was coming.

"You need to stick next to me and if we run into anyone, and I mean anyone, you say nothing."

"But what if they know me? This is my hometown."

"Why would anyone you know be wandering around the floors of this resort at eleven at night on a Monday?"

He was right. I doubted I'd meet anyone at this time. I shrugged my shoulders and we took off toward the back of the kitchen. "We're taking the service elevator, Ruth Ann," he said as we made it over to the elevator that was used for room service and housekeeping carts.

"So they're upstairs in one of the rooms?" I asked.

"Yes."

Just as we stood waiting for the elevator, I turned to see Steven staring straight ahead at the closed doors. Out of the corner of my eye I spotted movement and it was rushing toward us. I couldn't make out who it was until they passed the sidewall where the walk-in refrigerators and freezers were located. Inga and Sherman (he was truly trying) were running in and out of appliances and the counters. Steven was oblivious to them sneaking up on us, but I wasn't. I felt a rush of adrenaline and decided it was best to keep him looking my way instead of sensing Inga's pursuit. I don't know how they got free, but I was thrilled to see them. "So, what floor are they on?" I asked trying to think of something simple to get him talking.

"You'll see soon enough."

"Are they alone up in the room or do you have somebody guarding them?"

He didn't answer, but stayed looking in my direction. I tried very hard to watch what Inga was going to do so I'd be ready for anything. Steven, after hesitating whether or not to tell me anything more said, "It's only Jimmy and me so that leaves your daughter and cousin alone." He quickly added, "But don't think they're able to free themselves on their own. I made it impossible for them to escape."

Before I could respond, and I have to say I really wanted to know why Lynne and Prunella could not escape, Inga rushed up behind him and smashed him in the head with a cast iron skillet from the counter. Steven gasped in shock then plummeted to the floor and hit his head as he fell forward just missing me on his way down. "Inga!" I cried out. "You did it, you knocked him out." I fell to my knees just to make sure he was out, which he definitely was.

"Did I kill him?" Inga asked, panting from excitement. I carefully felt his wrist for a pulse. "He's alive," I said.

"Too bad," she said. "He's a bad man and deserved to be dead."

"Inga, he said he didn't kill Bert or Helena."

"I don't believe him," she spat out. "He probably said Mr. Eklund did, didn't he?"

"Well, yes, I guess he assumed it was Axel, but I don't think it was him either."

"Wait, if neither of them did it then who did?" Sherman asked, finally making it over to us. He tried only up to a point, and then cowered!

"How did you get away from Jimmy?" I asked Inga.

"He left Sherman and me in the middle of the storage room and told us not to move. He's stupid if he thinks I would just stand there and wait while he took off to check on something in the kitchen."

"He went into the kitchen?" I asked, surprised. Why would he do that? Maybe he was checking on his boss to see if he was safe.

"Yes, but the minute he left my sight I grabbed Sherman's arm and told him to come on. I grabbed a hammer that was on one of the shelves and the minute he came back through the kitchen I was ready for him."

"You hit him with the hammer?" I asked.

"You betcha I did. He fell flat to the floor and I gave him a few hard kicks just to be sure and we bolted into the kitchen to find you by the elevator. That's when we snuck around by the stoves and I found the skillet. It's hard and I'm used to working with them. I noticed you spotted me and were trying to keep Svenson's attention. That's when I bustled over and whacked him in the head."

"You are a fighter," I said. "But, now that you're both here, and I don't think Axel's as guilty as I used to, we need to figure out who's lying. Or is someone else involved that we don't know about?"

"I'm not sure whom we should believe," I continued. "But I do know Lynne and Prunella are upstairs in a room. I bet Steven has a key in one of his pockets."

"I'm not searching him!" Sherman stated. "He's probably dead after Inga whacked him in the head."

Inga scowled at him and said, "He's not dead. You're being a sissy. I'll check his pockets." Inga bent over and I stood up and said, "I'm going to free Axel. You wait here."

"Wait, what?" Inga said, checking Steven's front pocket in his shirt.

"He's being held up in the catwalk, so I'll just climb up the ladder and see if I can set him loose. Stay here until I get back, hopefully with Axel."

"I hope you're making the right decision, Ruth Ann," she said. "He could be fooling all of us you know."

"My gut tells me he's not. I have to go by that right now. We don't have much a chance without another male." I looked at Sherman and added, "I'm sorry, Sherman. I meant another male besides you."

"I know I'm pretty useless, Ruth Ann. I'm not a fighter, I'm a butler. I hate all of this."

"It'll be over soon," I said as I rushed out of the kitchen and into the storage room. The ladder was ready for me to climb. I went up about ten steps then was able to stick my head through the large square opening. I didn't think I'd be able to hoist myself up into the tiny space but I had to try. I grabbed the top of the ladder and took hold of the sides of the opening. I didn't want to step on the top rung because the ladder would become unsteady. There were only about two feet from where my feet were and the entrance to the opening. I thought about calling out for Axel, but wasn't sure if he was alone. Also, I didn't see Jimmy on the floor when I came out of the kitchen. Did he get up on his own or did he have help? I was so confused I didn't know what to think or whom to believe anymore.

I was able to force myself up into the tiny space that runs over the ballroom. It was a tight fit and I wasn't able to stand, but I was able to crawl. The light was limited up here, but I could make my way by the light shining in from the air vents. I crawled a few feet forward but Axel wasn't there. I could only see clearly about five feet or so in front of me. I felt the hard surface on my knees as I crawled a little further. I was sure I would be full of bruises after this escapade up here. I didn't go much further when I felt a vibration under my hands and knees. Where was it coming from? I was soon given an answer.

Chapter 36

I kept crawling about five more feet, and then another five feet when I noticed the floor beneath my hands and knees shake violently. I was momentarily worried I would fall through the ceiling onto the ballroom floor. That had to be several feet down and I would surely be killed or seriously injured. I paused to see if my weight was causing the vibration. I waited and held my breath. I was happy to say it wasn't me causing the motion. Something else was making the tunnel move. "Axel!" I called out as I looked ahead and finally spotted Axel gagged and tied up in a little ball. He was bent in odd angles so he would fit in the tunnel. I hurried over to him and immediately pulled off the rag that was stuffed in his mouth.

He coughed a couple times then said hoarsely, "Thank God you found me, Ruth Ann."

"Sorry it took so long, but you should never have run off without us back in the bakery."

"I know that now," he said, regaining his voice. "I found that clue and I got excited. I thought I could end this matter if I came here by myself and surprised Svenson. If I would've waited for all of you, we might not have found them."

"But you didn't find them, did you?"

"No, Svenson and his thug, Jimmy, found me and dragged me up that ladder and down this tunnel." He swallowed dryly and said, "Let me correct what I said. Jimmy dragged me up here and stuffed this filthy rag in my mouth, and then tied these ropes around me."

"I'm just thankful he didn't use knots," I said, unwinding the ropes that bound him. "It's tight up here. I'm surprised that tall man made it in here."

"He's quite flexible," Axel admitted. "It's like he was made of rubber. He just rolled me through this tunnel and left me here alone. I really didn't know if I'd ever be found."

"Steven admitted to me that you were being held up here. If he didn't tell me I wouldn't have looked up here."

"But wouldn't one of you have looked to see if Prunella or Lynne were in here?" he asked curiously.

"No, it's a long story. Let's get you out of here and get back to where Inga and Sherman are waiting. They're standing over Steven right now."

"Wait, what?" he asked, thoroughly confused. "What about John and Judy? And what happened to Svenson? I sure missed a lot, didn't I?"

"Yes, you did," I answered. "I'll fill you in while we're getting out of here. This place is even small for me. I'm feeling a bit claustrophobic in here." Once completely freed, we crawled as fast as we could to get out of the tunnel. It didn't take long for us to get down the ladder and back to Inga and Sherman.

"You're back, finally," Inga called out as we made our way through the kitchen and over to the service elevator.

I filled Axel in with as much as I could spew out before we reached the elevator. I looked on the ground and noticed Steven was not only still there, but Inga had tied his hands and feet up with yards and yards of string. She stuffed a filthy dishtowel in his mouth, and stood grinning over him. "Well, I see you took care of him," I said. "Was that necessary?" I asked, pointing to the dishtowel that was stained with an assortment of leftover foods that smelled of soiled garbage.

"He's scum," she replied. "He was going to take you to a room upstairs and trap you up there like Ms. Prunella and your daughter."

"Ruth Ann," Axel interrupted. "You don't even know if your daughter and Prunella are *really* up there."

"Yes we do," Inga declared holding up the room key. "We just don't know what room it opens."

"It could be a ruse, Inga," Axel explained. "He may be playing another one of his little games."

"No!" I cried out. "He has to be holding them up there. I can't take much more of this."

"Let's wake up the fool and force it out of him," Inga suggested, giving Svenson a slight kick with her foot seeing if he would stir, but he didn't move.

Axel looked around the kitchen and said, "We have another huge problem. We don't know where Jimmy is."

"That's right!" I exclaimed. "Inga, are you sure you knocked him out with the hammer?"

"Oh, yes," she answered. "He was out cold."

"Well, he must have a hard head, because he wasn't back there when Axel and I came down the ladder."

"No way!" she protested in alarm.

"Maybe," Sherman butted in. "Just maybe there really is someone else helping them and we don't know anything about them."

"Sherman's got a point," Axel admitted. "But is it someone working with Svenson or somebody new we know nothing about?"

"Steven swore to me that Jimmy and he were working alone," I said.

"If he told you the truth," Sherman mumbled, but I heard him loud and clear.

"I really don't think he was lying. I usually can tell when I'm being lied to." I turned to Axel and added, "Even when you were holding me prisoner back in your Sweden estate you would tell me things and I believed you."

"I was telling you the truth when I told you all about my past with my family and first wife."

"I know you were," I said, meaning it. "Your personality changed when you felt threatened and went after Bertha and her brothers."

"Yes, and you, Prunella, and the others also escaped and went after me. I've admitted I was horrible and will apologize until each and every one of you believes me."

Inga eyed him differently than before. She wasn't fully on board with the whole Axel reformation, but maybe after what she just heard she might be changing her tune a little. Her look softened a bit, which is not easy for such a strong woman.

"So, what do we do now?" Sherman asked, trying to get us back on track. "We need to get out of here before that Jimmy character and whoever else is after us finds us standing over their boss."

"I agree," Axel said. "We need to find the room this key fits. We'll get Svenson out of sight and maybe Ruth Ann can use her overwhelmingly sweet personality to coerce the night clerk to divulge the number of the room. What do you think, Ruth Ann? We need to give this a try and see if Prunella and Lynne are upstairs somewhere."

I grabbed the key Inga held in her outstretched hand and took off. I turned around as I was leaving and said, "Wait here." Axel nodded and I exited into the main dining room of the resort.

The room was dark and empty at this time of night. Steven kept saying he only had an hour to get me to convince Prunella to give him the necklace before he followed through with his plans over at the high school with John and Judy. I wondered what they were doing over there all this time after abandoning us here. At least John could've told us where they were heading. Maybe Judy told him there wasn't enough time to go back to us first. I wouldn't put it past her to do that. She really is a piece of work!

With the lack of time, I was positive Lynne and Prunella were somewhere here at the resort. I didn't waste any of it in the dining room and hurried out into the hall that led into the lobby. I knew Carol wouldn't be on duty since Steven admitted to slipping her a drug to mimic the flu or food poisoning. If she was working I felt sure I could get her to give me the room number, but that would also force me to tell her what was going on, too. The hall I entered also housed the entrance to the grand ballroom. I ran by the set of doors to the ballroom and ended up in the lobby. I peeked into the room and it appeared quiet and the chandeliers were emitting a dim glow that turned the once elegant room into an eerie crime scene. I didn't see a soul until I reached the front desk.

There was only one person sitting behind the check-in counter. It was a middle-aged man I didn't recognize. I understood I wouldn't know who worked the night shift, but Deer Creek's a small town and I thought I knew every resident in town. I tried to regain my breath before walking up and disturbing him. I noticed him intently watching something on a small device he was holding in his hands. I was glad for the moment or two to gain my wits before I lied about this room key I was holding. What on earth was I going to say to convince this stranger to give me the room number? Think, Ruth Ann, think!

I had an idea and hoped this man would go for it. I walked straight up to the counter where he was sitting on a tall stool. I leaned my elbows on the counter and smiled. He didn't see me at first, but then suddenly he spotted me out of the corner of his eye. I was standing there waiting for him. He jumped off the stool and whipped the headphones off. I think I just got another idea!

"Oh, I'm so sorry, ma'am," he said nervously. "I didn't see you standing there.

"Yes," I said. "You were busy with that device of yours." I motioned to his mini tablet on the counter, its frozen picture glaring up at my appalled face. He immediately flipped it over and turned beet red.

"I, I don't know what to say, ma'am. It's not a habit of mine to watch this kind of material," he said, rambling away about the inappropriate image that caught my eye. "Please, you won't tell my bosses will you?" That's my ticket! I knew I could get whatever information I needed out of him now.

"Well," I started to say. "I am very good friends with both Carol and Richard."

"Please, I can't afford to lose my job," he pleaded. "I live thirty miles from here and drive out here only twice a week to cover the late shift. They've been so kind to me I don't want to disappoint them. Can you pretend you never saw what you did?"

"I don't know," I said, contemplating his words even though I knew I would never tell Carol or Richard. "Maybe we can help each other," I said suggestively.

"Yes, yes, what can I do for you? Please, tell me, I'll do just about anything." I watched his dark brown eyes nervously twitch and his hands tremble as he held them out in the air begging for anything to get him out of this improper circumstance.

I held out the room key and slapped it on the counter. "I need to know what room this belongs to." I waited as his look went from worry to horror.

"I'm not allowed to give out room numbers. It's illegal," he said frantically.

"I'm not doing anything illegal, if you must know. I'm looking for a family member of mine and I know they're here at the resort. I just want to go up and make sure they're okay." Hopefully, that would convince him to give me the number. Or, "If you feel you need to wake Carol or Richard, then go ahead. They'd give me the room number no questions asked."

"Really?" he asked, perplexed. "I don't want you to call them. Carol's sick with the flu. She was supposed to be covering this shift tonight. They called me last minute and since I needed the work I hauled myself over here right away."

"I know. I heard Carol was sick. I doubt she'd want a call from me, right?" I said, emphasizing the last word.

"Oh, yes, you're right," he said, taking the key off the counter and turning to his computer and quickly typing on the keyboard. "Here it is," he said smiling. "Room 410. It's a beautiful suite."

"Suite?" I asked intriguingly. "I wonder why he booked them a suite?" I mumbled quietly to myself, but he overheard me and said, "Because the resort's full."

"Oh, that had to cost a pretty penny," I said to him.

"$550.00 a night, plus tax."

"I didn't know the suites were that expensive."

"It's high season now so the owners can get away with it," he replied with an evil smirk on his face. I didn't much care for this man. I had a strong feeling he wasn't the type of character I usually dealt with. Even though I promised not to mention the indecent material he was watching, I may just question them about employing him. He watched me closely and said, "Especially if the place is booked solid."

"I guess so," I said, wondering if Richard was the one who might price gouge the rooms at their resort. I didn't have time for this. I needed to get back to Axel and the others so we can check out this suite on the fourth floor. I thanked the desk clerk and headed back down the hall into the kitchen.

"About time," Inga said anxiously. "What took so long? You didn't get caught, did you?"

"Easy, Inga," I said, smiling and holding up the card. "I've got the room number. It just took me a few extra minutes."

"Why?" Axel asked me. "Did you run into anyone you know?"

"Nope, not at all. Only the night clerk whom I've never seen before."

"You know everybody in this town!" Sherman protested. "Isn't it suspicious that a stranger's behind the front desk?"

"No, not at all," I replied. "The man lives pretty far from here and only works a couple of nights to help out Richard and Carol. Nobody really wants the overnight shift. It's a hard position to fill."

"And wasn't Carol supposed to work tonight?" Inga asked.

"Yes, but after Steven drugged her, Richard contacted this man and he rushed over here. I guess I'll give him that much."

"As long as he's not one of Svenson's men," Axel suggested.

"I didn't even think of that," Inga cried out.

"No, I told you Steven said it's just him and Jimmy," I said, frustrated.

"I'm not sure I'd believe a word he said, Ruth Ann," Axel said. "He's a crooked lawyer to begin with, remember?"

He had a point, but I didn't think the night clerk had anything to do with Svenson. He's just a dirty, middle-aged man who gets to watch his filthy movies during the middle of the night. Oh, and get paid for it by my dear friends.

"What are we waiting for?" Inga asked, changing the topic. "Let's go check out room 410."

I looked around the floor by the elevator and noticed one important change. "Hey, what'd you do with Steven?"

"He's safely tucked away," Axel said, grinning over at Inga.

"What did you two do?" I asked suspiciously.

"Me too!" Sherman bellowed. "I helped them stuff that creep in the closet."

"Sherman!" Inga yelled at him. "Do you want the entire resort to hear you?"

"Sorry, but everyone assumes I'm useless," Sherman said, lowering his head feeling sorry for himself.

"We don't have time for this!" Axel snapped. "Sherman, you're not worthless, you're old."

"Easy, Axel," I said, pretty sure he made matters worse. "Sherman, you're about the same age as Axel."

"Yeah, I am," he said poignantly. "Then why is he so much more active than me?"

"Years of keeping myself in shape, Sherman," Axel said, eying the chubby butler. He was in great shape for a man around seventy. He's tall, lean and muscular. I can see why Prunella was attracted to him. I'd be attracted to him if I met him under different circumstances. However, I still think he's too old for Prunella. She's only in her early thirties and should be having kids of her own.

"So, what closet is he in?" I asked, changing the subject.

"The garbage one," Inga answered pointing to a door near the back exit to the parking lot. "I doubt anyone will go in there for a while. Most of the garbage from the above floors gets thrown down the chute."

"The smell in there is atrocious," Sherman announced. "I wonder when they have pick-up. It must be tomorrow because the dumpster in there was full."

"We'll have him out of their way before the morning," Axel said. "We just need him detained for a short time. Hopefully, that chief and detective of yours will return and we can clean up this mess."

"It's not their fault they're over at the high school," I mentioned. "Steven admitted to leaving them a specific clue so they took off."

"Without telling us!" Inga protested.

"I'm angry at them, too," I admitted. "But they'll be back after they realize they were played, *again*." I knew John was going to kick himself for falling for another false lead.

Axel pushed the elevator button and we waited for the service elevator doors to open. "They better be up there," Axel said, after hitting the fourth floor button and watching it light up.

"Where else can they be?" I asked. "Steven was on his way up there with me to try and convince Prunella to give up the location of the necklace. Nobody knows where it is."

"Not even you," Inga said, eyeing me.

"No, not even me," I said, disappointed. I thought Prunella would've trusted me a little more by now and divulged what she had done. I was just as surprised as everyone else to find out she had a separate safe built in the garage and only she and Sherman knew about it.

The service elevator didn't run as smoothly as the public one. It shook and rumbled making it up ever so slowly. "Why's this elevator so slow?" Inga asked impatiently.

"It's used to haul large items like food and laundry carts, and other service related things. I figure it's used a lot more than the guest elevator and constantly gets banged up pretty bad," Axel suggested. "Look at the scratches and dents all over the walls. It must run slower to safeguard the items it transports."

I wasn't sure where on the floor the doors would open up, but I wasn't too worried about running into guests at this hour. It was nearly midnight, and most guests here were pooped from hiking and skiing all day. There were always the rebel rousers that stayed up late and partied, but Carol closed the bar early during the week. The bell rang and the door slid open. I peeked my head out before anyone else to see where we were located. It appeared we were at the far end of the hall near the stairwell. Axel grabbed a hold of my arm tightly and pulled me back. "Don't do that!"

"Why not? I was just seeing where we were," I said angrily.

"What if there's a guard standing outside their door? You'd be seen immediately."

"I only stuck my head out, geez."

"At this hour the elevator noise sounds like a loud siren going off. If there was anyone out there, they'd look over at the elevator and your head would be popping out."

"Oh, I guess you have a point. Sorry, I didn't even think about that."

"I'm holding the button to keep the doors open. Maybe if the guard, if there is one, did hear the elevator ding, he would give up after a few seconds if nobody stepped out into the hall."

"Don't hold it too long," I said. "The buzzer will go off and that'll be much louder than any ding."

I watched Axel as he waited about ten seconds. He let go of the button and stepped into the hall. He looked to his left since we were at the end and there were no rooms to the right just the door to the stairwell. It didn't take him long to wave us into the hallway. "Hurry up," he snapped. "The elevator is going to buzz soon."

We moved into the hallway and hovered near Axel. "I don't see anyone around," I said quietly.

"No," Axel replied. "I would think if Prunella and Lynne were up here, there'd be a guard outside their door."

I became a tad frustrated with him and repeated, "I've told you, Axel, that it's only Steven and Jimmy. He said he wasn't working with anyone else and somehow he felt assured the girls would not be able to escape."

"I wonder what that means," Inga butted in. "What if he has them tied to dynamite or some other kind of explosive device?"

"What?" I exclaimed too loudly.

"Shhh, Ruth Ann," Axel barked. "Keep your voice down."

"Sorry, but that would be the last thing I'd ever think of. You don't think Steven would do such a thing, do you?"

Axel raised his eyebrows in surprise. "I thought *you* told me he didn't commit any murders? Why would he set Prunella and your daughter up in anything that could accidentally explode?"

"Or intentionally explode," Sherman mumbled.

"Yes," Axel agreed with Sherman.

"You're right, that's silly. I'm sure he's just got them tied up with a gag in their mouths. In any case, let's get down to suite 410."

We hurried down the hall and found the suite in the middle of the floor. "Here we are," Axel whispered. "I'm not sure if we should just break in or what?"

"I think we should just kick the door in!" Inga suggested, eager to go in. "I can try."

"No, you won't," Axel snapped at her. "We'll wake up the entire floor if you do that."

"Good point, but what are we going to do then?" she inquired.

I pulled out the room key and said, "Or we can just open the door and walk in."

"Risky," Axel replied. "Too risky."

"No, it's not," I said. "It's just going to be Prunella and Lynne in there, and I'm anxious to get in there so I'll just do it."

"Wait!" he said with force, but quietly.

"Just do it, Ruth Ann," Inga said impatiently. "We don't have a choice. We've got to go in anyway."

"Yeah, you're right," I said, ignoring Axel's protests and sticking the key in and turning the handle gently. We heard the click and jumped a little. The slightest sound was so loud it startled us. "Here we go," I whispered, and then turned the handle a little more and pushed the door slowly.

"Just whip the door open, Ruth Ann," Inga said excitedly. "There's no turning back now!"

I agreed and flew open the door of the suite and the four of us stood in the doorway staring into a pitch-black room. "I can't see anything," I said, trying to adjust my eyes to the darkness.

"Maybe this was just another one of his jokes," Sherman said, standing at the back of the pack. "It wouldn't surprise me if this suite was empty."

"Only one way to find out," Inga said, shoving Axel to the side and reaching around the wall to find a switch. "There," she said, as she flipped the switch and a wall light flashed on.

Ugh, my eyes went from total black to blinding light. I snapped my eyes shut for a second then re-opened them. I stared into the front foyer of the suite. "How big is this room?" Inga asked, looking around the spacious foyer filled with a cushioned bench, a wood armoire to hang your coats, and a beautiful antique chest and mirror. I'd never been in this particular suite, but noticed the familiar furniture already. "Hey, this stuff came from my store!" I said proudly.

"That's great, Ruth Ann," Inga said, not really caring. "Let's get out of this room and head into the suite." She treaded forward down the narrow hall that led into the main living area of the suite. I knew the layout well because most of Carol's suites had the same floor plan. There was a foyer, and then a hall that opened into a nice sized living area with a small kitchenette. The bedrooms (one or two) had doorways off on the sidewalls. The only suites that had a balcony were the ones on the back and end I believe.

"Wait, Inga, we should go in together," Axel said, catching up with her. It was too late. It was only a short distance into the main room after passing a bathroom.

"What the…" was all I heard from Inga before I caught up and saw exactly what she was referring to.

"They were here," I exclaimed. "But, but, where are they?" I asked, whirling my head around the room. "The ropes are here," I said, indicating the pile of ropes thrown in the middle of the room. I frantically eyed the kitchenette and figured there was nowhere to hide in there.

"Check the bedrooms," Axel ordered Sherman and Inga. They hurried together and disappeared into the first bedroom on the right. He looked at me sympathetically and said, "Don't worry, we'll find them."

"But they must've just left," I called out, lifting the ropes and noticing a couple dents in the plush couch. "They were on there," I said to Axel. "It's still warm!" I shouted out, feeling the dents with my hands.

Axel was too busy looking in the bathrooms, around the round, wood table and chairs next to the kitchenette, the entertainment center, and disappearing into the opposite bedroom that Inga and Sherman were searching. I stood alone in the suite and fell onto the couch. I couldn't take this anymore. Where were they? I felt as if it was one dead end after another when out of nowhere there was a loud bang that came from the front foyer. I rolled off the couch onto the floor and crawled as fast as I could to the backside of the couch. The couch faced toward the hall and if I didn't get off in time I would be spotted instantly.

I stayed as low as I could and hoped that Axel, Inga, and Sherman knew to stay where they were until we knew who just entered the suite. I tried to listen for any footsteps or voices when I spotted Axel in the doorway of the bedroom. He must've heard the noises too because he was anxiously watching me as I crouched behind the couch. Our eyes met and he mouthed, "Stay there, don't move."

I knew I had to take a little peek over the back edge of the couch. I had to know with whom we were dealing. Maybe it was Lynne or Prunella! I nodded over at Axel and went on my knees as I grabbed the fabric on the back of the couch. I ever so carefully pulled myself up enough that I could stick my head up to see who was coming. Axel was furious with me I could tell, but one of us had to see what we were dealing with. It's been one painful situation after another, and I wasn't going to sit on the floor and wait for someone to find me.

Just as I glanced over the edge, Inga and Sherman walked into the room as if nothing was going on. They were fighting with each other and oblivious to what was going down in here. I looked over at Axel, who was on the opposite side of the main room in the second bedroom doorway. He was waving his arms up and down trying to get their attention, but they didn't glance his way or see his frantic motions.

"Stop!" I yelled, standing upright and screaming over to Inga and Sherman. I hoped the shock of my scream would deter or hold off any quick actions from the person coming into the room. Inga froze, grabbed hold of Sherman's arm and shoved him to the ground so forcefully I thought she either knocked him unconscious or broke a few of his aging, brittle bones.

Sherman stayed silent on the ground while Inga ran over to me and was about to tackle me to the ground when the stranger entered and shouted, "STOP!"

I whipped my head around and saw John standing in front of the TV entertainment center with his gun aimed at Inga and me. He realized who it was just before Inga was about to throw me down. He immediately lowered his gun and hollered, "Ruth Ann!" Within a second he was at my side.

"John," I exclaimed, thrilled that it wasn't Jimmy or Steven Svenson who was standing next to me shoving Inga away.

John nearly knocked Inga over the back of the couch when she regained her footing. "Hey, watch out."

"Sorry, Inga," John said. "I didn't know what was going on in here when Ruth Ann screamed."

"John, how did you find us?" Axel said, walking casually into the room near us.

"Eklund, you're here now, huh?"

"Yes, Ruth Ann found me earlier."

John eyed me suspiciously and for a quick second I thought he was jealous of Axel. "Axel found that clue back in the bakery and thought he could end this by himself. He thought he would find Lynne and Prunella without any of us getting hurt."

"Well, that doesn't appear to have happened," John said, with a brisk tone. "Where's Svenson?"

"Where's Judy?" I asked, curiously looking toward the short hallway that opened into the foyer. "Is she out there?"

"No, she's checking out the rest of the resort."

"Wait," Axel interrupted. "How did you find us up here?"

"Yeah," Sherman agreed as stood back up. "How did you find this suite and know we were in here?"

"You okay, Sherman?" Inga asked him. "I didn't mean to hurt you."

"I was just stunned for a moment. I'm good now."

John ignored their conversation and said, "I got it out of that night clerk downstairs."

"He told you what?" I asked curiously.

"After Judy and I realized we were led on *another* false lead we came back here and I marched right up to the front desk. Carol wasn't there and this man I've never seen before was sitting behind the counter. After questioning who *he* was I asked him about anything he might've seen or heard tonight. He had a bizarre look on his face like I was about to arrest him. I don't trust that guy, but after he sweated quite a bit, and I told him he could be held liable for leaving anything out, he fessed up."

"What did he tell you exactly?" I asked, wondering if John found him watching that lewd show like I did.

He looked directly at me and said, "That you showed up demanding to know a room number for a key you handed him."

"Then he told you the suite number, right?" Axel inquired.

"Yep. I ran up the stairs and found the door ajar. I pushed it open and you know the rest." He looked around the room, disappointed, and said, "So, no Prunella or Lynne, huh?"

"No, we were just looking around for some clues," I said unhappily. "They were just here, though. The couch was still warm and there was a clear indentation on it."

John eyed the couch that had long since regained its shape and asked, "Have you found anything else up here?"

"Not yet," Axel said. "You came barreling in this room before we had a good enough look around."

John glared at Axel with daggers and barked, "Then let's get back at it. Judy should be here any minute then we can figure out what's next. I'm hoping Lynne or Prunella left us another clue."

"How many clues can those poor women leave us?" Axel asked, irritated. "We're like a group of bumbling idiots!"

"Easy, Axel," I said, not wanting this to turn into a fight between the two men. "I'll look in the living room area. Inga and Sherman can go back into the master bedroom, and Axel, you go back into the second bedroom and continue."

John agreed with me and started his own search first in the kitchen, and then the bathroom, and lastly the foyer. Nobody talked; we just searched for quite some time when I looked up from rummaging under the couch cushions to see Judy's smug face staring at me. "Well, Ruth Ann, I found where you stuffed Svenson."

"You found him in the kitchen? Is he still unconscious?"

"He's not in there anymore."

"What?" I bellowed loud enough for everyone to come back to the living room.

"What's happened?" Axel inquired.

Judy spoke before I could answer him and said, "Svenson's escaped."

"No way," Inga shouted. "He was tightly bound and unless he had help, there's no way he got out."

"My guess Jimmy reappeared and found him," Axel said. "We never did find him after Inga knocked him out earlier."

"That's right!" I exclaimed. "So, now what do we do? They've left us again!"

John said, "My guess is Prunella and Lynne are fully aware of our chase and are giving those two a difficult time. Why else would Svenson keep us running all over the place?"

"Because he's disturbed. He's buying time until Ms. Prunella discloses where that necklace is," Inga said furious. "But she won't tell him."

"Never!" I added. "She won't ever tell him. She'd rather make him run around and have us follow them. One of these times we'll catch up with them and we outnumber them."

"So, you think they left the resort?" Sherman asked, looking exhausted with his unshaven, tired face. A look that he would normally never be caught dead with.

"Possibly," John answered him, also showing signs of exhaustion. Come to think of it, I'm exhausted too. I can't remember when I slept last. I thought for sure we'd have found Lynne and Prunella by now. It was close to midnight and if we didn't come to some conclusion soon we would be going a second night without much sleep at all.

"Then we'd better look closer to see if the women left us a sign of where they're headed next," Judy said, stammering off down the hall toward the foyer of the suite.

"What if they didn't or couldn't leave us a clue?" Sherman asked nervously. "Then we're sunk."

"No, I know we can figure this out," I stated. "This is getting ridiculous."

Inga asked John, "They wouldn't have gone to that high school you and Judy were just at, would they?"

"I don't see why. That was just a ruse to get us out of the way so Ruth Ann could meet up with Prunella and force her to tell Svenson where the necklace is hidden."

"Hey," I said out of the blue. "Maybe we're going about this the wrong way."

"What do you mean, Ruth Ann?" John asked curiously as he opened up the mini refrigerator in the kitchen. He pulled out a water bottle and opened it up. He took a long swig of the cool liquid and held out the nearly empty bottle to me.

I shook my head and replied, "Maybe, just maybe, we should be forgetting about looking for Svenson and," I was immediately interrupted from a distant yell, "Are you serious?" Judy barked. "That's the dumb…" John stopped Judy before she finished her nasty sentence.

"Judy! Let Ruth Ann finish what she was saying."

Judy appeared back into the living area full of rage, but I ignored her for the moment and said, "Why don't we change direction and instead of looking for Svenson, which he thinks we'll be doing, and go after the necklace."

"What? No way," Judy snapped. "That's crazy."

"No, no it's not, Judy," John said, smiling brightly at me. "I see where Ruth Ann's going with this."

"Yes, if Steven thinks we're just going to keep chasing him, he'll keep eluding us. We know eventually they'll end up wherever the necklace is. Maybe we should cut out the cat and mouse game and go for the cheese! Get it?" I asked, glancing around at my audience with their mouths hanging open. "You know, the cheese is the necklace?"

"Ya, ya, I get it," Judy replied sarcastically.

John wasn't so quick to speak. I could see the wheels in his brain going round and round with my idea. Several times he was about to talk, but snapped his mouth shut. Finally, after several seconds he said, "You know, that might work."

"No way, John," Judy asserted. "They could kill them both before ever retrieving the necklace."

"How's that?" I asked her curiously. "Prunella would never tell him where it was. She would make him take her, and my daughter with them until they knew they'd be safe."

"I agree," Axel announced from the doorway of the second bedroom. "I'm just mad I didn't think of it."

"Thanks, Axel," I said, grinning. I turned my head back to an astonished Judy and said, "Well?"

"I'm not as sure as the rest of you, but I guess it could work."

Sherman did a little cough to get our attention. When he had our attention he said, "The problem with this course of action is that we don't know exactly where the necklace is at this time, correct?"

"That is a serious problem," John said. "It wasn't in the original safe or that second safe she had built in the garage."

"Wait a minute," I yelled suddenly. Sherman almost fell back to the ground with my outburst. "Sorry, I just had the most amazing thought."

"What's that, Ruth Ann?" John asked inquisitively.

"How do we know the necklace *isn't* in the original safe?"

"What? How? Hold on," John mumbled. "I thought the necklace was missing from the safe back in the house. That's when we discovered, from Sherman, that there was another safe built. That safe was also emptied."

"But we don't know if Prunella put it back into the original safe. That would throw everyone off, wouldn't it?" I asked, waiting to see their stunned and confused reactions.

"When would she have time to do that?" Inga asked.

"Well," I started to say. "She was acting strangely Sunday at lunchtime. That's when Axel contacted her to meet at the guesthouse. Prunella sensed trouble and took the necklace out of the safe. We only *assumed* she put it into the garage safe."

Sherman interrupted me and blurted out, "No, no, I went with her, remember? I was with her when she took me over to the garage."

"Sherman, did you actually see Prunella put the necklace into the safe?"

"Why, yes," he said with a weird, scrunched up look on his face. "Actually," he said, trying to think hard. "I never *saw* the physical necklace. She had me keep watch near the doors of the garage to see if we were followed."

"So, you never saw her put the necklace into the safe?" I asked, getting excited.

"No, no, I didn't, but that's why she went up there. Why wouldn't she?"

"To throw us all off," I said. "She wanted you to *think* she put it safely away. However, Prunella knew that you would most likely cave and tell us about the safe. She didn't know who would be caught or threatened to open the safe up."

"You're saying Ms. Prunella didn't trust me?" Sherman asked furiously.

"No, she didn't want your life to be in danger," I said quickly.

Axel stormed into the living area, obviously irritated, and said, "You've got to be kidding me? We've gone all over the place and risked our lives to find out the necklace might be back up in my estate safe?"

"It's possible, don't you think?" I questioned. Inga's mouth was hanging open, and John was grinning proudly at me. Axel was fuming mad, while Judy stood frozen in her spot glaring at me. Sherman was still sulking over the fact Prunella might not have trusted him as much as he thought.

I waited and waited until I became exasperated. "C'mon! Someone say something. We're wasting time!"

John was the first one to respond. "Ruth Ann's brought up a viable theory. I think we need to check it out."

"Are you telling me we have to go back up to Eklund's estate?" Judy asked, irritated by John's suggestion, mostly because I came up with the idea.

"Yes," I answered for John. "Aren't you tired of chasing all over the place? We're no closer to rescuing Prunella and Lynne than we were in the beginning."

"But you're suggesting we give up chasing after them." Judy protested. "That makes no sense."

"Yes, if we know where the necklace is we can either wait for them to show up, which they eventually will, or send them word that *we* are now in possession of the necklace."

"Yes, yes, good plan, Ruth Ann," Inga said excitedly. "Let's go now!"

Sherman nodded with a little more enthusiasm, and even Axel was ready to check it out. The only one who was against my plan was Judy. I didn't know if it was because she truly didn't care for the plan or that I came up with it before her. John overruled her so we left the suite and headed back into the empty lobby. Well, empty except for the night clerk whom John and I had confronted earlier. I put in the back of my mind to talk with John about this man and see if we should warn Richard and Carol about him. I knew if it was my employee I would want to know.

"Hurry," Inga said, reaching the front door of the resort first. "Let's get out of here."

We quickly made our way to John's police truck parked in the resort's parking lot. It was way at the back of the lot since the resort was nearly full, and by the time we reached the car we were frozen and out of breath from the frigid night air. "Turn on the heat!" I shouted out to John from the far back seat.

I looked around for a moment before I realized we were missing one person. "Hey, where'd Axel go?"

Frantically, John got out of his truck and ran around the immediate area. When he came back he was out of breath. "He's gone again all right, but where to now?

Judy said, "Who cares where he is? Let's get up to his estate before he does. I think he knows where the necklace might be."

"I'm sure he does," Inga replied from the back. "It's his house!"

John, giving up on locating Axel, turned the engine over and headed down Main Street in a frenzy. The only part of this plan that wasn't sitting well with me was leaving the resort. I didn't care too much about Axel at the moment. I wasn't sure where Steven was taking Prunella and Lynne, but if they were at the resort and we were leaving, I would feel horrible.

But, we had been through one disaster after another. We were just lucky nobody was seriously hurt tonight and we were together, well most of us. "We'll be there in ten," John called out. He was halfway up the mountain where Axel and

Prunella's massive estate was situated. The roads were clear and dry. If there had been any snow or ice on the road it would've been a dangerous ride at the speed John was traveling. He didn't turn on his lights. Not only was it very late at night, but also I didn't think he wanted to alert anyone that we were heading to the estate. I was deep in thought when Inga, who was sitting near the window next to me, shrieked, "Hey, you just missed the turnoff!"

John slammed on the brakes and the truck spun around on the now, freezing pavement. "Hang on," he yelled trying to regain control of the truck. It was too late; the truck kept spinning and then slid over the edge, precariously hanging over a bluff. I was in the backseat being thrown toward Inga, then back to Sherman. It was pretty dark, but the one thing I could see was the fear in Sherman's terrified blue eyes. They pierced mine as I held on to whatever I could grab as the truck spun out of control. "Ruth Ann," Sherman cried. "We're going to die!"

"No, Sherman," I tried to say as I suddenly stopped being thrown around. "Look, we've stopped!" I said as the motion halted.

John, very quietly, but authoritatively, told us not to move an inch. "If this truck veers too much to the front, we're all done for."

"What do you mean, John?" I demanded from the back seat as I froze, the front half of my body on Sherman and the other half sprawled over Inga's lap.

"I misjudged the road being dry. We must've hit a patch of black ice and that's why we went spinning."

"The truck's hanging over the edge of a cliff!" Judy exclaimed, peering over the front dash of the vehicle.

"I'm brutally aware of that fact, Judy," John replied, irritated at her for blurting out our dilemma. "Now, what do we do about it?"

"I don't want to die this way!" Sherman cried out from the back seat. "Please, get us out of this. I promise I'll tell you everything I know about where the necklace really is. Just get me out of this alive!"

Well, if I could explain how stunned we were with Sherman's announcement, it still wouldn't be enough to describe the shock on our faces. John slowly turned his head toward the back seat. His eyes took on the shape of thin, but opened, slits. If looks could kill, this would definitely be one of them. Inga and I were staring from John to Sherman and back to John again. "What did you say?" John asked through gritted teeth in a low, terrifying voice.

Sherman, realizing he'd blurted out a very regrettable statement, said, "Um, no, no, I didn't mean what I said. I'm just afraid to die." He quickly amended his comment and said, "I'm afraid to die this way."

"That's not what you said, Sherman," Judy announced. "You just admitted to us that you've known all along where the necklace was."

"Sherman," I said, hoping to get the truth out of him. "Please, tell us the truth. Do you know what Prunella's done with our necklace?" I carefully grabbed his arm with my hand and pleaded with him again. "Just say it, I won't be mad at you."

"Not me!" John bellowed, louder than he should have. The truck moaned, gave way to a slight rocking motion, and then halted still precariously perching over the edge of the bluff. I wish I could've sent John ESP up to the front seat advising him to control his temper. We weren't going to get anywhere if he threatened Sherman. Sherman's loyalty has always been, and will always be, to Prunella. My light brown eyes gazed his way and our eyes met for a second. John turned his head away from me and looked out the front window. I could now see the terror lying ahead of us. The night was dark, but I could see our dangerous position from the view of the headlights. Our vehicle was closer to going forward over the edge than backward toward the frozen, grassy area behind us.

John remained silent for a minute, and then blurted out, "I have an idea. I think my weight, with Judy is too much for the front end of the truck. I'm going to gently lift myself up and put my weight into the back."

"But that leaves me up here alone," Judy protested. "I'm lighter, let me go back first."

"Fine" John said, knowing it probably didn't matter who went first, but getting the weight distributed into the back was urgent. "Carefully lift yourself up and go through the opening in the middle. Try not to move too fast or wiggle too much."

"Hurry up," Inga exclaimed excitedly. "We need to get ourselves outta this so I can kill Sherman!" Sherman's howl sent the truck rocking again. "Be quiet!" Inga barked at him. "You're making matters worse."

"Everybody shut up!" John growled in a low voice. He turned to Judy and told her to go. She carefully unbuckled her seat belt and waited to see if there was any movement with the truck. Once she felt safe, she slowly swung each of her legs around, resting them on John's lap for a brief moment. I could've sworn I spotted an evil grin on her face as she rested her legs on his. John grabbed each of her legs and moved them toward the opening between the two front seats. "Use your hands to lift your body up and over the opening." Judy's legs were now squished into the back seat with her body just beginning to make its way to meet up with her legs. I noticed each of us was holding our breath until the transfer was complete. It felt like forever for her to get into the back seat with Sherman, Inga, and me. There wasn't enough room for us to sit side by side so I found myself resting more on Inga's lap than the seat. John held up his hand motioning us to not say a word. He put his finger up to his mouth and quietly said, "Did you feel that?" None of us crammed in the backseat knew what he was asking.

"What?" I whispered.

"The truck tipped back a little. I think it's going to work if I can get my weight into the back, too."

"But you won't fit back here," Sherman argued just as Judy's foot smacked him in his stomach. "Hey, that hurt!"

"I'll climb on top of you if you don't shut up!" she barked. Sherman's mouth clamped shut and we waited as John turned and twisted his well over six foot, meaty body around to fit through an opening that wasn't large enough for his arm to go through. "Nobody move," he said, getting one leg, then the other into the back of the truck. His head was shoved up against the roof and his behind was aiming at the dashboard. He was stuck.

"Okay," he said. "I don't think I'm going anywhere, and if I go back I'd be afraid it would give the truck momentum to go over the edge. Let me shift as much as my weight as I can to see if the truck will move back some more. Than we can jump out of the truck and hope it doesn't go over."

I listened to what John asked and waited to see if the truck would shift in our favor. The problem was if we got out of the truck, John would still be stuck in the middle. He could definitely make it into the backseat if we moved out of his way, but would that be too late? My fear took over as I grabbed his arm that was stretched out in the middle of the back seat and yanked it as hard as I could. John didn't see this coming and he yelped in pain. "What the?" Judy shouted as John came flying on top of her. Well, most of him came flying on top of her. His legs were now laying the wrong side up on the middle console of the truck and his body was twisted, backside up, on Judy.

"We're going to go over!" Sherman hollered. "I'm getting outta here."

He was about to open the door when I shouted, "No, Sherman, hang on." I noticed the truck shifted itself into a solid position and we weren't rocking anymore. "I think we're on frozen ground!"

"I think you're right, Ruth Ann," Inga said, peering out the window she was plastered against. "I'll open the door." She didn't wait for John to give his approval as she grabbed the handle and yanked open the door. She tumbled out of the truck onto the ground and jumped up. "It's good, the truck's safe. You can get out." She brushed some snow off of her from the light layer that had recently begun to fall.

I shoved everybody off of me and rolled over and out of the truck. I was ready to fall onto the ground and kiss it when John exited his truck and grabbed me tightly. "Thank God we're all okay," he said, out of breath. "I really thought we were goners!"

"Thanks for telling me that!" I said, too happy to stay mad. "Now what?"

John looked around at our surroundings and said, "We're only a short distance from the road. I must've hit an icy patch and spun around several times before we skidded off the road and landed here on the bluff. We're just lucky we didn't go over right away. With all this ice, I'm surprised we didn't." I looked where the tire marks came from and we must have come down the slight slope doing circle after circle. I was so scared I didn't pay much attention to it at the time, but looking at the imprints in the ground, we really were fortunate to still be alive.

"Can we get your truck out of here or is it too dangerous?" I asked him.

John ignored my question and stomped off to the other side of his truck. He flew open the back door and yelled, "GET OUT!" We knew who he was yelling at and, even though he deserved it, I felt a tad sorry for him. When one gets on John's bad side, it's usually an ugly scene. Judy was next to him holding out her gun. I stepped through the snow and hardened mud and snapped, "Is that really necessary?" I inquired.

"He's been lying to us all along, Ruth Ann," Judy answered. "He's been keeping the whereabouts of the bloody necklace from us and now he's going to pay by getting himself arrested."

"Nonsense," John bawled, grabbing poor old Sherman's arm from inside the back of the truck. "First, he's going to spill everything he so conveniently excluded us from, again, and then I'm going to haul his pitiful, sorry, weak-minded, ass to jail and throw out the key!"

"Whoa," I said, trying to pull John away from Sherman. "What Sherman did was wrong," I hesitated, and looked at him for a moment then added, "seriously wrong, but it wasn't Sherman who committed the murders and kidnapped Prunella and Lynne." I could see the sweat beginning to form on the poor guy's forehead as he gave me a crooked smile for helping him. I didn't return the smile, but said, "Don't misunderstand me, Sherman. I'm plenty ticked off at you. We could've avoided all this running around and rescued my daughter and cousin by now!"

"I'm sorry, Ruth Ann," Sherman said from the back seat. John had released the grip he had on his arm and took a step back to cool down. "I didn't have a choice."

"What?" Judy yelled at him from just outside the door. She stomped over to the opening sticking her head inside where she could put her face within inches of his. "Why don't you tell us what you mean by that?"

Sherman wiped a drip (or two) of the sweat that had trickled down the side of his face, even though it was freezing outside. He was terrified and knew his reluctance to divulge important information was over. John and Judy were not going to let this go any more. He asked if he could join us outside since he was so hot in the truck. Judy reached a hand out for him to grab as he swung his trembling legs around and outside onto the frozen ground. "Thank you."

Inga was next to me, standing a few feet away from the truck. I figured it was best for John to interrogate him first. Sherman really blew it this time. I wasn't sure if he did it for the right reasons, but I do know his loyalties have always been with Prunella. He must've had a really good reason to keep her secret this time. Inga didn't appear so forgiving. I could feel her fury building, as she stood motionless glaring at her friend, Sherman.

John, Judy, Inga, and I remained silent as Sherman brushed himself off nervously and coughed repeatedly as if he had a tickle in his throat that left him unable to speak. Finally, after several long, grueling seconds, John shouted, "Enough! Start talking. We're wasting too much time. I still have to get my truck outta this mess."

"Fine," Sherman answered with one last clearing of his throat. "I, I don't know where to begin." His pleading look over at Inga and then me was begging for our assistance. I shook my head back and forth slowly while Inga didn't make any motion that she was going to help him out of this one.

"Now!" Judy spat out, giving his stiffened right shoulder a nudge. "No more waiting for someone to help you. This is on you."

"Yes, yes it is," he said, regaining his composure enough to speak clearly. "I need to make one thing very clear. I didn't mean everything I said when I yelled out what you all heard. I thought we were going to die. I panicked."

John, about to jump on him, gritted his teeth so tightly I thought he'd break each and every tooth in his mouth. Very quietly, but angrily, he said, "Are you trying to tell us that you don't know where the necklace is? That you panicked when you thought my truck was going to go over this cliff?" John paused and pointed toward the sharp drop off that we almost experienced firsthand. Each of our heads followed John's stiff-arm as he wound it around to exaggerate the direction. "Is that what you're saying now?

Sherman waited until John's arm was back at his side. "No, I mean, yes," he muttered confused. "I meant that I know a little more than I've disclosed to you. I don't *exactly* know the specific location of the piece."

"So, you hollered out like a little baby when you thought you were going to die that you knew where the necklace was, but now that you're safe on the ground you claim that was an *exaggeration* of the truth?"

"No, I mean I know the location of the necklace."

"I'm getting really tired of this, Sherman," John said, frustrated. "So you do know where it is?"

"I said I know the *location* of the necklace, but not specifically where Ms. Prunella deposited it the last time she had it in her possession."

I couldn't take this cat and mouse game anymore. I blurted out, "Sherman, is it back at Axel's estate like I thought it might be? Back in the original safe?"

Sherman turned toward me and answered, "It's at Mr. Eklund's estate all right. But," he began to say, but hesitated long enough to glance over at John making sure he wasn't going to jump down his throat again. When he realized John was acting impatiently, but willing to let him continue he did. "But, I don't know that it's actually back in the original safe."

"Finally," Judy stated, letting out a groan. "We need to stop wasting time thinking Sherman's going to tell us everything. Whether he claims to know or not, that necklace is somewhere back at the estate. We need to get up there fast. By now, Svenson could've swiped the necklace and taken himself and Jimmy to the airport!"

"Judy's right," John said before I could protest. I wanted to know, if what Judy had stated was correct, then what's happened to my daughter? And Prunella. "I need help getting the truck moving again. I see we were stuck in some mud and I might need some help with some pushing to get us where I can drive it back up onto the road."

"You want us to push you out?" I asked, surprised. "The only ones strong enough to manage that are Inga and you."

Judy let out a laugh. "I think I can handle it too, Ruth Ann. I'm still young and quite strong." She glared at me with such a sadistic grin I wanted to slug her.

"I assumed you were capable, too. I didn't think Sherman or I are able to push a truck out of this muddy ditch."

She wiped the smirk off her face and seriously replied, "Oh, okay. I misunderstood you."

John ignored our bantering once again and went back inside the truck and tried to turn over the engine. It had no problem starting up. That was a good sign. Next he put the truck into reverse and tried to give it some gas. The wheels spun around and splattered wet muddy ice in all directions. I was fortunate to be paying attention to the wheels and once I noticed what was happening I jumped as far back as I could. Unfortunately, Judy and Sherman got the brunt of the mess. Inga escaped splashing mud, and once she saw Sherman and Judy, she grabbed her mid-section and bawled in laughter. "Serves you right, Sherman," Inga said between bursts of laughter.

Sherman, stunned by the wet, dark, filth on his long coat, glowered his dark blue eyes staring at her. The look even startled Inga, who doesn't scare easily. She immediately stopped laughing and clamped her mouth shut. Sherman, satisfied with the reaction, started frantically brushing away as many of the chunks of mud and ice that he could. Most of it smeared and spread across the front of his wool coat, but he kept at it until John reappeared at the back of his police truck. "Sorry about that," he said, noticing what he had done by gunning the gas pedal. "I had to give it a hard go because I was afraid I'd slip a little forward first." Ah, he was worried about moving the truck in case it went forward and over the edge! "It only moved about a foot before the wheels got caught up in the sludge."

"We see that!" Sherman yelled at him. "Do you see what you've done?"

John, amazed at the effrontery, spat out, "Excuse me?" He waited for an apology from Sherman, but Sherman wasn't about to give one. "You have no say in this matter. You're the reason why we're in this mess in the first place!"

"Me?"

"Don't start with me, Sherman," John replied with a reddening face. "If we knew the necklace was up at Eklund's estate, we would've searched the place from top to bottom and not gone chasing all over town."

I couldn't help but say, "Ahem, John, we still would've had to go into town to search for Prunella and Lynne."

"No, Ruth Ann," John hollered at me louder than was necessary. "They would've come to us. Prunella was playing just as much a dangerous game as Svenson. She made that man run all over town and risked many people's lives in order to protect her precious necklace." Before he could let me speak, he added, "And I'm up to here," John raised his arm and hand over his head to emphasize his point, "in this nonsense over a silly necklace. No material item should cause this much of a mess!"

"Wow," I muttered more to myself than anyone else. "I don't have any words right now. If you're trying to put some of the blame on me, I won't have it. I didn't take and hide the necklace or kidnap or murder anyone!"

John, without apologizing to me, turned on his heels and walked over to Judy who was standing near Inga. He whispered a few words into her ear as she stared at me intently. "Fine," was what she replied back as John went into his truck and restarted the engine. Judy marched over to Sherman and grabbed his arm under strong protest. "Hey, what are you doing?"

"We're going to go around to the front of the vehicle and push it as hard as we can when John tells us to. Inga, I need your help, too."

"What about me?" I inquired. "Can't I help a little?"

"No," A voice shouted out from the opened window. John immediately answered for Judy. "You stay off to the side."

"But," I began to say and then realized…I didn't want to help push the truck. I looked at the horror in Sherman, and even Inga's, face as Judy led them toward a small piece of flat land right before the drop off.

"Are you insane?" Inga asked, carefully looking over the ledge. "Our feet could slip and we'd go over the edge."

"You have plenty of room," Judy replied, standing in the middle of the front end of the truck. "Sherman, you go to my right, Inga, to my left." Judy barked out her orders and didn't leave room for any arguing. Sherman reluctantly stood next to Judy while Inga took position on the other side. Judy gave a thumbs up to John when I saw him reach for the gear to shift into reverse. I closed my eyes. I couldn't help myself.

It only took a few hard pushes, which I heard from the grinding of the wheels and the grunts from the pushers, before the truck's wheels took hold and finally moved far away from the edge of the bluff.

"You did it!" I shouted. I ran over to the truck and pounded on the front passenger side window. John reached over and opened the door, "Hop in." I pulled myself up and inside the truck and fastened the seatbelt right away.

Judy, Sherman, and Inga followed suit and shoved their way into the back of the truck. Poor Sherman was crammed into the middle with Inga and Judy in the window seats. Sherman looked like he'd been through a small war. His coat was wet and dirty, and his face bore the expression of a wild animal ready to pounce on anyone who confronted him.

John backed the truck up enough so he was able to turn the vehicle around and head up to the main road. I was thankful that we didn't have any more problems getting onto the road. I didn't think our group could handle another stuck truck!

Once John was on the road he backtracked a short distance and pulled off onto the gravel road that led to Axel's estate. I was wondering if Axel had already made it back. I knew he was desperate to get to Prunella and the necklace. However, I wasn't sure which was his top priority. John sped his way down the quarter mile drive until we reached the elegant entrance to the estate. In the middle of the circular drive was the covered fountain. Although the tan tarp covering the fountain looked cheap, it protected it from the harsh winter weather. John didn't pull around the circular part of the driveway. He stayed straight on the drive that led down and around the back of the house and the garage. He put the truck into park and turned to us. "Okay, I don't see any other vehicles here, but that doesn't mean Eklund isn't here or Svenson and that Jimmy character."

"It'd be great if Prunella and Lynne were here. I'm getting so frustrated I can't take much more of this," I expressed.

"There's no sign of them," Judy mentioned.

"They could've parked back near the garage," John suggested. "We can have a look back there first."

"No," Inga protested. "Let's just go in the front door and confront whoever's in there. We know they may be there so just be prepared."

"I agree with Inga," I said. "I'm tired of the wild goose chases. Our luck would be we run into another diversion if we go toward the garage first."

John looked over at Judy and shrugged his shoulders. "Fine with me," he replied, pulling out his gun and making sure it was ready to fire. Judy reached over me from the middle of the truck and popped open the glove compartment and grabbed her gun. It was within inches of my face. I didn't show any reaction because that's what she wanted.

"Good to go," she said. "Let's do this." Judy plopped back into the back seat and grabbed the door handle. She was the first one out of the car. I waited for John to give me the nod to go ahead and exit the truck. Sherman and Inga were already waiting at the back of the truck for John's orders.

"You three will stay by the fountain until Judy and I get inside and make sure we won't be ambushed right away."

"It's freezing out here, John," I said. "Plus, it's the middle of the night and dark. Nobody can see too much out here anyway."

"The front lights are on and it's pretty well lit up, Ruth Ann," Judy explained. "It'll just be a couple minutes."

I didn't respond to her, but grabbed Inga and Sherman's arm and walked over to the fountain. John and Judy went up to the front door and I saw John reach for the front door handle. Before he could even make an effort to open it, the door flew open.

Chapter 37

"**W**hat the?" John yelled, fumbling to get his gun in his right hand. Judy was hunched over ready with her gun between her two hands and extended arms.

"Don't shoot!" cried a voice from within.

"Eklund," John hollered, lowering his arm. "It's just you."

I hurried up the front steps and made my way to them. Inga and Sherman were right behind me. "Axel," I called out. "You're here."

He eyed me and smiled. "Yes, I've been here for quite a while, but," he said, glaring at John. "What on earth took you so long? You had a head start on me."

Sherman, who finally made his way up to us, panting, said, "The Chief got us in an accident."

"What?" Axel exclaimed. "Are you okay?" he asked, looking at the mess on Sherman's coat.

"Yes, yes," John answered. "We just slipped on some ice and had to get ourselves out of a ditch. Nothing much."

"Nothing much?" Sherman bellowed. "Look at me! I'm wet and full of mud from that vehicle of yours. Plus, you almost took us over a cliff and we could be dead right now!"

"Easy, Sherman," I said, patting him on the back gently and carefully. He was quite wet and I'd have to imagine, cold. "We're all fine. It was scary, yes, but we managed." I turned to Axel and asked him, "How did you get yourself up here?"

He looked guiltily at John and Judy. "Umm, I noticed as we were running out of the resort that there was a cab driver sitting in his car not far from where you were parked. It was a spur of the moment decision, and, now that I heard what just happened to you, I'm kind of glad I made it."

"You hailed a cab driver and drove up here?" John asked, surprised. Probably because he didn't notice the cab parked near his own truck.

"Yeah, why not?" Axel asked. "I pounded on the window of the cab and woke the guy up." He looked around at us and said, "Not that *any* of you noticed I wasn't in the truck at first, right?"

I was furious with him now and demanded, "Why did you do it? You could've just come along with us. What you did was wrong, plain and simple." I tried to calm down by taking a deep breath.

I did finally agree that it was a hectic moment and we didn't notice he wasn't there right away. Axel, obviously aware of my disappointment with him continued, "So, I asked him if he could take me up to my house. He said he was getting some shut-eye after dropping off a guest at the resort. Something about the guest's plane being delayed and the poor driver had to wait for hours, unpaid of course, until he was able to take them from the airport to the resort. I realized he was trying to con me into paying way more than a typical fare would be. I needed to get up here, so I offered him double the fare. He sat bolt upright and drove me lickity-split up to my house."

"But why did you have to try and beat us up here?" John asked. "You knew we were on our way, too. In fact, we should've been here before you. So what's with the constant separation from us, Eklund?" John stood within inches of Axel with his arms crossed over his torso. The gun, I noticed, was discretely put back into his holster.

"I panicked, that's all, nothing more to it."

"Doesn't make sense, Eklund. You're not the panicky type of person," John argued. "You must not want to not be seen with us, but why?"

"Fine, you're right, John," Axel admitted. "If Svenson was up here waiting for you I didn't want him to spot me, too."

"Why would that matter?" I asked him, a bit confused. "We're better with all of us confronting him anyway."

"No, Ruth Ann," Axel said. "I was hoping I could negotiate some kind of deal with him."

"What kind of deal?" John asked suspiciously. "Were you going to offer money or yourself in exchange for your wife and, hopefully, Ruth Ann's daughter, to be released?"

"I hadn't made up my mind yet. I wanted to see if I could talk the lunatic down and hope for him to do the right thing."

"Seriously?" Judy asked mockingly. "Svenson's not exactly a reasonable man. He's a murderer and a kidnapper."

I interrupted briefly again and said, "He said he didn't murder Bert or Helena, remember?"

Judy threw me a nasty glare and replied, "Like he would tell you the truth."

"Actually, I did believe him," I snapped back at her. "We're missing one piece of vital information."

"And what's that?" she asked me.

"There may be someone else involved."

Everyone present turned and stared at me. "What? Steven Svenson implied that to me."

John amazed at my naiveté, smiled and said, "Ruth Ann, more than likely he was lying."

"I'm usually pretty good at spotting when someone's lying to me. I would swear on my life he wasn't. He didn't kill anyone. Yes, he's a kidnapper and criminal, but no murderer."

John, obviously taking a moment to think about what I said, tried to speak, but snapped his mouth shut. Judy, on the other hand, was quick to reply to me. "That's ridiculous. Svenson murdered the butler and housekeeper. There are no other suspects."

John regained his voice and said, "Now hold on there, Judy. Ruth Ann may have brought up an important point. What if there's another party involved that we've ignored? I think we need to give it some merit."

"C'mon, John," she replied furiously. She shook her head violently and walked around us in a circle. "It's not likely, it's highly improbable," she muttered over and over.

"But not impossible," I added quietly, but Judy overheard me and for a split second I thought she was going to lunge at me.

"Enough for now," Axel interrupted. "Get inside and let me show you what I found while you all were dangling over a cliff."

John snapped back into our present situation and stormed inside the house. I assumed the coast was clear since Axel didn't mention anyone else being up at his estate. "Where we going?" John inquired.

"My library," Axel answered, walking past John in the luxurious and expansive foyer. John, Judy, Sherman, Inga and I followed him through the large, wooden double doors of the library. "Look," Axel said, pointing toward the wall of shelves behind his desk.

None of us had to ask what Axel was pointing at. The shelves were ransacked and books and knick-knacks were strewn all over the floor. "Someone was looking for a way into your safe," John said, hurrying over to the area behind Axel's desk. "What about your safe?" John questioned.

"I checked that right away," Axel answered. "They couldn't get in there. I assume that's why the shelves were searched. Whoever tried to get into my safe tried to find another way."

"Oh, like a secret combination written in a book or piece of paper with the combo stuck in one of the books?" I asked.

"Yes," Axel responded. "Or one of my collectibles." Axel sadly looked on the floor to numerous broken objects. "Most of those were quite expensive and irreplaceable."

John, who had ignorantly stepped on many of the broken objects, cleared his throat and said, "Sorry about that, Eklund. I'm sure whatever you have was heavily insured."

"Yes, but it doesn't mean they can be replaced. Money isn't everything to me. Even though you and your detective think it is." Axel moved his fixed stare from John over to Judy who was ignoring him completely. She was standing in front of the safe staring at it and putting her hands up to the keypad just itching to press some numbers to see if she could be the one to open it up.

Axel went and stood next to her after gently removing the picture that was hanging off the wall to hide the safe. "This is not a fake, it's an original oil painting from a family artist." He carefully walked over to the other side of his desk and leaned it up against his desk. "Stanley Lilgestrom."

"My uncle?" I asked him strangely. "I have many of his paintings myself, but how did *you* get one? And how is he a family artist to you?"

Axel came back to the safe and gave Judy a slight shove and replied, "I should've said it's one of Prunella's relatives."

"That makes sense," Judy said. "You and Prunella are cousins, maybe a bit distant, but nonetheless cousins."

I wondered why I never noticed the painting before. I had been in the library many times, but didn't even recognize the painting. I knew my great uncle used different mediums of art, but his paintings were usually of places he and my great aunt visited. This one was not his typical work. It was smaller than the ones I had; a library with bookshelves, and tables with chairs around them. Hmm, I'll have to look into this at some point. I knew he did a lot of artwork for some Bibles also; maybe this was something I never heard about. There was only one man sitting at one of the tables reading over a large book. The table was piled high with other books. I walked away from the safe while the others chatted about Axel's high tech safety precautions with his safe and looked closer at the painting. I was curious; what the book the man was reading. I had to admit I was rather shocked when I saw the title, *A History of Swedish Viking Ships.* How strange that Axel had a painting in *his* library painted by my great uncle about Viking ships! If he told me the truth, then it was actually a picture Prunella would've had in her possession. Something about that made me shiver. I'm not sure if it was the picture or that my uncle painted a picture like that and Prunella ended up with it. I know he did sell paintings for a living, but how did it end up in Sweden and then in Deer Creek, Colorado? Prunella will have to explain that one to me when we finally get her and Lynne back to us.

Axel turned and saw me on the floor staring at this small painting. He walked and stood over me. "What's up, Ruth Ann? The painting is good, is it not?"

"Yes, but how on earth did you and Prunella obtain this? I thought I knew where most of his paintings were except for the ones he did in Bibles."

"It's appropriate for my line of work and Prunella told me she had a distant relative that was an artist. She recalled seeing this picture at her parent's house when she was young. When they passed away she grabbed it. That's really all I know about it."

"Quite the coincidence, don't you think?" I asked him.

"I guess so. I never thought too much about it, sorry."

"Hey, Eklund, let's get inside this safe, huh?" John called out to us. "Worry about that painting another time."

Axel hurried back over to John and said, "I was already inside there. The necklace isn't in there."

"But, when did you do that?" Inga asked.

"When you all were in your precarious position over the cliff."

"We were gone a long time," I said. "He had plenty of time to come in here and open up his own safe."

"Exactly," Axel answered. "But I haven't looked anywhere else."

John and Judy turned their attention away from Axel and over to Sherman. "Well?" John asked him. "I think you'd better start talking now."

Axel looked confused and asked, "What are you talking to Sherman for?"

"Prunella and Sherman were in cahoots the whole time," Judy answered.

While we were talking, Sherman quietly edged his way over to the doors to exit the library. There was no way he would get away with it since he was old and slow. "Hey,"

Judy shouted, noticing he was getting close to the doors. "Get back here!"

Sherman stopped for a split second then turned and ran faster than I would've ever imagined possible. Inga was the one who tore after him in a hurry. She caught up to him just as he took his first two steps into the foyer. She grabbed him by his wrinkled, white collar and dragged him back to us. "What're you trying to do, Sherman?" Inga asked furiously. "Enough of this. You've got to stop protecting Ms. Prunella. She's not here, and you know more than you've told us. Spill it!" Inga brusquely deposited the old butler in one of the wingback chairs in front of the desk. He looked pathetic with his wrinkled suit, splattered with the mud that had seeped through his coat.

Sherman tried to sit himself up and straighten his jacket and shirt. It was basically useless, but Sherman was a proper man so I wouldn't expect anything less. Once he felt he was suitable he said, "I wasn't going to trick any of you. I wanted to check a few places privately, then I would've come and found you."

"Yeah, right," Judy commented. "Try again."

"Truly," he said. "I wanted to leave a few places secret just in case Ms. Prunella needed to use them again."

Axel stormed over to Sherman from the other side of the desk and stood directly over him. He was fuming mad! "And why would you think Prunella would need to hide something from any of us, especially me?"

Sherman squirmed in the chair and didn't like the close encounter of his boss. "I, I didn't mean it that way, exactly. Ms. Prunella trusts my indiscretion and the last thing I want to do is betray her trust."

"Circumstances have changed, Sherman," Axel said, backing off a little, not a lot, just not inches from his face.

"I know, I know," he said, finally coming to realize that he had to include us in his secrets with my cousin. He stood up and said, "C'mon. I will take you to where Ms. Prunella has hidden things before."

"Wait a minute, Sherman," I interrupted. He stopped in front of the chair and turned to me. I was leaning against the side of the desk and something suddenly dawned on me. The others stopped and waited for my next question. "I'm confused. Prunella hasn't been here that long so what on earth could she be hiding? And from whom was she hiding these things?"

"That's a good point, Ruth Ann," Inga said, standing right next to me as if we were one.

"We're wasting too much time!" Judy snapped. "Sherman, just take us to wherever you know. We can chit chat about the rest of it later."

John agreed so I put my questions on the back burner for now. But sooner or later I expected answers to why Prunella felt it necessary to hide things from me (and her husband with whom she supposedly reunited).

As one group, we left the library with Sherman in the lead. I was waiting for him to head up the main staircase, but he didn't. He went around the stairs and headed down the hall that led into the kitchen. We walked by the entrances to the formal living room and massive dining room. Sherman passed through a closed door and we found ourselves in the middle of the kitchen. "What are we doing in here, Sherman?" John asked him. "Don't tell me you had a safe installed in here?"

"No," he replied. "Ms. Prunella and I thought it was a safe place to hide things. Nobody would think to look in my kitchen!"

"You're probably right," Judy admitted. "So, there's a safe in here somewhere?" Judy turned around and eyed the entire kitchen area. I followed along with her view and looked to the right where a long, rectangular wooden table was located with eight chairs meticulously placed around it. Along the walls were a few cabinets and a large bay window on the back of the house. There were some shelves full of cookbooks and other kitchen related knick-knacks. "I don't see anything out of the ordinary on this side," Judy said.

We turned our attention to the left and that was when my mind realized there were many places Prunella could construct a hidden safe. The large white and gray swirled marble island had many drawers and cabinets that could hide a secret compartment. The L-shaped cabinets and counters along the wall also could have a safe built in them. I noticed the door to the pantry. We've been in there before! Maybe it was in there.

Judy thought the same thing I did as she walked over to the closed pantry door. "It could be anywhere in here so take us to it."

"Fine," Sherman replied and walked over to the pantry. He opened the closed door and stepped inside. John caught up to him so they wouldn't miss anything he was about to uncover. There wasn't enough room for Axel, Inga, and me to watch so we stood in the doorway peeking inside. Sherman flicked on the light switch and out popped shelves of food, small appliances, and kitchen supplies.

"You could last months with all the food in here." John mentioned, looking around the loads and loads of canned, packaged, bagged pastas, vegetables, and sauces. There was even room enough for a large freezer at the back wall probably filled with an entire cow!

"I like to be ready for surprise guests," Axel called out from the outside of the pantry. "This place is always ready for dinner guests."

"I didn't know you liked to entertain, Axel," I stated curiously. "You didn't live here long enough to make a lot of friends."

"I was this way in my household in Sweden, too. It's probably because my parents entertained a lot."

John gave Sherman a little push and said, "Well, go to wherever you hid stuff for Prunella."

Sherman walked deep into the long pantry and stood to the right of the freezer. He turned and looked at the onlookers and shook his head. "This is wrong," he muttered to himself. "She'll never forgive me."

"Knock it off!" John yelled, walking at least ten feet to stand behind Sherman. "Just show us where there's another safe and open it up. We need to know if that bloody necklace is in this place. I'm sick and tired of chasing after this thing."

Sherman looked over John's shoulder and caught my eye. I looked around at the others to see if he was actually trying to get their attention. Inga and Axel looked at me while Judy turned around and glanced my way. Judy, who was standing in the middle of the pantry snapped, "What was that for?"

I was truly surprised and said, "I, I have no idea. Why are you looking at me?"

"Because Sherman gave you a funny look," Judy replied. "Almost as if you know what's in here?"

I was extremely offended and said, "How would I know? I didn't know this hiding place even existed. Why don't you ask Sherman why he glanced over at me?"

Judy whipped around to face Sherman and John again. "Well, Sherman?"

"What'd I do?"

"We saw you look past John to give Ruth Ann a pleading look."

"I didn't mean anything by it. I was hoping Ruth Ann would come to my aid and get you to understand why I'm so hesitant about disclosing certain information."

"Information?" I asked curiously. "I thought we were here to see if the necklace was hidden in here. We need to find out if Prunella and Lynne have been here with Svenson."

"If they've been here and the necklace is missing, then we know that Svenson got a hold of it," John added.

"But if that's the case, where are Prunella and Lynne?" I asked. "Wouldn't they be released then?"

"Not necessarily," Judy commented. "He may still have them for reassurance."

"Reassurance of what?" I demanded.

"So he and Jimmy can get safely out of the country," Judy answered, irritated that I couldn't figure that out.

"What?" I cried out. "You think they may take them back to Sweden?"

"We just don't know yet, Ruth Ann," John said sympathetically

I suddenly felt as if the walls were closing in and I couldn't focus. Axel pulled me back from the doorway and held me up as I did what I hated to do. I swooned like a bloody fool. "Ruth Ann," Axel called out, but I could only vaguely hear him. I felt as if my world was crumbling out of control and I couldn't figure out how to save it. Lynne and Prunella were still missing and possibly out of the country with a mad man. I tried to inhale deeply so I didn't pass out. John came to my aid joined Axel. "Ruth Ann, you need to breathe. It'll be alright."

I heard them talking, but my body kept slowly sinking down to the floor. A nasty thought entered my brain. I wasn't going to give Judy the satisfaction of me acting like a weak female. That was exactly what I needed. I pushed the helping arms away from me and stood up. "I'm fine," I stated. "I'm just overtired and hungry. I'll be fine."

"Ruth Ann's right," Axel said. "We haven't had much sleep in the last two days."

"And no food," Inga protested. "Maybe I should make something while you get Sherman to come to his senses."

John agreed and left me leaning against the wall next to the pantry door. He marched over to Sherman. "Ruth Ann's not going to tell you it's okay to keep us in the dark for whatever it is you don't want us to find."

"But," Sherman stopped and Judy barked, "No buts, you don't have a choice. If you don't give us the exact location, we'll tear this pantry to bits and *you* will be the one to clean it up!"

Sherman conceded and lifted his arms up to the shelving unit on the right backside of the wall. I tried to see what he was doing, but John, Judy, and Axel blocked my view. John ordered me to stay out of the pantry and sit down until Inga prepared something to eat for us. I didn't listen of course and walked right into the pantry behind the others. Nobody paid any attention to where I was because they were focused on Sherman's actions. "Axel," I whispered. "Can I stand in front of you so I can see, too?" He acknowledged me and grabbed my arm and gently put me in front of him. We turned our attention back to Sherman who grabbed several boxes of cereal and dropped them right on the floor. He reached far back on the shelf when John asked him, "You had a safe built in the wall behind all that cereal?"

Sherman ignored his question and continued dumping several other items out of his way. A few boxes of rice dumped and the box split open and rice spilled over the floor. "Be careful, Sherman," I called out stepping on the rice that landed as far as where I was standing.

He ignored what I said and concentrated on his own movements. Finally, after a large part of the shelf was cleared away, Sherman exclaimed, "Got it!"

"Got what," I begged. "You found the necklace?"

John glared back at me and motioned me to be quiet. He turned back to Sherman who explained he came across the item he was looking for. "What, what did you find?" John asked eagerly.

Sherman pulled out a large tin container, like the kind you put Christmas cookies in, but taller. I couldn't figure out if he was going to drop that item also or open it up. He backed John and Judy away and then walked right past Axel and me. "Hey," Axel said as Sherman exited the pantry. "What do you think you're doing?"

Sherman walked over to the marble island and set the tin box down. Inga had prepared an assortment of sandwiches and they were piled high on a large serving platter next to the container. Inga eyed the tin box strangely and asked, "What's this?"

Sherman waited for us to gather around the island before he would speak. "Now," John demanded.

"Yes, I need to explain what this is before I open it up. You need to understand that I was forced to keep this a secret and I want each and every one of you to promise me you won't be upset with me."

"Besides you keeping this from us, why else would we be mad at you?" I asked him, wondering what Sherman had been hiding for so long.

"I'm warning you, it's big."

"Okay, now you got our attention. Tell us quickly because we've wasted too much time," John replied, willing to listen to Sherman instead of grabbing the tin and opening it up himself. His impatient eyes left the tin and made their way up to Sherman's face.

Sherman cleared his throat and nervously started to tell us the most unbelievable story. "You'll understand why I've been so loyal to Ms. Prunella after I tell you this. It's been a secret for many years, but it's time to reveal my relationship with her."

"Relationship?" John questioned him, appearing confused.

"Yes," Sherman said quietly. "Please, let me get this out. I already feel guilty for what I'm about to disclose. So if you don't mind, please no interrupting or asking any questions until I'm finished."

We nodded, and to keep ourselves quiet, we each grabbed one of Inga's deli sandwiches. As we chewed Sherman went into a long, shocking story about his past with Prunella. I will summarize some of the conversation because Sherman did a lot of pausing (for effect), and clearing of his throat.

"I've known Ms. Prunella for a very long time." Sherman looked over to Inga to see if she would disagree. Inga and Prunella also had a long association. Inga stayed steady and chewed her ham and cheese sandwich. "Okay, well, we've had a personal connection that goes back to when she was just a baby. I was living in Sweden with my parents at the time. Ms. Prunella lived in an affluent household with her parents." He stopped and directed the next comment to me. "Ruth Ann, I don't know exactly what she told you about her childhood, but she came from a wealthy family and her parents employed my parents. My parents were the head butler and housekeeper for them. I was apprenticing to become a full-time butler. I started later in life with this career because my parents wanted better for me. So I finished basic schooling and tried to work in a financial firm, but it wasn't for me. I guess service is in my blood and I wanted to come home and convince my parents to let me work alongside of them. My father was getting older and he needed help. So I offered myself to Ms. Prunella's parents. They readily agreed because they knew my father wasn't performing his duties as well anymore. He put up quite the fuss, but my mother convinced him to cut back his workload and let me fill in for him."

Sherman took a bite of his own sandwich and chewed ever so slowly. I was anxiously awaiting him to continue his story. Finally, after he ate half a sandwich, he continued.

"It wasn't long after I took over for my father that he passed away. We were living in a guesthouse on Ms. Prunella's family's property. My mother and I were up at the house for the day when we returned one evening to find him in his favorite recliner holding a newspaper. At first, we both thought he had just fallen asleep reading the paper. However, after a few minutes, my mother discovered he was dead."

"That's terrible, Sherman," I said. I quickly said, "I'm sorry, go on."

Sherman smiled sweetly at me then said, "Ms. Prunella was only a baby at the time. Her parents didn't spend a lot of time with her so my mother kind of took over the nurturing role while I took over the fatherly duties. Ms. Prunella and I grew very close as she grew up. I was over thirty years older than her so she treated me like a close, older relative. That's how we are connected. We grew to love and trust one another as father/daughter or uncle/niece. She never treated me like an employee, not once."

Sherman looked around at us and realized he had our full attention. He grabbed the other half of his sausage sandwich and ate it more quickly this time. He knew time was limited and John's patience was growing thin.

Before he finished swallowing, John, couldn't help but ask, "I don't get why this is such a secret? What's the big deal? So you two knew each other her entire life."

"Ah, but that's just setting up for what comes next," Sherman said grinning, making us wonder what was coming. I have to admit; I wasn't prepared for it.

"When Ms. Prunella was in her early teens, her parents experienced a devastating change in their lives. One day, she came home from school and marched into the kitchen like she always did. I was waiting for her with our new cook. I forgot to mention that my mother had also passed away about a year after my father. She couldn't go on without him and just gave up. I was devastated and worried I would lose my position at the house. I was reassured that would never happen especially because I had been so good with their daughter. So, Ms. Prunella's daily routine after school was to come into the kitchen and sit with me at the table and eat cookies while she told me all about her day at school. This was a normal day as far as we knew until her father marched into the kitchen and sat down next to us at the table." He waited for us to react, but none of us knew the importance of that move. "Don't you understand? It was unheard of for the head of the household to sit at the table with me, a lowly butler."

"But he may have just wanted to talk with his daughter?" Inga asked enthusiastically.

"No, no, that's not what happened at all. Ms. Prunella's father wanted me there when he broke the news about what happened to their family."

"C'mon, Sherman," Judy exclaimed. "Get on with it!"

"I am," he pronounced angrily. "Stop interrupting me! I lose my train of thought."

"Fine," she stammered.

"The importance of it was that her father knew how close I was with her, and when she found out they lost all their money and their home, they thought I could soften the blow for her."

"What?" I yelled. "Sorry, go on."

Axel almost choked on his sandwich, but caught himself before he couldn't speak. "Wait a minute, Sherman!" he tried to shout. We turned our attention from Sherman to Axel. John and Judy appeared confused, but I had a strong feeling I knew where this was heading.

"Yes, Mr. Eklund, I do believe you know what I'm about to say."

"Enough of these subtle hints you're throwing out. What are you saying, Sherman?" John asked, putting his hand up to stop Axel from speaking.

Sherman stood as tall as he could with his five-foot five frame and pointed his wrinkled, stubby, but perfectly manicured finger over at Axel. "It's all *his* fault! His family ruined Ms. Prunella's family fortune."

"Huh?" John questioned baffled, but I knew what Sherman was implying.

"Eklund Industries destroyed Ms. Prunella's family name and they lost the family business and any money they had. Ms. Prunella's father had to go to work as a janitor in Eklund's shipping business. It was degrading, but it was the deal he cut with Eklund's father."

Axel looked guilty. I had a feeling none of this was a surprise to him. Why wouldn't he know? It was his wife's family that his family conquered and destroyed, but why? I had so many questions running through my brain that I didn't know which one to ask first.

John beat me to the punch. "Eklund," John said, turning his attention to Axel. "Is this true?"

"Well, yes," he replied. "But it was my father's doing, not mine."

"Did you know about it?" John asked.

Axel hesitated for only a moment and then answered quietly, "Yes, I did know. But you don't know the entire story. You're only hearing Sherman's viewpoint." He waited for us to ask, but nobody said a word. "Isn't it my right to give my side?"

Finally, I spoke up since nobody else did. "Of course, Axel. Why don't you try and explain to us why your father destroyed my cousin's family and took all their money. Oh, and don't leave out this 'deal' Sherman said was worked out forcing Prunella's father to be a janitor in *your* building."

"Is this getting us anywhere?" Judy interrupted. "Why don't we hold off on this lovely family reunion and open up the damn tin!" She took a cleansing breath in and added; "I've had it with all of you! Enough lies and hidden relationships...move on!"

"No, Judy," John said. "I want to hear Eklund's quick version of what happened. It shows to what extent Sherman has lied and taken valuable time away from us finding Lynne and Prunella."

Judy huffed a little then stepped back waving her arm in front of her body sarcastically allowing Axel to tell his side.

"My father was ruthless," he started with. "I'm pretty sure that's where I get my cutthroat tendencies." Nobody argued with that point! "However, I do strongly believe I have a softer side, a more understanding side, due to my mother. She was a wonderful, forgiving and patient woman. She had to be living with my father. He would've driven most women straight to divorce court. However, my mother stuck by him no matter what he pulled and who he trampled. Prunella's father was one of those people."

"What could Prunella's father do that was so horrible that your father had to destroy him and his family?" I asked.

"Prunella's father, also named Stanley, ran his own business that was quite profitable. He made some of the metal components we used for our ships. Stanley didn't like my father low-balling the prices he was paying for their parts."

"Then why didn't he just raise the price or not do business with them?" Sherman asked.

"He couldn't. Stanley was put in a no win situation. My father ruled the area. Nobody would do business with Stanley if he went against or protested against my family, which is exactly what he did."

"So your father destroyed Stanley's company," I acknowledged.

"Exactly what he did." He waited a moment, concentrating on what he was to say next. "It was terrible, really. I never approved of how he crushed people without a care of who he was truly hurting. This time it was Prunella and her parents. Stanley refused to do business with him unless he paid a percentage over cost for his parts, and when my father refused, Stanley told him to basically stick it."

"Uh-oh," I mumbled.

"Yes, Ruth Ann, nobody told my father that. He was furious with the small business owner and took him down, along with his daughter and wife's comfortable living. My father told Stanley that the only work he would ever be able to find in their town was a janitorial position at Eklund Industries. Stanley, of course, flatly refused."

"Then why did he end up doing it?" I asked.

"Because after months and months of trying to get another position and being rejected he didn't have a choice."

"Why was he rejected?" Inga chimed in.

"Because when somebody was ready to hire him, my father would step in and threaten them, too."

"Wow, this is incredible," I said, stunned and surprised Prunella never told me about this.

Sherman, who patiently waited, finally spoke. "That's why I've protected Ms. Prunella from him her entire life." I noticed the wear on his face, but also something else. I couldn't put my finger on it, but I will. There was a strange look upon his face that told me there was more to this than he was telling us.

"Why was this your job, Sherman? Shouldn't her parents have taken that role on?" I asked.

"They were too busy before they lost their money, and after they lost their money, they were too busy trying to survive."

"That's why I came to work for Mr. Eklund," Sherman announced. "I wanted to be near Ms. Prunella when she became involved with him."

"I have a question," I said. "Did Prunella really associate with Axel to get back at him and his family for ruining them or for the feud with the necklace?"

"Ah, good question, Ruth Ann," Axel answered. "I can say that at first, I thought she was a young, ambitious woman who won my heart. Then I discovered her background with the necklace and thought she was going to kill me for it."

"Never!" Sherman bellowed. "Ms. Prunella would never kill anyone! She came to your acquaintance for both reasons, if you want the truth. She was devastated when her parents lost their money, but she was also on a mission to get her family's necklace back. That was all her parents had left that was of any value."

"Okay, Sherman, we've heard enough of the background. Why the hesitance in opening the tin?"

"Because there were other items in there that Prunella wanted to stay hidden away, forever."

"Really?" I asked excitedly. "What else could there be?" Maybe this would answer the funny feeling I had about Sherman withholding information from us.

"I've said enough about her past. Can we just move on and let me be the one to look inside?"

"No way, Sherman," John exclaimed. "I'm the Chief of Police and I will be the one to open it."

"NO!" Sherman yelled and grabbed the tin and held it close to his body. "I'll die before I let any of you take this from me."

"What on earth is in there?" I asked, stunned at Sherman's outburst.

"Private things that have nothing to do with the necklace. So why don't you let me look inside and I'll tell you if it's in there or not."

"Sorry, Sherman, but even I don't trust you completely anymore," I said sadly. "You've explained yourself for each incident, but it's been too much."

"But Ruth Ann, you of all people should understand family bonds."

"You're not her family!" Axel shouted at him. "I'm her family, and Ruth Ann and her girls are her family. You don't have any rights when it comes to her."

"Oh yes I do," Sherman bellowed. "I'm in her will." The look on Sherman's face would've said it all. He made a huge blunder blurting that significant piece of information out.

"What did you just say?" John asked, stepping ever so close to Sherman. In fact, if Sherman lost focus for even a second, John could reach in and snatch the tin before he could react.

"I don't have to repeat myself. That was a mistake. Forget it!"

"Seriously, Sherman?" I questioned him. "You just told us that Prunella put you in her will."

"When did she do that, Sherman?" John asked. "Before or after Ruth Ann met her?"

"Before, of course," he said. "I'm pretty sure she was planning on changing the whole thing and putting Ruth Ann as her Executor instead of me."

"So let me get something straight," John started to say. "Are you just her Executor or are you also a recipient in her will?"

"Both."

"So, that's what this is about," Axel said, grinning. "You don't want anyone to see her will, is that it?"

"Are you afraid she won't survive this, Sherman?" I asked him curiously.

"No, yes, I'm confused," he said, grasping the tin even tighter to his chest. "I know Prunella will make it out of this. She's a strong woman, and no, it's none of your business what's stated in her will. It is *her* will!" If you noticed, Sherman stopped using Ms. Prunella and started call her just plain Prunella!

"But it's my business, Sherman," I mentioned. "I'm her family, and Axel's her husband. When was this will written?"

"Years ago after her parents died, and she received a hefty sum from their life insurance. It left her comfortable."

"And don't forget about the necklace," Inga added. "You're a thief! All you want is that necklace for yourself. How do we know that *you're* not the murderer after all? Ruth Ann believes Svenson when he told her he didn't murder Bert and Helena. What about that?"

Sherman started to sweat. His face turned beet red and small perspiration started to build on his wide, crinkled forehead. "I didn't kill anyone! I'm not capable of that, however, I did want to protect that necklace from him!" Sherman pointed at Axel who was only a few feet behind John.

"Me? It's my necklace, too. I have just as much of a right to it as Prunella does. That's what we decided a couple days ago when we got back together. Her family and my family fought over the thing and we thought it best to share it."

"Really?" I asked, surprised I didn't hear about any of this. "What about my right?"

"Of course you have a say in it too, Ruth Ann. Prunella and I were going to speak with you."

"Oh," I said, wondering if he was telling me the truth. "But, Sherman, why do you think you should get it? And why protect it from Axel?"

"I'm in the will to inherit everything."

"Everything?" John asked suspiciously. "This isn't making you look guiltless, Sherman."

"I'm only culpable for protecting her will, nothing else."

"So, the will is in the tin with her necklace?" John asked him and Sherman nodded. "And you knew this all along?"

"No, not exactly. I knew the will was in there. We put it in there together. I really don't know if the necklace is in there."

"So, if she didn't tell you that she put the necklace in there, why are we even looking here?" Judy asked irritated.

"Because it's the last place anyone would search for it, right?" We nodded. "And it wasn't in the safe in the library or the garage. This is the only other place Prunella would use to be safe from everyone."

"I'm getting angrier and angrier," I stated. "I don't like what's been going on around here with all the secrets. I'm starting to regret ever finding out about the necklace, and Prunella!"

"Ruth Ann, you don't mean that," Axel said sympathetically. "You mean the world to her. She just has a difficult time trusting anyone completely. That's been her problem with me, too." He waited for a response from me, but I was still furious. "Look, her parents lost everything and left her to be raised by him," Axel pointed his finger over at Sherman. "Once she was old enough she went to school and then came to live at my estate back in Sweden. She's had a disruptive life without her family to support her."

"I supported her plenty!" Sherman bellowed.

"But you are not her parents," Axel explained. "She has a sweet, kind, soul, but lacks confidence."

I calmed down after hearing Axel's account, but when this finally was over, Prunella and I needed to have a long, serious talk.

Sherman didn't know what to say anymore, and I was still recovering from what I heard, when Judy stomped over to Sherman and grabbed the tin away from him without anyone noticing. The result put Sherman into a rage, John into shock, and Axel laughing. However, what we found inside the tin smacked the grin right off of his face.

Chapter 38

"Why did you do that?" Sherman screamed at Judy. "It's my personal property!"

"It's a police matter now, Sherman," Judy stated. "Back off," she said as Sherman rushed over and tried to retrieve the tin.

"Don't try anything, Sherman," Judy said, fuming. "I'm a police officer and you're posing a threat to me."

"Give it to me!" Sherman said, flailing his arms at Judy trying to get a grip on the tin, but failing miserably. He just didn't have the strength to fight anyone, but he did give it a valiant effort.

"John, a little help here," Judy asked, holding off Sherman while grasping the tin close to her body. John walked over, shoved Sherman away from her as if he was a toy puppy and took the tin from Judy and placed it back on the marble island. Sherman only made one minor effort to take it, but when Judy pulled her gun on him, he backed off admitting defeat by throwing his arms up in the air. "Fine, but Prunella will be furious with all of you."

"I highly doubt that, Sherman," I said. "Plus, we don't have a choice. We need to know if Svenson got his hands on our necklace." Like how I used the word *our* necklace?

"I agree," Axel said, hurrying over to the island and shoving his way between Judy and me.

"Hey, I want to see, too," Inga stammered trying to get close enough to look. She stood behind me easily able to see over my head. Inga was about a foot taller than me. I was only a smidgen over five-foot three while Inga seemed inches over six feet. She was a large boned, sturdy woman who would scare just about anyone who confronted her.

"Okay, the tin is safe on the island for the moment." John looked around at us and added, "if any of you try and stop me from opening it, I won't be responsible for trigger happy Judy shooting you!" The words did come out of John's mouth, but I'm assuming he was referring to Sherman only. I was about to protest when John gave me a slight wink, knowing I would probably open my mouth and protest.

Judy held tight to her gun aimed at Sherman. "I got it covered, boss," she replied, staring down Sherman. "I don't trust this guy anymore. For all we know he's completely capable of committing murder and theft."

Sherman spun his head around from staring at the lone tin on the island and slammed his fist down on the island. He momentarily forgot it was a marble island and cried out in pain. "Ouch!" He grabbed his hand with his other hand and bent over in pain. "That's uncalled for! I didn't murder anyone or commit theft. Prunella legally left me the possessions inside that tin. The will's the proof, so go ahead and open it. But you may not like everything you find in there."

"What are you hammering on about, Sherman?" John asked, exasperated. "Don't tell me there's more in there than the will and the slim possibility of the necklace?"

"I'm done speaking until we've opened it up and looked."

John shrugged his shoulders and grabbed a hold of the tin and pried open the metal lid. "Here goes," he said, reaching inside. He pulled out a long business envelope and held it up high so we could see. He laid it on the island and reached back inside. "Wait a minute," he muttered pulling out another small container. "What could this be, Sherman?" John held up a black square box about 4 inches by 4 inches.

Sherman shook his head and refused to speak. "Fine," John said, putting the box next to the envelope. "Let's see what else is in here," he said, reaching back inside and pulling out yet another black square box identical to the other one. "Why would there be two?" I asked curiously. John ignored my question as he set it down on top of the other box. "Should we see if there's another one?" He stuck his hand back in and pulled out a pile of pictures that were stuffed inside another business envelope. Sherman reached around and grabbed the envelope from John spilling most of the pictures onto the floor. "Why'd you do that, Sherman?" John bellowed. "It's just some old pictures."

Sherman dropped to the floor more quickly than I thought possible for his weakened body and started scooping them up as if they were pieces of gold. "Hey, that looks like Prunella," Axel called out spotting one of the fallen pictures. "I've seen pictures of her as a little girl. Who's that holding her on his shoulders though?"

Sherman stuffed the pictures back inside the envelope and crammed them inside his lapel pocket. "They're just old pictures of her when she was a young girl. I'm sure she doesn't want them ruined so I'll just hold onto them until I can hand them back to her."

John didn't care for his actions and demanded Sherman lay the envelope onto the island with the other items. He resisted at first, but Judy's gaze on him did the trick. "Fine."

Sherman pulled out the envelope and tossed it onto the island. "This is ridiculous. We're wasting time on this petty stuff when we should be trying to find Prunella and Lynne."

"I agree," I said. "Just tell me if the necklace is in there, please!"

John reached back inside the tin and the strangest look appeared upon his face. "What on earth," he cried out. He pulled out a small pistol and held it up in shock. "Why is this in here?" he asked Sherman.

"I, I don't know why."

"You're lying, Sherman," Judy said. "You've been hovering and protecting that tin like it's the most important thing in your life. I'll bet my own life you know exactly what's in those boxes and why Prunella put a gun in there or…or did you hide a gun in there?"

"Me?" He bellowed. "It's not my gun!"

"I don't care whose bloody gun it is," John screamed. "Prunella obviously felt threatened somehow or why else would she hide a gun?"

"I just want to see what's in those boxes, John. Open them up?"

"Well, I can tell you the necklace wasn't in the bottom of the tin. Nothing else is in there, so let's just see what's inside these two identical boxes."

"Why open them?" Sherman cried out. "It's her personal items and I think we're nosing around stuff we shouldn't be."

"What's the big deal, Sherman?" I asked him. "It's two black boxes and I want to know what's in them.

John grabbed one and he handed the other to me. "On three we open them up, got it?" I smiled and waited for his count.

"One, two, three!" I ripped off the top and what I saw inside took my breath away.

"No way!" Inga exclaimed. "There are two of them!"

"Two of what?" Axel said, frustrated that he couldn't see over John. He tried to push his way in to see the contents of the boxes, but John blocked his view. "Please, let me see," he begged.

John moved a smidgen over to let Axel in and when his eyes caught site of the objects, even he was speechless.

"What on earth!" He exclaimed. "There are *two* necklaces?"

John picked one of the infamous necklaces up and held it close to his face. "Are they real or fakes?"

I held the other one up and stared at it for longer than I thought when Axel nudged me. "Ruth Ann, can I hold it?" I came back to the present and handed it to him. John was touching the one he had and weighing it in each of his hands back and forth. "I honestly couldn't tell you if this one is real or a replica. Why would she need *two* fakes though?"

Axel studied the one he held for several minutes when he asked John if he could hold his. John carefully handed over the necklace and said, "No funny stuff, Eklund." Axel grabbed the item gently and gave John a funny look. "I don't know what you mean, John."

"Don't try and make a run for it with both of the necklaces."

"Seriously?" Axel said, bellowing out a loud laugh. "I've got Judy standing two feet away from me with a gun. How could I make a run for it?"

"Yeah, yeah," John said, realizing what he said sounded stupid. "Just examine them and tell me what you think."

Sherman, John, Judy, Inga, and I remained silent as Axel held one in each hand weighing them, touching them as if it was a piece of fine silk that needed to be caressed, and holding them up so close to his eyes it would have made me cross-eyed. "Well?" John asked impatiently after Axel repeated these motions over and over.

"Amazing," Axel mumbled to himself. "I just can't tell, really I can't."

"Can I?" I asked him. "I've worn the real one quite a bit. Maybe I could tell?"

Axel handed them over to me and I gently received each one in my trembling, outstretched hands. "You know, Ruth Ann," Judy started to say. "Maybe you never truly had the real one around your neck."

I reeled rapidly around and threw her a look that could kill. "Don't be ridiculous, Judy." But something hit me at that very moment. What if Prunella had been fooling me all along and I never really had the genuine necklace in my possession? What if she'd been lying to me from the beginning?

Axel, John, and Inga saw the expression on my face go from anger toward Judy to fear and then shock. It was Axel who spoke up first. "Prunella didn't do that to you, Ruth Ann. She would never willingly deceive you. The only reason you would've worn the fake one would be if she felt threatened for your life."

That did make sense, my rational side of my brain was telling me. We had to admit there'd been an awful lot of drama surrounding this damn necklace. Yes, I swore. This necklace had been nothing but a pain in the butt, and outside of meeting new friends and family, I wish it had never existed.

"Ruth Ann," John called out. "Are you okay?"

I got my senses back in order and said, "I'm fine. I don't know exactly what's happened with this necklace, but I feel confident saying that Prunella would never knowingly hand me the fake necklace unless she felt I was in some sort of danger. Which, I have to say, has been and is a distinct possibility."

"Good for you, Ruth Ann," Axel stated. "I couldn't have said it better."

"Yeah, me too," Inga agreed. "Ms. Prunella would never deceive you for her own gains."

"Huh?" Judy asked, confused.

Inga explained in a simpler way, "She would never try and pass off a fake necklace just to be mean to Ruth Ann for no reason."

"Oh, I guess I agree with that declaration."

"So, Ruth Ann, what do you think about the two necklaces?" John asked me. "Can you tell any difference?"

I studied them like Axel did. I touched them and held them up around my neck to see if either felt different. "No."

"No?" Axel asked me, wondering if I would explain.

"No, I think these must be fakes. They don't feel as heavy, and the two feel the same. I would think that if one of these were real, one would be slightly heavier or lighter than the other."

"Yes, I agree," Axel, said. "But you've worn it before. Does it feel like it did before?"

"Feels like I remember," was all I could say. "I'm confused now. Plus, why would the real one be in one of these simple black boxes?"

"To throw a potential thief off," John answered. "It's simple really. All Prunella had to do was make it look like it's one of the fakes, but it really isn't fake. A thief would see two black plain boxes and assume they're both fake so he leaves them alone. Maybe that's what happened here?"

"So, you think Svenson was here with Prunella and she led them to the box and showed them these two necklaces? He took her word for it that they weren't real and left them behind?" I questioned.

"In a nutshell, yes."

"Then where would she lead him after this and why would she do this if he's threatening to kill them both?" Inga asked, appearing totally confused.

"Maybe to buy more time until we finally catch up with them?"

"So, you think Prunella and Lynne are leading them on this wild goose chase until we find them?" Axel asked John.

"Good chance that's what's happening."

"Won't their time run out?" I asked. "Then what?"

"I believe we shouldn't think that way, Ruth Ann," Judy interrupted. "Let's catch them before this happens."

"But, what do we do now?" I asked, becoming visibly upset with my shaky voice. "Where are they? And is one of these necklaces I'm holding right now the real one?"

"I just don't know if it's genuine or not, Ruth Ann. We need an expert if you or Axel can't tell them apart." It was at that exact moment; Sherman cleared a little tickle in his throat. I don't believe he wanted that to happen, but John turned and pounced.

"Sherman!" John hollered, scaring Sherman half to death. "Would you like to add anything?"

"Me?" he asked him, stunned. "Why would you ask me if I had anything to add?"

"Because you've constantly lied, and let us run all over town when you knew staying here and waiting for Prunella to lead her abductors to this very spot was what was needed," John hollered. "What's wrong with you? We thought you were on *our* side, but I'm really doubting anything that comes out of your lying English mouth!"

"Well," Sherman announced, shocked at John's proclamation. "I don't have to take this! I'll just leave you to yourselves and I'll continue my own search for Prunella and Ruth Ann's daughter."

"Oh, no you won't," Judy said, grabbing the old guy by the collar and whipping his crouched-over form to face her. "You will answer each and every question we ask you with nothing but the truth or so help me…" Judy slammed her lips together and inhaled through her nose (quite loudly I might add) to get herself calmed down. In a low, sharp voice she continued, "I do not have to remind you that if you resist us you will be placed under arrest and I will personally make sure you rot in jail for as long as the law permits." Each word she accentuated with anger and forcefulness. I watched Sherman closely as the look in his eyes went from anger to fear of this mean looking woman, Judy. At that moment, I saw why Judy was a successful detective. She had a way with her words that made a person feel about six inches tall. Sherman watched intently as Judy released her grip from his jacket, and then he brought his aging, wrinkled hand up to his lapel and brushed off what I would have to call "Judy germs". He straightened his jacket out and shook his head with an air of arrogance and finally spoke. "I will answer your questions to the best of my knowledge. I cannot help it if they will not satisfy your needs, but I will do the best I can."

I was perplexed. I truly believed I was close to Sherman and we were on close friendly terms with Prunella living here. Why was he behaving like a spoiled, English brat? Where was this attitude coming from? Maybe John and Judy were correct. Sherman may not be on our side as much as I originally hoped, but what made him change so drastically with us? I decided to reserve my judgment against him until I could see where this would lead. I was going to keep my mouth shut and let John interrogate him about the contents of the tin.

"I'm going to sit down if you don't mind," Sherman said, walking to the other side of the marble island and pulling out a stool to sit in. "I haven't had much sleep the last couple days and I'm not as young as the rest of you." I watched Inga closely. She was unusually quiet and I would bet it's because she was as shocked about Sherman's change in personality as I was. Inga leaned against the counter near the large sink. There was a large coffee maker next to her and she started busying herself making more coffee. We needed the caffeine for sure, and even though I was extremely anxious about finding Prunella and my daughter, I knew we needed to get complete and accurate information out of Sherman.

"So, Sherman," John began, standing directly across the island from Sherman. "Let's just get right down to the huge elephant in the room. Did you know there were two necklaces in the tin?" He held his hand up to stop Sherman from answering and said, "Wait, answer this first. Did you know there were any necklaces in the tin? I watched you as we opened the black boxes and my cop intuition tells me you weren't overly surprised with the contents. I knew you were adamant that we didn't find the will, but what about the necklaces?"

"Don't forget to add if he knows if one of them is genuine or not?" Judy added.

Sherman looked baffled. I have to admit; I was a bit perplexed. John threw out too many questions in my opinion. One at a time, but I promised myself I was going to listen and not speak (which is alarmingly opposite of my normal behavior).

John leaned over the island on his elbows. "Well?"

"I don't remember what I'm supposed to answer," Sherman cried, flustered.

"The two necklaces first. Did you know they were in the tin?" John ordered.

"Yes."

"So you answered my question directly. Now, answer Judy's question." He noticed Sherman was about to ask what her question was, but he beat him to the punch. "Do you know if one of them was genuine?"

"Yes."

Okay, even my patience was wearing thin. John's face turned from normal, middle-aged rough-skinned whitish to a deep shade of ruby red. If smoke could've come out of his nostrils, I bet it would've. It was time to intervene. "Sherman," I shouted, startling him. "Knock off the one word responses!" I glared at him and saw the look of desperation in his eyes. Maybe I was wrong about his abrupt change of sides. The appearance of "please help me" was written all over his face once again. I didn't know what he wanted from me. Help him with what? I decided yelling at him wasn't getting us anywhere. I was standing next to John. I reached out and grabbed John's back with my hand and gave it a little pat. Just a slight touch to let him know I was going to try a different approach with Sherman. John stood up straight from leaning over on his elbows and gave me a slight shove. I took this as an approval to go over to Sherman and try talking to him softly and calmly. We'll see what happens, so here I go.

I walked around to the other side of the island and pulled out another stool. I plopped my weary behind on it and touched Sherman's forearm. "I'm sorry for yelling. I'm just tired and frustrated. Can you please understand that much?" I waited for Sherman to answer, but he just started at me with his fierce blue eyes. "Okay, well, you have to understand our side, Sherman? We've run out of ideas on why and what Prunella's doing right now. I just want them home safe and sound and if you can help in any way, I would be eternally grateful!"

Sherman cleared his throat and took in a deep breath. "I know, Ruth Ann. I just don't want to betray any confidentialities that Prunella bestowed upon me."

"What?" John hollered. I quickly turned my head toward his direction, and in as nice of a voice I could muster, I said, "Please, yelling at Sherman isn't getting us anywhere. We must see his viewpoint." The last part I said with gritted teeth because I didn't mean a word I said. I was just as exasperated as John and the rest of us, but Sherman really didn't see it our way. He was tunnel visioned, caring only about saving face with Prunella. I had to keep calm and wiggle anything I could out of this older, very stubborn man. John could see the desperation in my eyes. I was trying telepathy with him and hoping he would get it. It was time to win an award for best actress!

"Sherman, forget John. In fact, forget everyone else in this room." I saw the look of horror in Inga's face from my side vision. I ignored her and continued. "I want you to talk only to me, can you do that?" Sherman hesitated, and then reluctantly nodded. "Good. Now, we know that you and Prunella have a very long history together and you're extremely protective of her." Sherman nodded forcefully. "But, if you don't help us we may never see her or my daughter again."

"But that's impossible," Sherman cried out. "They will surely escape this madman and return to us, unharmed."

"But we can't depend on what you *think* could happen. I don't want to bet one percent that anything bad could happen, do you?" Sherman shook his head in agreement with my statement. "Good. Now, if we can figure out whether or not Prunella put the genuine necklace in the tin, then we know she hasn't given it to Svenson and they're still leading him on a wild-goose chase. However, if both those necklaces are fake, then possibly Svenson has the real piece and dumped Prunella and Lynne off somewhere." A light bulb went off in my head so I added, "Hey, they could be stashed somewhere in this estate. Wouldn't that be nice? Then we could search for them before their time runs out."

"What do you mean by that?" Sherman asked, terrified.

"What if they're gagged and stuffed inside a closet? The air could run out (unlikely, but hopefully Sherman would buy it)."

"Oh, my," Sherman exclaimed. "We can't let that happen. We've wasted too much time already."

"Exactly!" Inga hollered startling us. "So fess up, Sherman!"

Sherman looked over at Inga, then at Axel, John, Judy, and then back to me. We waited as patiently as we could for Sherman's response.

"I, I want to help. I really do, but what if I tell you and it puts Prunella in more danger?"

"And Lynne, Sherman," John added, looking at me compassionately.

"Yes, of course, Ms. Lynne, too."

"Sherman, what could you tell us that would put them in more danger?" I asked curiously.

"I've already led you to the tin and the will. There's more to it than just the two black boxes with **fake** necklaces in them."

"*What did you just say?*" John asked, pronouncing each word slowly.

"Oh, no," Sherman cried. "I didn't mean to say that!"

"But it's okay," I replied. "Now we know that the real necklace is still out there, somewhere. We don't know if Steven Svenson already has his hands on it. If he doesn't, he's probably fuming mad with Prunella. I don't like this."

"Me either," John stated. "We need to know more Sherman."

"Alright. The two necklaces are fakes because she wanted Ruth Ann and herself to have one, so the genuine necklace would stay safe. Each of you stated that you couldn't tell the difference."

"That's right, Sherman," I said. "The necklace looks exactly as I remember it."

"That's the point. However, when Mr. Eklund came back into the picture, Prunella wanted to fool him with the fake one to get him off her back." Sherman glanced over in Axel's direction to see his response.

"Really?" Axel questioned. "This must've been before we reconciled."

"Obviously," Sherman replied rudely. "But Prunella still didn't trust you. We had a solid, binding plan to keep the genuine necklace safe until she gave the signal."

"Signal, what signal?" I asked, confused. "Is that what you've been waiting for, a signal from Prunella?"

"Yes."

"But how stupid are you?" Judy asked him, irritated. "How can a woman who's kidnapped give you a signal?"

"Do not call me stupid, you're a bumbling fool of a detective if you can't figure that out."

"Wait, what did you just say?" I asked before Judy could march over to him and pulverize the old butler.

"I just meant that signals could still be given if Prunella is the one leading that Svenson fellow around."

"Enough," John stammered. "Just tell us what the signal is!"

"I, I," Sherman hesitated and looked over at me for help.

"Hey," I said. "I'm not helping you with this one. Just tell us so we can get on with this."

"Fine!" He let his head drop toward his chest for a moment before he lifted it up and brusquely spoke. "This tin was booby trapped!"

"How?" John asked, puzzled. He picked up the tin and inspected it from top to bottom and side to side. "It wasn't locked or there wasn't a poisonous spider in there to stop me. So explain how it was 'booby' trapped?"

Sherman took the tin John slid across the island toward him. He opened it up and reached deep inside. He pulled out a piece of paper that John had not seen. "Hey, where'd that come from?" John asked, perplexed.

"The bottom of the tin pulls up. There's a magnetic strip of metal on the bottom." Sherman halted and glared over at Judy. *So that's what he meant by stupid cop, I guess.* Sherman held up the loose piece of metal that fit perfectly, well almost perfectly, on the bottom. "Underneath was this piece of paper." He held it up for us to view.

"Hand it over," John ordered holding out his large, firm skinned hand.

"No, it's mine," he demanded. "I'll read it to you."

"When you're done reading it, I want to physically see it," John demanded. *I'd have to assume John didn't trust Sherman so he wanted to make sure whatever Sherman read was actually what was written on the tiny piece of paper.*

Sherman agreed and unfolded the wrinkled piece of paper. It read as follows:

If you needed to pull this letter out, then unwanted persons are seeking the necklace and the fake ones have been discovered. Take this note to the Library and go to the bookshelf on the back wall to the far left of the desk. Pull out the title 'The Works of Stanley Lilgestrom'. Open the book and you will find a rectangular cut out inside. The lock combination is 11.14.11.24 (Birthday months and days of Ruth Ann and myself). Inside should be the real deal necklace. Protect it if I can't. Never give it to anyone besides our own family members. I trust in you, Sherman.

You are the only one who knows about this, and for good reason. You've been a trusted friend and Great Uncle. Don't ever let anyone see this note.

   Love Always,
   Your Great Niece, Prunella

Chapter 39

"Wait, what did you just say?" I asked, stunned and dazed at what Sherman just read.

Sherman didn't answer me. He lowered his head slowly as if he was ashamed at what he divulged. I only wondered if he was ashamed at betraying Prunella's confidence or telling us he was actually her Great Uncle?

John didn't wait for Sherman to speak. "You heard him loud and clear, Ruth Ann. Sherman is not just a family butler and Executor of her will, but her Great Uncle. Great Uncle on whose side, the mother or father?"

"Answer him!" Judy shouted. "So we can finally get out of this kitchen and head back to the library. We need to retrieve the *real* necklace. If it's not there, we're in big trouble."

That brought Sherman back to reality. "Yes, we need to move on."

"Not until you answer me?" John demanded.

"I am Prunella's grandmother's brother."

"Wow, so we're related too?" I asked rhetorically.

"Can we dive into the family drama later?" Inga interrupted. "I'm not happy about any of it, but right now we need to focus people! We need to get Ms. Prunella and Lynne back. Can we please hurry to the library?"

We agreed to table the family discussion until Prunella was back with us. It was certainly an interesting change of events though. So that's why Sherman was named her guardian and Executor of her will. He was family to her, not just by association, but also by blood.

Sherman couldn't look me in the eyes after he disclosed his family involvement. John grabbed my hand and tightly held it as we made our way out of the kitchen and through the grand foyer to the library. The doors were closed. John and Judy made the rest of us wait until they made sure the room was clear. It only took a second once they were inside to wave us in. I didn't think Steven would have Prunella and Lynne just waiting for us in there. I wanted to know if they *had* been in here, though. Maybe Prunella already went over to the bookshelf and took the necklace.

I expressed my thoughts out loud to the group and Axel said, "If it's gone, then I don't see any reason for them holding onto Prunella and Lynne. Svenson would've gotten what he came for and would want to flee the country as fast as possible."

"I agree, Eklund," John stated. "Let's find out." John walked over to the already searched bookshelf and started searching the floor and the shelves. We stood back near the desk and two armchairs, but after several minutes, I noticed Axel and Inga becoming impatient. They walked over and started looking at the hundreds of books that lined the shelves and floor. I decided to sit down in one of the chairs. At this point, most people would wonder why I wasn't as anxious or energetic in finding the book. Let me say it in one word, exhaustion. I'm not as young as I would like to think, and to go two nights without much sleep isn't easy on me. I've never been good without my six to seven hours of sleep. One may say I get a little bitchy to be honest, but I would rather call it 'off'. Yes, that's a much better word. I'm just 'off' when I don't get my regular sleep, and that could cause me to snap at people, not focus as wholeheartedly as I should, become a tad clumsy…I could go on, but why concentrate on that when my brain should be working on finding that book! I hopped out of the chair and hurried over to the bookshelf. The rest of our group was frantically sifting through books and I remember the letter specifically stated the book was on the far left side of the shelves.

"So, no sight of the book?" I asked, stepping over piles of books. I won't describe the glares I received by that simple question. I walked slightly away from where books were flying off the shelf and glanced at a shelf far to the left. There, plain as day was 'The Works of Stanley Lilgestrom'. "Hey," I called out grabbing the book out of the case. "Here it is!"

It was a hardback about 11 inches by 14 inches, so quite large. I stepped over several books on the floor and lay the book on the empty polished desk. If it weren't for the importance of the find, I would've been reprimanded for finding it so quickly. John was the first one to make it over to me. "I'll do it, Ruth Ann." He ran his hand carefully over the cover. "Is this your relative, Ruth Ann?"

"I think so. I don't know if there are many Stanley Lilgestroms that are artists."

"It looks safe enough," he replied. The others surrounded John and me.

"Open it," Inga cried out nervously.

"Yeah, John, what are you waiting for?" I asked, suddenly getting my second wind (or is it twentieth by now?).

John slid his long, thick fingers to the spine of the book then over to the opposite side and pulled it open slowly. I wondered if he thought it was booby-trapped and blow up or something bizarre like that? Well, he was lucky and nothing monumental occurred when he opened it.

"Well," he said, showing the rest of us the inside. "Prunella wasn't lying. It's not a book at all. Just looks like one from the outside. Look, there's a large opening inside and a metal lock box was fitted in it. The dials on the front do require those numbers. Ruth Ann, tell me them again?"

Sherman coughed to get our attention and rattled off the numbers before I could get one out. "11.14.11.24"

"That's right!" I exclaimed. "See, Prunella used my birthday and her own. That shows she and I are loyal to one another, Sherman. You shouldn't feel bad about telling me. Prunella would want you to."

"Hmph," he groaned.

"It's too late for regrets, Sherman old man," Judy said, slapping him heartily on the back. "We're finally getting somewhere."

John set the book flat out on the desk. He reached inside and rolled the silver metal numbers until the numbers were aligned correctly. "Okay, it should pop open," he said, waiting for some sign of a click. We leaned over and watched as he lifted the mini safe's lid open, and low and behold, a glimmer of light gleamed through the box!

"It's there!" I yelled excited. "It's still in there!"

John picked up the white gold chain and on the end was the magnificent, ice blue stone dangling exquisitely. "Prunella didn't take it out," Sherman whispered loudly. "Thank God for that."

"But where are they then?" Judy asked, puzzled. "If the necklace is here, that means they're still out there chasing after this necklace that John's holding."

We froze, and a sudden chill ran up my spine. If I was exhausted, this woke me up. "Where are they?" I asked, terrified. "You don't think Svenson did anything horrible to them, do you?" I asked John with a worried look, hoping he would tell me it would be all right.

"I, I just don't know, Ruth Ann," John said solemnly. "We've been all around town. They just have to be here," he looked around motioning to the entire estate, not just the library. "We'll search this place from top to bottom. Svenson may have given up and left them tied up somewhere."

"But why would he just leave without the necklace?" Axel asked, puzzled at John's assessment. "You don't know this man like I do. He would die before giving this up."

"Gee, thanks Eklund," John said, tilting his head in my direction.

"I'm fine, John," I said. "I really feel, deep in my bones, that the girls are okay. I just know I would feel it if they were..."

"You don't have to say any more, Ruth Ann," Inga said, grabbing my shoulders and squeezing them so firmly I almost fell over. It was a kindly gesture from her, but she really didn't know her own strength.

We passed around the necklace admiring its beauty. Sherman was even okay with us taking turns with it. I was only going along with this idle activity until I had the guts to start looking. I wanted to search the house, but I had to admit I was terrified at what we might find.

Inga couldn't take it any longer. She grabbed my arm and led me over to the library doors. "Can we please start the search? I need to know if Ms. Prunella and Lynne are safe."

John raced over to the door before Inga could exit. "Hold on, we're not just going to go off on our own and risk one of us getting into danger, too."

"We can break off into teams of two," Inga suggested impatiently.

"Let's see, we have Inga, Ruth Ann, Axel, Judy, Sherman, and me. I think it's safer to stick in larger numbers. So," John hesitated a moment to think of who to pair with whom.

"Inga, you and Judy stick together and bring Axel along." He didn't pause long enough for Inga to complain about being stuck with Judy or Axel. Neither one would've been her choice. "Ruth Ann, Sherman, and I will be together."

"Sounds good," I said. "Where we going to look first?"

"I think our group will start in the basement," John stopped and glanced my way since he knew, as did everybody, that I hate going into these basements! "And Judy, you take Inga and Eklund up to the third floor and search each and every inch of the floor. Once you're done with the third floor move on to the second. We'll meet up somewhere in the middle unless we find them." John looked around the group waiting for a response. Nobody said a word so John said, "Good, let's go. Oh, no one be a hero if you run across Svenson or his goon, Jimmy, got it? Just keep a gun on them and send one of the others to come and find me."

John opened the library doors and we piled into the foyer. Inga was the first to reach the grand staircase that led up to the second and third floors. Judy was right behind her, and then Axel followed. They started their way up and we headed down the hall into the kitchen. I wasn't thrilled about my assignment, however, I was happy about sticking with John. I felt safe with him and knew he wouldn't let anything horrible happen to me.

The three of us entered the kitchen and John marched straight over to the door that would take us down into the dark, cold, cement basement. I've been down there too many times. Being held prisoner in that secret room, and finding Helena dead in the same room, forces one to become a bit paranoid about what one might find down there.

John was about to grab the doorknob and take us into the basement. Sherman wasn't following us. "Hey, come on Sherman," I called out to him as he walked over to the island and dumped down onto a stool.

"I'm too old for this. You two go ahead and I'll sit here and wait."

John released the doorknob and marched over to him. "Get up!" John grabbed his arm and pulled him right off the stool. Sherman was so surprised by John's actions that he didn't resist. John dragged him over to the basement door and once again put his hand on the doorknob and opened the door. He was still holding Sherman's arm and ordered him to follow him. "Ruth Ann, you come down last. Sherman, you go after me. I don't want you to speak, just follow."

Sherman mumbled something incoherent under his breath, but John ignored him and headed down the uneven wooden stairs. He turned and told us to be careful not to trip, and he would turn on the light at the bottom of the stairs. I could still see in the darkened stairwell with the light shining in from the kitchen. John was well ahead of Sherman, who was stepping slowly down the stairs. John turned on the light bulb on the ceiling right at the bottom of the stairs. "Good," I heard him say out loud.

"Nobody's down here?" I asked him.

"Looks clear," he said, moving along the back cement wall aiming for the secret room. "Hurry up, Ruth Ann," John called out to me. I was only halfway down the stairs. I could've easily been next to John by now if it wasn't for Sherman's leisureliness going down the stairs. "I need you to help me locate the button that opens up the room."

"I'm trying," I said loudly. "Sherman, you can go a little faster."

He stopped, spun his head around and glared into my eyes. "I'm not as young as you or as physically fit. I don't want to fall and break a hip!"

"Easy, Sherman," John hollered up to him. "You're just trying to avoid coming down here."

There was no response from Sherman. He just kept taking each step as slowly as a snail gliding across the floor. Finally, after several minutes, Sherman made his way to the bottom. He leaned over and tried to regain his breath. This had to be an act, I thought to myself. I chose not to comment, but ignored him and flew over to John who was frantically trying to find a teeny tiny button that would raise a portion of the wall and inside is the secret, torture room.

I remembered, ever so vividly, where the button was located. I felt along the rough cement wall and found it immediately. A few rumbles later, a door sized portion of the wall rose and we were once again standing in the doorway of one of my most hated rooms. The police tape was still partially hanging from where we discovered Helena just a few days ago. "Don't look over there, Ruth Ann," John said to me. "I just had to take a quick look in here to make sure Svenson didn't leave the girls in here."

"Please check that hole before I have a nervous breakdown, John," I said, terrified they were thrown into a large hole in the floor. I closed my eyes as I stood in the doorway not entering all the way inside. I did peek inside long enough to make sure I didn't find Prunella or Lynne chained to the wall like I had been, but I didn't have the nerve to watch as John walked over to the hole.

"Anything?" I asked, with my eyes still tightly shut.

"No, it's all clear, Ruth Ann."

"Thank God," I said, opening my eyes and finally taking a breath.

"Can we get out of here?" Sherman inquired.

"Yeah, nobody's been in here from what I can tell," John answered walking over to me and leading me out of the room. "I know that wasn't easy for you, but you know I had to check."

"I know. Hey, what if they went through the tunnel to the guesthouse?"

"No, I put my own booby trap there and I don't see the clear wire broken. Otherwise, the basement looks empty. I think we can safely say Svenson didn't come down here." "Now where?" I asked. "Are we going to join in the search upstairs?"

"We'll check the entire main floor first," John answered.

We made our way back up the stairs, and I can say Sherman was much faster going up than down. So I can probably safely state that his out of breath reaction earlier was an act to gain sympathy, which we didn't give him. He was barely out of breath as we stepped into the bright kitchen.

"We're burning daylight here," John said. "It's been too long with this chase. It needs to be over tonight."

"I couldn't agree more," I said. "How do you propose that'll happen?"

"We just hope we find them here, and soon."

The three of us agreed the kitchen was already thoroughly checked so we went through the door into a small butler's pantry that led into the massive dining room.

"There's nowhere to hide in here," I said, looking at the china cabinet, linens, and silver.

"Let me enter the dining room first," John said, pulling his gun out of his holster.

We didn't argue and waited for John to stick his head back into the butler's pantry and wave us inside. "All clear in here," he said as we looked around the enormous, cleared table. "There's nowhere to hide in here so let's go into the living room next." We followed John out the other entrance to the hall.

The opening to the living room was large and there wasn't a door opening, just a large arched entrance into a beautifully decorated, formal living room. "I'll check around the couches and chairs, but I doubt they'd be in here," I said, walking and putting my knee upon one of the several couches. I heaved myself up onto the couch and looked behind it. There wasn't enough room in between the couch and the wall to hide a human. "Not here," I called out.

John looked irritated. "They're not in here, let's move on." We walked into the foyer and the only options left were the hall closet and the library, which we were just in. "Open the closet, Sherman," John demanded.

"But, I don't have a gun. What if that Svenson fellow's in there?"

"I highly doubt that would happen. Just do it."

Sherman grumbled and walked over to the double door closet. He shakily took ahold of the door and pulled it open. He took a step back, as if that would save him if they were in there, and then looked inside.

"Get in there and have a good look," John told him. He gave me a quick smile as he egged Sherman on. "All the way in!" Sherman disappeared from our sight, but reappeared seconds later.

"Nobody's in there," he growled. "Can we move on now?"

"Yes, yes," John said, enjoying teasing the poor man. "Let's head upstairs." He eyed the staircase and added, "I haven't heard anything from the three of them yet."

"Me either," I said, wondering what, or should I say if, they found anyone.

We headed up the wide, red velvet runner and made our way to the second floor. "I don't hear them," John said, beginning to look concerned. "They must still be up on the third floor." He hesitated, viewing the stairs up to the third floor.

"Maybe we should go up there and check on them," I said. becoming a bit worried myself.

"That's a good idea. They have a lot of rooms to look through so it could just be taking them a long time."

"That better be the reason," Sherman muttered fairly quietly, but we still heard him.

"What else can it be?" I asked, standing next to him on the landing about ready to climb up more stairs.

"Yeah," John agreed. "We told them specifically to come and find me if there were any issues."

"Maybe they didn't have time or they couldn't," Sherman suggested with a hint of sarcasm in his voice.

"Sherman!" John hollered. "Why don't you keep your mouth shut?"

Sherman smacked his lips together and gave John a nasty look.

It took me a second, but then I understood why John had reacted to Sherman that way. "Whoa, wait a minute," I said. "Are you implying that the three of them were caught?"

"No, that's impossible, Ruth Ann," John said, trying to crack a slender smile, but I caught his lower lip quiver slightly. "Judy's got a gun, and they have Eklund who's still pretty strong."

"Don't forget Inga," Sherman added. "She's a bully and I don't think she's ever been intimidated by anyone."

"Good point," I whispered, but remembered too well that each of them had been caught before. "But, why would you get so upset at Sherman then?"

"I just didn't want him jumping to any ridiculous assumptions. That's all."

"Oh, okay," I said, not so confidently, but willing to accept John's explanations. "Let's just go up and check on them, can we?"

John took only a moment, and then said, "Yes, let's go, but I'll lead." He grabbed the gun he was holding and took a firm grip on it. I could tell he was concerned about the silence as we got closer to the top of the third staircase. His steps slowed down, and he hunched over a bit, ready to leap forward once he reached the last step to the top.

"John," I whispered. "I don't hear anyone up here. Maybe they went somewhere other than this floor."

"I told them not to," he retorted with gritted teeth. "They better be in one of these rooms with the doors closed, and that's why we don't hear them." I could tell he was fighting himself, feeling either worried or furious. I really hoped they were just searching the closet or bathrooms in one of the bedrooms up here. The third floor rooms were used for the staff of the estate. Inga's room was up here and so was Sherman's.

Sherman didn't wait for John this time. He marched past him and walked down the long wide hallway. He was halfway down before John realized what he was doing. "Hey, don't go in there."

Sherman ignored John and reached for the handle of the room he was facing. It was his room. He disappeared inside and John yelled, "C'mon, Ruth Ann, we'd better catch up with him." John grabbed my hand and pulled me down the hall as fast as he could. I didn't need him to pull me, I was just as anxious to get there as he was. Once we arrived, John told me to stay in the hall until he made sure it was safe inside. I obeyed, but then realized I was alone out here in the dark, empty hall. It wasn't normally creepy, but I've never stood here under these circumstances with a killer on the loose holding my daughter and cousin hostage. I was going to rush into the room when I heard a noise coming from somewhere near. "What was that?" I said out loud to no one.

I told myself I was just chicken and to knock it off. I was fine; John was just a few feet away inside the room with Sherman. If I heard it again, I'd be prepared to figure out where it was coming from. Probably from inside the room I told myself. Wrong! I heard a slight knock coming from another room. It was far enough away that I knew it wasn't from the room I was standing in front of, but possibly the next room over. That was Inga's room, I believe. Do I call for John or just walk a few feet over to the next door and investigate it on my own? I wasn't planning on opening up the door, just putting my ear against it and see if the noise would happen again.

I stood still, fighting with myself when I heard the knock again, but this time it was a little stronger and clearly coming from Inga's room. Without thinking, I rushed over and stuck my ear against the door. I waited for what seemed like an hour when the knock occurred again. What or *who* was making that noise? Do I try and see if the door is locked or do I run back and get John? I was acutely aware what I *should* do, but as usual, my irrational side took over and I reached out to see if the door was unlocked. It was.

I gently turned the knob, but before I opened it, I decided I would peek in first, and then go get John. It could be something as simple as a branch knocking against the window. I didn't want to alarm anyone just yet, so after a moment I pushed the door open an inch or so. I stuck my eye up to the crack, but couldn't see much. The room appeared quite dark, but that could be the time of day. It was dark outside now and unless someone had been in there I didn't expect to see a light on. I had to admit my hands were trembling more than I wanted them to, but I really wanted to see what was making that noise. Just as I was about to open the door another inch a hand grabbed me from behind and went across my mouth. The person dragged me backwards and I nearly fell onto the floor. I didn't have time to react since my focus was on opening the door just enough to peek inside.

"What the..." I mumbled through tightened fingers across my mouth.

"Shhh," the voice whispered. It was John. He released his hand and told me not to talk. I wanted to scream at him for scaring me half to death, but he did have a right. I, once again, didn't obey his direct order to stay put.

"What are you doing?" he whispered angrily. "I told you to stay where you were, and you went off to another room?"

"I heard a knock. I was only going to peek inside, but it's dark in there so I couldn't tell."

John grew angrier with me and said, "Then you come and get me to check it out. You don't EVER go into a room when we're searching for a killer!"

I knew he was right. As I've mentioned before, I hadn't slept in days, and I wasn't thinking rationally. I explained this to him again, and he relaxed his face. "You've got a point, Ruth Ann. I should know better to leave you alone anywhere under these circumstances. It was my fault."

Shocker! John just apologized to *me* for not following *his* orders. No matter how wrong this seemed I'd take it. I was able to get John to forget about it because the knock occurred again and he clearly heard it. I quickly whispered, "Where's Sherman?"

John nodded back over to his room. He wasn't about to leave this spot and go retrieve him. He held his finger over his mouth advising me not to speak. He walked up to the door and reached his hand up to carefully push the door open a bit more. He shoved his face right up to the opening and tried to glance inside. He shook his head and decided to back away.

"Why'd you do that?" I murmured.

He didn't answer me, but pulled out his gun and held it with both hands. I didn't have to be a genius to figure out what his next move was going to be. He quickly, with force, kicked the door in and yelled, "Nobody move!"

I was stunned for a second, and then hurried over to the opening to see if anyone was in there. John had disappeared inside the darkened room. I didn't hear any fighting or commotion so I reached around the side of the wall and found the light switch. I flicked it on and the room lit up. What we found inside took my breath away!

Chapter 40

"**R**uth Ann, stay back," John yelled. I didn't listen because the shock of what lay on the floor set me running toward it. On the floor coming out from under the iron framed bed was a pair of feet. John was running into the bathroom and closets. I ignored his order and fell to the floor next to the pair of feet, with shoes, coming from under the bed. They were Inga's. I knew those heavy, black work shoes anywhere. I knelt down and tried to look under the bed. I was terrified at what I might find. Was she alive? Was she severely injured or bleeding? I had complete tunnel vision when I grabbed a hold of her ankles and pulled with all my might. John flew out of Inga's bathroom and disappeared inside one of her two walk-in closets. He glanced my way, but I knew he was looking for others or even the remote chance Svenson was hiding somewhere in here.

"Inga," I yelled. I had her halfway out when another pair of hands grabbed a hold of one of her ankles. I turned around and saw Sherman pushing me over a little so he could help.

"Is she alive?" he exclaimed, terrified.

"I don't know yet. Help me get her all the way out. I don't see any blood so far." We managed to get Inga fully out from under her bed. I was relieved to see her eyes were wide-open, frightened, staring straight up at me. Her mouth had been duct taped shut and her hands tied in front of her. Sherman untied her hands, and then ripped off the tape (probably enjoying every moment of her pain). She exhaled loudly.

"Thank God!" Inga cried, trying to get in as much air as she could. "I didn't know if anyone would find me."

Sherman bellowed, "Your feet were sticking out from under the bed!"

I had to intervene because the glare she gave Sherman was terrifying. "Sherman, I doubt Inga knew her feet were sticking out in the open. Her head was stuck all the way under the bed."

Inga nodded, but was still trying to get herself together. She had been through a terrifying ordeal and when John finished checking the room he made his way over to us. "Inga, can you tell us what happened? Are the others around here?"

She stood up and was able to sit on the edge of her bed with a little help from John. "Now, please, hurry and tell us what happened to you?"

"Okay, I remember," Inga stated, rubbing the back of her head.

"Wait," I cried out. "Did they knock you out?"

"Yes, yes, I fought them as hard as I could, but that big bully with Svenson, grabbed my lamp and hit me over my head. It stunned me long enough for them to tie me up and cover my mouth with duct tape. Then they shoved me under my bed!"

"So you weren't totally knocked out then, just stunned a little," John said.

"Yes, I tried to save them, I really did," she bellowed. "I'm so sorry, they got away."

"Who got away?" I asked.

"And where's Eklund and Judy?" John added.

"Mr. Eklund and Judy were in another room, I guess. I told them I'd check my room and we'd meet up in the hall. They aren't around?" Inga inquired, trying to get off the bed, but John held her down.

"No, just us three," John answered. "But *who* got away, Inga?"

She looked me in my eyes with distress. "Ms. Prunella was in here," she stopped, swallowed some air, and added, "And Ms. Lynne." Inga lowered her head in humiliation. "I'm so sorry, I really tried to rescue them."

"Oh, Inga," I cried. "It's not your fault. You gave me wonderful news!"

"Huh?" The three of them blurted out in unison.

"They're still okay! Don't you get it?" I was happy, not that we still hadn't found them, but that they were still unharmed. "They're alive and here in this house! That means Svenson's here somewhere and he won't leave until Prunella hands the necklace over to him. He must know it's here and now we're here. He's hiding somewhere with the girls."

"Yes, yes, Ruth Ann," Sherman said. "But where?"

"They could be anywhere," John said, standing up from next to Inga and thinking hard. "They must've captured Eklund, and…Judy."

The look of disappointment on his face was obvious. Judy, being his big shot detective, seems to screw up a lot if you ask me. He must've finally figured that one out, too. "So, not to add a different theory to what you just said," Inga spoke, trying to get our attention. "Maybe, Judy and

Mr. Eklund followed them and aren't actually captured. Why would this Svenson fellow need *more* prisoners?"

"Ah, you raise an interesting point, Inga," John replied. "I hope that's what happened."

"What are we going to do now?" I asked impatiently.

John looked at Inga and asked her if she was sturdy enough to walk and keep up with us. "Of course," she answered, hopping off the bed easily.

"There wasn't any sign of them in Sherman's room or in here," John said. "What other rooms are up here?"

"Helena's room, and…Bert's room," Sherman answered with a big gulp. "I presume we have to go in there?"

"Yes, of course," Inga said, pushing Sherman out of the way and heading for the door.

"Hold on," John called out. "This time, under no circumstances, do we separate. Does each of you (his eyes on me) understand this?"

"Yes, John," I answered for the three of us. "We promise."

We slid out of the room and headed down to the next room. It was Helena's room. John opened the unlocked door and ripped down the police tape that was still across the inside of the door. I was about to mention that if the tape was still up, I doubted anyone had been in here. John beat me to it and said, "They could've replaced the tape after they left."

John went in first. Inga followed, then Sherman and I went in together. I had to give Sherman a little shove, but then he willingly moved all the way in. "I don't like going into a room where someone was murdered," he told me.

"She wasn't murdered in here, Sherman," I reminded him.

"She was still murdered. It's creepy."

He had a point, but we had to see if there was any sign of Axel, Judy or the others. I stood in the middle of the room and glanced around. The room was very bright, even though it was evening. Helena liked bright colors and it made me very sad that this young woman was so viciously killed. John disappeared into the bathroom, but quickly came back out and went over to her walk-in closet. Inga was looking under her bed while Sherman and I just stood still looking around.

"Clear," John stated and told us to move on to the next room. "We're not wasting any more time. They're here so let's find them, fast."

The next room was Bert's. He was horribly burned to death at the Halloween party in town. There was no police tape on his door so John just flew inside his room with his gun aimed and ready. The three of us followed and before we could do anything, John said they weren't here.

"So now where?" I asked.

"We head down to the second floor and check your room, Prunella's room, and Eklund's room."

"Prunella's room is Axel's room," I reminded him.

"Are there other rooms on the floor?" he asked.

"Yes, a couple guest rooms and storage closets," Sherman answered.

"Let's get to it," John said, trudging down the staircase to the second floor. "I feel fairly confident the guest rooms will be clear. I think we need to check Ruth Ann and Prunella's rooms. Maybe they kept Eklund tied up in there if they caught up with him."

John let Inga lead the way to my room. He went in first. I should explain, again, why I had a room here. I was held prisoner here not too long ago by Axel. Once that was straightened out, and Prunella took over his estate, she wanted me to have a permanent room here for whenever I wanted to stay. This place was massive with plenty of rooms. So, I picked one and decorated it the way I'd like. I enjoyed bringing some of the furniture over from my antique store and being able to use it myself. So, I brought a beautiful king-sized canopy bed here that was from the nineteenth century. It was supposedly from a castle in England former contacts of mine told me about after a trip they took. They had stayed in the castle as guests and found out that the owners were moving and wanted to sell many pieces to help pay for their expenses.

I was lucky to purchase several of their pieces, some of which are in my room here at the estate. I followed John inside. My bed, decorated with my favorite color bedding (periwinkle blue), looked so inviting I almost forgot why we were in there. I was conflicted. I was exhausted because of lack of sleep, but on the other hand, full of energy, and hoping to find my daughter and Prunella. John noticed me gazing over at the bed and walked to me. "Soon, Ruth Ann. You'll be able to get some rest soon." He gave my arm a gentle squeeze and disappeared into my bathroom. Ooh, my bathroom…I hoped I left it picked up. I sure didn't want him finding anything he shouldn't. Such as the little box of hair color I use to hide those minimal grays I have! He didn't know I used that, and I sure didn't want him to. I was about to run in there to see if I had left anything I shouldn't have out when he rushed out and went to my closet.

I didn't see any funny looks on his face so I let it go (for now), and waited for him to come out of the closet. John declared my room was clear so we went down the hall to Prunella's room. John felt that if there was any room on the floor that could be dangerous, it would be this one. He held Inga, Sherman, and me back so he could be the only one entering. Before he grabbed the handle to enter, he turned around and reminded us of his earlier warning. "Do not go anywhere from this exact spot unless I shout for you to run." He didn't wait for our response, but turned and grabbed the handle with one hand, and gun in the other.

"I wonder if Axel's in there?" I whispered to Inga and Sherman.

"I hope so," Sherman replied. We could use the help."

"Come on in," a voice shouted from within. We entered the door, but John was not alone.

"Axel," I cried out, hurrying over to John who was standing next to Axel right outside his closet. He was rubbing his wrists with his hands. From the ropes on the ground, I figured he was tied up and gagged just like Inga.

"It's okay, I'm fine," Axel said. "They shoved me into my closet and I couldn't yell. I knew someone would find me eventually."

"Where's Judy?" John demanded. "Did they capture her, too?"

"I have no idea," Axel answered. "I was in here looking around when Svenson showed up. He had an ugly grin on his face. I've never seen him look like this before. He demanded that I tell him where that bitch of a wife hid the necklace."

"Really?" I asked, shocked.

"Yes, he figured out Prunella and I were getting reacquainted and assumed she told me where the original was hidden." Axel stopped, looked at John directly, and added, "He knew about the fake ones in the tin."

"That doesn't totally surprise me," John answered.

"But, why didn't he think one of the two fakes were real?" Sherman asked, confused. "Prunella could've told him one was real, and then he'd be off."

"I don't know, Sherman," John said. "Svenson's on to her and us. He's been one step ahead of us the whole time. However, he's getting desperate."

"How so?" I asked.

"He can't leave the house. He knows the necklace is somewhere inside here. All he can do is keep watching and catching us. I don't know if he knows we've released Inga and Eklund yet. For all I know, he's got some camera watching our every move."

"Nonsense," Axel retorted. "There's no hidden cameras in here. I would know about them. I think he's waiting for us to go to another part of the estate, and then he can come back with the women and try and force them to cooperate again and again."

"He'll get tired of them eventually," John said, trying not to look at me. "I don't want him to get to that point, so we need to find them, now."

"Let's get moving," Axel said. "Maybe they went through the tunnels to the guest house?"

"I totally forgot about that place, Eklund," John exclaimed. "The problem is if they're watching us they'll know when we head down the tunnel. They can sneak back in here and start their games all over again."

"What do you mean, John?" I asked, terrified.

"I just meant with whoever he catches, Ruth Ann," John quickly added. "If we go through the tunnel, he can bring Judy and the girls back here from the path outside. It's a vicious circle."

"Well, what are we supposed to do?" Inga asked nervously. "There's got to be a way of confronting them."

"There is," Axel spoke up. "Some of us have to stay here and wait for them. We know where the real necklace is, right?" Axel reminded us that the necklace was back in his library in the book. We kept it there hoping the others would return, and then we would catch them red handed. The problem is we left to search the house. John wasn't comfortable taking the necklace out since Svenson and Jimmy were killers.

"We can't separate," John bellowed. "Every time we separate, someone gets caught!"

"What else can we do?" I begged of him. "This has to end tonight."

"It will. I have an idea," John said, appearing excited now.

We were still in Axel and Prunella's bedroom, and his brilliant suggestion was that we go back into the library and wait.

"That's all?" I said, shocked at his plan.

"What if they don't come back there?" Inga asked, confused.

"They have to," John said. "Don't you see? Prunella has to tell Svenson where it is now. He's probably telling her at this very moment that all of us are prisoners of his, and if she doesn't cooperate, he'll kill us."

"Hey, that's good," Inga cried out, excited.

"Why didn't we do that earlier?" I asked him.

"Because my hunch is that Prunella and Lynne observed Inga and Axel being captured," John looked over at them and asked, "Did they?"

"Yes, yes," Inga said eagerly. "I saw them both!" Axel shook his head and said he didn't see them, but he was in his own room searching. "They were inside *my* room," Inga replied proudly referring to Prunella and Lynne being inside her room and not Axel's.

"So, you see now, Ruth Ann?"

"What if Svenson doesn't come into the library?" I questioned him.

"He has to, hopefully sooner now because he's feeling trapped here," John said. "Let's get down there and wait it out."

"What about Judy?" I asked, regretting the words right after I said them.

"My guess is she's either with them or possibly in one of the guest rooms up here."

"Aren't we going to look?" Sherman asked.

"Yes, on the way down the hall, we'll stop in each of the rooms and check it out. But, we stay together," John reminded us.

John led the way and stopped at each of the extra bedrooms. We went through three more in all, and there was no sign of Judy. She had to have gotten herself captured. I bet her mouth got her in trouble; she's such a loose canon. She fell right into Svenson's hands and thought she could capture them by herself. Ha! I thought to myself. I can't wait to see what she said happened.

Once John felt the second floor was secure, he directed us back to the library. He said it could be a bit of a wait, so he suggested we take turns resting on the couches by the fireplace. I wanted to stay with him by the double doors to the library, but he vetoed me. John politely suggested (coerced is the better word) that I should rest. It had been a long couple days and I would be better off rested when we get the women back. I did agree with him, I was exhausted, and maybe a short nap would revive me.

So I headed over to one of the couches near the fireplace and lay down just for a short time to rest my eyes. Inga and John stood by the doors while Sherman and Axel shared the other couch near mine. I didn't think I'd be able to sleep, but not long after I lied down I found myself deep in slumber. I had the strangest dream. I only remembered part of it, but here goes:

I was working in my antique store in town when a strange man entered the store. He was magnificent! Tall, dark hair neatly cut, with a sweater and khaki pants. He was looking for a particular antique necklace. He said it was lost for many years and he was searching every antique store in Colorado. Now, I know that sounds unrealistic, but it is a dream. He said his great uncle gave it to his great aunt on her wedding day when they came to this country years and years ago (sound familiar?). The necklace was stolen not long after they were married, but her family searched and searched for it for years. The reason that he got involved was because he received a mysterious letter from some distant relative far, far away stating the necklace reappeared here, in Colorado. He'd been to many antique and jewelry stores asking about this necklace, but nobody had it. That's why he ended up in my little antique store. I asked him to describe the necklace because I may have heard something about it. He said he never directly saw it, but it was supposed to be the most brilliant sky blue, emerald shaped, and massive. Bigger than any stone that shape and color that anybody had ever laid eyes on.

Well, you can imagine my dilemma. That sounded just like *my* necklace. Do I tell him about it or get him out of here as fast as I can? I was struggling with my decision when he pulled out a gun and aimed it directly at my face. I asked him why he was aiming his gun at me and he shouted he knew I was the owner of the necklace. If I didn't give it back to him he'd kill everybody in my family! I laughed so loud (remember it's still a dream) that I must've *actually* laughed out loud. I suddenly felt my shoulders being shaken and distant voices calling my name. I slowly opened my eyes and found Axel, John, and Inga standing over me.

"What?" I asked, a bit short-tempered. "Why'd you wake me up?"

"You were screaming then laughing," John said, worried. "You must've had quite the dream."

"I did?" I sat up and told them about it, but they wrote it off due to stress and exhaustion. It felt so real, as if I had another relative out there in search of the same necklace. Could that be true? I sure hoped not. I didn't think I could handle more surprise relatives in search of some long lost family heirloom!

Once I got my wits about me, I asked if there'd been any action in regards to Svenson. "No, not yet," John replied, disappointed.

"How long was I asleep?" I asked curiously.

"It's 5 am," John answered me. "So, you had a good few hours' sleep. I'm glad, you needed it."

"Wow, I did sleep! How about you, Axel?"

"I got in a few winks then let John and Inga get a few. We've been up for a while, well, all of us except him," Axel pointed to Sherman who was still asleep on the couch. "I don't know how he slept through your bizarre laughing. You were really loud."

"Sorry, I didn't know I was doing it."

John sat down on the couch next to me and motioned over to the coffee table. "Why don't you eat a sandwich?"

"Where'd those come from?" I asked curiously, noticing my stomach turning. I hadn't eaten in a long time, and I was hungry. I reached out for a peanut butter and marshmallow crème sandwich. It's one of my all-time favorite sandwiches.

John answered my question as he grabbed one of the same sandwiches. "Inga and I did a quick walk through on the main floor to check doors and see if there was any sign of them. While we were in the kitchen I checked the basement and the back doors, and she made a bunch of sandwiches. We need to keep up our strength."

"It's wonderful," I said with a mouthful.

"It's 5:30 in the morning now. I wonder if they got some shut-eye themselves before making their move," John suggested. "I think something will go down any time now. We need to be ready, so I'm going back by the door. Eklund, why don't you join me?"

I ate two sandwiches and drank a bottle of warm water. I didn't care; it was the best meal I'd had in a long time. I stood up and started pacing around the library. I had a strong feeling this was going to be over soon, and I was getting more and more impatient. Inga was right behind me pacing over the same path I took. We nearly bumped into each other as I rounded Axel's desk, but she stepped out of the way just in time.

I wondered if John's theory was correct. What if what we've been doing for several hours has been a waste of time? They could be out of the country by now, and we'd never find them. I was beginning to panic when I heard John tell us to be quiet. "Why?" I asked without thinking.

"Shhh," he said softly. "I think I hear something." John's ear was against the library door. Axel was listening against the other door. I noticed the two exchange glances. Axel walked over to Inga and me and told us to get down behind the couch. I tilted my head in Sherman's direction because he was still fast asleep on the couch. Axel shook his head, which I took to mean, leave him alone. I could tell Inga wanted in on the action, but Axel grabbed her arm and led her to the back of the couch Sherman was lying on. I joined Inga, and the two of us peered over the back edge of the couch watching whatever was about to happen.

I noticed John wasn't the only one armed. Axel was holding a gun firmly in his hand. I noticed a slight shake, but that could just be nerves. This was a tense situation with a lot on the line. Everything we've been going through came down to this moment. Who, if anyone, was about to walk through those doors?

Chapter 41

I could've heard a pin drop. John and Axel were positioned on either side of the double doors. Inga and I were on our knees watching from behind the couch where Sherman was still, yes still, sleeping. He was old; I guess no sleep for two days really knocked him out. It felt like hours when I spotted John raise his arm to alert Axel to be ready. I could make out a distant noise now. It was the sound of loud footsteps marching over the marble tile floor in the grand foyer. I knew that sound because I'd heard it many times before. The foyer was so large, that any noise reverberated around the room.

I felt nauseous waiting for the doors to open. I took in a deep breath, realizing I had been holding my breath. I felt better, but still a nervous wreck, waiting and waiting for this moment to finally come to a climax. Who was going to walk through those doors? Was it going to be Steven Svenson alone or with Jimmy and the girls? I felt like I was going to burst when the door on the left side (John's side) flew open. Who I saw enter blew me away!

The minute the man had one foot in the door, John whirled around and grabbed his arms behind his back and Axel stood in front of him aiming the gun directly at the center of his body. "Whoa," the stranger called out, raising his arms up in the air in surrender. John didn't let go, but reached around and pulled the gun from the man's hand.

"Who are you?" John demanded. "And what are you doing here armed?"

I popped up so fast I almost fainted from the blood rush. I caught myself quickly and recovered. I ran over to John before he could protest. "Ruth Ann!" he yelled. "Get back over there."

"No, no, I need to explain," I tried to say. "This is the man!"

Axel looked confused, "What man? We've never seen him before."

I tried to get my faculties together because it was so unbelievable I couldn't put what was happening into words. "This is the man from my dream!"

John and Axel looked from me to the stranger and back to me. "You just think it is," Axel said. "It's impossible."

"No, please listen," I begged. "I dreamed of a man, tall like him, with dark neatly cut hair, like him, and wearing a sweater and khaki pants, like him." They checked him out from head to toe, but still seemed unconvinced.

"Look, he was carrying a gun, like my dream, and he was in search of the necklace."

"Ruth Ann!" Axel shouted rather loudly for the circumstances. "Please, do you have to announce *everything*?"

Oh, I understood his outburst. I probably should've left out the part about the necklace, but it was too late. The man appeared stunned, and then he said, "Wait, how do you know what I'm looking for?"

I looked at the two men holding this man and said, "I told you."

"Strange coincidence, that's all," John barked. "Why don't you let this person tell us why he's here with a loaded gun?"

John took the gun and opened it up. Yep, it was a loaded gun. He stuck it in the back of his pants, but still held his own gun on him. "Can I explain, please?" the stranger pleaded.

John took the man over to the desk and released him into one of the chairs facing the desk. He plopped down rather hard, but recovered quickly. "I don't know what's going on in here, but I'm looking for a Prunella Eklund."

"Why?" John ordered.

"Why should I tell any of you? Unless one of you is a Ms. Prunella Eklund?"

"You're pushing it!" John exclaimed, getting his face close to the young man. "I'm the Chief of Police here, so you better start talking." John pulled out his badge and shoved it close to his face.

"Oh," the man said nervously. "I've been all over the state looking for an antique that used to be in my family." I almost fainted again! Axel and Inga each grabbed an arm of mine to hold me steady. "What's wrong with her?" The man said, looking in my direction.

"Are you okay, Ruth Ann?" John asked, worried. "Maybe you should sit down?"

"I'm fine, but did you just hear what he said? He said exactly what he told me in my dream, right before he held a gun on me!"

"This is too weird, lady," the man stated. "Look, I just want to speak with this woman about a piece of jewelry. Can you please tell me where she is?"

"In due time," John said. "From now on I don't want you asking any questions, just answer mine."

"Fine."

"So, you're here, out of the blue, for an antique piece of jewelry that was supposedly in your family? Just nod." The man nodded. "How did you end up here? You may answer this question only."

"I told you I've been searching this state, and asking lots of questions to see if anyone ever heard of or saw the particular piece of jewelry."

"But *who* told you to come look for Prunella?" Axel interrupted and asked. John nodded at the guy that he should respond.

"I ended up here accidentally. When I went over to the café here in town, some woman, I think her name is, Wilma." I looked at John and we both knew what he was going to say. Wilma's a huge gossip, and probably spilled her guts about my necklace. I wouldn't even put it past her to tell him where to find Prunella and me.

"Go on," John spurred him on to continue before I could interfere.

"She told me all about this famous necklace that was the talk of her town. She then went on to tell me where to find it! I was a bit surprised how willing she was to send me up here. She didn't even know who I was."

"Who are you?" John asked, irritated. He would have to have a little talk with Wilma when this was over.

"My name is Alex."

"A little more about your background if you would," John said.

"I live in Chicago and I'm related to a family, Liljestrom, from Sweden. I'm a distant nephew of the original owners of the piece. They're names are Beta and Axel Liljestrom."

"This is absolutely the most unbelievable turn of events!" I cried out.

"So, Stanley Liljestrom was your…" I started to ask.

"My great, great uncle on my mother's side."

"How old are you?" John asked the man. I would've said late twenties by his looks. He was a handsome young man, but didn't really look Swedish.

"Twenty-four."

"That's awful young to be searching this state far away from home," John said suspiciously.

"I, I had my reasons," the young man said nervously.

"Why'd you have a gun?" Axel asked.

"I was told, by Wilma, that the necklace was cursed, and that I should protect myself when I go to search for it."

"You've got to be kidding?" I asked. Wilma's gossiping has gone too far this time. Well, actually, it's kind of true, but how would she know what we're dealing with right now?

"No, no, I'm not joking," Alex, pleaded.

John had enough. "This isn't getting us anywhere." He pulled Axel (very confusing now with an Alex in the picture) aside. I sneakily went within hearing distance and listened to their conversation.

John whispered, "What do you think, Eklund? Could this guy be telling the truth?"

Axel replied, "As bizarre and far-fetched as this sounds, I guess he could be telling the truth. I'm not convinced about why he has a gun though. I think he was willing to steal the necklace and use the gun as his weapon to achieve it."

"You think he would've shot someone to get his hands on the necklace?" I asked from a short distance away. Both Axel and John glared at me and told me to back off, but of course I didn't listen.

Axel continued, "I don't know, yet. I think we need to ask him why he wants to find this long lost family heirloom."

"Good point, Eklund. I'll do that now."

"I'll go stand by the doors just in case Svenson catches us off guard. I'll grab Inga and have her stand with me."

John walked casually back over to the chair where Alex was still sitting silently. I went and leaned upon the desk and waited for John to ask the question I really wanted answered, too.

Inga was happy to go stand guard by the door. She's always up for a fight! I just hoped it waited a few minutes longer so we knew whether Alex was on our side or not.

"So, Alex," John began. "I have another question I want you to answer, truthfully. I'll be able to tell if you're lying or not." Alex nodded vigorously. "Why do you want the necklace? What made you travel and search so hard for it?"

"That's easy," the young man said. "I've heard about the necklace from my mother. She said it was worth a lot of money, priceless I believe her words were. I need a large sum of money so I decided to do a search for it on my own."

"Does your mother know what you're doing?" John asked.

"No."

"Why not?"

"My parents aren't alive anymore," Alex stated solemnly. He lowered his head for a moment before he said softly, "It was her dying words to tell me to find the necklace."

I could tell John didn't know what to do or think. I felt horrible for this young man. He lost his parents, and his mother's last words were to find the necklace. He must've needed the money so he went in search of my necklace. If this was all true, what luck for him to end up here with family!

I could tell John wanted to interrogate him and get more out of him, but we didn't have the time. Axel alerted us that he heard muffled voices outside the library. He quietly said, "I don't think they are coming from the foyer, though. I think they're coming from further away."

John left Alex and me and went running over to the doors. He told Inga to take Alex and me and hide behind the couch again. I knew what we were doing, but Alex had no idea what he was in for. He didn't want to move, but I promised him I would fill him in on everything that was happening once we were safe. "Safe!" he blurted out noisily. John threw an evil glare in our direction and I put my hand over his mouth.

Alex tried to get my hand off his mouth, but I was being stubborn and wouldn't move. "Not until you promise to keep your mouth shut," I murmured, then released my hold after he reluctantly nodded. He looked around the room from John and Axel standing with guns by the doors, to Inga and myself kneeling below him now. Inga was about to grab him and lower him down when he willingly sank down in between us. He eyed the recumbent figure on the couch in horror. I shook my head and pulled him down behind the couch.

"He's not dead," I said quietly. "He's asleep."

"Through all this?" he asked, surprised.

"He's old, hasn't had much sleep, and may be avoiding what's about to happen," Inga snapped.

"Shhh," Axel hissed. "They're out there." John nodded and motioned to Axel to have his gun ready.

"When they open the door, don't hesitate, just pounce on whoever it is immediately." Axel nodded at John's whispered orders.

Inga, Alex, and I peered over the edge of the couch hidden from the doors of the library. Whoever entered wouldn't be able to see us until they were further into the library, and I'm hoping at that point John and Axel would've subdued them. Alex looked terrified, but I tried to calm him by grabbing his thick forearm and gently squeezing it. I so wanted to tell him I was his aunt or some distant relative to him. After, I said to myself, after this was finally over.

I could hear the voices now. They were very close to coming into the library. I was trying to make out if there were any female voices, but it was too muffled through the closed doors. It didn't take long before both doors swung open and the first individual came into focus.

"NOW!" John screamed and lunged at the man who entered first.

It was Steven Svenson. He was so caught off guard that the gun he was holding fell to the floor just as John threw him to his feet far away from the fallen gun. "Jump on him Eklund," John ordered. Axel threw himself on top of the face down figure of Steven. There didn't seem to be a struggle with him since John probably knocked the wind out of the man when he threw him. Axel had no problem handcuffing the man and twirling him around to face him.

John didn't watch Axel and Steven because he was standing out of my sightline just outside of the library. It didn't take long to see what was going on, and I have to say it was not what I expected.

John was backing inside the library holding his hands high in the air. Axel was busy with Steven so he didn't see what was going on. I saw perfectly clearly now. Jimmy was holding a gun aimed at John with the two girls following him into the library. I was so ecstatic to see my daughter and Prunella that I flew out from behind the couch and rushed over to them. John screamed at me to stop, but it was too late. I lunged at Jimmy, not even realizing he was physically ready to fire the gun at either John or me. He was so stunned by my actions, he hesitated one second too long.

John took this as his cue and grabbed his wrist so hard the gun fell to the floor. "Pick it up, Ruth Ann," John shouted. I fell to the ground and grabbed the gun and stood up and aimed it at Jimmy.

John twisted the man's wrist to the verge of breaking it. Jimmy screamed in pain trying to use his other hand to release John's grip, but John wouldn't budge. He noticed I had Jimmy's gun in my hand and so he quickly dropped hold of his wrist and snapped the gun from me before Jimmy could get to it.

This all occurred within a matter of seconds. Nothing was planned, it just happened, and thank God it worked out in our favor. I didn't care what was going on with Steven or Jimmy; all I could see was Lynne and Prunella. Inga ran over and we took the two women away from the ruckus and sat them down on the couch (obviously not the one Sherman was still sleeping on!).

Inga gently pulled the duct tape off Prunella's mouth, and I did the same with Lynne's. Their hands were tied behind their backs, and it was Alex who came over with a pair of scissors he found in the desk and cut them free.

Lynne and Prunella eyed the man strangely, but I said, "I'll explain that later. Right now I can't believe you both are finally here, with me, safe!"

Lynne had tears in her eyes and a huge smile on her face. "Hi, Mom," she said so normally.

"Hi, dear," I replied.

"I knew you'd come to our rescue!" Lynne said laughing.

"I did too," Prunella cried out to me. "I'm just happy we're all here, safe and uninjured." Prunella looked over to the still, non-moving form of Sherman. "Is he okay?" she asked, worried.

I walked over to him and gave him a little shake, "Okay, Sherman, you can stop pretending to be asleep. It's all over now."

Prunella, Inga, Lynne, Alex (who was still confused), and I were leaning over the old guy now waiting. For a second or two, I became worried that there was something seriously wrong with him, but my fears were quickly washed away when he rolled over from his side and smiled at us. "Oh, it's all over?" he asked, trying to act sleepy.

"You can't tell me you slept through the whole thing!" Inga said to him skeptically.

"I had a little secret," he said, pulling a small pill bottle from his inside pocket. "I took one of these." He held up a bottle full of sleeping pills.

"You took a sleeping pill?" Inga asked, fuming mad. "How could you? What if we needed your help?"

"I'm no good with fighting," he said selfishly. "I would just get in the way, so I figured I'd get a few hours of sleep, and then I could be useful in the kitchen. I knew when I woke up, this would all be over, and it is!"

Leave it to Sherman! He had a weird way of showing his loyalty, but in some strange way, it worked. Prunella was so relieved; she bent over and hugged the poor guy. "Glad to be back, Sherman."

"It's great to see you!" he said. It was at that moment; I remembered everything between Sherman and Prunella. I knew I had to bring up the topic, but now wasn't the time. It was time to celebrate us being together, as one big, crazy family!

Chapter 42

John and Axel handled the two men handcuffed on the floor. We had all forgotten one person, Judy. Where was she? John questioned Svenson until he finally caved. "She's in the hall closet. The woman wouldn't shut up! She's lucky I didn't kill her like I killed Helena."

"So, you just admitted to murder on top of all the other charges, Svenson," John said, reading his rights to him. "I suggest you keep your mouth shut until you have one heck of a lawyer." I was severely disappointed with Steven. I usually can spot a liar, but he clearly played me as a fool! Never again.

Steven slammed his mouth shut, and John headed out to find Judy. Within a few minutes, they both walked into the library. Judy was rubbing her mouth from the duct tape and looking a tad foolish.

"Judy," I said, smirking. "Nice to see you again!"

"Ruth Ann, I'm not in the mood for you right now. I know you can't wait to gloat over how I got caught once again." She turned to Sherman and spat, "You could've found me when you searched the closet. I was way in the back behind a pile of coats that were on the floor. Why didn't you search the pile?"

Sherman shrugged his shoulders and said, "I didn't think the pile was important, sorry." She threw him a disgusted look and turned to me.

"Judy," I said, wiping the smile off my face. "I truly am grateful you're okay." Judy smiled and went back to John who began barking out orders. "Call it in, Judy." Judy turned and stormed out of the room to make her calls.

I went back to my little group by the couch. I tried to explain about Alex, at least as much as I knew, when Alex stood up to leave. "Where are you going?" I asked him.

"I'm just interfering here. I'll go and leave you to reunite and to live your lives. I don't need to find the necklace, it's obviously in the right hands."

"No, wait," Prunella called out to him as he started to walk away. "You're family, now. I'll show you the necklace when…" she looked at me, I nodded my approval, and said, "Whenever you're ready."

Alex smiled and nodded. "Thank you. I really don't have much of a home to go back to anymore, and I'd sure like to see what all the fuss has been about!"

"Get ready for a long story!" I laughed.

"Once we've settled down, you can tell us all about your family, but for now, we believe you and want to welcome you to *our* unique family," I said.

John laughed at my comment and added, "You can say that again. I have a strange feeling this isn't over. I don't know if it'll ever be over when you're involved Ruth Ann!"

The End

About the Author

Karin Richardson graduated from The University of Iowa with a communications degree. She currently resides in a suburb of Chicago with her family.

Richardson's aspiration has always been to complete a series of mystery novels for readers of all ages. *ICE QUEST* is the second book in this Deer Creek Mystery Series. Look on Amazon for the first book, *BLUE ICE*. When she's not in San Juan holding a street vendor's pet iguana, Richardson is hard at work on book three!

www.ingramcontent.com/pod-product-compliance
Lightning Source LLC
Chambersburg PA
CBHW051928020726
47501CB00001B/32